THE ATHEREON

Winter's War

Daniel Frearson

First Published by Kindle Direct Publishing in 2017

The Athereon: Winter's War 3rd Edition
ISBN-13: 978-1549690280

Also by Daniel Frearson
(Grouped by Series)

67-49

Classified

The Ghost

Tightrope

Consequence

THE ATHEREON

Winter's War

Day of Reunion

Midnight

Era of Man

Revolution

DEAREST ROSE

Dearest Rose

Letter's Lost

ATHEREON TALES

The Last Dragon Slayer

The Doll

INDEPENDENT SHORTS

The Anarchist

INDEPENDENT NOVELS

The Night of Angels

Set in Stone

A Message From the Author

In this third edition of the Athereon Winter's War, in addition to the updated formatting and corrected spelling and grammar in the manuscript, between fifteen and twenty five percent of it has been completely rewritten.

While being as faithful to the original text as possible, new details have been added, old ones have been edited or removed, repetitions have been dealt with and the overall readability of the text had been greatly improved.

In my opinion, this is how the Athereon Winter's war should have been released in the first place.

And with my years of experience since it's original publish in November of 2017, I believe that the book as a whole is a massive step up from the original version released 3 years ago now.

A word of warning however. The story is thankfully largely unchanged. But that includes the lack of speech in the events that occur.

My intent with this rewrite was to improve the quality of my work. Not to try again. I did not go into this project planning to turn it into my best piece of work. Just something at least slightly less unreadable than it was before.

And if you haven't already discovered them, the rewrites of Day of Reunion and Midnight are coming later in 2020 prior to the release of The Athereon - Time of Prophecy - Volume 1, later that same year.

So as a personal gift to all of you long time fans of the series, I give to you the third and final version of my first published novel.

I hope you enjoy and continue to do so for years to come.

PROLOGUE

The Uninvited guests

It had long since passed the stroke of midnight by the time it happened. In fact, the clock hanging on the wall then was just mere moments away from striking two when those visitors finally came knocking at the door.

The skies above had turned black with clouds of rain. Rain that now poured down relentlessly unto the world below. Drenching the village. Drenching the homes. Drenching the people.

Chimney smoke, steam and engine exhaust lingering in the air. The potent stench of human society – the mark of their long-trusted machinery – corrupting the serenity of the land around them. Leaving behind nought but a sensation. One that could be felt everywhere. By everything.

The birds knew well to keep their distance. The dear and rabbits too. Foxes and hens hid from the noise and taste of the world. Even the snakes knew better. They just slithered away.

The homes of humans had long since been devoid of wildlife. And yet, on this night, in this town, the wildlife was there to stay. Almost as though someone, perhaps even something, was encouraging them.

But the animals weren't the only unlucky souls that could feel the stench of humanity that night. The people of the town were all too aware of its presence.

However, as luck would have it, this stench did not stay for long. A slight breeze from the west soon approached, moving the fumes away from the houses and off of the land. Cleansing it with the smell of the woodland from whence it came.

Nothing else now remained to take you away from the beauty of the country. Nothing but the sound of impacting rain drops against the glass of the windows and the ever-approaching footsteps now marching up the hill.

Heavy boots bashed against the cobbled path on that night. Boots belonging to men. Those men belonging to the war.

A platoon of soldiers they were. Slowly encroaching upon the household atop this hill. Fully armed and ready for a fight that each one of them feared would come.

Body armour covering them from head to toe. Pistols, grenades and rifles strapped all over their bodies and carried in their hands.

I had known from the moment they entered my village that this bunch would be just like the rest. No matter how heavily armed they were, humans, no matter where they come from or what they want, always behaved in the same way once they were inside that house.

They always believed that they were above us, that just because they had guns and chose to shout rather than speak that they could order us around.

But their authoritarian manner wouldn't get them very

8

far in that house. The only people in charge of what goes on within its walls were those who occupied it. And knowing those two like I do, I can safely say that deciding it was appropriate to be disturbing them at such an hour was their first mistake.

As they too would soon learn.

Two knocks on the door is what she heard. Two loud, strong and impatient strikes emanating from the old oak frame. The door shook violently, loosening the screws and releasing the nails slightly with each knock. Then when no one came running to open it for them, the humans in their arrogance, just walked on in.

The unlocked door handle turning. The door itself creaking as it was slowly opened with caution. And as they peered around its edge, in came the men from before.

The smell of cheap cigarettes and sugar filled chewing gum flooded the room with their presence. The distinct markings of the American military. Marks that she had learnt to identify so many years before that she was almost disappointed to find it was the same country yet again.

They certainly weren't the first and unfortunately for her, they wouldn't be the last. Visitors always ended up at that house sooner or later, it was only a matter of time before the next ones would come knocking once more.

The smell of those men stewing in their own sweat came through next. Followed swiftly by the rain as it poured down from their soaked boots and clothes. Drenching now, the rugs and the floor panels. An unnecessary annoyance that she would have to clean later on before the floor could stain. But first, she had some rather unpleasant guests to attend to.

The lights coming from torches the rifles were seen first. Beams of glistening unnatural white light entering through the door one by one.

Before long, those lights had begun to be pointed away from her as those humans started to sweep the entrance just as they always did.

They hadn't noticed her yet but she could feel their primitive eyes as they scanned the entrance to the building for threats. She could see their scared faces and the look of a nervous child in their eyes. Even through their helmets, she could tell that they were afraid.

They knew that they were in over their heads but still forced their way in regardless of their fear. Whether it was an act or if they actually believed it, they remained calm and made it seem as though they were in control of the situation at hand.

Everything was mostly silent for the first few seconds even. Not one man spoke a whisper. At least not until one of the grunts who had entered at the front shouted to the rest of the men behind him.

"Clear." He said.

He released his left hand from his rifle and lowered it slightly. It wasn't long before he was waving that arm in the air, gesturing with his hand, sending signals to the men.

The apparent leader of the group pushed his way to the front and entered the property as soon as this man was finished.

He wore nothing but combat boots, trousers and a jacket. No armour or helmet. He must have been in charge to be that brazen in the face of danger. That was the only explanation for his lack of protection that she could think of.

Not that it would have helped.

And showing no regard for the priceless artefacts within the building and no care for the painstakingly clean and hand-crafted Persian rugs on the floor, he barged his way further into the household the moment he had his bearings.

He marched his way through the main entrance and into the long hall connecting it to the rest of the lower floor. It was there that he first saw her. A woman standing at the other end of the hall in front of the mirror, waiting patiently for this man to arrive.

She could see the barrels of the guns pointed at her. Feel their anticipation as the room went silent and the chill of the night swept its way in.

From their perspective, all they saw was a young woman standing in front of them. A girl no taller than five foot nine, no older than thirty-four. No more muscular than any other woman her age would have been and no more special than any other human either.

She was thin with barely a muscle on her. A slim and curved figure from head to toe. She hardly had a scrap of meat on her at the time. Yet another part of her disguise – make yourself look frail and people often believe it.

They saw long brown hair dangling from her head, resting on her shoulders and covering her upper back. They saw her young face and the look of innocence that it gave off the longer that you stared at it. However, that look soon faded when they re-aimed their guns and pointed them at her forehead. After that the look of a scared housewife soon consumed her face.

And all of these features were contained within a stunning blue dress, worn especially for this occasion. To

11

them, she seemed normal, however odd it was for them to have met a woman at the time, they didn't think that she was too out of place.

But she was anything but normal and was defiantly not afraid. She wasn't startled, nor was she surprised. She had expected these men for many days at the time and in truth, the only surprise that she experienced was in knowing that they had taken so long to find her.

The outside air soon rushed in, flooding the building like water out of a dam. The candles danced in reaction to the cooler air, glowing brighter and filling the room with the aroma of an exceptionally wealthy household.

The flames flickered violently as the temperature and air pressure equalised. Shadows created by them moved across the floor like a wave of snakes; shifting their form as each candle changed its output ever so slightly over time.

The rain continued to pour its way down, now falling within the house thanks to the open door behind the men. The sound of rain drops was faint but quite apparent. Knowing that this would eventually rot the wood flooring, the woman began to experience frustration but never showed it on her face.

Hiding your emotions is just as important as being able to fake them. She had appearances to keep and her frustration was of little importance at the time. The men pointing guns at her came first.

The man at the front had now buried his initial shock at the woman's presence and was quietly approaching her at quite a pace. He obviously had little patience. Most humans do.

She took a few steps to the right, hiding her movements

12

under the pretence that she was intimidated by his own as he came towards her but in truth, she knew exactly what she was doing.

She was leading them to the living room. After a few seconds of retreating backwards, finally, she stopped moving. Standing still and watching as the men gasped in awe of the priceless antiquities that decorated the room in which they now stood.

The china and the paintings. The furniture and even the fireplace. All of it was old and all of it was a highly sought-after antique of some kind.

The paintings belonged in an art gallery due to their rarity and value. The same went for most items in that room as well. The house was more like a museum than a home. With so much on display, it was hard not to think that it had been set out on purpose.

To most visitors, the house did not look like a house at all. Once inside, the layout and the items on display made it look just like an ordinary museum or prestigious art gallery. But it was more than that.

It was a home, a place of living and a place of admiration. The house itself was the true object on display, not the ones within it. The owners had taken great pride in designing it and even more pride from decorating it. To them, it wasn't just a collection of priceless artefacts, it was one single display of art. Running through every room as though the rooms themselves had been a part of the display all along.

And now that the visitors were contained within the walls of the living room, staring at this art, she knew that she could control what they saw and where they went.

The soldiers soon gathered their thoughts and took

control of their faces once again. Their looks of surprise and awe soon faded and their attention quickly focused back towards their goal. Their purpose for being there in the first place had yet to be revealed.

The leader of the group, a sergeant, judging by markings on his uniform, directed his attention back at the woman. It was odd for a man of such a low rank to be in charge of an entire platoon but I guess that they were desperate, at the time they probably couldn't spare any more men or resources than they already had.

"We're looking for a man known only as The Athereon, we have been told that he resides within this home." The sergeant said loudly, almost shouting in her face. Waving his arms in the air as he spoke.

She smiled, taking yet another step back and continuing to grin. Her perfect locks of hair blowing in the gusts of wind, her dress fluttering in the breeze and her hands placed firmly together in front of her. Holding nothing but her temper, she simply continued to stand, smiling at the man and ignoring what he had just said as though it had passed right through her.

"Something funny, is it?" The man asked, holding his hand on his firearm as the rest of the men spread out and started searching the various rooms of the mansion for the man they had come in search off.

"Tell me…" She said. "You seek the Athereon but what exactly do you think that the Athereon is? A mere title perhaps?"

The sergeant's face changed then. It became cross with anger, almost completely enraged. However, she had expected this. These types of men always have a short temper and an even smaller amount of patience for timewasters. Let alone a women.

"Is this some kind of trick, some game?" He shouted, unlatching his pistol from its holster.

A warning, a mere show of arms perhaps? The few men that were still in the room already had their weapons drawn, how would pointing a mere pistol at her have affected the already existing feeling of hostility they gave off?

"No games." She replied. "But you must answer all the same. What do you think the Athereon is? This question should be simple if you have come this far in search of him."

She leant in closer, almost as you would if you intended to taunt the person you were speaking too. She continued to grin, seeming unfazed by the man's attempts to threaten her.

"I don't have time for this." The man sighed.

He raised his weapon and pointed it at her head. Unfazed yet again, she stood there, still grinning and not scared in the slightest. Even if he had tried to fire the gun, he would have been dead long before his finger had pulled the trigger.

"Answer the question love, it's for you own good."

She leaned in even closer than before, placing her head up to the barrel of the gun and continuing to smile she started staring directly into the sergeant's eyes.

The rest of the men in the room whispered something to each other and then suddenly all of them had gathered as a singular group standing behind the sergeant.

Even the ones in the other rooms had rallied to their position. It was a dense group of weapons, nothing more. It didn't matter if the firing squad was made up of people, as long as those guns were pointed at her, their lives meant nothing.

The sergeant lowered his gun, possibly out of shock or perhaps he didn't have the balls to shoot an unarmed and non-hostile woman without good reason. But finally, and to her relief, he attempted to answer the question but as expected, he gave her the same answer that every human did.

"The Athereon is an ancient warrior, a mage belonging to the old world and the only person known to exist that is capable of winning the fight that we now face."

He put his gun back into his holster and knelt down before her. She noticed this act and returned to standing up straight in her confusion. Relaxing a little now that the gun had been removed from her forehead, she eased her posture and stood her ground.

Not more than two feet away, the sergeant was on the floor in front of her – slowly drying off from the heat of the candles and the fire as he knelt. One knee on the floor and one in the air. Just as you would if you were to propose to someone, his posture was armature and poor. He had never done this before and it was obvious.

"Madam, if you know where he is, I beg of you. Summon him now, for all our sakes. We cannot win this fight alone." He pleaded.

The man lowered his head and looked at the floor that his drenched clothes had dampened. Perhaps in an attempt to show respect.

Though, on the other hand, a more likely reason for lowering his head was so that he could stare at her feet rather than her hips. It would have been seen as quite rude to stare at someone's groin for no reason other than that it just happened to be there.

She enlarged her smile for a moment, expressing joy, finding his answer as hilarious as his attempt to ask for help. Then she let out a large sigh as she gave her response, one that she had said many times before and one that she had memorised well.

"You humans, you always answer that question wrong." She smirked.

She looked to the table behind her for a moment. Drawing the attention of the men towards that same direction. She clicked her fingers and one of the chairs next to the table suddenly moved across the room towards her. Giving her a convenient seat for her to rest in.

There, she relaxed for a moment, taking her seat comfortably. She took in her surroundings and studied every man before her as they stood in awe of what she had done.

She then continued to speak, almost as if she was teaching a class of children, something that she was quite proficient in doing as it happened.

"The Athereon is not a warrior and is most certainly not a simple mage. A mage like myself could never hope to compare to one such as him. He's simply too powerful for that to ever happen. Furthermore, the Athereon is not a mere soldier that you can command; he is not simply here to go into battle at your behest."

The sergeant's head lifted to face hers, a look of confusion and frustration evident on his face. He knew that she was being purposely cryptic and yet, he still did nothing to stop her.

"Then what? What the devil is he?" The man snapped,

standing up once again, changing his posture to one of a defensive nature.

"Hope. Your last hope to be exact. Whenever there is a threat that humanity cannot control or contain, he is there. When there is a war that humanity cannot win, he is there. When the suffering of the masses becomes too much to handle, he is there. Not because he was asked to, not because he was forced to but because he chose to."

She raised her head a little and faced the crowd of men with their rifles and pistols still pointed at her. All nine of them were prepared to fire but not one shot ever left their clips. However, they still continued to point them her way, they had just had their fears confirmed after all. She was a mage and they were scared of her because of it.

"The Athereon is not a fighter nor is he a pacifist, the Athereon is and always will be our protector and our guardian. It is up to him to decide whether to help or not and it is up to him to decide if you are worthy of that help. It is very rare that humanity's wars ever actually interest him."

"So we are to be tested then?" He asked her in reply.

The sergeant then placed his hand back on his firearm ready to raise it once again.

"You already have been." She explained.

"When? All we have done is find and travel to his home, where does a test come into that?" He asked.

The sergeant seemed confused, removing his hand from his firearm and waving it in the air as he spoke. Just like a lot of simpler beings would do, humans always preferred to talk and gesture at the same time.

A mage was more sophisticated than that, we use our voices and our faces. What more did we really need in order

18

to emphasize a sentence? Waving your hand around only accomplished one thing. It distracted others.

"There are three tests that are performed when the Athereon's help is requested. First, you were tested by your ability to find this home. Only one man in the village below will tell you how to get through the barrier and the test was to see how quickly you could find him. A test that you failed."

"Failed? We found this house in less than a week!" The man snapped.

Again, the sergeant's face went back to one of simple anger. The confusion had faded despite what he had just said and was replaced only by the emotions that he had been trained to feel. Rage and hostility.

"Had you been more prepared then you would have brought a mage with you, they would have found this house in less than a day. To us it sticks out like a beacon. A pillar of light for all to see, a mark of his power and a warning for us to stay away." She explained.

Still, the sergeant maintained the illusion that he was confused by what she had told him. She could tell that he was possibly preparing for a fight, so she continued to explain. Buying herself time and creating a false sense of trust between them the longer she spoke.

"Second, you were tested when you entered this property. Seeing how you simply barged your way in here and drew your weapons immediately, not a shred of respect for his privacy or possessions, I would mark that as a fail as well." She continued.

"And the third?" He asked in a somewhat angered voice.

"Me and my question. The third test is how well you

treat me as a person and how well you answer my question. Should it be asked that is." She said. "By threatening me with violence and by answering my question in the same manner as you always do, you have failed. It is at this point that I must ask you all to leave. Or would you rather suffer the consequences of trespassing in a mage's household?"

The sergeant had not liked that answer. Tensing up, preparing for the battle that was to come, he opened his mouth once again. Probably moments away from attempting to fire his gun.

"Tell me, mage. What makes you so special?" The sergeant asked as he drew his weapon once again. Pointing it directly at her face, just as he had done moments before.

"Excuse me?" She replied, a hint of disgust given off by her voice. Her rage slowly building and unaware to them, her magic energy slowly pooling, ready for use.

"Why are you so important that not only do you live in his home but you yourself are also a part of his test? Who are you exactly?"

I have always enjoyed this part. Watching her show off has always been so entertaining to me and so frightening to them. I suppose that's just one of the perks of knowing her. Her body itself was beautiful but her rage was exquisite. Never had I known a more attractive woman than her. Nor do I intend to.

She stood up, clenched both fists and placed them by her side. Her magic power awakened and began to manifest. And from that moment on, she not only told them but she also showed them exactly what she was.

Shards of magic energy manifested around her. Small green shards of crystal floating and orbiting her body as she spoke. Gusts of wind, not unlike those from a tornado, spiralled around her, carrying those shards through the air. The intense strength of this wind served well to scare the men. It even made them lose their balance, preventing their ability to aim or fire their weapons.

"I am not someone that you should be so carelessly trifling with." She warned them. "You asked who I am, then I'll tell you. I am Katiana Illisidel, Crown Mage of the Magic Council. And more importantly, I am more than strong enough to wipe you all of the face of this Earth within a heartbeat if I must. You asked what made me special, why I live here and why I am part of his tests, then maybe you should have looked at the ring on my finger."

The shards began to multiply and pulsate with every word, intensifying in strength and surrounding her like a shield. The wind now blowing around the items in the property, like a storm inside a house it began to devastate everything around her.

"I am his WIFE!" She screamed.

The shards exploded, racing outward in every direction, shattering the windows, the vases and shredding the furniture. But not without purpose.

Each one that flew towards those humans did so with a target in mind. Their weapons. Smashing them into unrecognisable pieces on the floor with each and every impact from those shards.

As usual, the soldiers ran out of the door in fear. But at the front of the line was, as expected, the sergeant who had acted tough throughout the engagement.

Cowards as always, they never stop to notice that not one of the shards had actually hit them or even come close to doing so.

Out of the thousands surrounding her, none had been used to harm them; none were used in an attempt to attack them. That spell was simply intended for scaring the target, not injuring them. However, it could have done so easily if she had wanted it to.

I stood at the bottom of the path leading to the house, just outside of the barrier I had shown them through earlier. None of the men had noticed my presence; then again, they hadn't really noticed me since they met me over a week ago.

If they had, they would have never entered that house to begin with, they wouldn't have needed to.

Not one of them ever takes the time to actually think through what they were doing. Had they only brought a mage with them, they would have spotted me in a second. After all, all those who are sensitive to magic can see, I am far too powerful to be any ordinary mage.

I smiled as they ran past me, running back to their tanks and cars in an attempt to look tough and protect themselves as they gathered more of their weapons.

And then just as the last man had passed the barrier, I waved my arm and closed the hole that I had made once again. With myself safely on the other side.

I began to walk up the hill with laughter in my heart as expected. She had done exactly as she always does, scared them senseless, they hadn't even noticed that all their ammunition had been piled up on the wrong side of the barrier. Exactly where I had put it.

I was only five or six steps up the hill as they began to try to break through the barrier with their fists and knifes. Desperately trying to get back that which I had taken.

Even if they had regained such weaponry however, it wouldn't have helped. No projectile, not even their strongest bullets, would have been powerful enough to pierce a barrier as strong as that one. Something that was created with magic can often only be destroyed with magic.

They had no chance of breaking through, once a barrier of my creation is closed, there are only two people that can go through it and only five people who can open it again.

There were plenty of people capable of destroying it but that takes time and a lot of energy. If you ever come across a barrier and realise that it belongs to me, the best option you have is to request entry rather than force it. I have seen many a mage collapse from the exhaustion of trying.

I soon approached the door and pulled back the knocker. I knocked three times, taking a step back and bowing both my body and head.

The door soon opened.

"Forgive my intrusion madam but may I come in? I have important business to discuss with you." I said.

I lifted my head and returned to a standing posture as I awaited her response. Showing dignity and respect, not being forceful or suggesting that I should be in charge.

"Why of course, but tell me, why is it that you have come to me?" She replied. Moving away from the door to allow me through.

I took a step through the opening, removed my raincoat and placed it on the hooks to my right before I said anything. I didn't want to dampen the floor any more than it had already.

"May I start off by saying what a lovely home you have." I said.

I took a moment to turn my head all around, taking in the surroundings and admiring the artwork on the walls.

"Thank you." She giggled. "However, I cannot take all the credit, my husband chose most of the interior decorations."

She closed the door behind me and proceed to show me through the house and into the living area. The mess from before had already been corrected as I entered.

"And what a lovely job he did, miss?"

I reach out my hand, showing that I respect her as a woman and that I am genuinely interested in hearing the answer to the question that I had just asked.

"Katiana." She said, placing her hand on mine.

"A pleasure to meet you, Katiana."

I raise her hand to my lips and kiss the very edge of her knuckles with the most tender of touch.

"Such a beautiful wedding ring you have there, I dare say that I have never seen anything quite like it."

The ring had just caught my eye as I released her hand. A simple piece but quite obviously hand crafted. A spiral of silver and a pattern engraved throughout. A blue jewel on the front, sparkling in the light, sapphire perhaps.

I looked back to her face then to find her smiling before she spoke.

"My husband spent six weeks making that for me before the wedding. He could have used machines to do it faster but he did every step by hand and only when he was sure that I wouldn't catch him doing it. He wanted to surprise me on the day you see."

She lowered her head to stare at the ring. Admiring it as if she had never noticed its beauty before.

"Tell me." I said. "Would your husband be home by any chance? I would quite like to meet a man of such talent."

We stopped walking at that moment, only just steps away from entering the living area where the destruction from only moments ago would have awaited us.

"Why, no." She sighed. "He left many hours ago and I haven't a clue as to when he might return."

She raised her head back towards me, expressing a feeling of worry on her face. I ignored the lack of devastation in the room as I entered. I felt that it would be rude to mention its absence. Instead, I continued the conversation as if I hadn't noticed it.

"Such a shame, perhaps you could give him a message for me upon his return?"

I turned my attention back towards the hallway and subsequently the front door at the other end to signify that I intended to leave after that.

"Of course, however I can't promise that he will hear it any time soon." She said with a look of genuine sorrow appearing on her face.

She must have been truly worried about her husband's absence. I knew it to be an act but I still pretended that I thought it was genuine anyway in order to keep up appearances.

"Then by all means I will be on my way, please tell him that a soldier by the name of Terrance stopped by. Please tell him that I am staying at the Fox's Tail down the road. He can meet me there if it pleases him. Tell him that this concerns something that I believe he will understand; tell him that this is a matter of importance for the one known as the Athereon."

I bowed once again and bid the fair lady goodbye. Taking in every aspect of her figure and memorising her scent. Such a woman should be cherished even if you are forbidden to do so.

"You don't have to leave so soon." She insisted. "The kettle boiled not too long ago, at least allow me to make you a cup of tea before you leave."

She grabbed my arm and gave it a slight pull towards the room I assumed would be the kitchen.

"I am afraid that I must be off, I wouldn't want your husband to get the wrong idea if he came back while I was here. A beautiful woman like yourself must have quite the jealous man by her side, I know I would be."

"Yes, I suppose your right; perhaps it would be best if you did leave."

She released my arm and allowed me to leave. A look of genuine disappointment appeared on her face as a walked towards the door.

I grabbed my raincoat and reached for the door handle. Just as I latched onto it, I turned towards her with a smile on my face and asked her the question that finally broke the character I had been playing since I entered.

"So how did I do?"

She couldn't help but to let out an even bigger smile than mine, almost as if she was competing with me. I didn't see this as a game, despite how little we cared for taking it seriously, these rehearsals were important to us. They were a way of calming down and having a little fun after our latest rude guests had been thrown or scared out.

It was our way of making sure that we remembered what these encounters should be like even if they never would be.

"You passed as you always do. Now, come here." She ordered, pointing at a spot on the floor in front of her. "And comfort your 'beautiful woman'. I've just had the worst visitors that you could imagine, just look at the state of carpets."

I dropped my coat and she ran towards me before I had a chance to move to her. I opened my arms and she jumped for my face, assaulting it with an array of kisses and love bites. I almost lost my balance for a moment but soon regained it and began to walk through the house and up the east staircase.

I carried her to the bedroom, trying not to suffocate while she continued to tear off parts of my cheeks and beard. I kicked open the door, no regard for its value what so ever as I knew it could be repaired.

I approached the front of the bed and dropped her onto it. And with her now resting with her legs over the edge of the mattress and her back laying flat against it with her arms out to the side leaving her vulnerable, I took off my shirt and… well. You can guess what happened next. I know that if we had had neighbours, they could have.

JULIAN

Expectations. All of us have them at one time or another. They are formed from past experiences and act as a way for our primitive minds to predict events yet to come without so much as a thought.

To some, they can be useful. But to me, there were merely something that I had come to avoid back then. I wasn't the kind of person that would go through each day expecting events to unfold exactly as I had predicted them to or how I had seen them happen before. I enjoyed the spontaneity of life. The not knowing kept me intrigued. I wouldn't have wanted to ruin the experience by already knowing what was about to happen.

I wasn't someone who expected much from life at all to be honest. I knew that with every passing day some new event would occur somewhere in the world that would eventually work its way down to me and change my life whether I wanted it to or not.

I had come to accept that other than the choices and actions that I made and took, I was completely powerless to anticipate the rest of the world.

There were some things that I could control, some that I could predict with enough effort and information but there still remained much that I could not.

I wasn't a believer in fate at the time. Our lives are what we make of them. That was my belief. And even not, after all I have seen to contradict such a faith, I still remain sceptical.

But if there was one thing that I knew to be certain, one thing that remained true no matter what the circumstance, it was that everything in life happened for a reason.

Whether it be divine providence or mere luck – some force unseen and unfelt – it didn't matter. Every encounter that I had ever experienced, every event and every choice had happened for a reason.

While I couldn't comprehend why or how it happened, I knew this to be the case. And despite this view on life, despite what I believed to be true and how pointless I knew it was to expect events to happen as you imagine them, I had still allowed myself to expect the soldiers from that night to come marching back to my door.

Even though I shouldn't have made such a prediction, even though I knew that predicting events was as pointless as trying to anticipate the next earthquake or tornado, I still allowed myself to create such an expectation.

I had expected to see their return long before the next time a visitor came in search of my help. I was almost certain of it.

I had expected to see a small army of men and machinery at the border of my barrier within a week of their departure but that never happened.

It never would have. I later found out that the men had turned tail and ran. They never had any intention for coming back. And they certainly weren't about to speak of those events to anyone ever again. Even if they had wanted to return, even if they had wanted to tell someone, they wouldn't have been able to.

Unknown to them and most people really, there was a separate barrier surrounding the entire village. It didn't stop you physically, in fact most would have said it did nothing at all. But in reality, it effected each and every person walking through it mentally.

When people entered, nothing happened. But when they went back through it to leave, every memory of me and my home is wiped from their minds.

Within a few hours of the men passing through it as they ran, they wouldn't have remembered the house or my wife. They would have just remembered visiting the village and then leaving. Nothing in-between those events would have remained for long.

They would have eventually noticed the gaps in their memories and questioned them but by the time that they realised what was missing, they would have probably been dead.

It was unfortunate that such a precaution had been seen as necessary but with how well hidden I have tried to remain in the past, I wasn't going to simply allow people to leave with the knowledge of where I lived still intact within their minds.

With how obscure and feared I was to humans; I couldn't allow any who had met me or my wife to retain that information after they had left.

This wasn't for my protection or for my wife's in truth. It wasn't for the sake of the village or its inhabitants either. It was purely so that I could keep my privacy. There wasn't a single situation that you could put me in that I couldn't get myself out of with a little effort.

But if my house were to become a tourist location then I wouldn't have been able to get out of that so easily. That was my home, if I couldn't retain my privacy even when within its walls then I would have never had a private life again.

It's bad enough that mages can spot me from miles away. Imagine if they knew how to find me at all times regardless of sight.

So it was to that end, that I made sure anyone who came and visited me, anyone who had requested my help, wouldn't remember doing so unless I had allowed them to.

However, there were exceptions to this of course. In order for the barrier to actually take effect, you had to actually pass through it. For a mage, there were many ways of crossing distances without physically moving an inch.

For any person who knew even a slight amount of magic, the barrier wouldn't have been very effective. Then again, it wasn't really intended for use against mages, I designed it to keep the humans away from me and the complexities of my life.

There were only a handful of governments in the human world that even knew of magic's existence back then; even less that knew of me. If the soldiers had been allowed to remember, then they would have returned with guns and even more heavy machinery to force their way in a second time having confirmed both my existence and my residence in a single night.

If they had done this, they would have eventually started firing their explosives at the invisible barrier covering my house. If they had done that, there would have been immense repercussions in the human world.

Something like that, is not so easily forgotten or ignored. If they were to publicly attack my home and reveal magic to the rest of the world, the conflict that would follow would be too much to contain.

Humans fear what they do not understand. Tell them that magic exists and they will instantly start hunting it. Desperately trying to contain and control it in order to keep themselves on the top of the food chain.

And back then, humanity wasn't ready to learn the secrets of magic. Not by a long shot. Though, even now I'd have stood by that statement. Humans weren't ready.

But it wasn't like I was left with a choice in the end.

And neither would they have been.

If such an attack had been carried out on my home, the government behind it would be the ones I went after first. They would have known this. They at least had the common sense to stay away from me after I had said no. They feared me too greatly to have even considered it.

If the men from that night had returned to whatever base they had come from seeking a fight, then I suspect that one of their superiors would have told them to let it go in that instant. Telling them that if I had said no, there wouldn't have been a point in going back. Surely they know by now, if I say no, they won't be granted another audience with me again.

Then again, never has a single member of any military been allowed to leave knowing where I was. Never had anyone of the thousands who had stepped through my barrier ever come back after they left. So who can say what would've happened?

And yet, even though they always forgot, every time that

the guests are turned away, I always felt as though they would be coming back the next day.

It was strange to think that way, I knew that it was impossible for them to do so and yet I still woke up the following morning expecting it. My knowledge of how aggressively humans reacted to me seemed to have been more important than the fact that I knew they wouldn't be returning, even if they had left wanting to.

Even though I knew that none of them could have possibly remembered where the house was or how to get to it, I still anticipated their return for days after they left.

I'm not entirely sure as to why I did but it still happened. Perhaps I was getting bored of my peace and longed for a fight. Not that any meaningful battle could ever come when going at it against a people like the humans. It wouldn't have lasted more than a handful of minutes if I was at my top strength. An hour at most if I was at my worst.

But my need for bloodshed and battle could wait. It always did. And so I returned to my normal life, keeping that desire for battle in the back of my mind and going about my day to day business as though nothing had happened.

And just as I knew it would, my door remained silent that entire time. No visitors came from either world. And not one request for me to help the humans or the world of mages were made either.

It was quiet for a time after that night. Almost too quiet.

The night of their visit soon faded into nothing but a memory and three weeks quietly passed us by. The war in the east violently grew worse as it entered its second year of existence and with nothing else to do that day, I finally decided to look into it.

34

THE ATHEREON: WINTER'S WAR

After reading about it in the papers from the village and talking to a few of my more cooperative sources in the human world, I soon understood why I had been sought out by the military in the first place.

Not because I was required or needed but because the U.S. military knew they couldn't win and tried to use me as a way of ending the conflict and declaring them as the victor.

They had summoned me selfishly as always. I wouldn't have needed to attend even if I had agreed to talk to them. The war was wide spread and devastating that much was true but alas, that fight was not my kind of affair.

The fighting was too petty for me to intervene; I would have been more of a problem down there than the war itself. But if out of nothing but my own curiosity, I did eventually visit the battlefield of course. Just to take a look.

I stayed perched above one of the main areas of battle in an abandoned church for days and all I saw was a pointless conflict over land. Humanity's constant struggle for power wasn't of any importance to me.

I chose not to do anything about it definitively that day.

I chose to stay out of the fight entirely. And this choice wasn't made for my safety, nor for the sake of the humans that I would have killed to resolve the conflict but simply because I would have had to choose a side. One bunch of humans or the other.

It was my chosen purpose to be nothing more than the protector of humanity; therefor I am always supposed to be on their side.

How could I have done anything? I would have been against humanity no matter what side I chose.

However, if one side had been made up of the worst humanity had to offer, people who would have harmed a great many more than their own lives could tally, I would have gladly butchered them all.

While it was true that humanity could be a great and honourable species, most of them never come close to achieving this state of existence.

They start wars, pillage homes, and murder countless millions of their own kind all because someone disagreed with someone else over the way they did things.

If I hadn't already seen what humanity could become if they tried hard enough, I would have given up on them a long time ago.

So, I ignored the conflict and returned to my life of solitude. Three weeks passed after the night that our uninvited guests had left and nothing had become of it since. I was about three or four seconds away from finishing the repairs to the floor in the hallway when I heard it.

Three knocks in quick succession at the door. Not too quiet that they wouldn't have been heard and not too powerful that they would have damaged the frame. The knocks were just right, enough to be heard but not enough to startle those inside.

However, despite how appropriately loud they were, the knocks had managed to startle someone in the end. Because they had startled me.

At first I was shocked, simply dropping whatever I was holding and letting it break on the floor. I'm not sure what it was, a vase or pot of some kind maybe as I was putting everything back in its place. I can't remember. I was in a state of disbelief.

It shouldn't have been possible for someone to be at the door, the barrier was still closed to guests, Katiana and I were still inside and none of the others capable of opening it were in the country. If they were, I would have known. There was an order to things after all.

My wife was the Crown Mage of the Magic Council. If anyone with that level of strength had entered the country, she would have been warned. It's not common for a mage of sufficient power to be considered dangerous to have been allowed to walk around freely. Anyone powerful enough to break through one of my barriers, the same ones used to secure our prisons and the magic world itself, would have been closely watched and considered to be a deadly threat at all times.

And even if such a man did stand at the door, that didn't change the fact that I would have felt the barrier collapse if someone had forced their way through. With how sophisticated and powerful this particular barrier was, I would have at least heard someone break it down. Any spell powerful enough to break through one of my barriers wasn't going to be a quiet one. Such devastating destruction would have been so obvious that I would have felt its power building up long before the spell was activated.

I looked at Katiana as she came towards the hallways in response to the door's summons. Both of us were surprised to hear the knocks. To the best of my knowledge, this was the first time we'd been caught by surprise at the appearance of a guest.

This had never happened before and her face showed that fact quite adequately. Although, I would think that she was more upset at the sight of me breaking whatever I had just dropped than she was surprised to hear the door.

Never before had a caller come knocking during the day and never before had it been while I was still at home. Normally I would have to bring the guests to the house, passing them through the barrier myself. I would have pretended to be a simple mage and mention to the visiting soldiers that I would be capable of taking them where they wanted to go. It was a lie that I had told many times before and one that I was quite good at convincing people was the truth.

But that hadn't happened and instead a complete stranger now stood at the door. I closed my eyes and got a brief sense of him mentally. At first I was confused. Nothing about him made me think that he was a mage, at least there wasn't anything to suggest that he knew that he was. There were no signs of magic energy in his body and he didn't have the sense of a strong mind about him.

I thought that he was human for a moment but he was too sensitive to magic for him not to be a mage. So much so that I could feel him resisting my own senses. He was literally barricading his mind from me the more I peered in. Something that a human couldn't have done in a million years. Alost proving that he was more than what he at first appeared to be but even so, I still didn't think he was a mage.

I couldn't be sure. There was something. It was extremely week and hard to detect against the walls he'd erected around his mind but I sensed something odd within him. Some strange force that I had not felt before, something that led me to question him even more.

His lack of magic energy puzzled me too. It was so low

that he could have passed as human but there was still something about him; some strange feeling that his presence created. I couldn't get a good read on him because of it. It was like he had a wall of magic protecting him but it didn't feel like any magic I knew. I was familiar and yet wrong.

He certainly didn't seem human but I was almost completely sure that he wasn't a trained mage. If he had been, I would have sensed him before he arrived at the door. Magic energy isn't so easy to conceal when someone as potently powerful as me goes looking for it.

While I could sense some faint fragments of magic within him, he contained no magic circuits, no signs of training and nothing that would suggest that he even knew what magic was.

He felt like a child in truth. But I could clearly tell that he had the body of an adult. An adult capable of passing through my barrier, not displaying any signs of magic and could easily hide himself in a room full of humans.

He was an irregularity that I had never encountered before. A person that would have normally had no importance or interest to me yet I couldn't help but be curious about him. I couldn't understand what it was about him that made him so odd but I was surely about to find out, after all, he was stood on my doorstep.

I nodded at Katiana after I had finished sizing him up and then made myself scarce. Hiding myself away and out of view, sticking to the way we would normally did things as much as I could. To that end, Katiana was the one who opened the door while I remained hidden and kept my watchful eye on the both of them.

The first thing that I noticed when the door swung open

was the weather though. It was supposed to be calm and clear that day but something seemed off when the door opened. There wasn't a bird in sight, no chirping, no wind, no warmth and no cold. It was as if nature itself had stopped in his presence as if even the planet didn't agree with him.

After that, my eyes were drawn to him. The puzzling man standing at my door. He seemed so frail, barely a muscle on him. Scruffy blond hair dangling from his scalp and a poorly groomed beard hanging from his jaw. He looked like he had been living on the street. But for a mage, that wasn't possible.

The magic world had no economy at the time, simply power. The stronger you were and the higher your rank, the more unrestricted access you could have to the luxuries that a mage's life would give you.

Even if you didn't have enough power for a place to live, the various academies would always offer you a bed even if you weren't a student.

They were a haven for all who were akin to magic, offering a safe and secure environment for all who chose to reside within their walls. Seeing a mage living on the streets in this day and age was a result of only one thing.

Branding.

A banishment that is reserved only for the criminals who are deemed too dangerous to be locked up. The mark of this is a circular brand on your neck. Something that this man did not possess.

The brand itself is more similar to a curse than a spell. Leaching the magic energy from the mage until it reaches a point where it would be unusable and then keeping it there. Normally this would incapacitate the mage but the brand keeps you going. Turning you into nothing more than a human, forcing you to live amongst them, never to return to the world that you had once known and never to use magic again.

But nothing about this young man suggested that he was a criminal, in fact he seemed too innocent to have even committed a crime in the first place. He hadn't struck me as a thief or a murderer. He didn't strike me as being anything really. I couldn't get a sense of who he was at all, he was just too plain. Too ordinary.

He had an odd aura about him. A sense of clarity and purity that surrounded him like a blanket that hid him from the world.

In terms of his inner appearance, he seemed like a new born. His mind was too clean and his presence was too pure for him to have been an adult. Something about him simply didn't sit right with me.

I turned my attention to the clothes he wore too. They were old and tattered from use but I could still tell that they were a mage's clothing. The only thing that was odd about them was that no one had worn that design in over a hundred years. They were formal, a set of robes designed to be worn at special events or ceremonies.

I hadn't worn mine in a very long time and I'm not even sure that Katiana owned a set at the time. Not that she would have needed to. In all our time together, I'm not sure that we had ever attended a formal event of a high enough calibre for it to have been appropriate to wear them. With the exception of the odd celebratory meal, never had we gone to an event of a formal nature that would have required them.

But that's beside the point.

Now that the door was open, I could finally get a good look at him, no more of the parlour tricks I had been using to assess him through the walls. Now that I could physically see him, I was only causing my confusion to grow inside.

The thing that stood out most other than his appearance was his stance. He was bowing, that was the first thing that started to worry me. He was bowing in the same way that I did, just as those seeking my audience are expected to do. It was a formal bow, arms, legs and back kept straight, bowing from the hips alone. He was a particularly strange individual. I was certain of that much.

The words he spoke are what frightened me most.

"Pardon my intrusion ma'am, my name is Julian, may I come in? There are urgent matters that we must discuss." He said to her calmly.

He raised his head slightly to make eye contact, but still he bowed in her presence. Doing exactly as he should have done, as if he had seen it done before.

Katiana realised that he wasn't our usual type of guest, so she attempted to test him on the spot. Managing to go as far as opening her mouth to speak but before she had a chance to utter even a single word from her mouth he stepped in and said something most peculiar.

"I'm sorry but I must insist." He blabbered. "If I do not sit down soon, I may collapse where I stand. That is quite the barrier you have out there. I must say that I'm impressed. Getting through it wasn't easy."

Not only had he interrupted my wife as she attempted to speak but he had also revealed that he had knowledge of magic. While I had contained my suspicions at the time this only confirmed them. So much so that I couldn't help but utter the word from my mouth as I came to the realisation of what he was.

"Mage?" I whispered under my breath. Initially not realising that the word had left my lips but once it had it was already too late. What was said had been said but in spite of my luck, no one had heard it.

"Yes, yes come in."

Katiana showed him in and shut the door. Rushing him to the dining room and pulling him a chair to sit on.

He took off his winter coat as he came in and all I could focus on were the holes in the robes that he was wearing, revealing the scares on his back.

Four circular indents, much like those left when you lose a limb. Thick layers of skin covering what seemed to be an out of place bones all surrounded by the markings of a whip and the bruises of chains.

The four holes puzzled me the most, it wasn't something that I could explain. However, the lashes and scars surrounding them, those markings were rare, both in the human world and even more so in ours.

I often wondered where those marks had come from, where he had been treated so poorly. They were the marks of torture but the other marks, those four holes on his back, they didn't make any sense.

I didn't understand how he of all people could have such things at the time.

So I stayed hidden and watched from afar. I was the one who had designed and built the house, so of course I could hide in it. Staying hidden in the dark corners of doorways or up on the support beams in the larger rooms.

In my house, I was as hard to find as a shadow in the dead of night.

And realising that the man had at least some knowledge of magic, Katiana changed her tactic somewhat. No longer questioning him as she would have done a human, she asked him questions that only a mage could have answered.

"Tell me, mage, how did someone as untrained as you get through my husband's barrier?" She asked.

She crossed her arms and sat on the chair across from him. Staying cautious and not getting too close. An interesting tactic to use. I had often wondered how she would react when the day came that a mage would be knocking at the door and now I had been given a chance to find out.

It was a very rare occurrence for a mage to visit and it was even more uncommon for that mage to have been uninvited but never had we had an intruder.

"While it may be an impressive barrier, one that most people would have had to destroy in order to pass through, it has only one flaw. It is designed to be invisible wasn't it? Unnoticed by humans and by nature?" He asked, watching as Katiana nodded. "Therefore, it was designed so that animals could still pass through it unhindered. I assume the same goes for wind and rain?"

While that was true it still didn't explain how he got through. I saw no feathers or claws on the man. No fur or tail, nothing that would suggest that he was an animal or that he could have tricked the barrier into recognising him as one.

No mere mage could trick my barrier so easily regardless of his appearance anyway. I had been creating them for thousands of years and in all those years I have refined the process to a point far beyond everyone else.

Not one other mage could have made something so complex and powerful as quickly and as large as I could. Any other mage would have difficulty creating a barrier half the size of mine let alone being able to make so many rules and exceptions for what it would allow in and out.

In terms of creating a barrier, I was completely unrivalled – the same could be said for most of what I could do actually. When you've been around as long as I have, any skill can be mastered given enough patience.

"You didn't answer my question." Katiana replied, unfolding her arms, leaning on the surface of the dining table to get closer to him in order to create a feeling of urgency with her question.

"This means that if one were to have every nearby bird fly through all at once, a hole would open to allow their safe passage. A hole that would be just large enough for an 'untrained' mage like myself to teleport through unhindered."

He responded with a sense of pride in his voice. A look of accomplishment on his face. He was obviously proud to have gotten through the barrier. Even if he had cheated in order to do so.

'This amateur knows teleportation magic?' I said to my wife accidently.

Me and her, we shared a physic link, more telepathic than anything else but it allowed us to communicate over distances great or small.

Telepathy was a common skill for a mage but our link was special, it was private and very strong. Put enough effort into it and we could even share what we were seeing with each other.

I confess that I must have let the words slip unknowingly. I had believed that they had been nothing more than a self-contained thought, not knowing that I had unintentionally broadcast that thought for all to hear.

Even if it had been accidental, the message should have only been heard by Katiana, it wasn't sent publicly but privately. The only people capable of hearing it should have been those who already shared a private link with me but it was what happened mere moments after that thought was sent through the air that filled me with a sense of both amazement and fear.

"This 'amateur' knows many things." He said.

His words startled me, his look confused me and his intellect continued to allude me. I saw his head shift and soon I knew where he was looking all too disturbingly.

It was up, straight up at the ceiling, peering directly at the centre of the wooden support beams, exactly where I was standing at the time.

This was not just any standard form of telepathy that he possessed. It was on a level that actually might have rivalled my own.

So strong that he could hear a private line without even trying and then track that private line back to its source. That shouldn't have been possible.

A telepathic message is a disembodied and boundless voice playing in your head. A voice that doesn't give off a sense of direction when it's heard.

No one listening to that message should have been able to find where I was standing simply by hearing it. Telepathy didn't work that way. There was no physical or mental connection between where you are standing and the message itself. I didn't even know that tracking telepathic messages was possible and I was the one who had invented modern telepathy in the first place.

Besides that, the fact that he had managed to hear the message in the first place was astonishing enough. Such a skill is hard to learn and even more difficult to teach. If he had been sitting there the whole time trying to listen to every telepathic communication on purpose, it would have been obvious.

Such an action takes a great deal of concentration to perform. So much so that he wouldn't have been able to hold a conversation at the same time. He wouldn't have even been aware of his surroundings.

It didn't matter how he had done it in the end though. All that mattered was that he had.

He had managed to surmise that I was there, he had found me and now that I had been discovered I wouldn't be able to avoid the situation anymore.

Now that he had seen me, I had been left with little choice, for once I would have to do the interview myself. It had been many years since I had done this, going back to the days when I had first built the house. I couldn't remember a time where someone hadn't done this for me since then. Throughout my entire time living at that address, I had always had someone to do the interview on my behalf.

Otherwise I would be putting myself in the line of fire of whatever had entered the room. This wasn't for my safety but for the visitors. If they had started shooting, I would have killed them in response. Not because I wanted to but because I was simply too powerful to stop their injuries from being deadly.

It's hard to restrain yourself when you're as strong as I am and even more difficult when the thing that your fighting against was as easy to kill as a human.

The others who had done the interviews for me were a little less trigger happy, I guess. If they did lose their temper, it wouldn't have resulted in them accidently killing the guests, only injuring and scaring them. I didn't want to be known as a killer, so having others perform the interview for me seemed like the better choice.

But once I realised that I had been discovered, I decided to stop beating around the bush. If this man had sufficiently impressive skills and enough knowledge to get in here then I needed to deal with him quickly before things got too out of hand. I made my way down, teleporting from the ceiling to the floor, and landed behind Katiana having placed a hand on her shoulder. Politely telling her to leave.

"As you can see, I might be a little underqualified to properly assess this one." She said.

"It's all right. Could you get us some tea perhaps? I think that our guest here might need it quite desperately." I asked her.

She nodded and teleported her way into the kitchen. A little unnecessary given the distance but I suppose that it was faster than walking.

Now that she was gone and I was closer than I had been thus far, I took a long look at the man before me, realising that I should have been calling him boy all along. While he wore a beard and had a sufficiently tall build, he was no older than nineteen at the time. Still nothing more than a kid, not a single piece of wisdom or experience yet laid into his soul.

I took the seat that Katiana had left behind and began my own interview of him. Assessing his knowledge and power as best I could while the conversation continued. Desperately trying to figure out why he was here and how he knew so much about how to get an audience with me.

"Tell me Julian, by your assessment alone, what am I?"

"Blinding." He said. "But also magnificent and frightening. Threatening almost. Is there a reason that you carry those swords and wear that armour? Are all your guests greeted with the same hostile attire when they meet you?" He asked.

He was trying his best not to look at me for too long. Just as you wold do if you looked at a bright light or directly at the sun, he wouldn't keep his eyes on me for more than a second. It was as though he couldn't, as if by doing so created a sense of pain or fear within him. Is that what he meant when he said that I was 'blinding'. Was there something about me that made me difficult to look at? Was I giving off some form of invisible light that only he could see?

"What?" I replied in an intense state of shock.

That one statement alone had forced me to go from trying to figure out why he was here to trying to understand where he had gotten that description from.

It had completely shifted my focus. I now no longer cared for why he was here or who he was, I only cared about understanding what he could see. The only explanation that came to mind was impossible and yet it was the only one that made sense. This boy amazed me, an untrained mage obviously full of potential and unfocused magical power. He had skills that most were capable of possessing already and yet on top of that he had ones that were impossible for others to obtain.

'What's your story?' I often wondered.

What he had told me he could see shouldn't have been what he actually did see. I knew exactly what he was looking at and was only left with one question. How?

How was he able to see what he could, how was he able to do the things that he did and how did he know everything that he knew?

"Tell me." I said. "What exactly do you see when you look at me, I'm guessing that it doesn't look entirely human?"

I leant back in the chair, letting him have a good long look patiently awaiting his next words.

"I see a set of beautiful white and silver armour, immaculately pristine and crafted by someone who defiantly knew what they were doing. It is adorned by an irregularly shaped and very colourful amethyst crystal on the chest plate. Small red stripes of fabric hanging from the shoulders and elbows, a mark of your rank no doubt.

I see silver hair flowing perfectly out of your head and down your back, shining valiantly in the light of the sun behind you. Of course, I can see the two short-swords on your hips and the four, pretty impressive, wings coming out of you back.

Are they ornamental or do they actually work I wonder?"

'What is he?' I thought, greatly disturbed by what he could see.

I sat quietly in my chair, trying my best not to show the

feeling of shock too obviously on my face while I thought though everything that I knew about this boy.

Not only could he do things that even Katiana had difficulty doing but he could do something that shouldn't have been possible. He could see my true form. The one that I hardly ever wore at the time, the one that resides in a separate dimension to our own and the one that should have been impossible to perceive from this side of the gate.

It didn't have a physical presence in the real world. Nothing tangible to see or touch unless I was wearing it. When he looked at me, all he should have been able to see was my human body. No more strange or out of the ordinary than anyone else. He shouldn't have been able to see what he had.

I thought of questioning him about this but I had come up with a possible explanation as to how he could see me by then and in order for me to test my theory, I needed to know more about him first.

Starting with how he knew where I lived and how to get in. Not only through the barrier but also through the door. There wasn't a problem with him being able to see my other body, it was just a shock is all. I could have focused on that for the rest of the conversation but there were other things I needed to know at the time, his vision could wait.

"Julian, why are you here?" I asked.

I did my best to focus on the conversation but the whole time all my mind wanted to do was think through what was going on. For whatever reason, I wanted to think though escape plans, how I could contain him if I had to and what method of disposal would be best for the body.

I thought about warning Katiana, telling her to run in

case I had to do something that would have posed a threat to her. Harming her would have been something that I would only later regret.

But if I had, it would have tipped him off and I couldn't take that risk. While my wife and I were supposed to be the two most powerful beings on the planet, she was nothing compared to him, his power, his untapped potential, it frightened me.

The more I learnt about this boy, the more I began to consider him as a threat just because he existed. Never had I seen such outstanding and overwhelming potential in anyone else before. And all of this was before he had even been trained. It was more like looking at another one of my kind that it was a mage but that would have been impossible.

He was a mage, he had to be, my kind were long gone, but he was far too powerful to have been an ordinary one.

"I am here in the hopes of becoming your student." He said. Placing his palms together and dipping his head as if he were bowing in his chair before me.

A moment later and Katiana had walked back in with a tray of tea in her hand. Steaming hot water evaporated out from the spout of the pot by the second, drawing my attention to the tray and the items upon it.

Three of our more basic cups, a large pot of sugar, spoons and a small jug of milk. Inside the cups were tea leaves, natural and home grown, none of that instant ground up powder that the humans used.

Everything required to make tea was on that tray and she wasted no time in making each of us a cup once she had entered the room.

When she looked at me she saw nothing but the look of shock on my face, a look that was not often worn upon it. Not only that but she also saw the boy bowing before me as he pleaded for my help. What thoughts must have gone through her mind? How had she interrupted the situation in that moment, did she jump to conclusions or look at that moment objectively I wonder?

Either way, she stood at the other end of the table and poured each of us a cup of tea as our conversation resumed, closely watching the situation as it continued to unfold.

"You sought me out specifically, why is that?"

Julian returned to his previous posture, barely holding himself up on the chair. Before he had even been given a chance to speak the drinks were ready. Katiana handed me and him a fresh cup of tea and placed the tray at our end of the table.

Of course, I put a fistful of sugar in mine as soon as I could reach it, not because I prefer my tea to be sweet but simply because I needed a lot more sugar than most people do throughout their day. It was only eight fifteen in the morning and I was yet to drink or eat anything at the time. I had originally said that I would finish the repairs before I started on our breakfast but obviously that hadn't remained true for long.

If he had only arrived a few minutes later, I would have finished the cleaning and would have been properly prepared for his visit, even if I hadn't expected it. I would have been better groomed and full of energy after eating my toast and drinking my tea at the very least.

As it was, I had been wearing my paint stained dressing gown the whole time, something that it seemed Julian was incapable of perceiving. At least Katiana had thought it best to wear something other than her nightgown once she had woken up. Otherwise we would have greeted this stranger as if we had only just gotten out of bed, when in truth we had been awake or over three hours by the time that he arrived.

"I came here following the instructions given to me by my mother when I was born. I guess I'm lucky that the information wasn't out of date."

He stirred his tea, seeming as though he was waiting for something. The cup to cool perhaps or maybe he was waiting for the milk and sugar to mix in with the rest of the brew.

"Born?" Katiana asked as she sat down beside me, tea cup in hand.

"Imprintation. It wasn't too long after my birth, my mother passed on a great amount of her knowledge to me, however I was too young at the time to take it all in so small parts are missing or fragmented. The instructions that she left on how to find you are perfectly clear though, as if she wanted them to be intact above all the others." He explained swiftly, seemingly unaware of the implications of what he just said.

He seemed more relaxed now, sipping away at his tea and leaning back into his chair. However, that didn't make it any easier to accept what he had just said.

"Imprintation? Julian, are you sure that what she called it?" I asked, surely mere moments before Katiana did. Now that Imprintation had been mentioned, this conversation was as much to do with her as it was to do with me.

"Why, is that not a common skill?" He asked, seemingly

surprised that Imprintation was so rare. He didn't even know what the spell was and yet he knew how it worked. The information in his head must have been fragmented indeed.

"By law, only two people in the world are allowed to know how to preform Imprintation at one time." Katiana said as she forced her way in front of me in the conversation.

"Julian, do you not know why that is?" I asked him.

"No, that information was never given to me."

He drank more of his tea, slowly approaching the last of it. The pot was still on the tray beside him yet he never poured more from into his cup. With how thirsty he seemed, I was surprised by this inaction but at the time, more important matters were being discussed. He was probably too distracted to even think about the tea in that moment.

"Imprintation is a spell that my husband invented in order to preserve the workings of the Magic Council. Only two people are allowed to know it at a time, the Crown Mage and their chosen successor. Julian I must ask, what was your mother's name?"

Katiana waited for a response but at first, all we got from him was a look of sadness on his face. The thoughts that consumed his head attempting to answer that question had invoked a feeling of grief within him. It wasn't long before I found out why that was.

"Frances Ealton."

The words left his lips with such softness and grief that I knew exactly what was getting him down when he said them. There was only one feeling in the world that could have created such emotions. His face turned sour, the mere thought of his mother had brought about deep feelings of pain. Of course it would, his brain had been modelled on her memory fragments. His connection to her, while he wouldn't have understood it, was the same as it would have been if he had known her growing up. To him it was as though he had grown up with her all along. He had been given such a large chunk of her memories that in a sense, he was her.

I took a moment to gather my own emotions before I thought to respond to his words.

"Frances." I whispered into my cup.

"You knew her?" He pleaded, begging for me to tell him more.

"Frances Ealton, was the granddaughter of my predecessor, she was supposed to be where I am now." Katiana replied on my behalf.

She seemed to have no problem discussing this information for me but then again, the topic was more suitable for her to explain than it was for me. The inner workings of the Magic Council and the Crown Mage were topics that I understood but only because Katiana had explained them to me in detail.

I guess that I was lucky to have married a woman of sufficient political stature to become my inside man on the Magic Council. However, I never expected that when she received word that she had been accepted within their ranks that she would come home from that meeting and say that she had been chosen to replace the Crown Mage himself.

"My mother was supposed to be the Crown Mage?" He asked, a look of excitement and shock on his adolescent face.

"Your mother went missing some thirty years ago, leaving her grandfather behind in ill health to find another suitable replacement to become the next Crown Mage. After a decade of looking, no one could ever find her, not even me. I'm sorry to say that after those ten years, we were instructed to stop wasting our time." I told him.

Then it hit me, the realisation of why I never found her.

"Julian, you don't have to say anything, just nod. Your mother, did she die shortly after your birth? Complications from delivering you perhaps?"

He nodded, a small tear forming in the corner of his eye.

"How old are you Julian?" Asked Katiana as she picked up on what I was getting at.

"Twenty-nine."

He said those words in sadness but had only enlarged my interest in him and sparked even more thoughts and theories about him as a result.

I learnt then and there, that even though he didn't realise it, he wasn't a normal mage. His physical appearance did not match his age, the only thing that can cause that was a form of magic that had been temporarily outlawed at the time, one that I had long suspected his mother to have been using before her disappearance.

He was under the influence of a life extension spell. One that had before then been very widely used.

The spell was temporarily outlawed not long after it was discovered to also be usable as a way of committing suicide. Any spell that can be used as a way of self-harm is almost always a forbidden one.

However, due to how irreplaceable this spell was and how much the Magic World needed it in order to survive, the law was soon overruled. While there are many ways of extending one's lifespan, this was the only spell that could do so permanently.

Granting the receiving target with an additional two or five hundred years to live depending on how successfully it was cast.

The spell had only been illegal for a matter of months by the time Frances disappeared and by the time we stopped looking it had already been legalised again.

Now some of it was starting to make sense, the reason that I could never find his mother, the reason why no one could. Was because she had died before we even started looking. She would have had to have given birth only weeks after disappearing if Julian was to be as old as he claimed to be.

We only started our search after the first month, she was supposed to be on a private holiday at the time and it was believed that she would return on the date she was expected to do so.

After that date passed, everyone started looking. The Crown Mage and their successor are practically royalty, everyone wanted to join in with the search after we realised that she was missing. But we never found her.

If she had used such a spell like that then the rest of Julian's story made a bit more sense. A spell like the one she probably used would have caused complications during the pregnancy. Life extension spells are difficult to remove and never play well with children.

To have such a spell removed would have required permission from the Council. Something that she wouldn't have gotten at the time given the unstable nature of the law. In an attempt to remove it herself, probably to avoid any punishment if anyone ever found out, she most likely only managed to shift it onto her son. That still didn't explain why she had used it in the first place, it still didn't explain her disappearance or why she was dead.

Then a more important thought crossed my mind, one that confirmed his story of being her son somewhat. The clothes that he wore, most likely inherited from his mother, who would have done the same with her grandfather. They fit the style of the Crown Mage uniform from back then and it would have made sense that he would wear them. If he was really her son then they would have once belonged to her and would have been all that she was wearing when she disappeared.

Those clothes combined with the knowledge that he possessed all but proved his story. He knew too much about me to have not gotten that information from a reputable source like Frances. He wore clothes that fit the style of what his mother would have worn at the time and he didn't give off any sense that he was lying.

While his story had holes in it, while it was one that I had to piece together bit by bit, I accepted it.

This boy was the great grandson of the fifth Crown Mage, son of the second strongest mage on the planet at the time, entitled to a seat on the Council and completely untrained.

His origin was beginning to reveal itself a little but was still nothing more than a mystery at that moment. And to be honest, I only did what I did next out of my curiosity to solve that mystery.

But if you are the kind of person who believes in fate, then perhaps it was destiny that had brought him to me, perhaps the events of that day had all been preordained by some god millions of years ago.

But I did not believe such things and instead I believed that everything I did was because I had chosen to do so. A belief that I still carry to this day.

There was still so much that didn't make sense about the boy. His abilities and the strange feeling that I got whenever he was around were things that I still couldn't explain away.

But I saw no problem with taking him on as a pupil. He didn't appear to be dangerous. He didn't seem to have an ill intent. There was nothing about what he had done thus far to make me say no. In fact, everything that he had done up until that point only made me want to say yes.

He had potential, an outstanding amount of it. He had exceptional knowledge about subjects that are normally difficult to teach and then there was the fact that he was an enigma.

I wanted nothing more than to train him, to find out more about him. I wanted to solve the mystery of who and what he was and if everything he had told me ended up being true, I wanted to be the one who turned this novice into a master. To have the chance to teach someone so powerful and promising, I wasn't about to let it pass me by.

All that was left to do was to figure out if he was ready for training. If he was worthy of it. A test, just like those performed on my regular visitors. I needed to know what he thought I was.

"Julian. I believe you and would very much like to teach you but I have just one more question before I make my decision. Choose you answer well, because if you answer it correctly, it will mean that you not only get to stay here with me and my wife.

Not only will I train you as I would have done if you had been formally initiated into a mage's academy, I will also become your sponsor. Granting you access to any magic collage or school, any source of information or knowledge that has to do with the Magic World and disappearance of your mother. Choose your words carefully because your entire life is about to be defined by them."

He grinned eagerly, awaiting the question that was to come. Not realising what was truly riding on his answer. I soon set him straight, warning him of what would happen if his answer failed to impress me.

"But." I said. "Should you answer this question incorrectly, I will not be here the next time that you come looking. Neither will my wife or the house. We will disappear and you will never find us again. Get this question wrong and that's it, no second chances."

I was probably a little harsh by threatening him with such an action but that didn't matter. Little did he know that this threat was an empty one. This house wasn't moving any time soon for various reasons but in an attempt to scare him into actually trying his best, I gave him the treat none the less.

"Understood." He responded, still eager to get on with it.

"Very well, now take your time, you only get one answer and it better be the right one. You with me?"

He nodded.

"Okay then. My question is this. Who and what am I?"

I moved my chair back from the table, leaning on my legs with my elbows. Getting as close as I could to him, trying to get a good sense of what was going on in that head of his.

Katiana performed a similar gesture. She was probably a

little sceptical about his story and my decision to train him. No doubt she was thinking through what she was going to tell the Council when we were finished.

She leant over the table, patiently awaiting his answer. Mimicking me almost. Underneath all of her concentration and the look of deep thought on her face I could still see it. Her undeniable beauty. The radiance of her face that lit up the room with her smile, her soft cheeks and her tender lips. It didn't matter what the situation or circumstance, her beauty was always clear to me.

It took Julian a moment to respond, maybe an entire minute for him to come up with his answer. Silence filled the room and soon all that could be heard were our own thoughts. Finally, the suspense ended and he opened his mouth, declaring his answer and shocking both me and my wife even more than he had already.

"As for who, I would surmise that you are the one known as the Athereon. Judging by your appearance and your authoritarian manner, that is all that would make sense.

As for what, assuming that you are in fact the Athereon himself, you are a man of great wisdom, the origin of all magical knowledge on this planet, a teacher and a profit. A man of great power and great respect. A protector and a guardian to the human world and the one and only true overseer of ours.

You sir, are the man that I have been searching for all my life and now that I have found you, I will do anything to remain by your side.

It is with great honour and fear that I request you take me on as your student. Allow me to become your weapon, use me how you wish and help me become all that I am capable of being.

It is this that I beg of you, your majesty."

He placed his empty cup back on the tray, fell down to the floor at the end of the table. He forced his posture to recover and knelt down before me, just as the people of England once did back when I went by the name of Merlin.

But that was a very long time ago. I'm not even sure that I even know where Camelot is anymore. It burned to the ground hundreds of years after I left it. While its name has been remembered, the truth behind what it was has been lost to the sands of time.

Not one person alive, other than myself, knows of the utopia it once was. A place free from slavery and captivity, no poverty or wars. A land that had accepted magic and one that had thrived because of it.

With my careful guidance that nation turned into a beacon for humanity and that was when I saw what humans could one day become. I was treated as a king back then and the people bowed to me as such, just as Julian was doing now.

His right hand on his heart, his left arm behind his back, his left foot on the ground and his right knee beside it. A somewhat amateur royal bow if I say so but the gesture was appreciated.

And while the solute wasn't spot on, his answer... his answer was perfect. Never had I heard someone other than Katiana answer that question so perfectly.

But unlike her, he hadn't been chosen to join this life, he had been born into it. He did not come seeking my protection or aid as the humans do, instead he came seeking my knowledge and my skill. He came seeking my expertise as a mage and as a teacher. He had come to learn, nothing more.

I gave him a pat on the back after the moment of shock passed. Katiana was as dazed as I was after that. She didn't quite know how to react and just poured herself another cup of tea and forced it down. In all her years of asking people what I was, she had never heard a response like that.

If it had been her who had asked the question, I don't know how she would have reacted. She had never had someone get it right before.

So I congratulated him and helped him back on his feet. He was still a little weak but the tea would soon take effect and he would be fine after that. A little sugar and caffeine is all that you need to get through a day of hardship, at least that's what my mother taught me.

I wasted little time after that and took him for a tour around the house and the various buildings surrounding it. In part, I did this so that I wold have a chance to change my clothes on my way passed the bedrooms.

After that, I showed him to one of our various guest rooms, the one that was now to be his. He had a bed, a wardrobe, an en suite bathroom and various decorations dotting the room.

And of course, an east facing window to wake him up in the morning without harshly blasting his face with the sun.

I gave him that room rather than putting him in the dorms over in the school because I felt that it would be more homely and comfortable to be living in the main house rather than the alienated building out the back.

The school itself was mine, a private teaching area for my

own students. It was located behind the house, maybe two or three hundred meters beyond the gate at the end of the main garden. Three reasonably sized buildings and a large square field to serve as the courtyard.

These building made up my own personal school. A safe place, away from the watchful, controlling eyes of the Magic Council, a safe place for my students to learn and a home for up to fifty of those students at a time.

I originally built it not long after I found out how much land I actually owned. Since this was a human village, the ownership came down to payment and when I originally paid the mayor of the town for the land at the top of the hill, I hadn't expected him to give me the entire thing.

With so much extra space and the fact that I enjoyed teaching, I decided to build a school. A small and private one but probably the best place in the world to learn about magic.

I was the teacher after all.

At first, Julian was as dazed as I was and it took him a while to get a sense of where things were. So I allowed him to take his time and understand the layout of the house and made sure that he did not mistake his room with any of the others. There were nine more rooms in that same hallway for him to confuse his with unfortunately. They all looked the same. It took time to remember which one was which.

After that, I continued his tour, showing him to the most pertinent buildings and rooms around the property. But not all of it. That kind of tour would have taken days, the place was quite vast and painstakingly difficult to traverse in a sensibly ordered manner.

Besides, I didn't think that he had enough strength to

visit all the various fields and farm land that I owned at the time. And even with his new role as my student, I was hardly about to show him the vault.

So I took him to the training dojo, my personal library and then the student's one. The difference being that my library was in the house and had far more texts on forbidden spells but the student's one was attached to the dorm rooms and had only what they would need to cover the lessons I taught.

I showed him the brewery after that. A large, musty room under the house where I made all my various wines and beers personally and naturally, no spells or machinery involved. After that I had showed him everywhere he needed to know existed and everything that he needed to be able to find while he stayed with me.

I welcomed him into my home as a pupil and treated him as such until the day that I came to know him as a friend. Katiana treated him as an unknown for most of his stay though, only getting to know and like him after his fourth month of living with us.

It didn't take her long to report him to the Magic Council, not to brand him as a criminal or have him arrested for a crime but simply so that the case file for the disappearance of his mother could be closed.

However, for legal reasons, she never spoke a word more of it to me beyond explaining what I just said. She had her secrets and I had mine, we didn't go around trying to figure them out because there wasn't any point, we both trusted each other so there wasn't a reason for us to ruin that trust by revealing what we didn't want each other to know.

Katiana's plans aside, I made my own and planned to

teach him for many years to come. Together we would train, bettering his skills and knowledge, allowing me to understand more of what made him so strange and so odd and allowing him to understand the world through a proper mage's eyes.

That was the day that I met my most talented student to date. That was the day that I met Julian for the first time. That was the day that I met a true friend. The day that changed his life forever and helped redefine my own.

DAY ONE

Tucked away from view behind the majesty of main house, across from the rose petal lined gardens and the cherry blossom petties falling from the trees, hidden from the rest of the world behind a forest of tall arch trees, was a small patch of land separated from the rest.

A plot of land that was set aside a long time ago for its singular purpose. Land separated not only by distance but also but yet another protective barrier. Keeping it hidden from senses. Hidden from view. Hidden from the elements.

Protected in every sense.

Perfectly suited for its use.

And within this dome shaped shield to the back of my land, were three large buildings assembled by hand. Made from stone, wood and brick, these buildings stood firm under the eternal protection of their barrier.

Their existence remained unknown to most and hidden from the rest by the obscuring view of the other buildings which I owned.

In between all three of these buildings lied a large patch of grass covered land acting as a courtyard of sorts. Equipped with a running fountain and walkways. Benches and even a plaque. Embosses brass plated upon steel. An epitaph of names. The names of the first people to ever set foot behind its stone.

Three buildings, a courtyard and a plaque. Put all of these together and the result is a well looked after and well protected private school. A place of learning and a place of great mystery. Those who knew of it were only those who had studied within its halls.

The school was smaller than most but was just as prestigious as any other. Offering great knowledge and training to any who learnt there.

And while it was only made up of three simple buildings, their layout and contents were anything but basic. The closest one to the house, the one of the left and the one made primarily of wood, was that of the sparring dojo.

No larger than any sparing hall would have been but far more important than the rest. Because this dojo was mine and as such looked unlike any other dojo in history.

It was crafted by my own hands to fit a set criteria of needs.

Built to withstand constant abuse and most notably, built to serve as much more than just a place to fight. It was also a shelter. The strongest of the three buildings. The one sure place to outlast the rest should anything have come to attack.

The second building, the one furthest to the right of the three, contained the classrooms, my office, two sets of toilets in two separate gender split rooms and a seating area designed for relaxation between any of my rather trying classes.

And the final building, the one located in-between the other two, held the dorm rooms on the upper floor, the dining hall that every student simply referred to as a cafeteria on the lower floor and the student library in the basement.

Within this library were all manner of ancient scriptures about spell casting and the historical origins of various forms of magic. They all ranged in difficulty both in understanding and use. Anything from the most basic of instructional books to the most cryptic of barely readable passages, containing various incantations and spell techniques for the students to decipher on their own.

But other than this candle lit library secluded beneath the earth to hide the students from the sounds of battles occurring above ground during training sessions, the cafeteria was where any number of students would spend the majority of their free time.

They called it a cafeteria since that was what all their previous schools and academies had called theirs, not that they were wrong to call it that but while it did look like one, it didn't function as one.

None of the food had to be purchased before consumption and when it was time to do so, there were no ques, no lines, all you had to do was sit down and wait for your food to appear. This was a magic school after all. No need to walk when you can make your plate fly.

And when I permitted it, most would often use the communal space as a place to make conversation and study during their lunch and dinner periods. But the main purpose for that room was for the preparation and eating of food. I insisted that they stuck to that whenever they were in attendance of one of my meals.

And while these buildings had been kept in perfect structural conditional and had been cleaned regularly as to always look their best, not one of them had been used for many years before Julian arrived at my door.

I had not needed to use it, not since my last batch of students graduated just over twenty years before that day. It simply wasn't time yet.

And while I was happy to take him on as a student, in truth, I would have preferred it if he had shown up a few years later with everyone else.

While I greatly enjoyed teaching back then, I also preferred to stick to a schedule, something that Julian had torn up the moment he arrived.

The school wasn't ready to be used, I was supposed to have many more years to prepare before it was time to open its doors again.

That didn't matter too much though, as long as I could train him with the supplies that I had on hand then his early arrival wasn't going to be an issue.

But then I thought more of how strong he was, his untapped power and potential, the way that his presence filled me with a sense of uncertainty, I wasn't sure how strong he would be once I started teaching him how to properly harness that power.

There was a chance that the barrier surrounding the school wouldn't be enough to contain him if things got out of control. The barrier was designed for basic protection more than anything else. Keeping the untrained mages away from the main property is crucial while they learn how to use their powers.

Having up to fifty students living in the same place, eventually some of them would fight outside of the tournaments in an effort to train more practically. And in that eventuality, anything can happen. And most of the students I've had in my past could probably destroy half the property if not kept in check.

I did only accept the best after all.

So I put up a more simplistic barrier to the one surrounding my home and land around the school centuries ago as a precaution. People and friendly magic could go through but only people can come back out and only when permitted to do so.

Any offensive spell or any student without permission to exit the school grounds would be deflected inwards and away from the house, protecting the rest of my land or the village down the hill from any damage that they might have caused.

But even with these defences in place and every precaution taken to ensure that students could train there unhindered by rules of barricades, I was still sceptical as to whether or not it would be strong enough against Julian. If what I suspected about him was true, then after some training, he might actually be strong enough to break it.

But there wasn't much I could do, the barrier was one of the strongest that I could make despite its simple nature and it had survived several hundred years of students before him. Making a new one might have been unnecessary in the end and in that case, I would have rather avoided the exhaustion than waste my time.

So I guess I was willing to take the risk.

I would make do with what protections and provisions I had on hand in order to train Julian. If that turned out to be insufficient, then it wouldn't matter in the end. The next batch of students weren't due to arrive for another five years. I had time to correct any mistakes I made now before the next time.

And while that stretch of time before the others would arrive did put me in a good position to be able to focus on training Julian one to one, it also meant that he would be learning alone.

He wouldn't be learning in a class of thirty to ninety people like at an academy. He wouldn't be learning to live amongst others and he wouldn't be learning any social skills.

The advantage of getting me as your sole tutor is a large one. But the disadvantages were plentiful as well it seemed.

However, the five years until the next group of trainees arrived would give me just enough time to get Julian ready before he would be mixing with those others. I could allow him to forgo social interactions for now. So long as he learned quickly later.

And in the state that I had met him in, he was very dangerous to both himself and others. A complete novice with some very powerful level twenty-five spells under his sleeve. Nothing could endanger others more than that. It was good that I would get to begin training him alone. He already outclassed everyone else in most areas. I simply needed to focus on the weaker aspects of his talents in order to get him ready.

And then there was the information he carried to consider. Secrets that most in the Magic World didn't know about. Spells and locations not available to the public. As well as instructions on how to successfully gain an audience with myself.

With everything that he knew and everything that he

could do, he was quite dangerous indeed.

Imagine a baby, holding a loaded gun. Now imagine that that gun is pointed at a large pile of explosives. What would happen if the baby were to pull the trigger?

The same could be said for Julian. He had no idea how to aim or fire his spells correctly, so like the baby, his power would be quite explosive and out of his control.

Before I could train Julian in anything, I would have to teach him how to control the spells that he already possessed. Such a teaching method was quite foreign to me; teaching him backwards that is.

I would usually teach students how to cast a spell before allowing them to learn how to control it. However, in this case, he had learnt the spells and could even use them but he was utterly hopeless at controlling them.

My normal teaching method would be to explain how to cast a spell from the very basic level. The feel of the magic energy flowing through you. The formation fo the magic circuits. The correct stance to hold.

After that I would see if any of the students could do it themselves without further explanation and practice. If they could, only then would we move on to the next steps. Only then would I ensure that they had absolute control over those spells once cast.

Julian however, he knew the spells and how to put them to use but had no authority over them.

My only evidence of this was what he had told me of how he had gotten through the barrier. He said that he simply willed all the nearby birds to fly through at the same time but it was more than that.

Basic levels of Feral Mastership, though rare amongst

mages, were simple enough to cast. Very efficient too. One need only define the parameters they require and after that it takes almost no effort at all to maintain the effects. But he'd gone above and beyond what he needed to in order to achieve his goal that day.

He hadn't just summoned the birds but had also managed to reflect everything else. Every nearby animal had vanished, fleeing from him as fast as they could, every spec of nature had gone still and even the wind had slowed to a snail's pace once he was done.

Considering that he only wanted to have the birds create a hole for him, this proved that his power was out of his control. A simple spell like that takes very little effort and energy. The fact that he had used up so much to cast it only furthered the theory that he didn't have control over what he was doing.

Therefore, I intended to start by teaching a little control. Ordinarily this would have been done for me. Most first year students are capable of this. However, without knowing exactly what he could do and what aspects of the spells he couldn't control, I didn't know what I would need to teach him.

At dinner on the night he arrived, I had told Julian to meet me in the dojo at nine a.m. sharp. Not a moment late and not a second early.

He was to begin his training there. Within a safe and protected area. The fact that he had the ability to cast a spell that could control nature suggested that he had immense potential for more. Because of this, I had to make sure that he wasn't a danger to himself and the dojo was the only place that made sense.

The dojo itself, due to its proximity to the dorm rooms, had its own barrier placed within it. This barrier was designed to be activated only when excessive magic energy was present. Levels that high indicated that a spell was being cast and the barrier would quickly make efforts to protect the outside world from whatever that spell might have been once they were detected. But unlike the main two barriers surrounding it, this one didn't stop teleportation from the inside.

You could teleport out in an emergency but there was absolutely no way to teleport back in. This was for the student's protection, nothing more. I wouldn't have wanted someone teleporting in and getting a face full of fire or ice now would I?

I already had a reputation for going too far with students. I couldn't just let them start hurting each other by accident as well.

During that dinner though, the conversation was mostly plain. We stayed silent for most of the meal, only talking when we had a question to ask or to answer one of Julian's.

There wasn't much to say to be honest. He was an unknown at that point. Even though he was my student, that didn't mean that I knew him or that I trusted him.

That first night, it was as if we had let a total stranger stay in our home and in truth, we had. However, had I not, then he would have never become the trusted friend that I know him as today.

When I decided to take him in, to train him, I did so mostly because of what he told me during our initial conversation. I was intrigued by his ability to see me and that was pretty much all that I needed to know in order to make my decision.

His relation to an old friend of mine or his inherent knowledge of me didn't make much of a difference. Even if someone else knew all of what he did, I would have turned them down.

Julian on the other hand, was something quite unique and if I was correct about his potential then I wanted to be the one responsible for training him. With training given to him by me, he would be much more powerful than he could have been in an ordinary school.

He would be wiser and stronger. He would be the best that he could be under my wing and I wanted that for him. Finding someone so unfocused and yet so powerful is very rare, in all my years I have only ever met three others with as much potential as him and only one of them was eventually trained by myself.

Knowing what others of similar skill had managed to achieve later on in life, I wanted to be the one to give him that opportunity. I wanted to give him the best chance he would have in order to become all that he could ever be.

I wanted to be the one to turn this delicate flower into a lion. And with my help and training, I wouldn't have been surprised back then if his power had rivalled that of my own one day.

And knowing the possibilities, I knew that I couldn't go as slowly with him as I would the others I had trained before. He needed to go at his own pace. And the best way for me to figure out what that was, was to throw as much at him as I could and wait until he starts to choke.

Thus, Julian's first lesson would be both simple and very dangerous. His first lesson would be an assessment, a basic evaluation of his abilities. I needed to see what he could do and how well he could do it before I started teaching him anything.

At the time, I hadn't seen him use anything more complex than telepathy and therefore had no way of grasping his true power and capabilities at his current level. But I could guess. And even my guesses worried me.

If I was even slightly accurate with me assumption of how powerful he was, then training him would be more challenging than any mage that I had trained in the past.

Eager to begin, I arrived at the dojo late in the night after dinner, taking my time to prepare for the worst as I always did. Re-activating the enchantments in the walls and floor, supplementing them with protective and reinforceive spells. Checking the barrier for weak points and then testing its activation speed by firing a few simple spells at it.

Anything faster than the speed of sound and the barrier wouldn't be quick enough to catch it, luckily for me, only a handful of the spells I taught my students were faster than that. Actually the number was seven but I was sure Julian didn't have anything that powerful or fast under his belt quite yet.

Most light-emissive spells are very powerful and because of this are hard to master; put both those facts together and any spells that meet that description are placed as high on the levelling system as possible. The higher the level of a spell and the less likely you are to know it.

High-level spells require you to be a high-level mage to be permitted to learn them. These spells are hard to control and even harder to master at the best of times. So the likelihood of Julian knowing one was slim at best.

I then proceeded to upgrade the strength of both the barriers that protect my property to make sure that Julian wouldn't get through them without permission again. Something as simple as using an animal to create a momentary gap to teleport through shouldn't have been something that worked but since it had, I needed to protect myself against it in the future.

This unfortunately meant that I would need to limit how many animals could pass through at a time. This would make the barrier a bit more obvious if a flock of sheep or a migrating group of birds were to pass through. One or two might have been hit with a wall if they tried. But that number going through at the exact same time wasn't very likely. Unless they all flew in a line wing to wing with another anyway.

After that was done, I returned to the house and checked the time. I was only a few minutes away from midnight and had a long wait ahead of me, so I decided that it was about time that I drank my tea.

Mostly that was all I drank. As with every other mage for that matter.

Never a simple glass of water or the sweet taste of juice but tea. Not because I had a taste for it but more so because I had to drink it. My body reacted quite directly to modern drinks than humans did and the simplicity of tea seemed to be all that I could stomach safely.

If I was forced to, I could drink or eat anything, it wouldn't kill me but it would make me more than a little uncomfortable a few hours later. With the exception of coconut milk that is. I can drink that without a problem afterwards, the reason that I didn't was because I couldn't stand the stuff.

So I poured myself a cup form the pot, went upstairs and kissed my wife goodnight and then returned to the dojo. From there I waited, crouched on the floor, thinking.

The cold of the night soon swept in and I spent my time enduring it. I focused on raising my body temperature mentally rather than using magic. I found it relaxing. Meditation that is.

It was something that I had learnt from a Buddhist temple several hundred years ago. It was quite possibly the only thing that humans had taught me that I was actually glad I knew about.

So I employed my knowledge of meditation and focused my mind on the events of that previous day as I prepared for the one that laid ahead. I maintained my meditation for many hours before he came. Waiting patiently for his arrival and allowing myself some much-needed time to think.

Time to think over how I would train him, the teaching methods and the spells to focus on first. I thought about all that I would do with him in the years to come and then a realisation came to me.

If he was a complete novice then I wouldn't be able to train him anywhere past level one. With the exception of the spells he already knew, I wouldn't be able to teach him much more until he took the test. It was law. And I of all people knew what would happen if I went against this specific one for a third time.

So that became my goal and his. To train him as best I could and then take him for his entrance exam.

I was authorised to promote any mage above level seven as I sought fit but I was not allowed to initiate them. If he wasn't even officially ranked then I wasn't allowed to do anything about that. They only place that could would have been a school. A real one.

Despite his wishes and my own, he wouldn't be able to train with me forever. Eventually, he would have to go to the academy. He didn't have a choice. The academies are the only places for a mage to be initiated and receive their first rank and they was the best place to allow them to progress to a sufficient point for me to train them further.

As his sponsor and Master, I would be able to train him up until the point where he was ready for the test and then nothing more. There were laws to obey and I was the one who put them in place after all, how could I have ignored them when I had gone through all the trouble of enforcing them back in the day?

These laws weren't made out of spite, not out of an attempt to limit a mage's potential but in an attempt to allow him or her to achieve and surpass it. These laws ensured that every mage was placed in a school or academy of some kind if they wanted to pursue magic beyond the basics. And this also made sure that they would receive a proper education on top of their magecraft as well.

These establishments would focus on teaching them how to use new spells, how to control them, how to understand them and above all, it taught them how to stay safe.

Not only was a school the best place to go as a developing mage but it was also the safest. Not exposing the children to the dangers of the world unless completely necessary but still granting them a safe and secure space to practice magic.

So my eventual goal would be to get him ready for not

only taking the entrance exam but also passing it. After all, this boy showed potential and I wanted to send him to the best place available for realising and unleashing it.

If he was to be my student then there was only one place that I would be happy for him to go. After all, it wasn't known as the best academy of magecraft for nothing.

This decision was not mine alone however.

In order for him to attend this prestigious academy he would have to want to do so himself. I would have to convince him eventually. But not on that day, on that day he had only just started, no reason to worry him at that point. It wouldn't have been kind to tell him on the first day of teaching him that I couldn't continue to teach him for as long as he had wanted when we met.

So I focused on recollection after that. Thinking back on times past and long forgotten. Remembering what it was like when I first started teaching, the hardships and triumphs that were discovered and accomplished by those first few students. I thought back on my life of teaching and used all of that knowledge to formulate a plan for Julian.

He was to be unlike any other student that I had ever trained. He was stronger, obviously smarter and unranked. He had no official classification for his strength and ability and that made it hard to decide on what action to take.

I thought about how I first trained Katiana, someone who like Julian had shown a natural talent for magic. Someone who had a large surplus of untapped potential and someone who was completely untrained.

Training her was quite different however, back then, I didn't have the school, I wasn't an official teacher. By the time that she was sent for her official entrance exam, she was far passed level one and received more than one caution because of it.

That was the last time that I ever entered a student into an academy above the required level. After all, if the first-year students join at the same level of strength as the fifth-year ones, it created quite a disparity in the hierarchy of the school.

The world of mages desired power above all else and only associated a person's worth based on that power. When Katiana joined the academy, she was probably as strong if not stronger than most of the teachers. I guess that is to be expected after nine years of training with me.

I wasn't going to make the same mistake with Julian though. If I wanted to keep him hidden from the watchful eye of the Magic Council and ensure that his time in the academy was an enjoyable one, I had to make sure that he fit in with the food chain.

First-year students should be at the bottom of the pile and only those in the final years should be the strongest. I taught at that academy once and I have to say that out of everything I didn't like about it, I was at least glad that the students were learning where they fit in in the world.

For a mage, if someone is a higher rank and therefore stronger than you, avoid them. They are the ones in charge and not getting along with them would be a big mistake.

So that was the plan. Prepare him for the exam and not teach him too much before he takes it. By the time that this plan had been fully thought through and the end goal realised, almost eight hours had passed and the time that I had told Julian to meet me was quickly approaching.

And before he arrived, I had one more thing to prepare.

The tea.

I could hear footsteps quickly approaching the dojo a few minutes after I was done and I knew that it was time for the lesson to begin.

Nine a.m. sharp, not a moment late and not a second early, just as instructed. He opened the main door of the dojo, slowly pushing against its thick and dense frame. Gently making his way inside.

The old iron hinges squeaked as the dark oak door slowly swung open. The light from the morning sun swept in and illuminated the room much more than it had done through the windows above me too. I could feel its warm embrace on my face as the light hit me.

It was refreshing, filling me with clarity and peace of mind. And with it there, I could feel Julian's shadow as it was cast throughout the room. Moving from left to right as he made his way inside.

By then I could already sense it, his eagerness to begin, his excited state of mind and his willingness to learn.

I knew that he had already seen me but I did nothing and simply stayed in my position on the floor, my eyes closed and my breath silent.

As he drew ever closer, I began to notice more about him, soon I was able to feel more than just his excitement. I could feel his nervousness, his raised heart rate, his sweaty face and his unbalanced movements. He was far too excited and it was painfully obvious.

He was probably confused as to what he was supposed to do in that situation. He had only taken a few steps into the room by the time that he stopped. I could sense his presence, the same feeling of uncertainty and the clouded aura surrounding him as he stood there for that moment as I had felt in previous students before.

He was probably thinking that I was asleep or that I hadn't noticed him yet. So I continued to observe him mentally while he inspected his surroundings. I was interested to find out what he would do first.

He took his time and studied the room more closely than he had done the day before. Assessing the enchantments on the walls, running his finger up and down the ancient symbols etched into the wood.

I don't know if he understood their structure or meaning yet but he would do eventually. That was my new job after all. Master and teacher. It was my role to train him to understand it all.

Then he moved on, inspecting the weapons on display to the far side of the room. And on his way back towards my position in the centre of it all, he finally noticed the tea sat by my side.

The twin cups still steaming, filling the room with its aroma by the second. Two gold plated antiques and one pot sat on a silver tray next to me.

By that time, the door had already closed and we were alone. Nothing but the sounds of our breathing to listen to and nothing but what was in the room to distract us.

He approached me further, walking slowly and quietly. He made the decision to sit in front of me, copying my pose and waiting patiently. Just as I had expected him to.

I stayed silent and still, not showing any sign that I had noticed him.

Then I waved my hand at the tea.

"Drink." I told him with a whisper.

Not opening my eyes or even taking a breath. I sat there in peace. Unlike Julian. He sat there almost giddy, he was deeply excited for his first day of training and had the heart rate to show it.

For most people of his apparent age, he would have a raised heart rate, its natural, but considering that his outward appearance didn't fit his actual age I was a little shocked to see him act as though it did.

He took the cup closest to him and drank the tea as instructed. I picked up mine and did the same. Taking short but frequent sips, never opening my eyes and not paying any obvious attention to Julian. This was his first test and he knew nothing of it.

I sat patiently allowing him to finish the drink before I asked my first set of questions. He was entirely unaware that the moment he entered the room, his lesson had already begun.

He had probably suspected that I would be quick to get things started but he wouldn't have expected things to begin the second that he entered the room.

"Tell me Julian, what do you make of this tea?" I asked.

Finally, I opened my eyes and crossed my legs, relaxing my posture and actually sitting on the floor for the first time in hours.

And now that I could see him, I could actually see what he was doing rather than sense his movements by monitoring his muscles as they moved.

I saw that he was wearing the sparing uniform that I had given him as expected. He had tied the various laces on the chest and legs a little poorly but alas, he was wearing it at least.

The sparing uniform was a simple set of thick white robes made from fabrics I had accumulated over the years. These gave the wearer ample protection during training as well as a suitably smart look and a good amount of insulation from the elements too.

They were comfortable, well made and very versatile. You could have worn them as regular clothing and no one would have noticed.

In addition to taking the time to put the uniform on he had also shaved the scruffy beard that I had met him with the day before. Washed and straightened his hair, holding it in a ponytail behind his head. He was well prepared for his first lesson apparently. I was actually impressed.

Now th.at he had tidied up his appearance somewhat, he was starting to look like a mage, one in training at least. He had a long way to go before he would earn that title but I knew that one day he would get there.

I suspected that if he tried hard enough, he might even become the next Crown Mage at some point, he was certainly capable of it. Strength, knowledge and blood, he's be a first pick for most.

And after finishing his tea, he then placed the now empty mug back on the tray as I had done. Thus, the lesson commences.

"It is tea, sir, nothing special, a mere collection of plant leaves and hot water. Why? Is there something different about this tea?" He asked me curiously.

He looked down at the pot of tea, inspecting it, trying to find a reason as to why it would be special or different. But looking wasn't going to reveal its secret.

"What would you say if I told you that what you were

just drinking didn't exist for more than a minute before you entered the room?" I pondered.

"I would say that this is some kind of test." He replied.

I smirked.

"Correct. This is a test but the test was not the tea. The test was whether or not you believed it to be tea, a test that you both passed and failed." I explained.

I crossed my arms and looked deeply into him. Assessing the looks on his face as they appeared. I imagine that this would have made him quite uncomfortable doing this but he never expressed any obvious signs of discomfort.

"How have I accomplished that then. sir?"

He sat there, seemingly unaware of the meaning of this test. He seemed slightly confused at first but I later identified this as curiosity rather than confusion.

I uncrossed my arms and raised a finger in front of my face, signifying the number one as I spoke next.

"Firstly, you will address me as Master or Teacher from here on out, is that understood?"

I then waved my finger in the air to emphasise this order. Enforcing the master student relationship is crucial at this stage. It forms respect and keeps him in line. He nodded and corrected himself, this time calling me Master instead of sir.

I then raised my second finger, this time signifying the number two counting both visually and verbally as I continued to explain the test that I had just performed.

"Secondly, you passed when you called the drink tea. However, you failed when you did not recognise that this tea wasn't natural." I revealed.

Someone as sensitive to magic as him should have noticed the foreign signature of the tea, in truth I was a little disappointed that he hadn't.

Perhaps he had picked up on its odd sent, the way that it didn't quite feel right on the tongue. Maybe he had noticed it but was too naïve to tell that those senses were due to the tea being fake rather than it tasting bad.

"Are you saying that you created tea out of magic? But that's not possible, is it?" He asked, truly amazed by what my explanation had implied.

Of all the things he knew about me, it seemed that this wasn't one of them. Somewhere in that head of his was surely the information that when I am the one casting the spell, various impossibilities are more than possible.

"There are many things in the world of magic that are both possible and impossible at the same time. The magic that I used to create this tea is known as Creationist Magic, a skill that only I possess. In the past, it has been speculated that Creationist Magic is the same type used to create the universe. However, considering that I am the most powerful mage on the planet and all I can do is make a simple pot of tea, I cannot imagine the level of power required to create an infinitely expanding space." I told him.

He seemed even more intrigued at this point. Almost like he was a child learning about magic for the first time. This led to him asking numerous questions at the time. Like a thirsty animal drinking water, he continued to soak up information until he was satisfied.

"Why only you?" He asked.

"Because Creationist Magic is a level twenty-five spell. The spell itself is both very difficult to teach and at the same time far too dangerous to teach." I explained.

He ignored the reason as to why it was difficult and

dangerous to teach and moved on to me instead. I would have gladly told him that due to its high level, only the Crown Mage had a sufficient rank to learn it but even Katiana hadn't managed to master it, it was simply too complex.

After all, in order to create something from scratch like that, you need to know every finite detail about what you are trying to make. The chemical and elemental composition of the material, the structure of its atoms and the exact shape of the finished product, right down to the atomic and subatomic levels.

Even if I was allowed to teach people how to do such a thing, where would I start? The only reason that I could make the tea was because I had been drinking it for thousands of years. After such a long time, I had memorised everything there was to know about the beverage. All of this could have been explained to him but he insisted on asking more questions instead.

"So that makes you a level twenty-five mage then, Master?" He inquired.

This is a question that I had heard many times before. It is exactly what I would have expected a novice like him to say. The second I mention that I know a spell with a sufficiently high level to make it illegal to teach, people instantly assume that the level of that spell is the same as mine.

"No Julian, I am closer to level forty while human but that isn't certain. After all, there's no one to compare me to. The levelling system doesn't even officially go past twenty-seven as it is." I explained.

But this explanation only led to more questions with

every answer I gave him. No matter what I said, he would always have a question to ask after it.

"Then what level would you say I am Master?" He asked.

"Officially, nothing. You have no rank, but in terms of knowledge, you are barely level one. But by skill you are on par if not stronger than Katiana, making you at least level twenty-one. Based on the spells you know that is. But there is much more to a mage than just the spells that they possess. So this is where your first lesson comes in. Show me what you can do." I told him.

I had expected him to stand up and start casting spells at that point but still the conversation continued.

"You mean, you want to assess my abilities?" He asked, seeking clarification.

"Correct, you have already claimed to have an ability to control animals and to teleport at least a small distance at will. Furthermore, you exhibited signs of being able to hear telepathic conversations without even trying and there is that other thing." I said.

I scratched my beard at this point, unsure of what exactly to call the ability that he possessed.

"Thing?" He asked.

"Your sight, your ability to see my other form without even trying, as if it comes naturally to you. I don't even know what to call that. The fact is, it shouldn't be possible. But since it is, I have to ask, how do you do it?"

"Purely by accident Master." He replied.

His head dropped in shame, almost as if he had been worried that I would ask that very question sooner or later. I had already come to a pretty sensible theory of how he was doing it but in order for me to test that theory I decided to ask him first.

"How so?" I asked.

"When I was first figuring out how to cast spells, it was difficult. Only having bits and pieces of information and nothing more to go on led me to make many... mistakes." He said reluctantly.

Then I figured out the answer myself.

Unfortunately, my theory was close but not correct. I had thought that he had willingly done what he did but if it was accidental then it was a complete fluke.

If he only had fragments of information then I knew what he would have done to try and fix that. It was something that I had seen many a novice do before. But never had I heard of someone doing it after being imprinted on.

"Let me guess." I said, removing my hand from my beard and dropping it to my lap. "You thought that by forming magic circuits in your brain that you could unlock any fragments of information that might be in there through use of concentrated bursts of magic energy directed into your neurons?"

"Exactly." He nodded.

'How naive.' I thought

"And when you tried to do it, it quickly backfired and the circuits ended up in the wrong place. Your eyes to be exact?" I asked next.

"Yes Master, but how did you...?"

"Okay then, forget about showing me your talent, instead, answer me this. What is a magic circuit?" I asked him quickly.

The answer was simple, even the most amateur of mages knew it. At least I thought they did.

"It is a conduit for magic energy, allowing our bodies to control its flow and focus it into certain parts of that body to cast and amplify our spells." He replied.

"Almost correct." I said.

He was so close. I remember feeling quite disappointed when I heard the answer, then again, I don't know exactly what I should have expected. He had received no formal training and only had his mother's memories to go on. What information did I think he knew?

"Almost?" He asked.

Since he didn't know the answer, I decided to tell him, not knowing whether or not he would understand or remember. But since he didn't know, I at least knew what to make our next lesson about.

"Magic circuits do more than simply allow magical energy to flow through them. When they are formed densely enough and in the right pattern and order, the circuits themselves can be used to cast spells internal to your body.

By trying to plant them within your brain, when you have never done so before, you probably didn't realise how densely you were trying to create them. The brain is a very cramped space after all. So when your body redirected them to protect itself and they manifested into your eyes, they became something that is most peculiar."

Even though I knew what and how it had happened I still couldn't understand why the result of these actions had allowed him to see something that wasn't even there.

"So my inexperience allowed me to create a circuit that shouldn't be possible… entirely by accident?" He asked.

Now he was getting there. A little slowly but he was learning. He understood what I had told him so far and was

94

ready for more.

"Correct. But I must know, is there anything else that this sight can do?"

I was genuinely curious, since this was a new phenomenon, I needed to know the full extent of what it could do and be sure to document it. However, to my disappointment alone, the truth was pitiful.

The formation was exceptionally special but only seemed to have a use for looking at me, something that you can do with the naked eye just fine.

"Other than allowing me to spot a magic barrier at five thousand paces, no, nothing." He said.

So the circuits were confirmed to be otherwise useless and I decided what to do in an instant, there was only one course of action to be taken anyway. I didn't want my student to only see me as a man armed to the teeth.

"They hurt, don't they?" I asked him.

"Master?"

A slight look of confusion now appeared on his face.

"Your eyes, they have a constant feeling of burning, something that keeps you awake at night, am I correct?"

"Yes Master, the pain is on the edge of being unbearable at times but it is something that I have learnt to live with." He explained, expressing some amount of sorrow.

I had thought so. When magic circuits are placed in a part of the body as delicate as the eyes, it has to be done with the greatest of precision. Just forcing them in there would have caused some serious damage and having magic energy constantly flowing through them would have been extremely uncomfortable for anyone.

"Would you like me to take the pain away?"

"You can do that?" He asked with a look of joy now removing the confusion and curiosity from before.

"It will hurt more than you can imagine but only for a moment, after that, you will see me as everyone else does and the pain in your eyes will fade within a day or two." I told him clearly.

I warned him of the pain but only that. I had neglected to tell him the full list of risks in case he changed his mind. After realising that the formation was useless, I knew that he was better off without it. I certainly was.

"If it takes away the pain then do it. Just tell me what I need to do."

He sat there, preparing himself for the pain that he was about to experience. However, no amount if preparation could possibly ready you for the level of pain that he was about to go through.

"Stay still and close your eyes. Breathe normally and do not flinch. Not even the slightest movement, it would only endanger you more." I told him.

He closed his eyes as instructed. I placed my hands on each of his temples. I pressed in hard and told him to relax. Tensing up would only have made it hurt more.

Burning off magic circuits is normally a very delicate procedure but in this case, I wasn't focusing on a defective section or a miss aligned circuit. I was simply targeting them all.

I forced a little magical energy through my fingers and into his circuits to connect myself with them. Once I was in, I realised why I hadn't noticed them before, they were in the cornea. A spot that is so biologically complex and small that I wouldn't have been able to see them without knowing where they were in the first place.

But with the magic was in, I was ready. He wouldn't have even felt that I was in there at first. However, what I did next, that was something that he defiantly felt, how could he not? The procedure was called 'burning' magic circuits after all, there was bound to be a lot of pain.

Once the magic energy had fully engulfed his circuits, I burnt them. Quite literally mind you. I used the magic energy to create a quick flash of intense heat on every circuit all at once. It would have lasted less than a moment.

He yelled in pain, surprisingly staying perfectly still during it and then there was nothing. He went completely silent.

Luckily for him and for me, he hadn't moved. I had hurt him but at least I hadn't done any serious damage. It was only after they were gone that I noticed, his aura, it had disappeared too.

I'm not entirely sure what was creating it in the first place but it must have been connected to his eyes in some way. But now that they were gone, the sense of uncertainty that it created dissipated too and then I was left with a feeling of normality.

There wasn't anything strange about him anymore. Just a lot of untapped power lying within him, that's all I could feel now.

I removed my hands and told him to open his eyes. The procedure was complete and as far as I could tell it had been successful.

"What do you see?" I asked.

"It's difficult, everything's blurry. No wait, it's coming into focus now. I see; I see what I presume to be your human form Master."

This was a good sign but I needed to test that his eyes were working normally.

"Describe it to me."

"Short black hair with a hint of grey in parts. A young face, a short black beard and a sparing uniform much like my own." He said.

"Good, that went better than expected." I told him.

I placed my hand on the back of my head and began to scratch, the same thing that I always did when I'm trying to brush over a serious topic. It's some form of nervous response or something like that. I'm not a psychologist and I'm not sure that human phycology even applied to me anyway.

"There was a slight chance that you could have lost your vision from that." I said, laughing as I glossed over the true risks involved.

"How slight." He said defensively.

"Twelve percent, maybe fifteen." I said, pinching my fingers in the air a little to signify this amount.

"You could have warned me." He said as he rubbed the water from his eyes.

"You could have asked." I replied logically.

"Okay, what's next?" He asked, intent on continuing.

That's all the confrontation I received for my actions. This was surprising to me; I had expected that hearing the news that he could have gone blind would have made him a little more hostile towards me. But no, I was wrong about him yet again.

"Well now that you have had circuits removed, I cannot recommend that you use magic for the next few days, your body needs time to recover. So perhaps we will leave this assessment for a later date.

Meet me in classroom 1A over in the main building. Perhaps a more academic lesson will be sufficient to pass the time while you heal up." I told him.

I went back to crouching for a moment; I pressed my hands together and bowed towards him. He did the same and after that we both left. He went straight to classroom 1A as instructed and I got myself changed into some more formal clothes before I did the same.

Normally I would have stayed in the sparing uniform in case a student wanted a fight later on but with Julian unable to use magic for a while, I saw no point in wearing it. Julian on the other hand had left his on. He didn't need to but I suspect that at that point he hadn't noticed the clothes that I had put in his wardrobe. He probably still thought that the uniform was all he had.

Ten minutes passed and finally I arrived at classroom 1A. I entered to find that he had already found his seat, third isle up, last seat on the right. The one with the nicest view of course. From up there you could just about peer over the cusp of the hills and see nothing but countryside for miles.

"Shall we begin?" I asked him.

He nodded and sat himself up straight.

"Well then, our first lesson of the day will be on the history and origin of modern-day magic." I said. "Take it to heart. This isn't something I'll come back to again."

It was a good starting point for any novice. Not too demanding mentally while teaching him a lot in the process. Once he had an understanding of what magic actually was and where it came from, I would be able to start teaching him about spells.

Teaching him about enchantments, the incantations required for certain higher-level spells, magic circuit structures, how to use and cast defensive or offensive spells, you name it.

I would be able to teach him anything I thought he was ready for after that. But only to a certain point, one day soon he would need to get an official rank to progress any further.

So that was how it started, me and Julian, in classroom 1A. Every day after sparing at eleven a.m. exactly.

We would stay in that classroom until lunch and then return in the afternoon. Every day he would learn something new and impress me even more with his ability to grasp what I was teaching him so quickly. He absorbed information like a sponge, almost as if it came naturally to him.

His ability to do most basic tasks before I had explained how astonished me at first and then impressed me as day after day he continued to grow as both a mage and a student.

He eventually became what is best described as the perfect student. Never late to class and never afraid to ask questions. He was so well suited to this life that I was ashamed that I couldn't have taught him as he was growing up.

He had potential and was more than willing to unleash it. I quite enjoyed helping him do that. However, all of that changed when the day came that his success would mean he'd to leave me behind.

ACADEMIA

With me as his tutor, Julian continued to make exceptional progress for most of not that entire first year he spent with me.

He consistently managed to amaze me. Finding new ways to outdo himself or to defy my expectations on a daily basis. With his ability to learn, the pace that he could take in and catch on to everything I taught him, he never once slowed down.

And his unparalleled skills in combat. Hand to hand, magic and fencing. He picked up more and more skills each and every day. I couldn't hide the fact that I was impressed by his progress. In fact, it was almost terrifying.

I kept Katiana in the loop whenever he took another step forward, and she too agreed, his abilities were beyond what anyone could have anticipated. His natural talent for magecraft was almost unheard-of.

I had expected it to take me two if not three years to get him ready. And yet he managed to do it, every lesson and every test I threw at him, he did it all in just a single year.

His mind had grown unbelievably during his time as my student. His understanding and his insight rivalled my own in some aspects. He could finally see the world as a true mage. And that was only the beginning.

His body had followed suit.

As his mind took form and strengthened over the months, so too had his physique. His muscles.

The frail and thin boy that I had met that day. Barely a scrap of meat on his bone. Badly broken and bruised all over from his life of hardship. It was all gone within a matter of months.

Before me now stood a muscular and meaty boy. Healthy as one could be. Smiling and bright as a ray of sunlight. He was in better shape than I was at the time. And to a point, he even surpassed me when it came to raw strength.

His training had brought him quite far indeed. Perhaps too far. But he was no longer the street boy that I had met him as. He was no longer frightened or held back by his past. Because with my aid and guidance, he had moved past it and suppressed it.

An apprentice mage, at least traditionally, is meant to act as subordinate and servant to their master. Following them day in and day out and always doing as they were instructed. Knowing that even when dull and demeaning, it was always for their betterment.

And as a man of tradition myself, I treated him as such in the beginning.

He followed me on my duties constantly.

Journeying to the boarder walls to listen to the reports and weigh in on how best to deal with protecting ourselves form current human affairs.

Joining me on my trips to the capital, walking the streets of the great magic city Tryless that stood central to our kingdom. Slap bang in the middle of the entire magic world.

Overlooked by the Magic Council in their citadel tower.

Guarded by mountains and river streams.

And home to some two million people at one time.

He perhaps enjoyed his visit there too much.

And then there was the other thing. My responsibilities when it came to mage law.

I wasn't permitted to enforce many of them, I didn't strictly speaking have a role within the Council's ranks, but when spells that had never been seen before made their way into the larger world beyond our walls, it was my role to identify and trace them.

That was perhaps Julian's first trip outside of the Magic World's walls. He certainly didn't seem used to breathing the air outside of them.

But he handled it all in stride and upon our return, he always seemed to have learnt something. Even if it hadn't intended the journeys to be all that educational.

In truth, he was the most impressive student that I had ever taught and I'm not sure that this world will ever be able to make another quite like him.

In all my years of teaching, in all my years of living, never had I met a student with such a natural talent for magic. Never had I met a person with skills so adept and well-tuned that they seemed too good to be true after such a short period of practicing them.

He was remarkable in every way, truly destined to become an exceptionally strong mage one day and it was so obvious that almost everyone who met him agreed.

No one with that much power and aptitude for magic could have possibly been anything but what he was becoming now.

DANIEL FREARSON

For the entirety of the time that I knew him, he never ceased to amaze and surprise me. He was and will always be my greatest achievement. My perfect student and my friend. He was and to this day still is the most powerful mage that I have ever taught. And that says a lot more than you'd think.

Not even my wife, a woman who had been trained by myself for over three hundred years was a match for him in terms of ray ability.

And this achievement of his, besting her of all people when that she was supposed to be the second most powerful being on the planet at the time, only made him even more impressive.

But alas, raw capability and skill are too different thigs in this world. And unfortunately, skill alone doesn't determine one's stature either.

Even if he was the most powerful mage on the planet, any spell he used that was too far above his level would have been illegal. And without practice, deadly.

But he had made tremendous progress towards his growth and had sadly reached his limit beside me rather quickly as a result.

In fact, it took him less than a third of the time it should have done. In just a single year he had already gotten as far as I could take him. I just wish I could have done more.

But rules were rules and the law was the law.

As the Council saw it, his time with me was over now that he had reached his current peak. Which meant that the time to say goodbye would soon be approaching.

We were only a staggeringly short twelve months into his training when Julian was ready for the next step. He had mastered the spells that he already possessed and had

104

shown a keen interest into learning more than the basic ones that I was allowed to teach him at the time.

He was even beginning to experiment with creating his own. A feat that not many attempt due to its complexity and yet he seemed to be on the right track towards being able to achieve it.

But no matter what he could have done beyond this point, his studies had progressed well and he had learnt all that I was able to teach him for now. In order for me, or anyone to take him any further, he would need to officially become a student of my school.

The only problem was that the next time that the school was due to be used wasn't for another four years. I couldn't open it just for one student and I defiantly couldn't open it for everyone else when they wouldn't have been ready for what I would be teaching them.

So eventually, the time came when I had to make the choice. I had to put one foot in front of the other and push him further towards greatness without me.

And when that day came, I chose to take him to a place that ordinarily he would be ill prepared to venture.

But since he had come so far, I thought it was finally time.

So I took him for his entrance exam.

I took him to a place of triumph, a place where he could prove himself, a place where he would be able to stand tall and strong above everyone else.

And once he had made it through this trial of fire, he would be ready to do all of that and more.

It was July fourteenth when it happened.

Myself, Katiana and Julian, packing our bags and

preparing for the long trip ahead. We weren't planning on staying there at the time but due to the nature of the exam, we always went prepared. If something were to happen, then at least we would have what we needed to stay a few nights.

But I hadn't spoken a word of what I was planning to Julian yet. We had discussed what he saw himself doing in the future before that point and had agreed that going to an official mage school would be best for him but I had never told him which one I would take him to when the time came.

All I had told him on the eve of the day before was that his next lesson would be unlike any I had taught him so far. I told him that it would be a challenge worthy of his full attention. A danger not to be taken lightly. And that a great victory awaited him.

Even with this cryptic version of what I really had planned, he would have still been able to guess what that lesson really was. I suppose that meant he knew what was going on, even if it hadn't registered in his head at the time.

I intended to tell him of course, I'm not one for surprises myself so I don't usually surprise others. But for whatever reason, I never found the right time.

I ended up retaining that knowledge. My own inability to share the events to come ensured that it remained as a poorly kept secret for as long as it took me to go through with it.

For days leading up to that night, for the various lessons that I had to slow his progress, I thought about telling him. I knew that he had a right to know, I knew that if I told him, there was a chance he might work harder towards preparing himself. But I also knew how excitable he could be when approaching such challenges.

I knew that there was a chance, however minor, that he would become so excited and caught up in the moment that he wouldn't be capable of passing. So I guess that in the end it was on purpose. I suppose I did do my best to keep it to myself.

Doing this allowed him to experience the surprise and suspense of that day unhindered. After all, it was supposed to be my last day teaching him for quite some time, I wanted to make it special. But, perhaps making it a surprise was unfair.

I felt like I was saying goodbye to a son at the time, he had lived in my home for so long that I had become attached to him and I could tell that a similar thing had happened to Katiana as well. Every night he would be all we talked about before bed.

She would ask what subjects I was focusing on in his lessons. How much I had taught him in the day and then ask how well he had absorbed the information. She would ask me if he had been progressing to my satisfaction every single night like clockwork and then proceed to ask about his wellbeing.

To find out if I had been too hard on him whilst sparing or if I hadn't been pushing him hard enough for him to learn how to cope.

She cared about him and if you ever needed proof of that then look no further than the day that she celebrated his birthday.

At the time, neither I nor Julian had expected it. I didn't even know that she had figured out when his birthday was and she never told me about her plans. Julian himself never knew when his birthday was either, at best he guessed that it was in May but he couldn't be sure.

Due to the nature of how he had grown up and the conspiracy surrounding his mother's disappearance, I never quite figured out how she did it but somehow, she did. On May ninth, Julian and I retreated from the dojo for lunch when we saw it.

Instead of our regular meal of sandwiches or meatballs, a great feast was laid out before us. A banquet fit for kings. Not people. There was roast turkey, duck, pork. Mashed and roasted potatoes. And various other vegetables covering the table from end to end.

It was an enormous meal for only three people, yet somehow, we managed to finish most of it.

When I asked Katiana why she had gone to all the trouble, she simply smiled and kept quiet. I knew she was up to something so I sat down and Julian did the same.

It was only when she came back out of the kitchen with two boxes in her hand that I understood. She was celebrating his birthday. Even Julian didn't understand. He had never known the exact date of his birth and couldn't comprehend how she had figured it out.

She handed him the boxes with the subtle look of delight on her face as she wished him a happy birthday.

Julian probably wanted to ask her how she knew but instead he focused on the moment and opened the boxes. The first one was small, easily fitting in your hand. It was square and plush blue.

It was a ring box.

When Julian opened it, even I wore a look of shock on my face. Inside was one of Katiana's oldest possessions, a ring dating back to before she was born.

A relic from my past, a gift that I had once bestowed onto her and something that she could never bring herself to wear. It carried too much significance and far too much power for her to feel comfortable holding it on her body.

I couldn't get a good look at it from my position but if memory severs me right, it was made from silver. Engraved with Nordic runes and gems.

It was ancient and very powerful.

The enchantment placed upon it was part of the reason that Katiana never wore it. When worn, it allows the wearer to mentally turn back the clock.

To replay memories in your mind at will, going as far back as you could remember them. For Julian, this ring was the perfect gift and the joy on his face when he was told what it could do was a look that I never intend to forget.

The next box was larger, at least a half metre long on one side. She didn't even bother telling him what it was, he could figure that out for himself.

Within this box was something that I hadn't expected to ever see. Inside were the clothes that he had worn on the day that he had met us. The old mage robes that were scuffed, ripped and muddy. At least they used to be.

When the lid of the box opened both Julian's jaw and my own dropped. They had been repaired, cleaned and re-dyed. They were in pristine condition and looked almost new.

Julian was overzealous with happiness after that, never waking up without a smile on his face, not even looking as though he could feel anything but joy anymore.

If that didn't say that Katiana cared then I don't know what did. Even when I asked her, again and again, how she figured out when his birthday was, she stayed silent.

She told me that secrets sometimes need to remain as secrets. After the ninth try, I just stopped asking. To this day, I still don't understand how she did it but that doesn't matter. He was happier as a whole after that day and now we knew exactly when to celebrate his birthday each year.

However, despite how much she cared for him or how much she had come to love him, she wouldn't be able to do much on the day.

For the sake of formality, she was required to observe the event but not as a teacher or a friend. On this day, she would have to represent the Magic Council in accordance with her duties as the Crown Mage.

Because of this, her mood was quite foul for days leading up to the event. She wasn't allowed to show affection towards him and wasn't even allowed to talk to him outside of the exam.

Julian had noticed that something was troubling her but I didn't tell him why. He could tell that she was intentionally avoiding him and yet, I couldn't even tell him that it wasn't his fault.

Instead, I asked her to try and find a way to spend as much time away from him as possible. It would only be for a couple of days so I didn't see any harm in asking her to distance herself from the two of us.

The Crown Mage is meant to be impartial you see. In order for her opinion to count for anything, she had to show that she wasn't influenced by or attached to him.

Unfortunately, this normally meant that she had to be quite mean to a student for a week or two.

But, fortunately for all of us, she had managed to find a

way to stay out of the house for most of the hours in the day.

She had spent her time staying busy, doing anything that she could that didn't require her to be at home each and every day leading up to the event.

I'm not sure what she did for most of it but for the final five days leading up to the trip she had been securing our rout into the academy that I had chosen.

Normally this would have only taken a simple visit and some paperwork but Julian couldn't teleport that far on his own at the time. When added in with the fact that he didn't know where he was going, I would have to take him there myself. This meant that there would need to be a larger exception in the barrier surrounding this academy than normal and that everyone would need to be prepared to start the exam as soon as we arrived.

Everything had to be perfect; he only got one chance at something like this after all. I wanted to make sure that this was a chance that did not go wasted.

I wanted to give him the best shot of succeeding, so I did what I must in order to allow him to achieve this goal. Treating the situation differently than I ever had done before.

Normally, I wouldn't care if the students made it in or not. Of course, I wanted them to succeed but I wouldn't have made a big fuss over it if they didn't in the end. The main purpose of the exam was to prove if they were capable as a mage. And sometimes, even the best teachers can't turn stone into gold.

But with Julian, everything was different.

It was as though getting him through this exam was the most important thing in the world at the time. I couldn't focus on anything else. I couldn't even look at him in the same way anymore. I knew that if I didn't get him through this exam, I would have failed him.

Of all the students that I had entered into that school, never had I made so large an attempt to ensure that they made it through.

Julian was strong and smart, that much was true but this academy was well known for being the best one in the world and for good reason. It only accepted the finest of mages.

Because of this, the ones who actually graduated were normally all in the top one percent around the world. If a mage, no matter who or where, is declared to be the best at something or the strongest in something else, it is almost always because they attended this academy.

I had seen great things in this boy and I wanted to ensure that he would achieve the status that he was both worthy and capable of.

So I made sure everything was ready, and when the time finally came, it began.

I looked at my watch to check the time. Moments before then the hands had just moved into position. It was ten fifteen exactly and we were all ready.

I nodded to Katiana and she teleported off ahead of us to fill in the final pieces of paperwork for me. Normally this would be the job of his teacher but I was sure they wouldn't mind a visit from the Crown Mage instead.

Then again, if I had gone in her place then it would have taken much longer as a result. My wife was well known amongst most of the magic world but I was known by all of it. My presence would have caused a riot or two. I do give off an aura of overwhelming power after all.

Perhaps I was being overly cautious at the time but the past is the past, I had made the decision to carry Julian in myself so Katiana did the paperwork in my place.

I suppose that it helped us both in a way. It allowed me to take him straight into the exam and it allowed her to be seen arriving by herself. No doubt, this would have helped her maintain at least some of her fleeting authority.

A few minutes passed and the time finally came for us to depart as well. I gripped Julian firmly on the shoulder, gazed down at his choice of apparel and prepared for the journey at hand.

Instead of wearing his more formal clothes – his robes or a suit – he had chosen to wear his sparing uniform. The laces were tightly tied together in more practiced and professional knots. The fit and finish matched his physique perfectly now and from the year he'd been using it, the only sights of wear and tear were on the sleeves that had begun to fray.

But that wasn't really a problem in any way. Such a slight detail was unlikely to be picked up on by anyone else but me. Other than the few wandering threads hanging from his arms, the uniform was in a pristine condition.

And as for choosing to wear it, there wasn't a more appropriate attire that he could have worn. The sparing uniform may simply look like a set of leather robes and a belt but they were much more than that.

By law, every sparing uniform must have reinforced fibres from top to bottom. However, as this was only a protective precaution, those fibres didn't actually need to be physical. So to save on the weight and make it easier for him to move, I achieved this by enchanting the set that Julian wore.

This made them lighter but still just as strong as any other set. The purpose of this law was to keep overpowered teachers like myself from killing the students should they get too carried away during a fight.

Some would argue that this made battles far too easy since the students couldn't sustain any real injuries but I prefer my students to still be breathing rather than have them six feet under after every punch.

"Julian." I said.

"Yes Master?"

"What are the three rules of a successful long-distance teleport?" I asked him.

A simple test to put him in the right mind-set and to calm him a little. Even from the distance between us, I could still tell that he was anxious, nervous even.

He did well to hide it but as I approached him further it only became ever more apparent. His blood was pumping violently and his sweat was swiftly soaking into his uniform. His posture was poor and his mind was elsewhere. This question soon got him back on track.

"There are four." He replied.

His nerves settling a little as he realised that I was testing him. Simply by saying those three words I could already tell that he was on top of his game.

If he hadn't been then he would have never spotted that I was testing him in more than one way with that question.

"Rule one, don't tense up. Rule two, keep your mind clear. Three. Focus only on your destination and the forth, when carrying a passenger, hold on tight." He recited form his memory.

"Very good my boy, now take a deep breath." I warned
114

him. "And relax."

He gasped in a full breath off air and of we went.

Traveling many hundreds of miles in less than an instant.

Soon we would arrive at the academy that I had chosen to enrol him at and the real test would begin.

In less time than it takes to blink, we would have travelled to another continent entirely, crossing three time zones and six international borders.

I don't quite know how to describe teleportation, it's not like you can see anything while you do it. The world around you goes black but only for a moment, when the light flows back into your eyes you would have already arrived if the teleport had been performed successfully.

You need to focus on your destination and envision a bubble of empty space around you. Then fill that space with energy and exert your will into it and force it to move to your destination.

If done correctly, you should be exactly where you expected to be. If not, there's no telling where you could end up. There aren't many things that can interrupt a teleport other than incompetence but if the fault was not your own then it comes down to one of two things. Your destination doesn't exist or a barrier was blocking your path.

As for what it looks like to others, all I know is how I to do it isn't quite how it looks when someone else does it. I'm not too sure as to how it looks when I did it but I would assume that its's at least mostly similar.

No one ever actually taught me how to teleport, it was something that I just did by accident one day. Since then I have been teaching it to others, you can imagine that teaching such an action was difficult in the beginning.

After all, it was an accident. I wasn't sure how I was supposed to make sure that others could do it on purpose. It took time. And over that time, I watched many teleports. And every one of them looked different.

But as for my own style of going from point A to point B, I have only ever been told how it looks. After all, when I do it myself, I can't exactly see the process. It's over too fast for that.

Within an instant, no more time than it takes for your eyes to blink or a heart to beat, the person standing before you is gone, replaced with a quickly dissipating light echo.

A bright blue hue perfectly shaped to their body.

That's all there is to see when someone leaves.

But arrival is far more interesting.

It's easy to miss unless you're looking but the arrival of a teleport is much easier to perceive than the departure. When landing, a quick jolt of energy, somewhat similar to lighting, fills the space that you are about to teleport to.

Like the bubble that you imagine when teleporting, it expands suddenly and then disappears with a flash of blue light. By the time your eyes refocus, the teleportation process has been completed and the travellers have arrived.

When a teleport is performed correctly, you and the bubble move in unison traveling as far as your magical power can carry you.

For someone as week as Julian was back then, you would have been lucky to make it a few hundred metres, let alone miles. But for someone like me or Katiana, we could probably visit the moon if it was possible to do so.

But simply having the power to go somewhere doesn't mean that you should. In order to teleport anywhere, you need to be able to picture it. For most, this means visiting your destination beforehand. But there were ways around this.

For some and I do mean some, it was possible to travel to a location simply by knowing its position on a map. Although you wouldn't necessarily be able to predict where you would land to any degree of accuracy, you'd still be close enough.

More commonly, when someone is told to teleport somewhere for the first time, they would use a picture as a reference point, an anchor if you will. A mental image to hold while you attempt to steer yourself to your destination.

I have never really thought too much about what exactly happens during this time inside the bubble but an old student of mine once speculated a theory that was most interesting to me.

She was such a bright girl back then; I'm not surprised that she grew up to become not only the sixth Crown Mage but also my wife.

Someone so smart and talented would have been wasted with any other man.

She speculated that, similar to how my other form is… for lack of a better description – hidden behind the walls of another dimension, teleportation worked in a similar way. She thought that our bodies move to this other dimension during the teleport and all that is left is an anchor point. The bubble of magic that we send to our destination.

She theorised that instead of us moving, it is instead simply our magic moving and that we are carried to its location when we re-enter this dimension. Almost as though instead of actually teleporting at all we are instead opening interdimensional portals at two separate locations and then moving between them.

An interesting theory to be sure but one that was unfounded and impossible to prove. Teleportation lasts for such a short amount of time that it's hard to make any assessment as to how it really works.

It's not like you can see or feel anything when your body doesn't even exist for the extent of the trip.

I had no clue as to whether she was right or wrong but I have never heard an explanation that made any more sense that that one did.

But then again, I had never heard any explanation prior to that to compare it to. In order for anyone to prove this you would have to be able to either slow or perceive time at a rate that was impossible to achieve.

Even with all my power and knowledge, the manipulation of time wasn't a possibly outcome of magecraft no matter your skill.

And besides that, the amount you'd have to slow time to be able to see anything would be astronomical. A single second would be equivalent to a century.

But theory doesn't matter much in this case.

We all knew how to use teleportation magic by now.

There's no need to understand how it works so long as it does.

And with our teleportation under way, it was less than a second after our departure before we arrived.

The teleport was complete and we were exactly where we needed to be.

I thought that we better get right down to business so I teleported us into the main sparing hall for him to perform his entrance exam right away.

The sparing hall itself was much like my dojo in many ways. A solid wood floor, protective barriers around the designated combat rings and enchantments fortifying the walls of the room itself.

However, where it mainly differed from my simple dojo was the fact that it was much larger. Not a simple wooden shack like mine, this one was designed for tournaments and more academic lessons.

The sparing hall at the academy was two if not three times longer and about fifty percent wider than my mere dojo.

The walls were made of stone, not wood. The support pillars for the floor above were scattered far and wide, extending upwards almost twenty-five meters, made of marble reinforced with steel beams in the centre and completely covered in defensive enchantments to keep them standing no matter what the students threw at them.

Weapons and armour lined the walls much likes those within my dojo. Each one on display for the visitors and students to lust over. They sat upon their own pedestals and weapon racks just as mine did but unlike my own, there were far more of them.

A vast arsenal of swords, pikes and bows filled the room. Enough weapons for over three hundred people to defend themselves, enough armour to protect a small army, enough power to start a war.

Other than the weapons, the similarities stopped there.

To the north side of the hall was a large array of seating for spectators. Seats that were already full when we arrived. Two maybe three hundred other students sat there in silence, patiently awaiting our arrival.

Preparing themselves for the marvel that they were about to witness. It didn't matter what reason I had chosen to visit the academy, I always received an audience.

To the other side of the hall, opposite the seats and against the respective wall at that end, were large wooden structures. Seating platforms, each one taller than the next going upwards like an arched pyramid until you reach the one in the middle.

This middle seat was the one that the Headmaster would use and the one with the best view and the most eyes focused upon it.

That seat extended maybe five metres in the air. All those next to it, slowly decreased in height as you went down the lines. Seats extended to the left and to the right, making an almost arch shaped pattern as a result.

Twenty-three seats with the Headmaster's in the middle. Reserved to staff and special visitors, these seats weren't for students to use.

The arch of the seats matched the shape of the tournament circle in front of them. Wrapping around the edge of the outer circle like a hand gripping a glass.

Unlike the spectators, these seats were much closer to the action and had a much better view because of this. They were also safer in a way, each of them having extra enchantments placed on the frame of the oak-wood structure, defending the occupants much more than the students at the other end of the hall.

Not that the enchantments were necessary anyway. It had been decades since the last accident and it wasn't even me who had caused it. As long as I stood in the room, no one was in any serious danger. I could at least control myself to some degree.

The room shook violently as the energy of my teleport amassed and then suddenly, there we were.

A quick jolt of energy suddenly lit up the rings of the tournament circle and then dissipated just as quickly. A quick breath later and there we stood.

Placed perfectly in the centre of the ring and facing the platform of seats in front of us.

We were perfectly on time and ready for what was to come. The judges and even a part of the Magic Council, including Katiana, were awaiting his performance and mine.

I released my grip of Julian and bowed to the Headmaster as soon as I could. Julian did the same.

Sitting beside this old fart of a man was my wife on one side and the defence governor on the other.

Katiana was there to witness the event and if needed, give her impartial opinion should anything happen that wasn't to the Council's liking.

As for the defence governor, he was there to ensure that I wasn't breaking any of the sanctions placed upon me. If I were to use a spell too powerful or one that was forbidden, he had the authority to launch an all-out assault on me. Not that they would have won such a fight, it was just his job to enforce the law and punish me if he felt the need.

There were various other people seated in front of us. Members of the academic leadership, teachers from the school and staff from various other establishments connected to it.

They were not of any importance. Or at least they weren't important enough for myself to have known their names.

However, the final five seats on the right of me contained the judges.

These people were the only ones other than the Headmaster that I paid attention to. They were there to assess Julian during this exam, I needed to make sure that throughout the entire thing they remained satisfied.

To the left sat a few less important people but they were still ones that I needed to keep an eye on. To the far left sat the representatives from the Council.

Most likely there to make sure that I didn't cheat, or kill someone during the exam. They were there to make sure that I hadn't taught Julian anything that he shouldn't have known yet and that I wasn't going to cheat his way into the academy.

While the judges were the ones that I was there to please, the Council members were the ones that I couldn't afford to anger.

We raised our heads and returned to our previous stance. A moment later and the Headmaster had raised his hand a brief second before he spoke.

This was something that he did every time that he had something official to say. Signifying that during its time in the air, no one will speak out until he lowered his hand again.

If any student or even a staff member should dare to do so, they would be punished in a most bizarre manner, they would have a silencing spell cast on them.

Making it impossible to speak until it wore off.

While this doesn't sound like much of a punishment, you must keep in mind that these spells last upwards of two weeks at a time and when cast correctly and depending on the caster they can be quite difficult to remove by force.

"Here today we are to witness the entrance exam of one Julian Ealton, last surviving descendant of the fifth Crown Mage, Titus Ealton. Currently a student of the Athereon himself, this individual has been granted special entry due to his master's stature. This exam is to be performed in three stages, endurance, knowledge and power. Stage one will commence when you are ready."

He lowered his hand allowing others in the room to speak; this included Julian and myself of course and it wasn't long before Julian had a question to ask.

"Where are we?" He whispered to me.

"Welcome to the Grand Archive and School for Magic, formally and publicly known as Academia. Today is the day that you have been waiting for lad." I told him with pride as he started to look around timidly.

I stayed facing the Headmaster and all the others sitting on the stand before me. I didn't dare take my eyes off of them. I didn't want to miss the Headmaster's hand being raised. I hated having to remove silence spells, they can be quite tricky and very keen to latch on.

I watched as Katiana began to smile in my presence but I did nothing in return. If I had given off any sense that she would be a distraction to me, then she would have been removed and I couldn't have that.

This was something that she had been waiting for and was something that I wanted her to see.

"You mean that this is my enrolment?" Julian asked, unfazed by the various faces staring down at him and seemingly unaware of the three hundred more behind him.

"Only if you pass." I said.

"What do I do to pass?"

"To pass you must complete two of three stages with two marks or all three stages with one mark. Stage one assesses endurance, stage two assesses your knowledge and stage three assesses your overall power." I explained.

"Stage one starts now then I guess.?"

"When you say the word, your test will begin. But know that I cannot help you. Once you start, you either complete the stage or you fail." I warned him.

He turned his eyes back to the Headmaster and proclaimed that he was ready to begin. Not hesitating in the slightest, he stood there and said what he had to say in order to get the process started.

He was as ready as he would ever be at that point, I guess. Not that he had a choice though.

"I'm ready." He said. Bowing to the bearded old man before him.

The Headmaster raised his hand once again and everyone stayed silent.

"Stage one will last no less than two minutes, you must stay both conscious and in the smallest of the five rings during this time. The use of any spell above level five is prohibited, this includes teleportation, telepathy and of course, it prohibits the use of the Athereon form.

Your opponent will be your Master. Unfortunately for you, your Master is the Athereon himself. Good luck. Remember that you do not have to beat him, only last a mere two minutes up against him. You will begin when both opponents stand in their positions marked on the floor." The Headmaster instructed, lowering his hand.

Julian looked down at the floor and saw the red circles

lined across it. Similar to the layout of my dojo back home, the floor is meant for sparing and as such as several rings were laid out for combat zones. The one that we were standing in was the largest, designed for tournaments not simple friendly sparing matches.

So we moved back from the position we had arrived stood in proceeded towards the edge of the smallest inner circle.

Every ninety degrees around this circle were smaller blue circles. These were the positions that we must stand in. Julian took his place, now doing nothing but stare at the crowd of students he had only just noticed and I walked over to mine and gave him a quick warning just to be fair.

"Julian, remember this is not about winning. Just dodge my attacks and you will be fine. However, everyone here has seen me fight before, since I am not allowed to go easy on you, they are here to assess whether or not I am fighting at my best." I said, giving him a heads up that I would be going at him strong and fast from the off.

I took my position and bowed at Julian, he bowed back and then the fight began.

We had spared many times before but never like this.

Not only was I not allowed to go easy on him, I mustn't. If he was to have any chance at entering this academy then I would have to forget the bond we shared. I must think of him not as my pupil but as my enemy.

This first task sounds impossible to most people when they hear about it, but in truth, it's not all that difficult. People think of me as an unbeatable warrior and while normally I am, not being allowed to use any spell above level five means that I cannot shift into my true form. It means that I cannot summon weapons or perform an enchantment.

Being limited to level five makes me just a strong as any other mage of similar rank, in terms of magic that is. In terms of combat skills, even with just my fists and some basic casting magic, I am still not an easy target to eliminate.

If Julian had thought that the lessons he had endured so far were tough, then he was about to learn a completely new meaning for the word difficult.

"Begin." Shouted the Headmaster, waving his hand downwards as you would at the start of a race or when firing artillery.

I looked towards Julian.

'He has no idea what's about to hit him.' I thought.

I clenched my right fist; placed it by my hip with the knuckles facing towards him and tensed my muscles.

I sprang into action a moment later, moving towards him at speeds no mortal man could have perceived. Almost as if I were gliding just barely above the floor, I approached him about to hit him in a way he couldn't have seen coming.

If I had been up against any other person, that attack would have landed in the gut and knocked him off his feet and out of the circle. My goal wasn't to purposely fail him but to give him the best chance possible at showing off.

If I fought at my best then when he completed the stage, he would have seemed even more impressive than he already was.

But Julian being Julian, he got lucky.

As I approached, I realised that he had already started to move. As if he had begun dodging before I had even starting hitting.

Just as my fist should have hit him, all I felt was air. Within a heartbeat, he had read my moves and evaded my attack. Something that I hadn't expected from him.

'Still full of surprises.' I thought

I stopped myself just shy of the rings edge, sliding across the floor as I went. I turned to look at him and what I saw surprised me even more.

He copied exactly what I had just done. Fist clenched tight by his hip, legs spread widely apart and his speed just slightly slower than mine.

I had never used that on him before, I was shocked that he could have copied it so perfectly after just one encounter.

I moved as fast as I could and deflected the blow. I saw an opening in that moment, his arms were to his right deflecting mine, leaving his head wide open.

I went for his face, putting all my strength and speed into that one blow but again, I had hit nothing but air. By the time my fist had reached his head it was long gone.

In the confusion, I too had left myself open. He went for a jab at my ribs, so I went for a deflection followed by a punch to the gut.

The deflection worked, he never laid a hand on me but yet again, my hit never landed. He moved backwards so fast that he just barely went out of reach of my arm.

Obviously, this fight wasn't going to be won with raw power alone. But without enchantments, that meant that we had no speed boosts, no reflex enhancements. I was limited to any spell below level five; this was going to make it difficult to gain the upper hand.

"Good reflexes, but let us see how you handle a little heat." I jested.

Fire magic, anything below the conjuration of pure magma is strictly a level two spell. I punched my fist into my hand and they both came a light with bright glowing flames. Dwarfing the light of the bulbs on the ceiling.

Not something that I agreed with but this academy was state of the art, it made sense that they had electricity there. I on the other hand preferred the glow of candles and a brightly lit fire to illuminate my home.

I changed my stance to allow him to come at me this time.

Ten seconds had passed so far and not a single hit had been landed. The crowd had only just gotten over their initial shock from when Julian managed to dodge the first blow.

I could hear their breaths, the gasps and anticipation after every attack. They were eager to see the fight progress and so was I.

He came sprinting at me this time, a look of determination in his eyes. As he grew closer, I realised something, he was going in a straight line. Making no attempt to slow and no attempt to evade anything. He obviously had a plan bouncing around in that head of his.

I placed my palms together than forced them into the ground. He was mere steps away when the floor below him began to light up, a mere moment away from bursting with flames. I channelled my energy into this burst and then again, just as it was about to hit him, he wasn't there.

He had jumped at the last moment and was now sliding across the floor towards me. I pulled my arm up to punch him as he reached me. But I underestimated his speed. My fist hit the floor, merely denting it but not even getting close him. He had gone straight through my open legs.

To this day, I am still disappointed with myself for leaving such a wide opening like that. It was purely amateur, not a single part of it suggested that I knew what I was doing. Making a mistake like that was completely childish, no sense of how to fight at all. How could I have been so foolish?

Now behind me, he was in the clear to perform an attack, or so he thought. He went for my legs but they weren't there by the time his hit passed me.

I jumped into the air and had no intentions for coming down, so I stayed there. While actual flight magic is a level nine skill and I obviously couldn't use my wings while I'm in my human form, creating an updraft with wind magic was still level one.

By that point, only fifteen seconds had passed and the fight was still going. To get one mark in this stage, you must last a minute at least, to get two you must last two. There was one exception to this however, if you were to knock me out of the ring, two points would be awarded no matter how long it had taken.

He looked at me from below, assessed the situation and that was when he actually realised what he needed to do. I was diverting all air upwards towards me. This created quite the breeze. He placed his had within the gale, and began to freeze it. He was trying to force me down by freezing the air around me.

I reacted a little forcefully in my opinion. I pointed my fists downwards and began to eject fire out of my hands. This wasn't the best idea and in the heat of the moment, I hadn't realised that Julian had already anticipated this act.

Hidden beneath the haze of the icy air was a little surprise he had prepared for me. The foundations of a wind funnel, a synthetic tornado, only inches above the floor.

When my fiery blaze hit the chilled air, it activated. Creating an uncontrolled funnel of gale force winds around me. Forcing me to spin in mid-air for a few moments.

But as I mentioned a mere moment ago, this was an uncontrolled funnel and was fundamentally still just made up of air. I placed my hand into the funnel of air and focused. Slowing the wind, adjusting the vectors controlling it and then transferring it towards Julian, a raging beam of high-pressure air racing towards him.

Yet again, he dodged.

The air missed him completely and hit the barrier protecting the rest of the room from us instead.

But with my own winds gone and his redirected downwards, I was now left falling to the ground and twenty meters below me was my target.

I clenched my fist, relit my flames and intended to get a good slam in on his head as I fell.

Still recovering from his previous dodge, I had only a moment to do anything before he dodged again. But it wasn't his body that moved, not one single muscle in his legs that extended, in fact it seemed as though he wasn't making any attempt to dodge it at all. To my own disbelief, he was instead attempting to block it.

As I drew closer, falling from the sky above, his right fist rose up to meet mine. He stayed crouched below me, channelling every muscle into absorbing this blow.

'He thinks that he can block a punch from me?' I thought as I continued to fall. 'If he wants to feel my power then by all means he can do it with that power at full strength.'

I intensified the flames and put everything that I had into that blow. Every muscle exerting immense force and power, every magic circuit channelling energy into the flames and every thought focused on landing this one strike.

It didn't matter what he intended to do, no matter what defence he had thought of, nothing he could muster could have withstood such a strike.

My muscles were stronger, my magic was older and my circuits were saturated with an unending supply of power. If this strike had hit any other person, they would have been dead.

But when our fists hit one another, I heard a sharp snap as his arm broke in several places, a gasp of pain as the force hit his core and shook his bones. But then something happened, something that I had never seen before.

My hit backfired.

Sending me flying through the air in the process.

The initial impact had detonated my flames yet the explosion only directed itself at me. The heat alone overwhelming me for a moment and then all I could feel was the force of my punch sending me sky high in less than a second.

To my astonishment, I had just lost, to my own pupil none the less.

At the time, I didn't understand how he had done it. Perhaps he channelled all his energy into a very small yet powerful barrier around his fist. On the other hand, maybe he had a protection enchantment on him somewhere that I didn't know about that meant that he couldn't be wounded without his attacker receiving the same hit.

DANIEL FREARSON

By the time I realised what had happened, I was already outside of the ring. Now that I had lost, I used real flight magic this time to slow and control my decent before I landed back on the floor.

I planted my feet down full of surprise and shock. I looked over at the judges and saw the exact same look on their faces as well; even Katiana had a shocked look on her face.

None of us, not one single person watching or participating in the fight had expected that outcome.

In less than a minute, he had not only come out with only a single hit taken but also as the victor. Against me no less.

I moved my gaze back over to Julian. He hadn't moved an inch. Still kneeling there with his obviously broken arm in the air. He turned his head towards me with a week yet promising smile on his face.

"So, how did I do?" He asked.

He coughed for a moment and then collapsed before me.

I rushed over to help him but there was nothing to be done. He was severely injured and all out of magical energy.

I'm surprised that he could even speak after exerting himself as much as he did. The best thing for him to do now would be to rest, a lot.

I did what I could for his arm but I'm no medic. I cannot fully heal a wound without a serious amount of concentration. Something that in that moment, I did not have.

The barriers lifted once he dropped and the real medics in the corner of the hall rushed into action. They carried him straight to the infirmary. I would join him there later, but for now, I would have to stay where I stood.

The Headmaster raised his hand and a feeling of fear consumed me in both body and soul for a moment.

"Stage one is complete. The obvious victor here is Julian. Stage two will commence if and when he recovers. As for how he won, Athereon, can you explain?" He asked of me.

He lowered his hand and I kept both of mine behind my back. I was pretty sure that the knuckles in my right hand were shattered as a result of whatever spell Julian had just used against me.

I didn't really want people to see much carrying such a wound.

"To be completely honest sir, I haven't the foggiest. In all my years of fighting, I have never seen anyone reflect my attacks, let alone withstand them." I told him.

The head judge, Mage Clanton Darley questioned me as to the legitimacy of his victory. Something that I expected to happen eventually and something that only he would have thought of asking.

"Athereon, if I may, by your assessment, what level would you say that that spell was?" He inquired.

I knew that this would be the first question he asked, he always questioned how my students do it when they pass the endurance stage. The simple truth of the matter is that I train them well. But in Julian's case, I didn't have a clue.

"Due to its potency and how it was used I would place it somewhere between levels five and eight. But as for how it was actually done and what it was. The only comparison that I can offer is that it was a variation of the Fatal Mirror spell." I explained.

He moved in closer to me, now leaning over the long table that he and the rest of the judges sat at.

"Enlighten us if you would please. What exactly is the Fatal Mirror spell?"

I should have expected that question as soon as I mentioned the spell. He was just looking for an excuse or perhaps evidence however slight or insignificant that would allow him to disqualify Julian.

"Fatal Mirror is a spell that officially doesn't have a level requirement to be taught. It is purely a defensive spell and as such is classified as level zero with the rest of them. But as I said, this is only a comparison, that spell was most certainly not Fatal Mirror." I told him.

The Headmaster raised his hand.

"How can you be sure, it certainly looked like it to me?" He said.

The hand lowered and I already had my response.

"Fatal Mirror is a spell that is only to be used in the most dire of situations. It protects the user from all incoming damage and deflects it back at the attacker.

This spell is only known as a 'Fatal' Mirror, because using it will drain you of all your magical energy, in some situations this can result in extreme pain or even death. The only reason that I would say this wasn't Fatal Mirror is because of his arm. It was broken. Had the spell been Fatal Mirror he would have been perfectly unharmed, which he is not." I explained as plainly as I could.

Again, I saw the hand of the Headmaster rise.

"Very well, we will assess the situation. As for now, tend to you student. I will grant him whatever reprieve he required before we continue. He still has two more stages to complete after all." The headmaster said.

I bowed and made my exit.

"Thank you, sir. I look forward to hearing the results of your assessment." I told him.

As I left the room, I contacted Katiana privately. Asking her to do what she had to do to get to the infirmary as soon as possible.

Our telepathic link was week when surrounded by so many mages; I had to keep it short and would have to tell her everything that I wanted to in person. I wouldn't want anyone else to overhear.

It took her only ten minutes to get to the infirmary from the hall on foot. Not bad considering the confusing layout of the building.

I on the other hand had to teleport in, something that the nurses didn't appreciate at the time. But I am something of a celebrity in the Magic World. Should word have gotten out that I was simply wondering the halls of Academia, there would surely have been a riot as hundreds of students rushed in to meet me.

But I sat by his bedside and took over from the nurse. Even when week, I can still heal a broken bone faster than she could have done. Now that the confusion of that moment had passed, I had time to think and time to concentrate. Now that I was alone, I could heal him much faster than anyone else could have done.

I just needed a little time to get my head back on track. Without my concentration I can't do anything. It's difficult to repair bones as it is, it's almost impossible if you're not able to concentrate.

There I waited for Katiana. By the time that she arrived, I had already thought through what I needed to say to her almost a dozen times.

She entered his room with a sad look on her face at first.

"What have you done now?" She said. "Go a bit too rough on another student again?"

I looked at her with a serious yet calm face.

She closed the door and sat in front of me.

"You saw what he did, didn't you? How he won?" I asked.

I returned to looking at Julian while I finished healing his arm. It was more badly injured than I had thought. He had torn a ligament as well as completely shattering the bones. As well as rupturing over twelve blood vessels and dislocating his wrist.

In the human world, such an arm might well have been amputated.

"Yes, I know what he did but not how?" She told me.

"That's just the thing, I don't know. It felt like Fatal Mirror but it was much too focused and far too small." I told her in return.

I finished healing his arm for the moment. He would need more than one mere healing spell to fix such a break. But at the time it wasn't going to kill him.

So I turned my attention back to myself and started to heal my right hand. The knuckles were both shattered and dislocated as a result of that spell.

"Are you saying that it was a spell variant that you haven't seen before?" She asked.

"No, I'm saying that it was a spell that I hadn't seen before. I couldn't even read the sigils." I said.

Sigils, they are a difficult thing to explain.

When a spell is cast, no matter what it is or how it is used, sigils are formed. These are a type of signature given off by almost every spell. Almost like a foreign language, these sigils are confusing and odd. Even if you could see them, you most certainly couldn't read them.

Only those who are extremely sensitive to magic can see them though. I only knew of three mages other than myself who could see them at the time but only I knew enough about them to be able to read them.

"A foreign spell, but how is that possible? You basically invented every spell out there today." She stated.

"That's what worries me. This boy has more potential than I like to admit and have you not noticed the fact that he looks nowhere near the age that he should? Just look at him now, he's supposed to be thirty. But he still looks twenty. Who else do you know that can invent spells and control his outward appearance at will?" I asked.

"Only …you." She gasped.

"Exactly." I said.

I released my grip on my hand; it was as good as it was going to be for a while. A wound like that would need multiple healing spells cast on it similar to Julian's arm. The break was too severe to fix in one go. The body can only cope with so much at once.

"But that's impossible. There hasn't been another Athereon born in thousands of years. You told me yourself, you watched them all die over twelve millennia ago." She said.

"And that's what scares me. He shares more similarities with me than any mage I have ever met." I said, pausing for a moment and looking closely at him. Assessing his scares and his markings and trying not to think of the only obvious reason that he would have them. "I can't help but wonder, what if someone was trying to create something that could equal me?"

I desperately tried to find another answer as to what exactly he was but I couldn't. I couldn't pull an answer out of my head by magic. I only had the evidence to go on and everything about this boy just screamed out that something about him didn't make sense.

"How and why would someone do that?" She asked. "I know the Council's tried to make people that could stand against you before but well... I of all people know how that ended up."

"I don't know, but looking at him, you can't help but think about it. The scares on his back are almost as if he had something removed. Like wings perhaps? And the other markings on his back, similar to ones from where my armour attaches to my spine.

And then there's the lashing scars, the marks of shackles of his wrists and ankles. I don't know what to make of them." I pondered.

"So you think that someone abducted one of the most powerful mages alive and what, tried to grow another... another you?" Shea asked.

She didn't understand the situation any more than I did but one thing I did know is that this conversation couldn't go on for much longer.

We had more questions than we did answers. Plus, anyone could have been listening in. That room wasn't exactly air tight and everyone in the building was a mage with who knows how many spells under their belt.

So I looked at her, making a face that was hard to describe.

I gave her a look that told her that we needed to stop and leave this for later as I said.

"I don't know what I'm thinking but I definitely don't like it. If only I knew more about where he came from then maybe we would have some answers." I told her, leaving it at that.

Little did I know then, that when I finally got those answers, I wouldn't be happy to know them. In fact, the only thing that came of them in the end… was sorrow.

THE HIDDEN CIRCUITS

Julian's arm managed to recover quickly with me at his side. Day after day, I would come and visit him at the same hour. I would sit with him for a few minutes, healing him gently with my spells as I waited.

I would do what I could on every visit. Encouraging bone growth and ensuring each fragment of his arm reattached in the correct positions little by little each day.

It wasn't a quick process to heal an arm like that. There were things to consider. Brute forcing my way through the process would have only further prolonged his suffering and exhausted my own supply of magic energy.

Healing spells themselves weren't complicated, but each wound required a different approach and this one was no different.

Even the most skilled medics in the Magic World didn't know how to fix everything. It required decades of study in various aspects of medicine and spellcraft. No one person could learn it all.

Unless of course, you were me. I've had the time.

I might not have been responsible for the invention of every healing spell and medicinal method of correcting wounds within the body, but I had created a good basis for them. Adapting my own methods, mages around the world and in varying cultures had time and time again come up with newer and more specific avenues of healing the body. And over time, learning as many of them as I could, I slowly became able to heal almost anything.

Anaemia. Organ failure. Infections. Broken bones. Deflated lungs. Even an aneurism could be corrected if I got to the patient soon enough.

Short of losing a limb, mages could survive almost anything given that someone proficient at healing the body was nearby.

But once the heart stops, there isn't much point.

Magic energy cannot flow through a body with no life.

And if the body no longer supports life without healing, unfortunately there is simply nothing that can be done.

If your heart stops and is not restarted, healing spells cannot affect you. And if you cannot be healed, it is unlikely that your heart will ever beat again.

Resurrection spells did exist but... the cost.

Maybe it's best that wasn't described.

But none of this was the case for Julian.

He had some broken bones, some internal bleeding and bruising and a severe case of exhaustion caused by the spell he cast during our sparring session.

I could heal him easily.

So I kept coming day after day to check in and do just that.

And then before leaving, I would always take the time to speak with his nurse when she arrived.

After much deliberation at first, we agreed that his recovery was going well. And by the fifth day we even

142

agreed that his arm had all but completely repaired itself by that point.

His outward appearance suggested that he was in perfect shape. Not a single thing was visually wrong with him. In fact, I even said that his arm looked perfect.

However, I couldn't say the same for the rest of him.

The amount of magic energy that he used in that one shot, the level of stress that would have put on his body, had clearly taken its toll.

Three weeks went by and all I could do during that time was wait. There was no rushing it. His recovery was more complicated than simply mending a broken arm.

He had injured more than his body with that spell. He had wounded his mind, perhaps even his very soul – if there is such a thing.

By casting that spell, by using so much energy so quickly, it had proven to be too much for his body and his mind to bear.

Most people discover their limits by accident and may even surpass them in time but Julian had ignored his limits and broken passed them several times over.

The fact that the spell hadn't killed him was nothing short of a miracle. Using so much energy in such a short burst would have weakened even a fully trained mage but with Julian, it was different.

The amount of energy that he used was more than he could hold even when fully charged. The fact that the spell was actually cast in the first place suggested that he had drawn the required energy from some other source to make up the difference. A worrying thought in reality.

But he didn't have the look of someone who had eaten

his way through their life force. There were no patches of black skin or excessive hair loss on his body.

But whatever that source had been, if it wasn't his life force, I had to question what else it could have been.

However, if it hadn't killed him, in the grand scheme of things it didn't really matter. What did matter was that by using the spell he had, he had left himself only steps away from death's door.

I was surprised, glad even, that he hadn't died from it but even so, he hadn't avoided death by much. Seeing him in the state that he was in, cold and still. Sleeping endlessly on a hospital bed with little signs of recovery, at first glance he might well have been dead. And that was not a sight that I ever wanted to see again.

He wasn't just my student, not just a boy that I was dutybound to be responsible for; he was a friend.

In the twelve months that he had lived in my home we had become more than student and teacher. More than master and apprentice.

He was funny, cunning, quick to find light in a dark situation and never one to stray from a fight.

He was much like my younger self in a way. Some personality traits of ours clashed from time to time but overall we got on like a house on fire.

He was the kind of person that I could see myself enjoying a drink with, the kind of person that I could rely on, the kind of person that I could trust and the kind of person who I could confide in.

He was much more than a student or even a friend in a way. To me, I saw him as family. But seeing him in that state, it was too much to bear.

144

I told myself day after day that he would pull through but I hadn't seen much evidence of that after those three weeks and it was becoming obvious that his mental state might be more dire than I had assumed.

Julian was strong both in will and in body. A natural born fighter and a very talented mage, but he wasn't invincible.

Everyone had limits. Everyone had something that they couldn't do no matter how hard they willed it to be so. And this was just one of those things.

His magic energy couldn't outlast his use of it and his body couldn't cope with the drain he had suffered because of it.

Ordinarily he would have passed out the moment his magic energy ran dry. But whatever had possessed him to cast that spell had somehow allowed him to ignore his limits as well.

And also any sense of self preservation.

That spell was far too strong for him to have used safely on his first try. In fact, I dare say that it was too strong for anyone to use without prior experience.

After seeing what it had done to someone who had only used it for a brief second, I was hesitant to even think of trying it myself.

For a mage, casting spells isn't as simple as flipping a switch. We cannot fire off a spell with the click of our fingers, it takes much more time than that.

Some but not all spells require you to recite the incantation. A sort of verbal command linking the spell to an action. Only more complex spells require such finesse and because of this we are always aware of the cost of each spell as it slowly builds up within our circuits before use. But a spell like the one Julian used, purely thought and will behind it's casting, it would have surely set off warning signals in his mind before he tried to cast it.

The spell was far too powerful for it to have been cast without thinking it through, he would have had to contemplate it. Envision exactly what he wanted to do and then give form to that image. He should have known that the spell was too taxing. He should have been able to feel it before he actually cast it. Forcing that much power through his arm like that, he must have known that he was going too far.

The spell was powerful, so much so that I would be more than a little cautious when trying to teach it to others – if I knew how to cast it that is.

It was dangerous, rivalling power equal to that of the most powerful spells in existence, even some of those that only I could use.

The Magic Council had caught onto this fact as well. They had seen how powerful it was and weren't prepared to let it go without a fight.

So in addition to visiting Julian every day, I also had to argue in inquiry after inquiry, stating that the spell he used was of a defensive nature and therefore was legal to be used during the fight.

But they wouldn't have any of it. All they saw was a spell that was capable of not only defending against me but also wounding me at the same time and that was precisely something that they would have wanted.

The Magic Council has and will always see me as a liability. While I might be acting as both protector and
146

guardian over the two worlds now, that didn't mean that I would always be.

They knew this. They had known this for a long time. And were constantly seeking new and more inventive ways to try and contain if not kill me should the day arise that such action needed taking.

But unlike a mere mage, I didn't age, I didn't grow tired after battle, I didn't die without significant effort and even so, I wouldn't stay dead for long.

They had been trying to find a way of protecting themselves against me for centuries, ever since I first formed the Council itself.

Back then, it was different. Far different. It was before the days of the official Mage academies. Before the days of the wall between the secrets of our world and aggressive nature the humans. Before we had even secluded ourselves away on this continent.

It was a very long time ago when I realised that with the population of magic sensitive beings continuing to increase, they would need more than a protector to keep them in check.

They would need a government.

If the human world was intent on persistently being incapable of understanding or coexisting with them – if they would never respect them – then they needed a world of their own. And any world requires order.

A governing force fit that need quite adequately in truth.

So in order for mage kind in harmony with themselves and away from the humans, I decided that they would need a separate government.

A completely separate world to live in.

So, when I felt that they were ready, I handpicked twenty-five of those who I trusted at the time. Twenty-five men and women coming from families of respect and power. Twenty-five men and women who could answer for everyone who would soon be within their domain.

And together, these men and women formed the first Magic Council. Electing of their own volition that their strongest member would act as the leader of the group.

Calling him the first Crown Mage.

Even abdicating that said mage should be considered royalty for a time.

The idea behind this, was that should there be a split in opinion, a perfect divide between the council members, the Crown Mage would have the authority to weigh in with the deciding vote.

So should twelve members of the council wish to implement a law and the other twelve didn't, the Crown mage would have to choose a side.

It was up to him or her to resolve the standstill.

That was the role that they played.

And as far as I could tell, this government was fair in the beginning. Listening to the people and doing what was in their best interest.

However, since that time, five other Magic Councils have existed, all with different Crown Mage's as their leaders.

Each council brought with it their own views and their own opinions.

And the latest one was quite different from the one that I had envisioned when I proposed the idea of a council in the first place.

They cared more about power and defence than the

welfare of the people. Their top priority was to ensure that I was under control. They saw me as nothing more than a threat and they wanted to deal with me as if I was one at every turn.

While they never made it public knowledge, they had been sanctioning what I could and couldn't do for centuries. Outlawing most of my strongest abilities and restricting my movements.

Making it law that every school and archive was surrounded by a barrier that I couldn't pass through without permission.

And soon enough, in a mere two hundred years, they had managed to restrict me from doing pretty much anything.

I wasn't even allowed to leave the barrier of my land unless it was absolutely necessary.

The Council was much more than just a governing force in control of the Magic World now. In a way they had also become its eternal overseers.

Acting as both law enforcement, judge and jury; they kept the mages of the world in check by force and fear mongering. And most who worked for the council were nothing more than mercenaries. Tasked with rounding up if not killing anyone of interest.

The Magic Council had turned into an unrecognisable group of savages since I first founded it.

The latest council had done nothing other than restrict my movements and powers. It was the first council that actually did the world some good. They elected to raise the wall between the species, separating our world from the humans, founding the first magic academies and creating the levelling system. They were the ones who shaped the world into what it is now.

While I did not always agree with their reasoning, I respected their decisions, trusting them to do what was in everyone's best interest.

Then the first council was disbanded and replaced following concerns that since I had chosen its members the council was biased in some way.

And now, fast forwarding a few more centuries, and the inquiries had started.

The original council would have never done something so pointless. Back then, they appreciated my opinion and respected my authority, fearing my power. But now, none of that meant anything.

Every day they summoned me again, asking different variations of the same question over and over without end. And yet all of these inquiries solved nothing, the one person who could tell them what they wanted to know was lying in a coma. But all they saw was power and they weren't willing to stop until that power was theirs.

And with how often they had become, I started visiting Julian a second time after the inquiries ended each day.

Teleporting into his room and once more ensuring that his recovery, while slow, was continuing.

And slowly, this is what my life became. An endless journey from one point to another as I went from Academia to the Citadel and back over and over again fir three weeks straight.

It was so exhausting that it took me all those weeks just to notice it. It took me three whole weeks to finally realise what was going on inside of Julian's body to keep him sleeping.

And when I did, I only wished that I had figured it out sooner. Something so obvious should have been easy to notice but with everything that was going on around me at the time, I'm not surprised that I missed it.

There wasn't anything immediately obvious about him that made it stand out. But once you looked closer, you couldn't miss it.

Using that much magic energy so quickly probably sent his body into a state of shock but even so, it shouldn't have put him in a coma. There was something more at work and yet, it took me far too long to notice what that was.

I theorised what was going on with him, discussing it with Katiana each night but never dwelling on the subject. Our relationship had been sketchy ever since she was appointed as the Crown Mage and I didn't want to do anything to draw us any further apart than we already were.

She had been staying mostly at home since the inquiries and was always curious to find out how the situation was developing.

But she stuck to her usual activates in my absence, reading novels from the human world or one of the various books that I had written in my time to occupy herself in her boredom.

And other than that, she pretty much didn't do anything but practice her magic in the dojo while I was gone. She wouldn't dare risk practicing while I was around though, I wasn't legally allowed to train her anymore.

She had been invited to every inquiry as it happened, well of course she had, but with her being so close to the topic of the inquiry she wasn't allowed to give her opinion.

So every day she refused the invitation. Even though she was supposedly their leader, in this case the rest of the council had the authority and she was the spectator.

So instead of attending an argument that she wasn't allowed to be a part of, she remained at home, visiting the dojo late each night before I returned from visiting Julian.

While she doesn't use her talents very often, she was quite possibly the greatest enchanter on the planet at the time. Capable of casting and writing enchantments faster than anyone that I had ever seen. Even capable of doing so from distances in excess of a mile, a talent that was something most mages could never hope to develop.

She was also quite proficient in both hand-to-hand and weaponised combat. Almost to the same point that I was. Thanks to first-hand knowledge from me and a private training course back when she was my student, she was just as powerful as I was in some areas at least.

When I first saw what she could do, back when she was still nothing more than my student, I gave her a gift that suited her talents perfectly, one that she continued to cherish and use every day after that.

The gift I gave her was my bow.

Not a mere object that fired arrows I assure you. The bow that I had given her was quite special; it had been enchanted so that it would never need tightening, never need repairing and so it would never need arrows.

A personal favourite of mine and a perfect match for her skills. Ivory strained black in every crevasse to give it depth decorated the bow from end to end. Pausing in the middle to revel an expertly crafted handle that perfectly fit the shape of a hand. A handle more comfortable than any I had ever felt in fact. One that I knew I would never see again.

And a bow more powerful than any I had ever seen.

This bow was unique and impossible to replicate – not that I haven't tried. The only reason I know that it's impossible to do is because after six hundred years, I have been incapable of accomplishing the same level of perfection.

I had come close from time to time but I had never been able to replicate it perfectly. That bow was one of a kind and I had placed it in good hands when I gave it to her.

And by gifting this item to someone who was a mere student at the time, I wasn't simply giving her a weapon. I was giving her a part of me, to cherish and to carry.

An object that held so many of my memories that it was as much an extension of my body as the wings on my own back or arms on my torso.

She would always have a part of me with her, no matter where she was or how dire the situation. All she had to do was look at that bow and she would know that I was with her, always.

I guess that when I gave her this weapon, I had already decided that one day I would marry this girl. We had known one another for over seven years by that point, knowing someone as well as I knew her, I guess that such a decision was going to be made eventually.

The shots that it fired came from her and her alone.

That is what makes her so special, like me, she can summon weapons in an instant. She was quite possibly one of the fastest summoners that I had ever met too. Capable of doing so with such finesse and perfection, she could summon any weapon to her side faster than any I had seen before and all of this while using as little magic energy as possible.

Every day that Julian spent in that infirmary, she had been practicing, a lot. With each day that passed, I would come home to find more and more arrows stacked up in the targets.

She never missed and most certainly didn't want to. With Julian in the infirmary the way that he was, it must have affected her more than she would tell me.

She almost never verbally told someone when she was angry, stressed or sad. I'm not sure that she even knew how to put such feelings into words at times. But then again, she didn't have to. Just one look at her and you simply knew exactly what she was feeling.

If her face didn't give it away soon enough, her actions surely did. Be it either an explosion of green shards destroying the furniture in an outburst of rage or arrows placed perfectly in the centre or head of a target due to something weighing down on her. Never had I needed to ask if she was alright, I could tell by what she was doing at the time if she was or not.

And with Julian the way that he was, the way that he had become part of our household for the past year like a son to us in a way, she was worried about him constantly. And practicing was her way of letting out some steam and wrecking my practice targets.

After so many years of building more targets after she had destroyed them, I think that it would have actually been easier to just have her fire at a wall and repair that. It wouldn't break as easily anyway.

But on the fourth week of waiting for Julian to return to

us, that was when something finally happened.

I was visiting him as usual, I would stay for an hour or two, get a sense of how he was doing and then leave. But on this occasion, I just happened to notice something, something that was so obscure and small that I hadn't seen it before it had gotten as bad as it was.

His arm. In the area where I had been healing him, it was wrong. Almost as though it were decaying. The skin was dark and the blood was thick. Even the bone had become brittle once again. It didn't make any sense.

So I checked him over as closely as I could, mentally scanning every nanometre of his body until I finally found the cause.

And the truth.

That was when I experienced fear for the second time because of something that Julian had done. Because unknown to me, under the muscle in his arm and then even more so all over his body in fact, were freshly formed and very powerful magic circuits.

I checked and then checked again but nothing could change the truth of that situation. He had covered almost his entire body in magic circuits. Like a nervous system made of magic, it covered him head to toe.

They were more powerful than anything a novice like him should have been able to make, in fact, they were almost as strong as the ones that I often dedicated to some of my most powerful spells. But he had them everywhere.

Magic circuits aren't something to be taken lightly.

While they might not have a tangible presence, they most certainly still had a physical one. While you couldn't touch them or actually see them, they were there, you could feel them.

They were so powerful, so potent and so fresh that they seemed as though they were still being formed and I wouldn't have been surprised to find that they were.

Even after a month, his body hadn't managed to finish what he must have started during the fight.

And with such a vast network of interwoven strands of magic, I was astonished that he was even capable of breathing. Such a sophisticated design, such a vast amount of space, it shouldn't have been possible to make it in one go.

He should have been dead already and yet, now that I had finally noticed, it was for whatever reason that his death was actually approaching after such a delay.

Realising what was happening and what these circuits would do to him if I didn't intervene, I called Katiana immediately.

This needed to be dealt with before the Magic Council caught wind of it and before it got to the point of funeral planning.

The Council would be more interested in dissecting him if they found out that this was what had killed him. For a mage to have not only formed such a vast network of circuits all at once and to have survived doing so for as long as Julian had, they would have surely wanted to know how.

It didn't matter that it was only five in the morning at the time, this needed to be done right away. So I called and she came running.

This would have been the first time that she had visited him since the day that he fell into the coma. She might have found the experience calming in some way had it not been

156

such a serious situation.

Forming magic circuits before you are initiated into an academy let alone one as prestigious as Academia is strictly forbidden.

If the higher ups had found out, he would have never gotten a place. Furthermore, if something wasn't done there and then, the amount of magic that these circuits would eat up in order to sustain themselves would have prevented him from ever recovering even with my aid.

The drain on his magic energy would have continued, keeping him asleep and never allowing him to wake up again, eventually leading him to his death.

Magic circuits are more than just a means of conducting energy, they are formed from magic and require a constant stream of it for them to function.

The only problem was that this energy requirement wasn't optional. If you choose to make magic circuits, you need to do so safely.

Only make circuits if you are sure you can survive their drain. Eventually your body gets used to the energy requirement and you stop noticing it. Perhaps you even surpass the you you were before and obtain a new level of magic energy production as a result. But that takes time, and Julian didn't have that.

What he had done, it was far more than reckless.

Forming so many circuits so quickly and so densely, it would have killed any other person. But Julian was still with us even after that. He was obviously stronger than he should have been, something was keeping him alive, but even that wasn't enough to last forever it seems.

The strain that those circuits had placed on him was too

much, he was still dying in the end. Suffering a death that only a mage can experience, he was going to die from being too devoid of magic.

Deficiency Syndrome.

A terrible condition.

One that I would not wish on anyone.

Use up to much magic energy too quickly and you can faint, go too far passed your limit and you can be put into a coma but run out completely, use up so much energy that you reach a point where you can no longer generate more and you'll die.

The body of a mage cannot function without magic energy. Running out of it is the one thing that every mage is taught to avoid and is a death that we all fear we will one day experience.

So I of all people knew the risks. The stakes.

And when Katiana arrived merely moments after my call, I explained what I intended to do straight away. And of course, she didn't like it one bit.

Not simply because it was a bad idea from the start, but because as the Crown Mage she represented the law and what I was about to do was defiantly against it.

"You want to do what?" She shouted, not realising that the door to Julian's room was still wide open behind her.

I swiftly closed it with a flick of my left wrist from across the room before anyone overheard our argument. Though, it was only wood. Anyone right outside could have heard every word.

"I want to make sure that he wakes up, we can worry about him getting a place later." I replied.

I looked at her, knowing what I was suggesting was

wrong but not letting that stop me. I was practically begging with her at this point.

"Yes, I understand what you want to do but doing it this way... it's not going to work." She said, showing no confidence in me at all.

She became purely furious with me after that. I could see the anger swelling up inside her and all I could do was feel even more attracted to her.

I gave off a slight yet smug smile, infuriating her even further. Not that I cared at the time.

"Don't look at me like that." She said, anger obviously contained with her voice. But I didn't care, I was simply giving her a look, it wasn't my fault that she took offence.

"I'm sorry, I can't help it, I've told you before that you're beautiful when you're mad." I said.

I turned my head away from her, attempting to wipe the smile from my face but this accomplished nothing.

"Can we please get back to the matter at hand?"

Her anger subsided and her cheeks began to blush, like a schoolgirl being hit on for the first time, her face was as priceless as it was unique.

"Right. Julian's entire body is covered in freshly formed magic circuits, he must have formed them accidently when he tried to use that spell. At least I hope it was an accident. I'll be sure to kill him myself if he did this on purpose." I explained to her, giving my best assessment.

I returned to my chair by his bed and kept an eye on him while we spoke. He was getting weaker by the minute. So much so that I was surprised to have been the first to notice his declining condition.

"Yes, I had guessed as much." She said.

Finally, she walked over to the bed and actually attempted to look as though she was considering it.

"Well obviously I can't remove all of them at once; I would either kill him or paralyze him much faster than the circuits would have done." I said.

'Or turn his brain into mush.' I thought.

"So instead you want to commit a crime and taboo... to wake him up?" She asked plainly.

She pulled up a chair from the corner of the room and sat at the foot of his hospital bed. Keeping her distance from me purposefully.

"So if I can't remove them, then I'll instead slow their growth and allow him to heal so that he can train and get used to them." I told her.

I moved in a little closer to her, an act that she wasn't too happy with. She crossed her arms and shifted over a little more.

"Yes, but in order to do so you want to forcibly infuse your magic with his. Not only is it reclus and insane but it's also forbidden, by you none the less." She told me, practically calling me a hypocrite, which I guess I was.

"If I don't do this, these circuits will continue to grow and consume him. Just look at his arm, its already rejecting the healing spells I've cast on it. It's practically refusing to heal at all." I told her.

"If something goes wrong, I cannot protect you and neither will your title. The Council will hunt you down till the end of time for this." She warned.

Finally, she looked as though she was coming around to the idea. Unfolding her arms and sitting more comfortably in her chair.

"I know but what can they do? Even if I die, I always come back." I chuckled. Resulting in a smile on her face as well, one that she tried hard to hide from me, almost as if she was embarrassed by it.

But I understood why she laughed. Back when she was still young and I wasn't as old, she used to be quite good at injuring me during her training.

After the first few times I told her to stop healing me. If she intended to understand me then she needed to see what happened when I died. And after a while, she turned it into a game, seeing how long she could keep me dead and how quickly she could do it.

If any other student had suggested this, I would have refused and probably sent them half the world away with the click of my fingers, but with her, I never felt like she was trying to actually hurt me, I never felt like I was in danger. She had that effect on people, a way of making people feel safe even when they weren't.

"Fine, why did you need me then?" She asked.

Finally, she had caught onto the point of the conversation. I didn't need her permission; I would have done the procedure with or without it if I needed to. I had asked her here for another reason. One that I was sure she would disagree with in addition to what I needed to do.

"You're not going to like that part either." I said reluctantly, watching as her anger soon returned.

"And why not?" She asked, re-crossing her arms and leaning backwards into her chair. She wasn't going to be so calm in a moment.

"Full body enchantment?" I said, shrugging my shoulders, raising the pitch of my voice and turning my

161

head away from her.

While she was already angry with me for what I had said before that moment, this suggestion would make her far more than simply mad.

"How can you be so stupid?" She shouted. Getting up from the chair and walking around the room in anger. "Full body enchantments are forbidden within Academia. Not only would he be expelled the second they found out, he would also be a danger to those around him, not to mention how difficult they are to make. I seem to remember you telling me never to attempt one unless my life depended on it!"

She stood in the far corner of the room by the door looking at the wall in protest.

"But Julian's life does, and he won't be found out, not if he could hide it." I said, not making any attempt to look at her in case she threw a punch or two. Even more so in case she decided to detonate the room. Her anger could be quite… explosive.

"How so?" She asked to my surprise. Turning back to face me but still standing in the corner with her arms crossed and her fists clenched tight.

"I only need you to cast a concealment spell and place it throughout his body." I said.

I looked at her, trying to get a read of how angry she was but this accomplished nothing. All I saw was the beautiful face of my wife. I couldn't detect any emotions even though I was trying.

"Why?" She asked.

"Because when his body rejects my magic, and it will, he will need to hide the pain that he's in. It wouldn't be very

162

pleasant but at least no one would know." I said.

I had thought hard about this decision and while it wasn't the greatest idea, it was the only one that had a chance of working.

When his body finally begins to expel my magic energy, it would cause a pain not unlike that of childbirth. If Katiana placed a concealment enchantment on him, this would not only hide the circuits that he carried but also the pain when it surfaced.

He would still feel it but no matter how much he wanted it to, it wouldn't show in his face. And with Katiana performing the enchantment, I was sure that it would be strong enough to also hide the signature of my magic as well.

"Hmmmm!" She huffed.

She finally sat back down, still keeping her arms crossed, pointing her disappointed yet still enraged face at me in protest.

"It would also hide his circuits should he ever use them." I explained.

"And why can't you do it?" She asked.

A valid question and one that she could have figured out the answer to if she had thought hard enough.

"Because I'm about to pump him full of my own magic, you know full well that concealment spells cannot hide yourself, only others." I explained further.

She thought hard about the situation, taking many seconds to come to a decision. Changing her angered face to that of someone who was fed up.

However, with me being me and her being her, I had already convinced her before she even disagreed with what I was asking. We were like that back then, the kind of couple that would argue about something even though they knew that they would agree in the end.

"Agreed. But you're cooking tonight." She un-folded her arms to say before she finally relaxed a little.

I laughed at her. "If that's the price I have to pay the so be it. You do know that my cooking is world class, right?"

She did, but I felt like asking just to find out why she had felt that having me cook was a suitable bargaining chip for the favour I was asking.

"Yes, but your ability to not make a mess isn't. Have fun cleaning it up when you're finished." She told me.

I smiled and chuckled a little inside. She obviously wasn't thinking like a mage in that moment. We don't need to clean things by hand, we simply click our fingers and they clean themselves. After a little effort is put into it anyway.

Realising that she had made up her mind and that the conversation didn't need to continue anymore I got back to the matter at hand.

"If the joking's out of the way, shall we begin?"

She quietened down, placed one hand firmly on his chest and the other on her heart. She put on a more serious face and began to make the enchantment. Etching sigils into his ribs with her mind as I did my bit in the background.

Such a complex enchantment of this size would take time to write, even for someone as skilled as her. So I knew that I had all the time that I needed in order to finish before she did. I placed one hand on his head and the other on his arm. I took a deep breath in and did what I had to.

The amount of magic that I was about to infuse into his system was more than my human form could hold. So first, I shifted into my other one.

The room shook a little as I did this, no more than it does when I teleport in, so this wasn't noticed by anyone thankfully. The shadow created by the wings on my back sent the room black as they blocked the lights on the ceiling. And shrouded in darkness and unknown to any of the nursing staff, I began to perform the procedure.

Once the room was darkened through, I noticed a light. A slight green hue surrounding both of Katiana's hands as she etched the enchantment into his bones.

Such a light is only given off when an exceptional amount of magic energy is being used, magic energy given off as waste energy in the form of light emissions. Obviously, the enchantment must have been more taxing that I had expected.

The same light would probably be given off by my hands soon enough, but unlike hers, mine would be of a golden colour.

The natural colour of my Athereon body's magic signature. Unlike the blue colour of my human form, this one was more primal, brighter, more mesmerizing and much more powerful. But before such a light could be emitted, I actually had to start the procedure.

I pooled my magic and focused it into my hands. Draining it from every magic circuit in my Athereon body. Doing this all in one go would mean that his system would so oversaturated with magic energy that he'd have no choice but to accept the power that I was about to throw at it.

And with my magic energy now ready, I sparked it. Sending it flooding into his body, overwhelming his new circuits and hopefully saturating them for long enough that his own magic could get used to their drain by the time that mine faded.

The room soon lit up in the golden glow of my aura, blinding me and Katiana as we continued to do our parts to save him.

I could feel parts of his circuits fighting the foreign energy for a moment at first, but they couldn't do so for long, I had thrown too much at them, they simply couldn't refuse it.

It would be like trying to stop a building from falling over with your bare hands, you can try but you aren't going to stop it.

Before long, every part of my body was running on empty and Julian was fully charged.

It was done and I was weaker than ever.

I shifted back into my human form and retreated into my chair while Katiana finished her enchantment. The golden glow dissipated from my hands and my vision returned.

I took one look at Katiana and knew that something was off. Her hands were glowing brighter than before, the amount of energy she was using had doubled while I had been forcing all of mine into Julian.

She was now using so much at such a fast rate that even her eyes had started to glow. She was defiantly using more energy than she should have done, something about that never quite sat right with me.

But she could handle it, unlike Julian, her energy reserves dwarfed that of almost anyone else. She could take the drain, for now at least.

I stopped worrying about her after I realised that she could take the toll and refocused my thoughts onto myself. I too had used a great deal of energy and I could defiantly feel it.

While I can recharge magic energy faster than anyone, after a drain like that; it would be a while before my Athereon form would be at full strength again.

It wasn't like I had just cast a spell or anything, I had just intentionally drained every spec of energy from that body and forced it into Julian. Everything that I had left over had been used up when I shifted back to my human form. There was nothing left to go back to.

But while I was sat there assessing how much of a setback my condition would be in the long run, Katiana soon finished what she was doing and the light from her hands and eyes quickly faded.

Not long after her eyes finally stopped glowing she removed her hand from his chest, I knew just from the feeling his body gave off that she had been successful. But at what cost?

She had left no scars, no pain and no blood. No signs what so ever that she had just etched an enchantment into his bones and with that enchantment no one would ever be able to tell what was hidden underneath. It was perfect.

But Katiana on the other hand, she was week, far more than she should have been. But I, in my trust of her own ability to decide when she was at her limit, didn't pay as much attention to this as I should have done at the time.

Instead, I focused on Julian and I didn't have to wait very long before he finally woke up.

With no more drain on his magic energy, his body was able to recover most of what he needed to stay conscious. The rest of it would have to recover while he was awake, this would be slow but with my energy running though him he wasn't going to be using his own anytime soon. If he tried to his body would use my energy instead as it desperately tried to get rid of it.

And when h opened his eyes, I was happy to realise that he hadn't changed at all. He was immediately punctual in fact.

"So, how did I do?" He coughed out.

"Welcome back my boy. Glad to have you with us." I said to him, completely ignoring the pain that Katiana was expressing on her face.

I knew what had caused it and I couldn't do anything but be aware of its existence. It's not like you can heal an injury that didn't physically exist.

I placed my hand back on Julian's arm to repair the damage that his body had suffered from my efforts to revive him. Not only did his body accept the healing spell much better than the last time but it seemed as though he hadn't noticed I was casting one.

"Back? How long have I been out?" He questioned as he realised his surroundings and recognised the feeling of his five-day stubble now covering his face and neck.

He gasped as he jumped back to full alertness. Sitting up as quickly as he could, springing into action, adrenalin surely flowing through his veins at the time.

"The fight! D… Did I win?" He asked.

I finished the healing spell and removed my hand, sitting back in my chair a little while I tried to push the pain from my other body out of my mind.

I had defiantly pushed myself a little too far. If I had stayed wearing that body, I would have surely lost consciousness already. That would have been interesting. The nurses would have freaked if they saw my other body laying in one of their infirmary rooms.

"Surprisingly, yes. You won." I said with a hint of embarrassment in my voice

I nodded to Katiana, she knew what to do next.

Now that he was awake, she would have to inform the judges and the Headmaster, the next stage of his entrance exam would be starting soon.

It couldn't be postponed any more than it already had.

She left the room on foot rather than teleporting though. I guess she was feeling a little week after that enchantment after all. I would have expected so at least. What little magic she had left was probably all that was keeping her awake at that point.

"So... I passed?" He asked, completely ignoring Katiana as she left through the door.

He paid no attention to it even when the door slammed behind her.

"The first stage, yes. You passed, gaining two marks. All you need to do is pass one more stage with the same marking and you're in." I told him with confidence.

He was straight on the ball. Knowing what to say as if the past month in the infirmary hadn't affected him in the slightest.

"Knowledge is next right?" He asked, already knowing the answer.

"Are you sure that you're up to it?"

Not that he had a choice in the matter, I asked this question regardless. He clenched his right fist and tensed up the muscles in his right arm.

The wound had obviously healed by that point then. Realising this, I saw no real reason as to why he wouldn't be ready. All he needed for the next task was his mind, his physical state didn't matter too much for the test that was to come.

"Yeah, I'm ready." He said with the upmost of confidence. "All I have to do is answer questions right?"

He was right, as if someone had told him beforehand but after all, it wasn't too difficult to figure out. The test was one of knowledge. Other than questioning someone how else would you go about determining their level of knowledge?

"I'm not allowed to say." I smiled as I shook my head. "Now though, you need to get dressed. Meet me in the hall outside when you're done."

I would have normally recommended some food before we headed out but he had been fed through daily intakes of nutrients and vitamins telekinetically encouraged into his stomach and down is throat since he got there. He was probably healthier than I was at the time.

I stood up after that and headed for the door of the room, he sat there in a daze, possibly trying to figure out how he won that fight but there would be time for that later.

"Master." He said.

I turned to face him just before opening the door.

"Thank you."

I smiled at him.

"I should be thanking you, it's been a long time since I lost a fight, and I rather enjoyed it to be honest. Now get ready. The others will be waiting for us."

I left the room and waited outside patiently. He was on a private ward on the top floor of the infirmary. The likelihood of students visiting here was low so I didn't think that anyone would recognise me if I waited there.

But I was a little surprised to find that not one nurse passed me while I was there. They hadn't been by to check in on him for a while. I wonder if they were busy with something else.

So I stood silently for a few minutes before he came out.

And when he did, a fresh set of cloths on, brushed hair and cleaned teeth, I knew he was ready.

If I had never given him a compliment before this would have been the perfect time to tell him that he is nothing if not time efficient.

I grabbed his shoulder and teleported us in. I wasn't about to go strolling around the campus while classes were in session, I would cause quite a mess as students rushed around desperately trying to meet me.

And then when we arrived, everyone was ready for us and of course, they had many questions to ask before we could get down to business.

So I stood there patiently and throughout the entire thing I had a consistent thought screaming in my mind.

'For the love of god, don't screw up this time.'

TESTS OF KNOWLEDGE AND POWER

When Julian and I arrived in the main hall, everyone was already in position. Everything was exactly as it had been almost a month before.

Lights illuminating us from above. A full array of staff and officials in the stands. Barriers erect around us for the protection of others. It was almost a repeat of the last time.

However, this time, news had spread widely about a boy who had beaten me unaided in single combat. And thanks to this rumour, the stage had been set. A live performance for all to see and experience was about to begin. Because this time, we had a much larger audience.

Although, this next part of the exam did not involve us needing to fight one another, so there wasn't much of an incentive to come and watch.

However, that didn't stop the two thousand or so students from wanting in that hall for a chance to see the boy who knocked me back by himself.

And while this number would seem large, it was nothing compared to the total student count or the maximum capacity of the hall. If need be, Academia had enough seats to accommodate all nineteen thousand students and still have room to spare.

In instances where a larger than normal audience had arrived, the design of the hall was more than capable of handling the excess of students lining the walls.

And even with so many, each of the combat rings, tournament circles or designated fighting areas in the room were a clear twenty meters away from any of the walls.

This allowed for as many seats as needed to line the room and allow the students to spectate the various events held within this hall in perfect safety.

However, that wasn't true this time. Because the seats hadn't been laid out on this occasion. With so little warning and an unexpectedly large crowd, I wasn't surprised to find everyone stood in a large group encircling our position when I arrived.

And even if they had thought to prepare, how would they know when to prepare for? No one was expecting Julian to recover as quickly as he did once he was awake. And it wasn't like anyone was used to the idea of spectators during an entrance exam. It's normally a quick and dirty affair. No more than ten minutes per person. They'd never had the need for an audience in the past.

And with how swiftly Julian's strength had returned now, seeming as they'd waited long enough, there wouldn't have been much point in delaying any further.

The barrier surrounding the tournament circle we were stood in had been raised long before are arrival. No doubt in an effort to protect both us from the spectators and the spectators from us once we continued.

However, with so many students in the sparing hall at the same time, they obviously couldn't all fit on the select few permanent seats in the room.

174

Most of the crowd had gathered around the perimeter of the barrier already, surrounding us as if they were a part of it. But at least with the barrier activated they couldn't come flooding in.

A barrier isn't something that can simply be turned on and off though. In order to raise and then lower a barrier, what you actually have to do is activate or deactivate the various rules that determine what can enter and what cannot. Similar to how enchantments work, these rules are written into the barrier and are controlled by changing the flow of magic energy between them. But unlike enchantments, in most cases they can only be controlled by the person who originally wrote them.

This could obviously lead to some rather unfortunate mishaps when t came to the barriers surrounding certain government buildings. Say perhaps, a school.

And in an effort to avoid any problems or liabilities from ever occurring, a new member of staff is chosen to rewrite each barrier every ten years. #

This was a contingency plan of course.

If someone were to murder the member of staff they believed to be controlling the barriers in an attempt to launch an assault against a now defenceless building, at least there wouldn't be a high chance that they had killed the right one.

The person in control of academy barriers is always a secret held to the highest regard. And in Academia's case, there were only three people would have known who this individual was at a time.

That being of course, the Headmaster himself, the Magic Council's representative appointed to the school and the staff member himself.

I suppose we took the protection of our young very seriously at the time. But it was better to be over cautious than it was to be ill prepared.

Having lost our relics and secrets to criminals in the past after they'd broken through various other barriers in similar manners to avoid the taxing nature of tearing them apart, it was only natural to take precautions against the same strategy being used somewhere else.

There weren't just lives at stake in a school. The texts on magic reserved for only the best and brightest were kept there as well. Spells and techniques that could lead to disaster if used by anyone not trained to practice the use of such power.

The barriers around this school severed to protect. The barriers inside of it too. And now that we were inside of one of these protective layers, the students safely stood behind it, theoretically we were incapable of doing harm to anyone but ourselves.

Though, theory doesn't always translate to reality.

I knew that all too well.

There was an initial sense of shock on both our faces once we arrived and saw that spectacle.

Neither one of us had expected such a sizable crowd to have gathered so quickly. But, like wildfire through dry grass, the flames had spread far and wide beyond anyone's control. And before we even knew the news had been spread, it had engulfed the entire student body.

But we didn't let that get in our way. Whether it would be two thousand or two million spectators watching us, we weren't about to let that stop us from completing the next stage.

Julian's entire future as a mage was riding on the next two tests we were about to undergo. And I wasn't about to just let him fail because of stage fright. And I doubt that he was about to just lay down in the face of such a challenge either. He would at least try his hardest first.

So in keeping with the long standing mage tradition of not wasting another individuals time whenever possible, we both quickly turned our attention back towards the wooden platform from before.

Staring at the crowd wasn't going to do anything but distract us anyway. It didn't matter if they were there or not, they had no significance and no impact on the exam, ignoring them was our best course of action.

So we turned our heads towards the staff members, judges and council members and prepared for what was to come.

Katiana was there of course, sat beside the Headmaster at the top of the structure. She was conscious and fully aware of her surroundings but that being said, she wasn't looking too good.

The amount of energy that she had used creating the enchantment that now concealed Julian's magic circuits had taken a lot out of her.

She'd be fine given enough time.

Time to rest and time to recover that is.

Visually, she didn't seem too out of place, to most there wouldn't have been even the slightest sign that she was as week as she actually was. But when you ignore the visual and focus on the emotional, her mental state, the level of magic energy within her, then you would see. If you looked deep down and used more than just your eyes, then you'd be able to tell that she was barely conscious at the time.

I contacted her telepathically to see if she would be able to cope under that much stress but I received no response. Instead all I got was a slight smile and a look of fear in her eyes.

She had heard my message but it would seem that she was too week to even use telepathy. Thus proving that her condition was exactly what I had thought.

She was teetering on the edge of full depletion and the minimal level of magic energy to stay awake. She was in no condition to do anything in the way of magic. Not even basic telepathy. A form of communication that used magic energy to send the brain signals through the air to another person. A most casual and inconsequential method of conveying thoughts in fact. Most could do it endlessly without suffering from any ill effects. But I guess that wasn't true for Katiana anymore.

Which would also mean that if she intended to get herself home, she would have to stay as still as possible and focus all her effort into generating more magic energy for herself. A trying task at best.

The obvious problem with that was that the next two stages weren't going to take that long to complete. As long as Julian was on point that is.

I could probably stall for a while without being noticed but that would only buy us another five minutes at most. She'd never be able to recover enough energy to go about her day normally. She needed an hour if not more and she wasn't gonna get it here.

The other option was that I stuck around long enough so that I could take her home myself but that would have been noticed.

If she was supposed to be stronger than any mage on the planet, then why would she need me to take her home? I'm her husband, not her servant. And I'm certainly not her chauffeur.

Whatever I chose, there still wasn't a way for me to do anything for her at the time.

I considered trying to prolong the stages rather than stalling but that idea quickly faded as I realised how foolish that would have been to attempt.

So I refrained from thinking of her any further if all I had were dead ends awaiting my every thought and quickly got back to the matter at hand.

I looked to the Headmaster and bowed to show my respect, Julian coping my every move and then it began.

He raised his hand soon after that and we raised are heads. He opened his mouth and out came the words that we had hoped to hear. He was getting straight down to business, beginning the next stage rather than announcing Julian's disqualification as I had feared.

"We are gathered here today to witness initiation student Julian during stages two and three of his entrance exam." The Headmaster said.

I smiled thinking that that would be it. But it would seem that I had celebrated a little prematurely. There was more to be said and I had feared that this topic would be brought up for weeks.

"However." Said the Headmaster.

'Shit.' I thought.

It was the only word that had come to mind in that moment. Not too impressive I'm afraid but it summed up my feelings quite well no doubt.

"In regard to the spell used to defeat the Athereon during the first stage, the representatives from the Magic Council, the judges and myself have determined the following.

Due to the nature in which this spell was used and that is shares similarities with a spell that we have seen before, we have classified it to be a level four defensive spell. Therefore, in accordance with the rules already laid out, it was perfectly legal for Julian to have used it during the fight. Which makes his victory as legitimate as it would have been for anyone else.

It is with great satisfaction that I finally get to say this for once. The victor of that first stage was not as records would dictate, the Athereon. Instead, I congratulate you Julian, you won the first battle. A job well done lad." The Headmaster explained.

'That figures.' I thought.

I understood exactly why such a sentence would bring joy to him. It was because that during his entrance exam he himself had lost to me. Miserably. But that was a long time ago and I had thought that he would have forgotten it by then. Or at the very least have gotten over it.

Nevertheless, the higher ups had determined the spell to be classified as level four, meaning that even though I didn't yet know what that spell was or what its true capabilities were, it was at least still legal to use it during the fight.

But now for the tricky bit.

Stage two was about to begin.

The Headmaster had not yet lowered his hand and we

were both still standing there patiently, not moving a muscle, not saying a word. Just standing still and looking up at the man before us.

"In regards to stage two. Though it has taken an unprecedented length of time to get here, we will continue as standard." He said. "Julian, this will be a test of your knowledge. You will answer all questions given to you by your master to the best of your ability. Answer all but one correctly to pass, answer all of them correctly to skip stage three should you wish to do so." He continued. "Rest assured that the questions are a set standard. So do not think that because your Master is the one asking them that he will be going easy on you." He warned. "With that said, are you ready to begin?"

The Headmaster finally lowered his hand. But before Julian was allowed to say anything, I had something to say, something that puzzled both Julian and the judges immensely as soon as it was let out.

"With the upmost of respect Headmaster, I have a request to make." I stated.

He raised his eyebrows at me. Shocked almost by the fact that I would dare to do such a thing.

"I request that you allow me to add an additional two questions to the test. I also ask that you take me at my word and trust me on this. I believe that you will want to hear the answers." I told him.

To my surprise, he nodded swiftly and so with my smile, I thanked him. I looked over to Julian, quite confused as to why I would want to make the test more difficult no doubt but he seemed to have no objections regardless.

He declared himself to be ready with a nod of his own.

The Headmaster waved his hand and with that action alone he had told us to begin.

So I turned to Julian and began the test by asking my first question.

"These questions are asked in a random and mostly irrelevant order. Take your time and do your best, you only get one chance." I warned him.

He nodded at me, signalling that he understood.

So I began.

While these questions are reasonably challenging, most students don't pass this stage on purpose. The stage itself was relatively important but the majority of students at the academy were there on their fighting skills alone.

Knowledge was secondary in that case.

"Very well then, question one. Please name the nine main archetypes of magic." I asked of him.

It took him less than a second to respond. Not that it would have taken him a long amount of time anyway. This first question was simple and something that he had learnt many months beforehand.

"Fire, Ice, Wind, Water, Earth, Enchantment, Summoning, Teleportation and Fortification." He said, listing them in the exact order that he had been taught them in.

"Correct." I said. "Question two. Which three forms of magic are most commonly referred to as the three T's?"

A second more basic question but one that still challenges your general knowledge of magic. Of course, this was something that even a teenager like Julian would know. But despite outward appearance, Julian was much older than that.

182

And he was even faster to respond that time.

"Teleportation, Telepathy and Telekinesis." He said.

The three T's in their entirety.

Teleportation, the ability to move to a given location at will.

Telepathy, the ability to communicate over large distances no matter where you are or what obstacles may be between you and the recipient.

And finally, Telekinesis. A form of magic that has no offensive capabilities on the battlefield but one that every mage could use with enough practice. Summarised as the ability to move and control an object's momentum, position and orientation from a distance. For some this could even be done through walls.

"Correct." I told him. "Question three. What is a magic circuit?"

This time he took a moment to think, hopefully to think back to that first lesson we shared together, where I actually taught him this answer.

"A magic circuit is a conduit for magic energy. They allow us to control the movement and shape of our magic energy to perform spells, activate enchantments or even enhance our senses."

A look of confidence appeared on his face while he spoke along with a slight hint of pride in his voice. He knew he had gotten the answer correct and he was proud of that fact.

He had remembered well. So well in fact that I smiled for a moment before realising that I didn't have time to be impressed.

"Correct." I said. "Question four. What are the three principles that all mages are sworn to live by?"

The answer to this question was something that I had only mentioned in conversation, never during a lesson. But he had remembered regardless.

"To protect, conceal and respect." He said.

"Please elaborate." I said hastily.

He had answered correctly but unless he said the full thing, it wouldn't be accepted as an answer.

During this exam stage, you are given one repeat, for lack for a better description. Should you answer a question correctly but not with enough detail for it to count as an answer, the examiner, me, can ask for the student to try again.

It was something that most do not use but in Julian's case, he had needed to. I suspect that he simply shortened his answer thinking that it would be acceptable and efficient but unfortunately, the only correct answer for that question was the full thing.

He realised his mistake and expanded on his previous sentence. Not realising that this too was all part of the test.

Of course, he might have been able to make it through with the previous answer but I thought that it was a bit too risky, so I decided to use his repeat for him.

"First. A mage must protect himself and his kin. Second. He must do his best to conceal the Magic World from humanity and all secrets that it holds. And third. A mage must respect the laws of nature, his peers and his master." He said faster, showing an improved sense of confidence as he spoke.

I looked over to the judges for a moment.

They seemed uneasy but hadn't said anything.

It took a few seconds, but suddenly I saw that one of

them had nodded. This answer had been accepted and I could continue.

I'm not entirely sure why they didn't accept it right away, perhaps because he had to say it twice or perhaps it was the speed of his words but it didn't matter. They had given the okay and I could continue.

"Correct." I said. "Question five. Name the three main magic types forbidden to mages. Those specifically forbidden to even the Crown Mage herself."

"Creation, Resurrection and Life Drain." He responded.

He was right. However I wish he didn't have to be.

There was still so much more that Katiana could have learnt from me but the Council had stated time and time again that I would have to follow their rules.

I wouldn't want to put her in any danger from the Council itself. Not only could she have lost her title and rank, if I had chosen to ignore the rules she could have even been branded, never to use magic again.

If I hadn't followed the rules, I would have all but killed her.

"Correct. Question six. What is the name the current Crown Mage?" I asked.

He responded immediately, not even needing to think about it. He had spent the past year living with the two of us after all. He was bound to know her name.

"Katiana Illisidel." He said.

That one was too easy, now for something that I had only ever mentioned once and briefly. If he had grown up in an ordinary magic household, he would have already known this thanks to her fame but he hadn't so he would have to make an informative guess.

"Correct." I told him. "Question seven. What form of magic does the current Crown Mage specialize in?"

It took some time for him to think of his answer, he probably spent that time thinking back to the one time that I actually told him, not that he needed to.

If you spent enough time around her, you would soon figure it out by yourself.

"Enchantment." He said gingerly.

He had a worried look on his face for a moment but there was no need for it. He was correct. However, if that look on his face or the sound of his voice was anything to go on, I would say that his answer was nothing more than a guess.

He must have forgotten that one time that I had mentioned it but he had answered correctly regardless.

"Correct." I said, reassuring him and allowing him to get rid of that stupid look on his face. There was no need for it, I was certain he would make it through without a problem. "Question eight. Other than raw power, what other main component determines the potency of a spell?"

"The caster's ability to channel magic energy into it and his continual control of that energy once it leaves the body. Simply put, the more adept the mage is at controlling the movements of his own energy the stronger the cast spell will be as a result." He explained perfectly.

'Well done my boy.' I thought to myself as yet another smile appeared on my face. Not only had he answered correctly, he had even given a shortened and more condensed form of the same speech I had given him on the topic.

"Correct." I told him aloud. "Question nine. Before you become a student at an academy such as Academia, what are prohibited from doing?"

This one was too easy for him as well.

"The use of any spell or enchantment above level one unless in the presence of my Master is strictly prohibited before entering into a school." He stated.

"Correct. Question ten. There is no wrong answer to this question so take your time. What do you hope to gain from enrolling in this academy?" I asked him.

This is something that I had never asked him before. He had probably never even thought about it but even so, it didn't take him long to answer.

"I seek both knowledge and power, enough so that I might one day achieve the rank of a level seven mage and enrol in your school when it reopens in four years' time." He said proudly.

"An interesting answer Julian." I said sinisterly with a smile and lowered head. "Well done."

I might have paused briefly to congratulate him but I swiftly returned to the examination after that.

In that moment, I had lost my place it seemed.

Normally, the test would have ended with that question and because of this I had taken a break as though nothing had changed. But something had changed and I had even more questions to ask.

So I re-aimed my thoughts and returned to the exam.

"Additional question one." I said.

His face turned sour as the fear of what questions I had added to the test settled in. He had no need to be scared but even so, these added questions almost cost him both of the marks.

"The spell that you used to defeat me. Were you taught it

or did you come up with it?" I asked, eagerly waiting to hear the answer. I'm sure that the Council representatives were as well.

"Neither." He said. "I had seen a spell similar to it before and attempted to replicate it, I had never done so prior to that moment and must have performed it incorrectly and pushed myself too far as a result."

That wasn't an answer that this question could accept. I looked to the judges and they shook their heads. I should have worded that question differently, I almost cost him his place because of this.

I had given him two choices and then he just goes with option three. In essence, he hadn't actually answered the question at all.

"Unfortunately, I cannot accept that as an answer. Get this last question right and you're still through to the next stage though." I told him.

He seemed saddened by this but what he didn't know is that there was no way to get this next question wrong. He had already made it in that way, the stage was passed regardless of what his next answer would be.

"Final question. Since you are the first person to have performed that spell. You have the right to name it. So Julian, what shall it be called?" I asked him.

He smirked and then went silent. Thinking hard as to what his new spell should be known as.

It took him a minute but he got there in the end. I was glad that he had taken his time; the name that he chose in the end was quite fitting.

"Assuming that this isn't already taken, I choose to have my spell be known as the Defensive Flare." He said.

'An interesting choice.' I thought.

"Julian." I said swiftly, pausing to build suspense. "That concludes this stage of your exam. Congratulations, you're through to the next one."

His face lit up with joy from the news.

We bowed to each other and then turned to the Headmaster yet again. As we did the slightest sound of chatter rose from the crowed. Probably as a result of knowing the name of his new spell.

I bet they couldn't wait to see it in action after that.

The Headmaster raised his hand as expected, the chattering stopped as a result and the room went completely silent.

Unnaturally so. I couldn't even hear anyone's breathing. It was as if all sound had just stopped. The room was far too quiet for me to bear.

"Julian Ealton. Congratulations for making it this far. The next stage is one of power. To do this you must perform the most powerful spell that you know how to cast.

But seeing as you have just invented your own, a feat not accomplished by most, we would ask that you perform that spell instead. You may begin when ready." The Headmaster instructed before then turning his head towards my position. Instilling me with fear and apprehension. "Athereon, for this stage, there are no limits on what you can do. Hit him as hard as you can, let us test the capabilities of this 'Defensive Flare'."

He lowered his hand and the crowd became even more dense than usual for this event. It's not every day that they got to see me at full power let alone up against a mage who had invented his own spell.

We bowed to the Headmaster then took our positions on the circle as we had done before.

I prepared for the fight as best I could. Realising that it was going to be a short one I felt that, while it was a risk, using my Athereon form would be suitable.

I was still week from helping Julian, so I would be hitting hard but not as hard as I could. On any other occasion I would have hit him with a flurry of spells that he had never even heard of now that I'd been given permission.

But due the state that I was in at the time, I didn't have much choice. My other body was still very low on magic energy but by that point I had recovered enough to punch him at least.

Julian altered his stance, channelling his muscles and energy into his right arm. Not realising that with my magic energy flowing through his circuits he didn't even need to try. This time the spell would be much more powerful than before and a lot larger. If anything, this time, the spell would be visible at least.

I prepared myself, shifting into my weakened yet still stronger Athereon from with nothing but a thought and displaying it for all to see.

It felt numb at first. The body was still not ready for a proper fight but it would have to do.

I chose not draw or summon any of my weapons in order to save energy. Even the ones that I had belted to my hips required a constant magic energy flow to use. That's what I get for only carrying enchanted weapons I guess.

Instead, I chose to use my fist.

But first I had some enchantments to activate.

Unlike the ones on my weapons, these didn't require a

constant energy flow, just enough to activate them. After that, their magic energy reserves from the last time they were used would take care of the rest.

And as each one sparked into action, my body began glow slightly, like the flash of a camera going off as each enchantment was awakened.

But for these enchantments, I had to activate them by voice command. Each one was etched into either my bones or the armour that I wore. And they were old.

They were written in such an ancient form of what we now call sigils that not even Katiana understood how they worked. Then again, they predated her by twelve thousand years or so.

And when I was done activating them, my armour and body would have had a slight orange-yellow hue around them. Not so much that I was giving off light but enough that I was outlined by colour.

Since these enchantments were old, activating them required me to speak the words in my natural language. Unfortunately, there isn't a way to write such a language with English letters.

I wouldn't even know where to start if I were asked to say each syllable separately. The words themselves are simply so far from English that I'm not sure it's possible to directly translate them.

So instead, I'll give you a shorter, roughly translated, English version of what I said.

"Speed, Strength, Reflex, Flight, Stronghold, Flare."

The corresponding enchantments activated and began enhancing my speed, my strength, my reflexes, my wings, my armour and finally my allowing me the use of Flare.

A confusing name for what it actually was. Flare was the name for my ability to jolt forwards at exception speed without a head start.

Put simply, Flare was my ability to go from zero to a hundred miles per hour in an instant but it didn't last long. I could only cover a distance of fifty meters before I slowed down. And once it starts to wear off, it does so rather quickly.

But now that my enchantments were activated, I turned my attention to my offensive capabilities. Finally deciding to light my fist with flames for some added kick to my attack.

While they looked similar to the ones that I had used during stage one, they were far from the same. They were hotter, stronger and more devastating.

Simply being near these flames would have made you sweat. If you dared to touch them, I would be surprised if you even had any skin left.

I only used something so strong because I intended to give this new spell of his a run for its money. I intended to see just how much it could block and just how much it could really reflect.

I wondered if I might have gone a bit too far. After all, if his spell hadn't been as strong as it was in the end, could I have killed him?

But now the Headmaster could see that we were both ready, he waved his hand shouting the word.

"Begin!"

I jumped into action, launching myself towards Julian at an even faster speed than before. I was confident that his shield could withstand my attack and that it would hurt like hell afterwards and he did not disappoint.

As I grew near, I could see his mouth start to move and heard the words as they left his lips. I realised that he had figured out how to cast the spell more accurately. Using those magic circuits he had created when he first tried to cast it. Even shouting its name.

It made sense I suppose. By attaching a name to the spell, he would be able to attach a word to the actions. Telling his body what to do rather than doing it himself.

I could just hear him say those words before it hit me.

"Defensive Flare!"

Suddenly his hand began to glow blue and a crystalline shield emitted from just in front of his knuckles in a flash of light. Growing violently as it spread outwards. Reaching a size many times larger than the one I had seen him use before.

I shouldn't have been surprised, with my magic flowing through him, I should have expected it to be stronger. And by the time that I hit it, the shield hadn't even stopped growing.

It was expanding so fast that it was probably going to completely surround him when it was done if I had allowed it to continue.

But when my fist finally did hit him, it was just like before, a brief moment where I thought I had gotten through and then a fiery explosion that sent me back several meters.

The force was massive, enough to pop eardrums and shatter glass if there had been any.

It was exactly as before, the exact force of my attack hitting me straight in the face.

If the first time felt like a sledgehammer then this time felt like a grenade. With so much more power placed into my attack, there was a lot more of it being thrown back at me.

An explosion of fire and pressure erupted from him. Expanding outwards faster and faster before being deflected back into the ring by the barrier surrounding us.

'Most impressive.'

That was all I thought as I went flying through the air.

When I landed, the pain I was in forced me to change back. I could no longer hold my form in its condition, so I reverted to my human one in order or recover.

With all the strength that I had placed into that punch, even with my Stronghold enchantment, it had still broken bones. With my Athereon body now injured and extremely low on energy, it wasn't going to be usable for a while.

If it were my only body, then I would have collapsed after that. Unlike humans though, if my body should be injured enough to lose consciousness then I can swap to the other before that consciousness fades but I still needed enough energy and time in order to do so.

This is why I always do my best to ensure that I have at least some energy left, just in case I needed to swap bodies at some point.

Leaving myself completely drained might not actually kill me but it would leave me weak enough that I might as well already be dead.

For example, if I were to put all of my power into a single attack and leave nothing in reserve, well what do I do if that attack wasn't enough and the fight was still going?

In that situation I would be done for, I wouldn't be able to cast a spell anymore or even swap bodies to continue fighting. However, I hadn't been in such a situation in many hundreds of years and didn't intend to put myself in one like it again.

And once I was changed back to my unharmed and mostly 'saturated human form, I looked back at Julian and saw the Defensive Flare in all its glory as it began to fade.

A crystal structure flowing in a spiralling pattern like a flower from the centre. And from left to right, all I could see on it was the crack that my punch had created during the attack.

Nothing but a crack.

I'm not even sure I could have broken it at full strength. I would have needed a weapon or two just to have enough power to break through.

More interesting was the look of sheer shock on his face. Possibly from the fact that he had survived that hit but it was more likely to be because he was shocked to still be standing. Last time it took a lot out of him.

And as soon as he released his fist, the shield lost integrity entirely. Shattering into a great many pieces. Falling through the air like sparkling dust before it faded completely.

And in that silence, all it took was one.

One person to start so that the rest could follow.

And once they started, the entire crowd cheered in unison in response to that display. Hell, even the judges clapped at what they had seen. But the Headmaster, what he did scared me.

He was laughing.

A great chuckle, the likes of which came from old men like him.

The crowd began to cheer even louder for Julian,

chanting his name and jumping all over the place. He was famous now, the only first year with his own spell and the only student to ever survive a head one assault form me during an unrestricted battle.

Even if it hadn't been at full strength, they were still impressed by it. I'm not even sure that anyone noticed I wasn't putting everything I had into that attack. They simply saw the explosion and my injuries and assumed that I had hit him as hard as I could.

It took a minute but everyone soon calmed down.

Julian and I bowed to one another. We turned back to the Headmaster who had already raised his hand. We hadn't even noticed until we saw it. But sometime before we bowed, the crowed had stopped making noise. I guess that we were lucky to have not said anything after that moment.

"Julian Ealton, as a reward for passing all three stages of your entrance exam, I can now officially welcome you as the newest student to join our prestigious academy." He announced.

We looked at one another with smiles on our faces but there was more to be said.

"In addition, as a reward for that most entertaining and impressive display, I hereby immediately promote you to a level two mage. Effective from the day you start your lessons, you will be granted all the benefits that such a rank holds." He continued. "Furthermore, for being the only student in history to have survived a full-strength punch from the Athereon, twice. I am personally placing you among our most elite. Hencceforth, you will be placed in Class One.

And I expect that you'll impress.

So welcome to your new elite status, Mage Ealton. It brings me great pleasure to name you as our new top student."

He lowered his hand. We thanked him deeply and made our way. The second that the barrier would drop, the students would have been all over him and me.

I took him home and he just couldn't stop laughing once he was there. He was still a kid, despite his metal age. His outward appearance was deceiving, he looked almost twenty but in truth, he was almost thirty.

I often wondered what could have caused this. Life extension magic is prohibited until you graduate. So to be safe he had been entered into the academy as a teenager. We didn't want to give reason for anyone to suspect him as a criminal but there wasn't time to question him on such a matter.

Celebrations were most certainly in order that night. It was a good thing that I was cooking, a three-course meal of his choice, anything from anywhere. My kitchen was quite well stocked and of course, I could teleport anywhere he wanted, within reason, and buy what we didn't have.

There was much to discuss about the past four weeks and little time to do it too.

Once you are accepted into an academy, your first lesson starts the following day. They don't waste their time and are quick to get you acclimated into your new routine.

Katiana arrived in the living room a few moments after us having said her goodbyes and possibly weighed in on anything the others had said in our absence.

But she was seemingly weaker than she should have been.

This was more than depletion at work.

There was something more to her lack of magic than just the enchantment she had cast. She had had almost thirty minutes to recover, it should have been enough for such a short teleport.

I knew that there was something more complicated going on with her but there would be time to figure that out later.

That night was the last night that Julian would be spending in our home for a long time. And we were going to make the most of it.

After I explained what I had done to him and got some answers of my own of course. I wasn't going to let him off easy. He had much to explain.

Starting with where he got the nerve to form those circuits in the first place.

THE LAST SUPPER

That night lasted for what seemed like an eternity. Every second passed as hours. Every hour passed as days.

At the time, I had thought this night would last forever. A single moment of peace and serenity amongst so many of hardship and loss.

It would have been uncharacteristically kind of the world I know to grant me such a gift. But alas, as with all things, nothing last forever.

And the repercussions from that night – the events that took place on that evening so long ago now – they formed rippled deeply interlaced into the world.

Even now, what was set in motion then can still be felt to this day.

Everything I had faced since that night. Every loss, every battle and every difficult choice I have suffered. It all started here.

Julian, myself and Katiana. Sitting at the dining table in the main hall of the house. Overlooked by the endless shadows cast by the tall trees outside the windows to our backs. Lit by candle and warmed by the fires. Everything since then, started here.

But we were celebrating at the time. We could not have known what was to come of the words said at that table. All we could see was what laid out before us. Plates upon plates of food. All of which chosen by Julian. All of which set in his honour as we commemorated his last night within our walls. And wished him a good farewell as he ventured out into the world on his own.

It seemed to go on forever. All of us sat at the table eating our candle lit meals as the local wildlife came scratching at our floor to ceiling windows in search of food.

Twin tailed white foxes, cats and even the occasional dear. They all lived in the forests surrounding my home at the top of the hill. All of them able to smell our food from miles away. All of them hungry. Begging myself and the others for our scraps every time we turned out heads their way.

It wasn't rare to see the odd creature of nature within the garden beyond my doors. But on this night, there were dozens of them. Many more than I had seen in quite a while.

But of course, there were the regulars that I recognised from their previous visits. Some of which I had even taken the time to name.

George, the somewhat adventurous bobcat who practically lived on the branch of the old oak tree he currently laid on. Mary, the twin tailed white fox with two mesmerising golden eyes and a somewhat of a sweet tooth. And even Katiana's favourite, Butch. A black cat from head to toe the size of a greyhound. Large enough to break our pottery and even nock over some smaller trees at times. But a softy down to the core who would roll over and expose his stomach to her whenever he came round.

Seeing any one of those three outside wasn't uncommon. But at the same time, and with their friends no less, that was a rarity.

But at least it went to show just how densely populated that forest had become of late. The magic energy emanating from myself and Katiana over the years much have acted as somewhat of a magnet to their kind. Animals had always been far more sensitive to magic than humans. They saw it as a sign of safety.

No wonder their numbers had grown.

And as they all sat outside the windows watching us, we were watching them. Watching as they salivated over our streaming food and the smells each plate had. Watching as we drank the finest of wines and beers from across the world. Watching as we enjoyed our time.

Watching as we said goodbye to our friend.

Enjoying what we believed to be our last night as a group together for what it was.

I even drank that night.

Though I did use my enchanted wine glass when doing so. It lowered the alcohol content by a small factor. Not enough to sacrifice the taste. But more than enough to make it easier on my body to absorb.

Alcohol on its own affects me far more gravely than most humans and mages of the world. Whereas for them it was a delicious poison that could be enjoyed in small quantities with only mild effects, for myself, the effect it had on my body was exaggerated somewhat.

I knew that the more I drank, the weaker I would become. My liver unable to process the alcohol efficiently and leaving a large quantity of it in my blood with every sip.

My kidneys unable to convert it into my urine and my mind suffering a great many detrimental effects as a result.

I knew full well what this beverage would do to me if I drank too much. But in that moment, it didn't matter.

Julian had just passed his entrance exam and we were celebrating. It only seemed natural to join them in the drinking of alcohol for that occasion.

I still stuck to weaker wines and cider mostly though. Even if I'm doing it just the once, I'm still not gonna overdo it.

I didn't even dare break out the vodka or the whiskey collection in my cellar. Anything over a certain alcohol level would have most certainly been a threat to my health.

It's always been funny to me though. How a naturally occurring substance like ethanol could be so devastating to my body despite everything evolution should have done to allow me to process it.

And yet, if I were to drink enough where a normal human would begin to feel drunk, then for my body it would already be too late.

My muscles would be too weak to support my weight, my mind would be too clouded to think clearly and my magic energy would be completely uncontrollable if I even tried.

So, in a sense, getting me drunk would be the one of the best possibly ways to guarantee winning a fight against me. The only time that I am at my weakest is when I've had too much to drink. That or when I'm severely depleted of magic energy. But even then, I still had my fists.

However, since we were celebrating Julian's achievements, I decided to have a glass or two. Maintaining appearances mostly. I had never told anyone about what alcohol did to my body before of course. Not even Katiana.

I wouldn't dare to.

If I were to simply let people know about what is most likely my only exploitable weakness, then eventually someone would have used it against me for real.

So I kept up the appearances I had long since set in place and sat at the dining table drinking the beverages like any other person would have done.

A magnificent banquet of food was laid out before us and a very chuffed young man sat at the other end of it was quickly scoffing it all down.

Katiana and I sat opposed to him so that we could be as little a distraction as possible that night. The food was largely for him. What laughter we had at the time could be done from a distance with ease in an attempt as to not take away from the spread laid out in front of him.

And as we sat at this table, toasting our drinks in Julian's name and saying words of praise, we congratulated him on his achievements, we told exaggerated stories of how he's defeated me in battle as one would have done a great feast in years past. And just as with a feast, we quite comfortably ate our fill of food

Savouring each bite as if it were our last the entire time.

It was the best we had treated the boy since he arrived. And it was only when we questioned him that we began to treat him as anything but our friend.

Perhaps I pushed him too far in the end but I needed answers and that was the best way to get them at the time. We didn't have long left after all. Once he left for Academia, I wouldn't see him again unless he graduated or transferred into my own school.

Those were the rules.

A mage in training cannot be allowed into the rest of the world. Unless of course, they had express permission from the Magic Council. Which would involve declaring what he was intent on doing with his freedom. And I doubted they'd be quick to accept the risk of a student walking free of the academy walls just to come and see me.

So, I had no other option.

Julian had to be questioned.

And while I didn't intend to, I ended up making it sound much more like an interrogation than a simple conversation than he might have deserved.

I suppose that there were other ways to approach the situation, different ways of wording the questions at the very least. And there were defiantly better ways of treating Julian.

I did my best not to seem hostile towards him but in the heat of the moment, I guess that I was a little too forceful.

This was a night to remember and I had turned it into one that I was sure he would probably try to forget.

We had been home for hours before I made my move though. We'd been eating for over thirty minutes before I started the conversation. Quietly enjoying our meals before I broke the silence.

So I guess there were at least some happy memories to be taken away from that night still.

He must have known that something was wrong before I started talking though, the night had been far too quiet and the atmosphere far too toxic before the meal started.

If the food hadn't come to interrupt that atmosphere, it

might not have ended on its own. But, looking back on it now, I guess that there wasn't really a reason to wait.

If I was going to ruin that evening anyway then why postpone it? The questions that I needed to ask, the answers that I needed to learn, I should have just forced them out the moment that we got home.

It was almost seven thirty in the morning when we returned from Academia and I waited until seven in the evening to say what I needed to say.

After everything that happened, all that had been revealed and all that had been accomplished, I almost couldn't do it.

It was Julian's moment of triumph, his victory. Finally he would become a ral mage. Given the title and a rank. Legally able to use magic. Legally allowed to learn more. To pursue his own goals from here on.

He had come so far from the day he come stumbling through my doors. And I didn't want to ruin that for him. He was beginning to become someone important to me.

An apprentice that I would be proud to call family one day.

But eventually, the time came when I could no longer put it off. I had to ask my questions now or I'd go forever without knowing.

And once I had started, I had no intention of stopping.

"Julian." I sighed. "Do you know what we're about to talk to you about?"

I moved to a seat further down the table to sit beside him as I asked this in a heavy tone.

After all, from my previous position it would have been hard to talk to him without shouting and it would have been even harder to convey any sense of tone or severity in my voice or on my face with such a distance to cover.

And besides, the food on the table had been served many minutes prior to the conversation and by the time that I started taking it had already been devoured to its entirety.

A feast fit for seven laid in ruins before us.

Scraps of meat on every plate and tray. Bones stacked up in pyramids on their corresponding platters. The table was littered with the last remnants of food. Pieces too small to bother eating but too many of them to ignore.

When you first looked at it, it seemed as though a wild boar had been eating off the plates, The table was a complete mess but I should have expected that.

With so much food and so little time to eat it before it went cold naturally, I should have expected there to be quite the mess in everyone's rush to finish it all.

Especially once Julian started sinking his teeth into it.

He hadn't eaten an actual meal in a month. His muscles were starting to shrink into nothingness and his skin was so thin that you could almost see through it.

He didn't look too good but other than a well cooked meal and plenty of exercise, there wasn't much that we could do about it.

And to that end, I had cocked most of the food just for him and him alone. And if someone were to tally up the plates, compared to him, we hadn't even made a dent in the total number of plates devoured that day

He had scoffed so much of it down so quickly that I was surprised that it didn't come racing back up. With how hungry he must have felt from that coma, plus the immense drain from his new circuits, I wouldn't have been surprised if he could have kept eating for days.

He certainly had the pace for it.

But Katiana and I had already finished eating both our main course and our desserts when I moved my seat. There was no longer a meal for my questions to interrupt on our parts. But Julian was the one celebrating and he was hungry. So he still had a much larger portion of food left to crush with his teeth and swallow down his throat before he could finish.

Even despite the amount of food that he had already consumed, he still had far more room to fill as it seemed. And after that, he still had his dessert to consider.

A mountain of half-melted ice cream or a five layered chocolate cake, or both. The idea of the meal was to make sure that he enjoyed it, so of course there was more food than there needed to be to ensure that he had as much to choose from and enjoy as possible.

I never really imagined that he'd eat it all but he obviously didn't get that memo.

"I assume it has something to do with what put me in a coma for three and a half weeks." He said.

Despite the fact that he was now talking he, still continued to eat. Not really paying much attention to me at all at first.

He was more interested in the roast pork and mushrooms on his plate than he was in my voice. But then again, I couldn't really blame him.

I had made the food after all. I of all people knew how good it tasted.

My cooking skills weren't over exaggerated, they weren't a lie and they weren't to be underestimated.

I had lived in the company of some of the world's greatest chefs and in all my years of living, one would come to assume that I knew what I was doing when it came to the kitchen.

"Yes, that and other things." I replied.

I interlocked my fingers and lent my arms over the table. Not looking directly at him, I approached Julian, getting as close as I could without making him uncomfortable.

This close proximity would make the conversation seem more important, hopefully making him take it a little more seriously than he had been doing.

"What more is there?" He asked.

Julian continued eating as the conversation endured, placing the final piece of meat on his plate in his mouth after he had spoken.

I could hear him as he chewed it, enjoying every flavour and every texture.

And with that done, he moved onto dessert, grabbing a large piece of chocolate sponge from the table. I guess that the ice cream wasn't appealing to him after all, it hadn't gone to waste though, I had greatly enjoyed the portion that I had from it.

Mint choc chip and raspberry ripple. There were selections of vanilla and chocolate there too but I preferred the flavours that I had chosen more than the others.

"I cast a spell that was way above me and it took its toll, that's it right, what more is there? I went above my limit and I ended up in a coma for it." He said, seemingly unaware of what he had done.

He began to dig into the cake slice on his plate. Not even batting an eyelid and completely ignoring the severity of what he had just said.

I knew that he understood the importance of the matter at hand but for some reason he had chosen to ignore it as if he were completely ignorant of its existence.

"Julian, that spell, it did more than simply take a toll. With how little I know about it I'm not certain of this but I dare say that it might have even been beyond a fully trained mage. But as for you, casting that spell almost killed you." I told him.

I still attempted not to make eye contact, enforcing my position that this conversation was far more serious than he was accepting. The expression that I was holding on my face and the tone in my voice should have been enough for him to take me seriously but for whatever reason, it did nothing.

He simply kept eating the cake on his plate.

"It can't have been that serious, it was my first time casting the spell and I was drained a bit more than I had expected, that's all." He said.

He responded like a child, ignoring the statement that I had just made, continuing to enjoy his cake as if nothing was wrong.

He was oddly ignorant of the situation given how smart he had proven to be in the past. As if he wasn't really thinking about it. It was as if he was in denial about what had happened but he had no reason to be.

"Julian, explain it to me. How did you produce that spell the first time? What did you base it one and what possessed you to cast in in the first place?" I asked him.

If he didn't want to accept that the situation had been as serious as it was then I would have to force him to realise it himself.

If you cannot convince someone that they are wrong then force them to come to that conclusion by themselves. It seems as though my psychology course wasn't wasted after all. However, it was around fifty years out of date at the time.

"Well I thought about what I wanted to do, focused my magic energy into my fist and imagined a small dome shaped shield above my knuckles. Then it just happened, as if my body just knew what to do on its own." He told me.

"That's not exactly what happened, son."

My face darkened, as if I was scared of telling him the truth. Still not making any attempt at eye contact, I remained still and faced downwards at the table.

Finally, he finished his dessert and turned to face me, realising that the situation was actually as serious as I was saying when he saw my face.

"Enlighten me." He said. His tome more direct and focused than before. His eyes focused on mine and his attitude towards the subject was as mature as it should have been from the beginning.

"When you cast that spell, more specifically when you tried to cast that spell, you realised that the level of magic required was beyond you, yes?" I asked him first.

"I felt my body resist the incantation, if that's what you mean. But the pain passed in less than a second and the spell was cast anyway. It can't have been that beyond me?" He said.

"So if you tried to perform a spell that you couldn't naturally conjure, what would normally happen in that instance?"

"If I lacked the skill to focus enough energy into the spell then my body would have…" He paused, possibly finally realising the truth.

"Go on." I said.

"My body would have gone to drain magic energy from my circuits. But I didn't have any so I… I formed enough magic circuits to divert the required energy from elsewhere in my body towards that spell…" He sighed, realising his mistake and the danger he could have and actually had placed himself in because of it.

"And?"

I still waited patiently for him to come to the conclusion himself. I wanted him to admit, in his own words, the mistake that he had made. I wanted him to understand just how serious the situation had been.

"With how drained I was afterwards combined with the amount of energy that the spell required, my body would have… Are you saying that I covered my entire body with magic circuits just to perform a spell for a split second?" He asked louder in shock.

Finally, he had come to the truth.

Realising the fatal reality of what he had done.

It was at this point that I finally looked at him. Now that he had told me that he realised his mistake, it was time to tell him the rest of it.

"I'm afraid so."

I leaned back and relaxed into my chair, removing my arms from the table and sitting a little more comfortably now that he was at least starting to understand the severity of the subject.

"Then how am I not dead, furthermore how am I qualified for entry into the academy?" He asked even louder than the last time.

He forced his words out as fast as he could, desperately trying to figure out how exactly he was sitting at the table beside me and not being lowered into the ground.

"That's simple, you have Katiana and myself to thank."

"You both… saved me. How?" He asked.

"Ah well…" I paused there when I saw her move.

Katiana had left the room. She hadn't approved of the risks that I had taken before. I would have been surprised if she had changed her mind on that decision since then.

She probably went back to the dojo to cool off.

She'd had a difficult day after all.

"Did I say something wrong, Master?" Asked Julian.

"I respect your concern but it's not your fault, its mine." I replied shortly after sighing.

I leant in over the table and interlocked my fingers again. I only do this when I'm saying something that is difficult to put into words or when it's something that I will regret saying. Either way, the act itself was worth mentioning, he had a right to know what we had done to save him.

"What she and I did, is outlawed right up to the highest level." I told him. "Julian. Your body had begun to shut down, rejecting my attempts to heal you and completely draining you of all your magic energy in an attempt to saturate the newly formed circuits with that energy instead. It had drained so much that your body couldn't function on its own anymore.

Simply put, what you did was stupid and what I did to save you was reclus. Your body was rejecting the circuits in order to save itself but it had done so too late.

They were already integrated into your system. The only

way to save you was to give them a surplus of magic energy to slowly release into you over time.

Obviously, with you in a coma at the time, I couldn't ask your permission to do this. So I did it anyway. I gave you every drop of energy I could spare. You still feel it now don't you? That overwhelming sense of boundless warmth coming from your heart?"

He nodded slightly but didn't say a word.

"Obviously with that much magic energy flowing around inside of you, it realised itself when you cast Defensive Flare earlier. Your body knew that you had too much energy and attempted to remove some of it once you began casting that spell.

But please do keep in mind that you will slowly expel my magic on your own and your body should be able to sustain the circuits from that point on. But you'll need to refrain from using magic carelessly. Your spells will be more powerful than normal because of this. Furthermore, the faster you drain my magic the less time your body has to get used to that many circuits. Should you run out of my energy before you can survive the drain by yourself, we will only end up back where we started." I explained to him further.

He looked at me, a mixture of emotions appeared on his face. But not those I had been anticipating at the time

I expected him to be disgusted. Forcibly ingesting magic energy into someone is the same act as rape for a mage. It is not simply a violation of the body but also of the soul, if there was such a thing. If he had been any other person, I would have been slapped right in face after telling him that.

But when he spoke, the words that came out were not what I had expected.

"Thank you, Master."

I gave him a look of confusion instead of speaking, an appropriate response in my opinion. I hadn't expected any thanks for this. I had violated him, in ways that only a mage would understand. And yet, he thanked me, not for what I had done but for why I had chosen to do it.

"Thank you for saving my life and thank you for doing it in such a way that it allowed me to impress my fellow students on day one." He said.

"Julian I, I hadn't expected that." I replied.

"But." He said. "How did Katiana fit into all of this?"

"Ah well um…"

'Where do I start?' I thought.

"You are aware that forming any magic circuits before becoming a student at an academy is strictly forbidden correct?" I asked.

"Yes but I still don't…"

"Julian, what do you think would happen if the Headmaster found out that not only had you done this once before but you had then done it a second time during your god dam entrance exam?" I asked louder.

"I would be incarcerated for my crime and striped of my rank as mage." He said.

"Exactly. So I had Katiana perform a very special kind of enchantment on you. A very specific form of concealment. Hiding your circuits from all but the most adept inspections and also hiding my magic signature as well.

It won't last forever but by the time it does eventually fade, you would have already been given permission to form circuits and my magic should have faded completely by then too." I explained.

"Let me get this straight. Not only did I cheat on my entrance exam but I'm also walking around with illegal circuits, a custom enchantment and your magic energy?" He asked.

"Basically, yes. Not bad for your first day eh?" I chuckled.

I had more questions to ask after that, more detailed and personal ones. I wanted to know more about his past, more about his birth. I wanted to find out where he had come from, what he was and where he intended on going next.

However, I never got the chance. When the moment finally arose for me to change the topic of the discussion and try to get some answers out of him, the moment was interrupted.

I was just about to ask him about these mysteries when it happened. Something else getting in the way. Again.

Every time I had gone to ask him in the past, something always got in the way. Whether it be lunch or an accident, something always prevented me from finding out more about his past.

The last time that I tried to pry into his secrets was during a sparring session. The moment the question came out of my lips, Julian collapsed from exhaustion, almost as if it had been done deliberately. Even purposefully.

He always found a way to avoid the question and right up until the day that I finally found out the truth, he himself, had never spoken a word of it.

So I guess that I had remembered it backwards then. I hadn't been hostile with him at the time but I had intended to be.

Looking back on it now, I'm not entirely sure what

would have led me to remember it that way. I have always had an impeccable memory, so why would I have remembered what I wanted to do as if I had actually done it?

My lapse in memory aside though, I had intended to ask Julian about his past in that moment and then something got in the way, as it always did.

That time the thing that had gotten in the way of my questioning wasn't Julian himself, however it turned out that he was still to blame.

The presence that I felt in that moment had originated from the perimeter of the main barrier. I ignored it at first due to how preposterous the idea was but the presence never went away.

It was only when that presence tried contacting me telepathically that I paid any attention to it.

A rare occurrence but one that happened from time to time nonetheless. I felt a sharp pain in my right temple as the trespasser tried to break into my mind.

It wasn't the first time that someone had done this but it was the first time that someone had managed to do so from the other side of a fully erect and sealed barrier of my own design.

It was only when I finally accepted that this presence I was feeling wasn't going to simply go away if I ignored them that I realised who and what it was.

If this person was intent on telling me something telepathically, then I could at least use the magic energy signature from that signal to trace it back to the source and get a sense of who I was dealing with on my own.

My senses couldn't make out much from such a distance, but it did give me enough to recognise a part of it. The part that screamed out that this person was in fact a student. And from Academia.

It wasn't clear to most people, but residual magic energy from those around you does linger for a time. Ans the energy around this person was densely packed. From thousands of different people.

Exactly the same as what I had felt back at Academia that morning.

This wasn't just some random visitor; it was someone who had managed to follow us back home and had been stuck outside ever since.

Attempting to follow a teleport doesn't always work, especially when that teleport ends up leading to the other side of a barrier.

In cases like this, the barrier would have defected the teleport and you could end up anywhere from right outside it to several miles away. That is the main reason why people tend to not follow others when they teleport if they know what's good for them. You have no way of telling where you could end up.

But with how persistent this person seemed to be and how long they'd most likely been stuck here, I left the house after their attempt to get into my mind to deal with them.

I did my best not to alarm Julian. Telling him to pack his things for his first day of Academia in the morning while I was gone.

And as I made my way down the hill, I noticed something about this student. Not only were they in fact from Academia, but I even recognised them from earlier in the day.

She was standing in the crowd with everyone else during

the final two stages of his exam. She was the only one who stayed silent and almost motionless throughout the fight. Making no attempt to celebrate or cheer when Julian won, not even showing a single emotion on her face.

She had only stood out to me because of this.

I kept thinking that she didn't fit. An oddity that I couldn't comprehend or explain. Obviously, I never intended to find out why she was so odd, I had merely taken notice of it. If she had never shown up at my doorstep then I would have never thought of her again.

But seeing her standing there, I exited the barrier rather than letting her through it and joined her on the other side.

I wasn't too keen on strangers, let alone a mage. There were thousands of magical artefacts and weapons in my home, any one of them could have been quite destructive in the wrong hands.

And it was only after leaving the barrier that I heard it.

Her voice, inside my head.

'Atheron, please forgive the intrusion.' She said.

She proceeded to curtsey, lifting her skirt up a little too far if you ask me. Not that I was bothered at the time, I was too focused on getting rid of her quickly to take note of her non-existent underwear.

Although, that being said, I guess that I did take note of it anyway if I remember it.

Her mishap aside, I looked straight at her, as though I were looking into her. Sizing her up, figuring her out and conducting little examinations of her inside my mind.

There was much to learn in that moment and I needed to understand all of it before it was too late.

And in those first few moments, I didn't treat her as a

visitor or trespasser, nor a student or a minor, I treated her as I would have done an enemy. Showing intense hostility on my face as I took in every detail with my mind and with my eyes.

Her scarlet red hair, flowing quite nicely down to her shoulders. Her petite build, the way that her uniform seemed a little too small for her and the various bracelets decorating her right wrist.

Something about her didn't feel right to me.

With the exception of her hair and her telepathic abilities, she was simply too dull. Too ordinary.

'My name is Katrina, I attempted to follow you as you teleported off earlier but I ended up in the village below as you can see.' She explained.

Her voice, still being projected into my head had intrigued me enough to talk with her. I folded my arms and lent up against the old oak tree next to me. Taking in everything about this situation one at a time.

Her looks, her utter lack of emotion and questioning as to her motive for being outside my home above all else.

"I'm impressed that you managed to follow me at all." I said. "But I am more impressed at your ability to break into my mind without me allowing it. Before meeting you, I wouldn't have thought that to be possible. But here we are." I continued, expressing the slightest hint of anger in my voice as I spoke, hoping that with enough time and enough hostility she would cut to the chase.

'Yes, that was rude of me. Forgive my intrusion, it's just that I haven't been able to speak for many years now. Not since, the accident.' She explained.

She stopped talking for a moment, and clutched her

bracelets with her left hand. They obviously had something to do with the accident she mentioned. But I wasn't interested in her past, only the present.

'But that's not important. What is important is that during your fight and as you teleported off, I was reading your mind. I'm sorry to have done so without your permission but I heard things that were most peculiar, all I wanted to say is that provided you can arrange a meeting between myself and Julian; your secrets will stay safe within my silence.' She told me.

Blackmail? Really?

I dare not think it at the time but this situation was horrendous and quite embarrassing. Being blackmailed by someone less than one percent of my age, how could I have let that happen?

I blocked off what portions of my mind that I could to control her intrusion after hearing how intrusive she had already been but this didn't accomplish much.

With what little of my mind barricaded against her now safe to use, dark thoughts started to surface.

I thought about removing her, forcefully.

I could make it look like an accident, playing it off as though she had died as a result of her teleport. It would have been an easy lie to tell. She had followed me during a teleport, there's no telling what could happen as a result.

I suppose I was lucky such action wasn't required in the end. Killing others in order to protect others is something that I can live with but killing an innocent little girl, I would have never gotten over that.

It wasn't long after thinking about killing her that I realised something, I could feel her presence now. It was so faint and subtle, I might have missed it if I hadn't been looking.

Now that I could feel her, I knew what parts of my mind she had gained access to and to my amazement, she had access to almost all of it, even the parts I thought that I have blocked off.

Knowing this, I intended to shorten the encounter, before she managed to find something that I would have to kill her over.

I nodded to her and sent her my own telepathic message. Using far more force than was necessary to do so, in an attempt to frighten her with the power of my mind as my voice screamed inside of her head but she did not react in the slightest.

No feeling of fear, no sense of pain. It was as if she hadn't noticed the potency of my message at all.

'You will have your meeting but nothing more. I cannot control him beyond that point, he is no longer my student after all.'

She smiled and nodded.

'That is fine, could you have him meet me at lunch under the grand tree tomorrow?' She asked.

This was an interesting place to meet.

Having him go to the most crowded place in all of Academia at the one time of day that the students have free reign of the campus?

How peculiar.

I wondered how she intended to make this meeting private but it didn't take long for me to realise. She would have whatever conversation she wanted with him telepathically, no one would overhear.

The area would have been too crowded by students for anyone to have noticed that the conversation was even taking place.

Realising that she had had no reaction to my forcible message from before, I chose to continue speaking aloud. Telepathy wasn't really my strongest talent and I saw no reason to use it any further.

She was mute, not deaf, just because she couldn't speak it didn't mean that I had to be silent as well.

"I can arrange that." I told her.

As I turned to go back to the house, thinking that the conversation had ended, she had one last thing to ask of me.

'Just one more thing. This place was further away than I expected it to be. I'm afraid that I don't think I can teleport back to Academia without draining myself too much.'

I gave off a loud sigh and grabbed her by the shoulder. I took a quick hop back to the administration office and left her there. At first, I did this only to scare her but in truth, it was simply because students aren't allowed to leave campus without permission.

I had taken her there to report her for using my teleportation exemption as a window to escape the school barrier.

I explained to staff why she had left, telling a slight lie when it came to the blackmail part and then I left. When I returned home, I gave Julian her instructions. I told him why it was so important that he meet this girl and then I went to see Katiana. Who had almost destroyed the entire dojo while I had been gone.

I guess that she saw me teleporting off with a nineteen-year-old girl and got the wrong idea.

Either way, her shards were in every piece of wood in the room. The supports were barely holding and the weapons on display in there were shattered.

I guess I should have told her before leaving then?

Nevertheless, Julian knew what he needed to and he was already asleep when I returned from cleaning the dojo a few hours later.

I helped Katiana calm down a little too. Taking her back to bed once she was in a better mood and helping her make an even bigger mess in there.

Either way, the day that followed that night was an important one. And it started early.

The academy was on another continent after all.

Nine a.m. there was six back at my home.

But that didn't matter to me, I could go two or three days without sleep. Safely at least.

I had gone up to five days without rest when needed in my past but my wife and Julian on the other hand. They were the ones who needed the rest, not me.

Besides, I had a broken hand and several ribs to heal thanks to Julian's Defensive Flare spell. Perhaps the rest was good for me as well. Even if I couldn't feel the pain at the time, I knew that it was still there.

Much like I knew I had this nagging feeling that I had just overlooked something.

Something important.

I wonder what that could have been?

THE DAYS BETWEEN

The day I had feared for over a year had come. Parting with my apprentice, parting with a friend – saying goodbye to him for who knew how long at the time. That day came. And then it went.

I took Julian to Academia, handed him to the waiting members of staff by the front gates, and then I left. Banned from re-entering that barrier again for the foreseeable future.

So I said my goodbyes, wished the boy good luck and went on my way.

It was quite surprising. How easy it was to say goodbye at the time.

I had expected there to be some part of me that didn't want to see him go, some part of me that would rear its head in that momenta and beg the world to let him stay.

But even if there had been, such wishes would have been nothing more than foolish dreams.

I knew full well where he was going. I knew more than anyone the progress he could make there. The achievements. The rewards.

I knew that given his capabilities; he'd never fail to amaze his teachers during his time there. I knew that letting him go was the right thing to do. But that didn't stop me from wanting there to be another way.

A talented and capable young mage is a rare thing in this world. Even more so are those who would wish to become an apprentice of mine.

There was some amount of accomplishment on my part for being his master that past year. And if he could have stayed with me even longer, if I could have thought him more, then just imagine what I could have made.

I had been handed a lump of clay and told to mould it to a pre-set shape. But had I the freedom, that clay in my hands could have become anything.

Every passing decade would have seen his understanding and endurance increase. His talent and skills improving. His ability to see the world from a mage's point of view guiding every move he made.

If I had been able to keep him under my wing until I felt he was ready to move on and pursue his own path, he could have been one of the most highly achieving mages of his generation.

He could have invented spells or even perfected those that already existed. Explored new avenues of magic that no one had ever explored. Come up with ways to surpass limits most thought were set in stone.

He could have done anything.

And yet, I had to hold him back.

I had to slow his progress.

Hand him over to a school who taught their students only what the Council dictated they were allowed to. A school that only hones the skills mages were permitted to master. A school that only trained their students in magecraft that they were allowed to teach.

He would be gravely limited as a student there.

Even with it being the most prestigious school of magic in the Magic World, he still could have done so much more.

And yet, I had no choice.

I saw his potential. I saw what he could become.

And the world forced me to ignore it.

I trained him as best I could. Giving him solid foundations and starting blocks towards his development and trusting that his choices and the world around him would allow him to only further improve.

The day he astounded me the most would have been one of the earliest.

A simple training exercise focusing on the identification and on the fly analysis of higher-level spells.

A test to see if he could identify the comments of the spell, isolate them, control them and them manipulate them to his own advantage.

Easy enough to learn with practice.

But he didn't need it.

I had tasked him with penetrating a barrier. A wall of magic energy not more than an inch thick that would have rejected anything and anyone who wasn't myself.

His objective was to study the spell, break it down into every basic component and then find a way to rearrange them to allow himself passage and yet not disrupt the rest of the spell.

He'd already shown an interest in bypassing my barriers in the past. I had no doubt in my mind that he could grasp the concept and figure it out eventually.

I'd estimated no more than a day to do it.

And yet, as I went to turn around and leave him to work

it out while I was gone, he suddenly stopped me.

No more than a minute after I tasked him with this challenge and explained exactly how to do it, he'd actually managed to pull it off.

Holding his hand against the barrier, using his own magic energy to do as needed to rearrange there spell and then passing that hand through it like it was empty air a moment later.

When I asked him how he had done this, how he had managed to complete a task that should have taken hours for a novice to grasp without prior experience in only a matter of seconds, his answer was short and simple.

"You asked me to find a way through and I did." He said. "I changed the rule pertaining to mage entry allowances and rewrote them to allow anyone through."

"Rewrote them?" I asked him quickly, not understanding how he would have even known how to do that yet. "Just finding that rule should have taken you the rest of the day, it's so deep in the incantation that you shouldn't have known where to look. And you knew exactly where it was. But... how?"

It took him a while to explain to me exactly how he had managed to do it but after that long conversation I understood. He thought differently to most, saw things that others could not and understood things that baffled most.

He said that he did not need to find the rule, he said that he had known where it was all along. By his account, all it took was one look at the spell to know where that rule was, simply by looking at the design of the barrier he knew exactly how and where it had been written.

He said that when I had asked him to get through it he

228

understood what to do. That because there was no need to break it down in order to step through, he would have to correct the rule preventing him from passing through. Simply by knowing that he had to be on the other side allowed him to find a solution from the problem preventing him from reaching the answer.

He'd heard the task, looked at the spell and just known what to do in seconds. No prior experience, no explanation required, no assistance.

He just understood.

A mage who can do something like that, take a look at a spell and understand everything about it in an instant, they're a rare breed. But his ability, with no training at all and little to no experience in spells of any kind, it was beyond what I had seen before.

I tested him more and more over the moths he stayed with me. Putting him through more and more tests, throwing more and more spells at him to try and figure out what his limit was for understanding the structure of a spell he'd never seen before. But there didn't seem to be one.

Whether it be elemental, enchanting, vector or anything else, he understood every spell I showed him. He couldn't cast them on his own, the magic energy flow techniques and internal incantations were still an unknown to him. But as for how the spell worked, down to whatever level of detail you could choose, he would always understand it with just a single look.

I guess that this would explain how he was able to cast a spell that seen or attempted before. He was tasked with solving a problem. He needed to defeat me in battle.

In order to do this he knew that he would have to use

something that I couldn't defend against, something that I had never seen before.

And somehow, using every spell he had assessed in the months I'd been testing him; he'd managed to come up with one of his own. Defining every part about it.

The magic circuit designs, the sigils positions, the magic energy flow and the incantation. He figured all of that out on his own so that it could match the spell he'd come up with to use against me.

If it didn't sound completely impossible then I would have said he was only able to cast that spell because he understood magecraft better than even I did.

The way he cast that spell though, the way he improved himself in order to do it. That had to be more than just an accident.

He might have defined every aspect of that spell in less than a second at the time, but that didn't change the fact that he couldn't cast it. His body wasn't capable of such a task.

He had defined a spell beyond his own capabilities and instead of trying something else, he corrected that mismatch and found a way to improve himself

Defeating me was the task and he was the problem. In order to reach his goal and knock me out of the ring he would have to fix himself and he certainly did do that.

The only question that still hovers over me, is how.

How was he able to do this? What mix of knowledge and talent had allowed this boy to come up with something so complex?

Creating as spell is no simple feat.

Just because I can do it doesn't mean that it's easy. You have to envision every aspect of the spell. The purpose, the meaning, the incantation and the feeling. You have to create a way of casting it, define its parameters, how it should be used, what emotion should trigger it and how it should behave.

In my entire lifetime, some fifteen thousand years, I have only ever done this two thousand and fifteen times. Adapting different variants of spell based of those I had come up with before. Completely unable to doing it again and again.

Spells are primal things. Magic energy is naturally occurring but entirely unobtainable through any natural means. Requiring great focus and practice in order to cast a spell from it. And creating one from scratch, is nothing short of the work of a god.

The only thing more complex that the creation of a spell would be teaching that spell to someone else.

Making them see the incantations as you do, to experience the feelings, attach the same emotional and physical meaning to it. To be able to make them see every aspect of your creation exactly as you do. It is and will always be the most difficult thing that a mage will ever do.

In the thousands of years that human mages have existed, only nine of them are responsible for creating their own spells, Julian now making that number a nice round ten.

With his remarkable way of thinking coupled with his talent and his ability to create spells of all things, I knew all along that he would only excel at the academy and I can say with the upmost of honesty that he never did disappoint.

If it wasn't for the fact that you can only increase your rank by completing examinations that are only held when the timetable says that they are, then I would have expected him to reach level seven within a week if he tried hard enough.

With his understanding and the spells he already knew, they'd label him a level seven mage in an instant once they saw his potential. But unfortunately, that's not how things are done.

You have to meet criteria and achieve a certain amount of goals. Ticking boxes one at a time just like everyone else.

Climbing the ranks takes a long time no matter how much you try and speed through it. And I guess that since there was no need to rush, Julian instead chose to make good use of his.

While I do not know everything that happened during his time enrolled within the academy, I kept close enough tabs on him and attended enough of the events held by the school to figure it out.

The rumours that circulated around that boy were enough to make anyone curious after all. With so many stories about him popping up year after year, I couldn't stay away.

In fact, I'm surprised I didn't end up knowing more.

Whether it be bad luck or providence, that boy was quite a hot topic around the mage community as a whole.

You couldn't go anywhere without hearing at least one rumour about him. Not the markets, the farms or the borders. Everyone was talking about him.

Some random shop in the heart of Tryless. The waiting area on the ground floor of the Citadel. The southern barracks near the border walls, if there were even a handful of mages within the vicinity then there would surely be

232

someone talking about him.

He was even more well-known than I was at one point.

His fame was only going to continue growing at this rate too.

Eventually it might have gotten out of hand.

But I kept in touch with Academia while he was a student there. Talking with the Headmaster whenever we met at the Citadel. He would be on his way to a meeting and I would be on my way back out of one. Leaving again and again as the Council summoned me to discuss some pointless idea of theirs to limit or reduce my powers every other week as I always did.

It didn't matter what they came up with, short of locking me up there weren't any further limitations that they could have placed on me.

And they were hardly about to do that.

They of all people knew how important I was.

But I still had power.

Standing.

And anyone with the ability to threaten their rule was a problem to them. But unfortunately for their endless efforts, I wasn't a problem that they could make disappear as easily as the rest.

However, seeing the Headmaster from time to time as he reported in did allow me some amount of relief after my visits. Although, since I didn't officially or otherwise have any relation to the boy, getting any information proved to be more than a little difficult.

I might have been his guardian for all anyone else cared but when it came to Academia, all I was to them was a threat to his wellbeing.

I had no blood tie and no legal reason to be associated with him. Even my stature didn't help me. Being the Athereon had many perks back then even with all the Council tried to put in my way but when it came to Academia, the staff would just sit there in fear rather than tell me anything.

I had thought that the Headmaster would be better than this, given our history at least, but it would seem that even he was under the leash of the Magic Council just like the rest of them.

Then again, Academia had some pretty shady ties to the Council at the time. Shadier than even my own relationship with the school. So I suppose that I should have expected their hostility towards me not to budge.

This reluctance to tell me what I needed to know went on for his entire stay there though. The Headmaster and his underlings only allowing me to learn what I wanted to after he was back under my wing as it were. Years after the fact.

So at the time, I had no choice but to respect their position. It wasn't my place to boss them around, despite the fact that I should have done.

In all the years that he was a student there, I only heard the reports that Katiana received every time the Council was concerned about something that he had done.

Legally of course, I'm not allowed to actually ask her about any matters to do with the Council. But that doesn't mean that I can't be in the same room when Katiana decided to talk about them.

This was my main source of information for a while at first. But eventually even she was being kept out of the loop and soon it became obvious what I would have to do.

If I wanted to know anything about what he was doing, I would have to ask him myself. Something that so long as a barrier remained in place around his school, was completely impossible on my part.

The public still spoke of him though. Speaking of a strange new student competing in and winning tournament after tournament.

A man who could use a spell that only he knew, a man who had overwhelming talent and power compared to his peers.

Even from that brief description, I knew that it was him.

Simply for managing to create a new spell he had already been placed at the top of the school. Joining the elite class and ranking up on day one.

If anyone was going to be capable of doing everything that I heard whispers about, it would be him.

I even got the change to watch one of those tournaments eventually. But only after a week long debate over whether or not it was safe to let me in.

He wouldn't have known that I was there, the crowds were too packed and I did have to blend in as to not draw attention to myself, but I did at least get to see his in action

I got to see how powerful and ruthless he had become.

I saw the medals that he wore when he was handed the trophy for the fourth year running. I heard of the prizes that he had won and the titles he had earned. Everything about him, Academia's Prodigy as he was known, was literally lining the gallery walls.

Pictures, plaques, trophies and medals.

They all had his name on.

Every sport you could think of and every competition.

He'd won almost all of them.

The only thing that I could think about throughout the entire event was that if I had been allowed to train him to that level then he would have already surpassed where he was by that point.

If I had remained his tutor, he would have been equal in strength to a fully trained mage by the end of his second year. But if I had done that, focused solely on his training and kept him secluded at my home, he would have never achieved all that he had. And besides, it wasn't legal for starters. No matter how much I disagreed.

I was only legally allowed to train a mage once they pass level seven and only allowed to partially train newcomers under the agreement that they would never pass level one while under my roof.

In order for them to ever make a dent on the world, I was forced to put them into a real school.

This was the Council's doing of course.

Restriction after sanction after restriction. That's all I got from them. A constant and steady flow of rules and regulations limiting the spells that I could cast, the places that I could visit and the students that I could train.

But I had to obey.

I had to listen.

If not, I would have been cut off from the Magic World. Outcast completely. Restricted from ever passing through our borders again.

The only way back in would have been by force and the Mage Defence Force, our version of an army, would have liked nothing more than to be in a fight against me.

It would have given them an excuse to use forbidden

spells. A legal reason to dust off the Planetary Firing Rings and attack me from orbit with a barrage of spells that I had been long forbidden from even acknowledging the existence of.

A series of powerful ring-shaped crystals infused with decade's worth of my magic energy and built to my design. They were originally intended for use against entire armies. They were designed to kill thousands. But if they were directed against a single combatant, fired on such a small target in a narrow enough beam, it would have surely been capable of killing me.

But in order to use it, to attack my home from orbit with a bright and perfectly visible laser fired from space, they would have to reveal its existence at the same time.

Letting the rest of the mage world know that there was a weapon capable of levelling cities in the hands of the Council and that it had been there for hundreds of years.

After knowing something like that, a rebellion would have surely occurred.

The Council knew this and they feared it immensely.

The only thing that had kept them from using it on me in the past were a combination of two truths.

The fact that if the public learnt of its existence the Council would be overthrown and the fact that I was still needed, despite how much they didn't trust me.

It was their arrogance, their fear and their lack of understanding that drew them from the path that we all follow.

Instead of trying to use me as a force for good, instead of recognising my wisdom and my authority, they decided to shut me out and control me.

Hide me away and call upon me when needed.

It was for this reason that they kept me in the dark. Banishing me from academies unless I was required to be there.

And it is for this reason that I was kept away from Julian while he was enrolled in that academy. It was because they feared what I might one day become. The horrors that I was capable of unleashing and the power that I held.

They knew as well as I did, that a protector had two ways of dying. In the line of duty or as a monster.

You can die a hero or see yourself live long enough to become the villain. Isn't that how it goes?

The Council saw me as a future threat and they wanted me taken care of. Be it through killing me or through controlling me. I knew full well why they did what they did and I accepted it. They didn't have to like or trust me, just accept that thy still needed me.

Unless of course, they wanted to take over the duty of fighting against the very force that had given me the title of protector in the first place after my repeated defeat of them.

I have guarded mage kind from humans for thousands of years. But I have protected this world as a whole for far longer than that.

A fight that never ends.

A fight that remains ever present. One that no amount of boasting, no amount of shouting and no amount of sanctions, will ever cease to exist.

So if the Council truly wanted to get rid of me, if they wanted me to leave – to lay down and die – then they would first have to prove to me that they could take over in my stead.

Which both myself and the Council as a whole knew was never going to happen.

I was exceptionally hard to kill.

Could they say the same?

So I accepted that they didn't trust me and I accepted everything they did to try and encourage me to take action against them. But I never did. I never even argued it.

And so I followed their rules and eventually I buried my curiosity in Julian as well.

As best I could at least.

And after that, I moved on with my life.

Returning to my seclusion and isolation, returning to the protection of my barrier, the cold empty space within its walls. And from there I was to wait.

To wait for Julian to finish his studies, to wait for a compelling reason to venture outside of my home and to wait for history to repeat itself once again.

After all, when Julian had left me to join Academia, I had four more years until this would happen again.

And once I had finally ended my foolish efforts to find out how he was doing at the academy, I had only two and a half years left.

Just shy of three years. Twenty-nine months. Twenty-nine months to prepare and to think.

Preparing for a day that soon approached. The one that I had always come to dread for years after its passing. The one that had repeated itself so many times before.

The day the fight resumed at last.

The day that, once again, the sky above our heads, cracks open. And through they come.

Ready for war.

THE DAY THE SKY TORE OPEN

Before I knew it, the day that I said goodbye to Julian had been left in my past. And almost four whole years had been allowed to pass me by since.

Four short years – barely even the length of a blink in terms of my own lifespan – that's all took.

Four years was all the time I needed for those months of having Julian both under my roof and under my wing to fade back into my memory.

Pushed away into the dark recesses of my mind as I focussed on more pressing matters. Events that would soon come.

It took me four years, but finally, when the time came, I had prepared myself. Prepared myself to go back to this eternal war all over again.

I couldn't even count how many times it'd been now.

But I could predict it.

Down to the day.

I always knew when it was coming.

And this time it was no different.

On the day that it finally happened, the day that the war started up yet again after so many years, history repeated itself as it always used to do.

DANIEL FREARSON

From the moment that the first shock was felt, the first moment that the light was seen in the sky above my home – I knew. I knew that it was for both myself and Katiana to finally reopen my school once again.

Unlike establishments like Academia, my school taught the students things that they were probably better off not knowing. The truths and secrets that I revealed to them, the inner workings of what kept the world in check – perhaps it wasn't my place to tell them. Maybe I should have let them ask, giving them the choice.

The choice of whether to find out the truth or to run from it the moment they sense the dangerous aura that surrounds it. Perhaps it had done, things would have been easier. Perhaps if everyone had known we would have had even more time.

But due to the nature of what I would be preparing these students to do, secrecy to the outer world and complete transparency to them was a requirement.

The danger and challenge of what laid ahead. It wasn't something that any ordinary mage could face. It wasn't something that children should be forced into fighting. But I needed the best. The most talented, the most reliable. The most resilient. And like it or not, whilst a mage's knowledge and understanding may improve with age, their capacity for magecraft does not.

The peak performance of a mage is often found before they turn thirty. Meaning that any spell they learn past then, would have been just as strong had they known it all along.

I couldn't have someone above a certain age do this for me however. I required a mind that could still be taught. One that would answer to authority. One that could be moulded. Manipulated.

And one that would see the benefits of what I would be offering them as a reward instead of simply staring down the barrel of the gun that was the danger they would be up against.

I needed to use children.

The younger and more promising the better.

It was the only way.

And I was forced to only accept the best of them.

Anyone below a certain skill level simply wouldn't be capable of grasping what I was teaching them. It would take far too long to train them to a suitable level. They'd have never survived.

And if I allowed myself to resort to simply training anyone with the required rank but not the required skill, then I would have gotten most of them killed before the war had even started.

So, every twenty-six years, Academia begrudgingly sent me the top two percent of their students for me to train.

Everyone and anyone over level seven in rank or above but specifically limiting that large number of their students to only the best of the best. Only those with skill equal to that of someone who had already surpassed level twelve.

And they did this, twenty six years apart every time, so that when the time came – the same day that I experienced every twenty-six years for almost my entire life – sixty-three students would appear on my doorstep, chosen and sent to me by the Headmaster himself knowing full well what they would be doing once they arrived.

These sixty-three would not have it easy however. Simply because they were qualified didn't mean that they could just walk straight in.

Those sixty-three would have to fight for the first fifty places and then those fifty would fight their hardest to survive the remainder of that following year.

And by the end of that year, just before the time came for their skills to be put to the ultimate test, only twenty-three would remain. Just enough for me to properly train for what they would face.

Those twenty-three would be just enough for myself and my wife, with a great deal of effort and practice, to turn into an army.

That's what they would be after a year with me.

An army.

No longer a class of students fighting for the best grades but a group pf trained warriors fighting solely for their own survival.

It wasn't as easy for me anymore. Teaching that is.

For me, teaching wasn't something that I chose to do now. It had become something that I had to do in order to prolong the existence of this world.

Because if I didn't train them, if I didn't prepare, then alone I would fall. And everything else would follow.

This was all because of one thing. One singular threat as old as civilization itself. And every twenty-six years, it comes back.

No matter how many times I push them back, no matter how many of them I slay, they always return. Over and over again they invade, over and over again they fail, and still, twenty-six years later, there they are again.

And on this day every twenty-six years, something happened. Something that forced me to seek out warriors capable of felling its power alongside myself and Katiana on the battlefield.

I did this because if I did not, if I failed to train them or didn't train anyone at all, there'd be no one else to take my place.

The Mage Defence Force may have been created to wage wars and protect our civilization from any outside threat beyond our border walls but they weren't capable of handling the enemy that I had faced for most of my life.

While as a whole that army of ours is strong. Individually they were weak. Nothing more than level fifteen at best. Men and women carrying enchanting weapons and armour and forced to rely on their formations and their tactics in order to win a battle.

They had no real skill or talent for killing.

They'd have never survived against this carnage and the Magic Council itself knew it. They'd known it all along.

That was the only reason that the Council allowed me to train the students to fight alongside me. It was because they knew as well as I did, that the fight that I was tasked with resolving could not be fought with strength and numbers alone.

The Council knew that the only person capable of teaching others to fight this war was someone like myself. Someone who had fought them before. Someone who knew the magic of the old world and how to teach others to use it.

And they knew that if I were to win this battle each and every time, if I were to fight on their behalf while they told the people of the Magic World nothing of this conflict, then I would have to do it my way.

Out of everything the Council and I had disagreed on in

the past, this was the only thing that we saw eye to eye on. They wanted protection from this war, they wanted victory and they knew that only I could provide that.

So out of everything I had every requested from them in the past, this was all that they had ever provided. Permission to build a school with the sole purpose of training warriors to fight in this war.

The only thing this government that I helped form had ever given me was the permission to take sixty-three students from Academia and turn them into ruthless killers.

They had only ever given me the permission to fight.

And once again, the time had come to repeat everything from the start. The coming day was just hours away from dawning and with it, the way had at last begun again.

The first signs that the war is on the horizon occurs on that day. The day that comes every nine thousand five hundred and eighty-three days like clockwork.

The war's arrival is signified by an event that was impossible to ignore each and every time. An event that would have catastrophic consequences if not taken care of quickly and efficiently.

And for me to have done this alone, to have fought against this war with just myself and Katiana on the battlefield, it was more than simply difficult to do.

It was impossible.

But it had not always been that way.

I used to have a partner. One who equalled me in more ways than just ability and strength. However, despite her power, despite her abilities and her skill, she was swallowed by the very darkness that she left me alone to fight against.

That is why the school existed. It was a training camp,

designed with a purpose, the creation and training of warriors capable of assisting me on the battlefield.

However, in the decades leading up to that day, the school hadn't really been needed. The previous event and the one before that were nothing compared to what I had faced in the past.

And on those occasions, the students were given their awards for passing the course and sent on their way. Not receiving any of the final training lessons that would have prepared them for battle and never knowing the horrors that they might have had to face.

But those more peaceful times when myself and Kat had been enough to hold back this army until they lost the strength to continue would never come again.

This time, when the first signs of the event started surfacing, I knew things would be different. The sheer scale of the initial attack was more than enough to tip me off that this one was bigger than the rest. That alone had me worried. But then... then it got worse.

I awoke in the middle of the night, my head throbbing and my senses confused.

My barrier was screaming at me. As though every one of the sigils lining the perimeter had been set off all at once thinking that there was an intruder.

Their combined alarms rang within my head like a fire alarm, compelling me to wake up within seconds.

Never had I felt such power, such an immense sense of of impending doom hovering just over my own home.

I had anticipated this day; it was already overdue by a few hours when I went to sleep that night, but it was only when I went outside to get a better look at what was going on that I saw it.

The full extent of what I was up against this time.

In my haste to get myself outside, I had forgotten clothes, simply teleporting from my bed and into the garden. Standing under the stars in my birthday suit, feeling the chilling crisp in the air, the unmistakeable dampness from the grass and the utter fear and shock that gripped my body whole.

It didn't matter what my body felt at the time. Whether be damned, it would have stood there nonetheless. Staring up into the sky. Peering deeply into the spectacle before me that remained far more pertinent than how wet my feet were or how cold my skin felt.

My sudden rush to the garden had awoken Katiana of course. She of all people knew that the day was coming. She had been expecting it same as I had. And there in the window of our master bedroom, she stared down at me. Probably not awake enough as to realise why I would be so concerned. But she knew I was scared.

But she couldn't see what I saw. At least not yet. It wasn't strong enough for a normal mage to sense it. It wouldn't be for a whole.

All she saw was her naked husband staring at the sky trembling in his fear.

But what I could see. It only filled me with fear. An overwhelming sense that one's mortality was about to be tested.

The look of a men standing in terror as he stared at the storm to come.

I gritted my teeth, clenching my fists as I stood there in complete silence, simply frozen by the image spread out before me.

A great big crack in the sky.

Invisible to all but the most adept of mages, perhaps even all of them.

And it was big. Bigger than I had ever seen it before. Almost too powerful for me to quantify.

At least five miles long, maybe one or two miles wide, suspended above my home at an altitude of one if not two or more kilometres up.

It filled the night sky, taking over all that should have been there. The stars, the moon, the clouds, I couldn't see any of them. I could only see the bright light emanating from the crack taking their place.

Just like how certain spectrums of light are invisible to humans, the light being given off from this crack was invisible to everyone. Except for me.

Even in my human form, my physiology doesn't perfectly match that of a natural one. I'm not sure about all the differences but I know that my eyes were at least one of them. I could see a broader spectrum of light than humans could. I could see things that went unnoticed by others in the Magic World too such as the sigils that make up our spells.

And I could even witness events that were invisible to the world as a whole. I could even see the flow of magic depending on how hard I tried. I could see its primal, energetic form in all living things as it came flooding out of the ground and became absorbed into everything through the air.

It was like an aura surrounding everything that was alive. The magic energy of the planet itself existing in everything that could breathe. And I could see it. I could identify it.

This was what had made me so much of an expert when it came to assessing another mages power just by glancing over at them. Because even when they weren't using their magic, I could still see it.

But what I could see on that night, the terrifying sight before me, it was unexpected and far beyond anything that I could have categorised.

In terms of power, it was beyond anything that should have been possible. It was far stronger than I had ever seen it before. Releasing a constant and steady flow of magic energy that came spewing out of it, poisoning the air, corrupting the land and playing havoc with my barrier as it tried to resist the foreign matter attempting to break through.

That would have been what set off the alarms, the detection of this energy would have surely confused it. I never designed it to detect such a treat, the barrier should have simply ignored it entirely but it wasn't the energy itself that it was reacting to, it was its potency.

With so much energy in the air, the barrier had been confused into thinking that there were thousands of mages surrounding it preparing for an attack and had responded accordingly.

There was so much power in the air that it had been recognised as an army. I didn't even know that that was possible and I made sure to correct that error in the barrier's makeup once I had the chance.

And while she couldn't see the spectacle itself, at least not yet, Katiana could sense the strain being placed on the dome protecting us. She could feel the power trying to work itself though.

By then, some twenty seconds after I stepped outside, she would have known what it was. She would have remembered what was going on. And even if she couldn't see it, the immense pressure of that invisible force surrounding our home was enough to make anyone scared.

But for those like us, those who knew what it was, we were terrified.

Unlike most magic energy, this one wasn't even remotely natural. It was dark, unclean, and rotten. This form of magic had no place in our world and even the planet itself refused to accept its existence whenever it appeared.

All it did was corrupt and destroy.

It takes away all life in its path, leaving only decay and destruction behind. It was a corruptive and formless force, created in an attempt to end a war long ago forgotten but, in the end, it only managed to eternally prolong it.

The crack it came from, I had never known what to call it, never known how or why it opened every twenty-six years or how to keep it closed, I only knew what it did as a result of its own appearance.

I have often heard those who fight with me refer to it as a Tear in the fabric of reality. A portal to another dimension floating in the sky.

But all I knew in that moment was that, this time, I wouldn't be able to deal with it as easily as before.

And realising how powerful it was, how uncontrollably large it had already become, I was forced to try and contain it then and there.

I reached my arms out towards it and began to do what I could. Focusing hard and using a great deal more magic energy that I had ever done before to place a spherical barrier around it. The strongest that I had ever created at the time. But I knew that even this wouldn't be enough to hold it back forever.

Nine layers deep, covered in defensive enchantments and fortified against the strongest of attacks. A barrier that should have held back the strongest of mages for decades. It was stronger than even the barriers protecting the Magic World. And yet, this barrier was still overcome by what it was deigned to hold back.

Any barrier is a difficult thing to make. Not only do you have to visualise its shape and provide the required energy to create it but you must also mentally recite the incantation and then insert rules as you make it.

Thousands of words and phrases make up a barrier, endless lines of text etched into every layer of the shell. And for a barrier this large and this powerful, the incantation was nothing special. Just fifteen thousand words. That's all it took to set it up. Designing it so that it would protect against everything and everything. Giving it no exceptions. No exemptions. Just making it so that nothing was to come through it. Not even air.

It was a small book's length of words that summed up to only two.

"No entry."

Even before it started to fail, I had known it would never be enough to survive for long.

I had never felt so much power in one place before.

Not even back when there were several million people like myself still alive in the world. Never had I felt so much power in such a small area.

And in truth, I didn't quite know what to do about it.

I placed a barrier to hold it back for the moment, rushed back into the house and managed to put some clothes on. And then before I could do anything else to plan or prepare, the unthinkable happened.

The Tear grew. It just got larger on its own.

For this to have happened so soon and so suddenly I knew that I wouldn't have enough time.

The barrier that I had placed around it was so large, so complex, that it had already drained me completely and yet, it hadn't been enough.

Only a minute after its formation, the barrier had already been placed under far too much strain to last the year it needed to.

But I had no idea how much strain it was truly holding back. I could only guess at the time. Nothing in that moment was certain so all I could do was guess at how long I had and even my worst-case scenario wound up being far too conservative.

The barrier lasted nowhere near what I had hoped it would, not even close.

But at the time, the barrier appeared to be holding, I knew I would have time to recover my magic energy and try again at a later date so I got things in place and prepared for my guests.

Katiana had already left by then.

While she wasn't quite as sensitive to magic as I was, while she couldn't see or feel it, she knew exactly what it took to get me in such a state. Only one thing had ever done so before and she had seen it right up close.

It was the look of a man who knew that he was about to

die. That was what she saw in me as I placed that barrier in the sky and that was precisely what I had scared her as well.

The same thing had happened ten years before. Six years before I had even met Julian, I had faced something that had put me in this state. And she was unfortunate enough to see it first-hand.

The events that took place ten years before the crack appeared left me afraid. So afraid that I thought that I would never feel that level of fear again.

And it was Katiana who found me amidst the blood, carnage and bodies littering the floor when that barrier holding me inside their kill box finally went down.

She never could forget the look on my face that day.

And it was the same face that I wore in that moment. The same face I wore in the first moment when I saw that crack above my head. And because of that, because of what such a look meant, even Katiana, was afraid.

Just from seeing my face, she felt the same fear that I did.

She knew that we both were about to die.

And even if most count me as immortal, I am not invincible. I can die. It just takes a lot of effort to keep me dead.

All I have is the ability to live forever and to resurrect myself when death occurs. But should there be no body left for me to resurrect, I might as well be dead.

While my consciousness would still exist and float around in the veil for eternity, I would never be capable of returning again.

So, if I were to allow my body to be completely destroyed, I would stay dead. This was the only way to keep me down. Cut off the head, burn the body and crush the

254

remains.

Destroy everything until there's nothing left but dust and then that's it, I would be dead and the world would be doomed.

I had never told anyone that before. Not even my wife knew what it truly took to keep me down. And even if it was unlikely for someone to put that much effort into killing me, I still knew that there were some out there in the world who were capable of doing so.

It was for that reason that anytime I came up against a fighter of sufficient strength to destroy me entirely that I truly felt fear.

I can live forever, grow back limbs and organs endlessly but there is no way to come back from a death like that. There's no way to come back when there's nothing left to come back to.

And the only times that I ever really get scared are the times that you and anyone else near me at the time should run for the hills.

Because if I recognise an opponent as one who was strong enough to actually kill me then that meant that anyone standing within a mile of my position was in just as much danger.

Anyone strong enough to kill me is surely too powerful to contain.

The men and women that I killed ten years before this day, the ones who came so close to actually keeping me dead. They were too powerful to be ordinary mages but I never got a chance to find out what they were during my fight against them.

From the moment they saw me and erected that barrier to

keep our fight contained, they attacked and they kept going until they had either ran out of strength or until I had torn off their heads.

Even after a five-hour bloodbath of a fight, one of them was still holding on. And after having to use hundreds of my resurrections to regrow the limbs that they blasted off of my body minute after minute, it was with the death of this final fighter that I at last managed to kill them all.

And when it was all over, it was Katiana that found me.

Kneeling atop a pile of bodies with gashes and shrapnel lining my entire body. Two swords in my hands and a look of a man who had just faced his own mortality on my face.

She had never seen me like that before. Seeing it again surely scared her just as much as what I was seeing scared me.

So she reacted swiftly.

Teleporting to the Citadel to summon the Magic Council. Heading to them first to relay the news. Telling them that the time had come.

And then she would have sent a message to both Academia and the other Magic Council bases around the world, giving them a warning them that it was starting once again. Expressing her fear and alerting them more than they would have usually been.

She knew that this one was different even though she had hadn't seen it, but she had seen me and she knew that the others needed warning.

The Council did its job as best it could; walling off the human world from ours completely by removing every exemption on the barriers at the time. And then defending what little they could if I failed to do so myself with even more barriers surrounding the village all the way back to the mountains.

That's all the Magic Council did at the time.

After that, Academia did what it had always done. They selected candidates and then sent me my fresh meet. Sixty-three warm and walking weapons.

My new students.

My future army.

Normally when I placed a barrier around one of these Tears, it would hold at least a year, enough time for me to train them. Enough time for me to prepare them for the war that was to come. But this time, I wasn't even sure I had a week.

And with the process already under way, that meant that in less than six hours, there would be just over sixty of Academia's elite standing at my doorstep.

In six hours, their training would begin and as far as I was concerned, from that same moment, so too did the war.

So I did what I could to prepare while I waited.

Grabbing myself a cup of tea and getting to work. Cleaning both of the classrooms over at the school. Repairing any damage, I could in the dojo, strengthening the school barrier and then taking some much-needed time to rest a moment and strengthen myself.

Creating that barrier had taken quite the toll on me, I knew that I would have enough energy to do most things by the time the students arrived but I wouldn't be anywhere near my full strength.

I needed at least a full day of not casting a single spell to recover that amount of magic energy and I certainly wasn't going to get that any time soon.

I would have to start drinking tea contently in the meantime then. Accelerating the magic energy generation within my body as much as I could as the drink did its work.

So I took a breather, and then made the beds and cleaned the dorms. Removing the cobwebs and the pesky spiders themselves.

Then I moved on making sure that the gender restricting enchantments still worked. Best to keep those hormonal teenagers under as much control as possible after all. Not that these enchantments would stop much. They were more of a deterrent than anything else.

If a student was adamant that he wanted to go into a girl's room or vice versa, he or she could still manage it with a little effort.

So before long, not even an hour after the Tear appeared and Katiana had left, everything was ready for their arrival.

And that was when things, as bad as they already were, became far, far worse.

As if what had happened so far wasn't enough, it seemed as though someone out there really wanted to make a crappy day as bad as it could have been at the time.

I heard a loud sound coming from the sky just as I left the dorms having finished the jobs that needed doing.

At first I believed that the sound was that of my barrier already beginning to fail – which would have been bad enough – but it was much worse than even that.

Think of the worst thing that could have happened given my situation at the time, then think of something worse. Not double that.

Perhaps you'd imagined that the Tear had grown, or that the army had already began to fall from it. But even those eventualities weren't even close to the truth of what happened in that moment.

I teleported from my position by the backdoor of the dorms to the middle of my garden once again to get an unobstructed look.

I didn't even care that I was too weak at the time I manage even that short jump safely, I just knew that I needed to get a good look that that was the fastest way to do it so I damned the consequences and did it anyway.

And from there, I looked up at the sky and I stared.

I stared and I stared for minutes. Mumbling incoherently as I saw what was right before my eyes. Unable to believe any of it.

But I didn't have to believe, belief didn't make the situation true, the events did.

That was why, despite what I thought and knew to be possible from my own experience, instead of seeing one Tear floating in the sky, I saw two.

Side by side many kilometres above me, there they were. The new one seemed smaller than the other but still just as powerful.

I did my best to react in the most suitable way given the situation at hand but my best wasn't anywhere near good enough.

It's a good thing that Katiana was back by then, I might not have been able to do anything without her helping me at the time.

Even when I'm at my strongest, even when I am wearing my other body, I would have still been too weak to do what needed to be done alone.

I thought about making another barrier alongside the

first, that would have made sense in theory, but they were too close to do that. Even if I had managed to find enough magic energy to make another, it would have fused with the first one before long, weakening them both or even making a hole.

I couldn't take that chance.

So I began to extend and enhance the barrier that was already there. I stretched and stretched, using so much energy that I almost collapsed and still it wasn't big enough to cover both of them.

I had hoped to hold them both at bay with a single barrier but even I couldn't make something that large by myself.

To my disappointment and embarrassment, I had to ask Katiana to help. I called to her, startling her at first but soon she was by my side.

She could see my hands in the air, feel the energy that was leaving them but couldn't see exactly what I was doing. The barrier was simply too far away for her to perceive its presence.

Realising that she wouldn't be able to help without being able to see it, I used the link that existed between us and shared my sight with her. Something that we had only ever practiced doing once and only in the bedroom.

She gasped as she saw the purple glow of the holes in the sky, she stepped back in fear and disbelief, but after a moment to recollect herself, she understood what she needed to do.

She could see what I was attempting and she soon began to help. With our combined magical strength, we were able to secure the barrier around the two of them.

But stretched so far and with so little magic energy between us to properly reinforce it, the barrier was a lot weaker than I would have liked.

However, once a magic barrier is formed you can only strengthen it if you are strong enough to do so. Since this barrier had taken the two most powerful mages on the planet to create, I didn't see a way of making a better one without doubling the number of mages trying to do it. Something that would have meant using a couple hundred weaker mages to equal the two of us in power.

But never before had a barrier of such scale been made by just two people and never before had such a barrier been put up against something as strong as the corruption seeping out of those cracks in the sky.

By the time we were finished, sitting on the floor of our garden staring up at the sky as we watched the sun rise behind our house, the students had started arriving.

One by one they showed up at my doorstep.

And before I could take even a moment to recover some magic energy, I had to begin explaining how their new course would work and get them settled in their new school.

Katiana retreated indoors and made some tea for the both of us. Not a drop of that pot went to the students. We both drank the entire thing in minutes.

We defiantly needed it. Not only was the beverage good for both the mind and the soul but it also helped the body of a mage recover from the pain of being drained. And as we had both just extended a large amount of our magic energy supply, we were both feeling the effects.

And since it was the only drink that had such healing capabilities for a mage, almost every mage alive at the time was accustom to drinking it regularly.

Not at all out of luxury but purely out of necessity.

So it was a good thing there were so many brands of instant coffee available on the market. We were never in short supply.

Though, if you wanted a proper brew, you'd need to grow your own tea leaves. But that takes time and space. Not many people want to commit to that. However, it does taste far superior to the brands you can buy in the human world if you do it right.

So the two of us drank our tea as the students began to pop into existence on the other side of my front door.

The first five students arrived within the first few seconds of each other. The rest had taken their time getting there which gave the two of us a much-needed reprieve.

I had already removed the teleportation limit on my barriers before they arrived but that didn't stop them from taking a while.

It was a long journey to make. They were probably double checking their coordinates before they tried it. Wouldn't want to end up teleporting into a wall after all. That wasn't too easy to fix.

But once they had all arrived and some of them had left, I would be replacing that particular enchantment on the barrier just as before.

I wasn't about to let my students run off now was I?

But, as per usual, the first five were put through straight away. Leaving the next forty-five spaces up for grabs.

After enjoying yet another pot of tea and emptying my now filled bladder, I went outside and got to work. Having those first five students stand beside me by the front door, making the rest of them wait on the hill while everyone arrived.

One by one they teleported in, all of then different in their own way. Ranging from the tall to the small, from the strong, physically or mentally, to the weak. The colour of their hair, the size of their noses, the fit of their robes.

Everyone was unique. Everyone was probably thinking something different as they first looked at me too. But none of them had any idea what was about to happen.

And finally, after two or three minutes of waiting, the final student arrived. I could already hear the chatter stirring by then. Everyone wondering why they were there, why I was there and why only five of their classmates were standing beside me.

They were about to find out.

"Students of Academia, I welcome to my home." I told them loudly, watching as they all shut their mouths to listen. "As you have probably already guessed, I am the Athereon. And from this day forth, I will be your new instructor!"

They all knew who I was, or at least suspected it.

When a mage first meets me, it takes them a while to shake of the feeling of fear that my presence creates. Not an intentional affect but an accidental one.

The sheer scale of my strength compared to theirs would have overwhelmed them. Similar to the feeling you get when you pick a fight with someone only to realise that they were on a completely different level than you.

Like a ripple in the water against a wave, it was obvious who was stronger.

They all smirked in response to my statement of course, thinking that they had just won the lottery or something. It was well known that my school was one of the most impressive establishments when it comes to the sophistication of the magic they would be taught here but what they didn't know is that the entrance exam, had already started.

"As you can see, five of your classmates stand beside me. They were the first to arrive and because of this, they are automatically accepted into the school. As for the rest of you, your entrance exam starts now!"

As everyone else began to grow nervous of what this exam would entail, I asked the five students to go and chose their rooms in the dorms while I explained what would happen to everyone else. Katiana was inside the house waiting to show them which way to go.

And after they were settled, they would meet me in the courtyard later for their first lesson.

And as they left, I could hear even more chatter starting up. Questions and rumours spreading quickly. I soon put a stop to that.

"Students!" I shouted. "I welcome you all to my home. And I trust that all of you will come to treat it with respect. While you are fully aware that I run a school for the elite every twenty-six years, what you do not know is its name."

I paused for dramatic effect, no point in just telling them, they were students after all, I was entitled to a little fun at their expense.

"Behind my mansion, lies the one and only Mages School for Enhanced Combat and Defence. More commonly known as Boot Camp." I told them.

They hadn't expected that.

I could see all of them questioning what to do. Some

would want to go back to Academia, some would want to stay but little did they know, they wouldn't get the choice.

I took a red flag out of my pocket, holding it up in the air for all of them to see. Pinching it ever so slightly, dangling it in front of me.

"This, is a piece of cloth!" I said.

I smiled, they laughed, nothing more to say.

"More importantly, this is the requirement for you to pass your entrance exam."

One boy at the front spoke his mind a little too loudly for his own good, something that he would continue to do throughout his stay at my school.

"What the fuck is he on about?" Said the boy.

However, while I say boy, he was twenty years old at least. One of the youngest of them but not quite young enough to be the youngest himself.

I ignored him though, I didn't have time to deal with him in the moment. For all I knew at the time, he wasn't going to be there for very long.

I'm saddened to say that I was wrong, he ended up becoming one of my students and one of my most talented fighters.

Though based on first impressions, I wouldn't have wanted him to be.

"In order to gain entrance to my school, you must take this flag from me before your opponent. You will all do this in pairs. After everyone has been up once, twenty-nine of you will have gained entry, leaving only sixteen more spots. For these spots the reaming twenty-nine of you will pair up again and again until all forty-five remaining places have been secured." I explained.

They seemed excited hearing about this news. Probably expecting it to be easy. Which was strange; normally they don't want to compete. Someone almost always insists they have the skill to be accepted. They always try to boast their way in.

Those are the ones I intentionally pair off against the more talented students.

"I will pick the pairs at random. You will both stand ten paces away from me, one to the left and one to the right. When I say go, do whatever you have to do to get the flag first.

Now who wants to have a go first?"

Almost all of them put their hand up in the air, begging to be the first.

So I pointed to two of them. They walked up and took their positions beside me.

"Alright, names?" I asked them.

"Victoria." One replied.

"Daron." Said the other.

"Round one, Victoria vs Daron." I shouted

I continued to hold the flag out in front of me, dangling it in the air.

"Begin." I yelled.

I watched eagerly, seeing the determination in their eyes. Their drive to make it through was admirable but pointless. This school wasn't for the kind hearted. Before long, they would be all but begging to leave.

Victoria moved first, immediately sprinting towards the flag. Daron didn't seem to move at all though. He had something up his sleeve instead. He allowed Victoria to think he was just going to stand there but he wasn't so still.

Behind his back I could sense the power building up in his palm. He intended to send the girl flying through the air, possible landing on her arse.

A moment later and his fist came out from behind him, garnishing a fire spell intended for ranged use. He fired the spell in the form of a flaming ball of magic energy heading her way but Victoria wasn't going to take this lying down.

She had originally put her arm out to grab the flag but now, she had clenched it into a fist, filling it with magic and stopping dead in place as I heard her shout the words.

"Defensive Flare."

Her hand lit up and a small dome shaped shield emitted from it. Deflecting the fireball and sending it right back at Daron. He dodged it but by then it was too late, Victoria had the flag in her hand.

I could see that Julian had been busy.

I saw him standing amidst the crowd, smirking at her pathetic attempt to use his spell. However, I was at least pleased that he hadn't kept it to himself.

Just because you invent a spell, doesn't mean that only you can use it, someone would have copied it eventually but this one felt taught. She knew what to do, as if Julian himself had told her.

"And the victor is, Victoria!" I shouted.

I grabbed her arm and put it in the air as if she had just one a wrestling match. Daron was pissed of course; he returned to the crowd and waited for his next try after he'd dusted himself off a moment later.

Victoria on the other hand was quite pleased with herself.

She grabbed her bags and made her way inside, from there Katiana would show her to the dorm rooms for her to take her pick.

The next few matches went by quickly. Round after round went by without a hitch. Everyone sticking to basic but effective techniques to slow the other. Softening the ground to make them lose their balance. Using wind or even lightning.

They did whatever they could think of to grab that flag.

And I got to learn a lot about each one of them as they did.

And then, after one hour, forty-three of the remaining forty-five spaces had been filled.

The remaining students were exhausted. Worn out from trying over and over again but what they didn't know was that none of them would be getting another go. I had left two particular students out on purpose.

I had intentionally left Julian for last but what I didn't expect was the other person who had also been left behind with him. It was the same girl form four years ago. The one who tried to blackmail me on the day he entered into Academia.

She was stood next to him, close by his side like a friend but looking closer it was far more than that. She wasn't just close to him, she was holding him.

His arm anyway.

I recognised this attachment and thought that putting them up against each other would be an interesting way of ending this little exam.

However, I never expected what occurred to actually happen the way that it did.

All I saw in that moment was an attachment, a very dangerous thing to have as a mage. If you have something to lose then someone will always take it from you eventually.

So I left those two for last in order to teach them that I wasn't going to go easy on them because they were cosy with each other.

Even if I considered Julian to be a friend, I wasn't about to make an exception. At my school, everyone is your enemy, even your friends.

I called them up by name this time. They took their places and prepared to fight for the flag. I shouted begin and they both did the same thing at the same time, resulting in quite the outcome.

They both stayed perfectly still, flicked their heads up towards the flag and suddenly teleported towards it.

With such a short distance to travel, I'm surprised they bothered, it would have been just as fast to sprint but the result of this was entirely unforeseen.

I suddenly felt a strong tug on the flag, I looked down to see who had grabbed it first and that's when I saw it. Both of their hands were on the flag.

They had grabbed it at the same time.

It was a draw.

This was the first time that this had ever happened.

I didn't quite know what to make of it. But I hadn't said it was against the rules to draw with your opponent, so an exception was made in their case.

They both got a place. Despite the intent I held by wanting them to go up against one another, the outcome threw that out of the window. They both got a place and my intent was forgotten.

The remaining students were quite upset as a result but I didn't leave them standing around for long enough for them to voice their concerns. I forcibly teleported them outside the barrier all at once and returned to the house to get back to more important things.

Normally, teleporting so many people all at once would be a death sentence in my condition but since it was such a short trip, I barely felt it.

With the teleportation block back in place on the barrier too, they weren't getting back in either.

I assume they went back to Academia eventually, however in doing so, I would never be seeing them again.

As soon as they returned to Academia, their minds would have been wiped of all information concerning me. Probably a little over the top but I liked my privacy and couldn't risk having a school full of students knowing where I lived.

This was just one of my conditions that Academia had to meet. In order for me to train these students, in order for me to fight this war, I requested, among other things, that all who get eliminated have their minds wiped clean of knowledge about me or where I live.

With that over and done with though, I congratulated Julian and his friend and made my way inside. Their first lesson was about to begin and even more surprises lied in wait for me there.

PROVING GROUND

.

With the entrance exam out of the way, I had been left with the fifty students that I'd been looking for. Fifty young and strong minds. Bodies ready to be worked into shape. Potential only just beginning to shine through.

These fifty students, these thirty-three boys and seventeen young girls, they would soon become the soldiers that would make up my army.

Soon these fifty souls, would be culled down to half their number, and prepared for the horrors that awaited them in the battle to come.

Each of them already had their own suspicions. Perhaps some could even sense the strange energy lingering in the air. Perhaps the strongest of them, Julian and this girl that appeared to be joined at the hip with him, maybe those two could already feel the presence of the pressure amassing right outside my barrier's walls.

More likely than not, most knew that something about their situation didn't quite fit right. The sudden change in their vocation and the urgency surrounding it all. Some of them probably saw through the lie.

But none of them truly knew what it was that puzzled

them so.

Even those who could tell that something about the environment wasn't quite natural, they wouldn't be capable of figuring out why. None of them had ever encountered corruption before now. And none of them had even the faintest ides idea of what that corruption truly was. They wouldn't have even realised what its presence in the airt meant for the world as a whole.

But it wasn't my place to tell them.

At least not yet.

These fifty students wouldn't have the stomach to accept what they were here to do if I told them now. They had yet to take the time to develop a taste for the carnage of battle.

These fifty students of mine were innocent souls. They had no place on the field of battle in such a war. Which was why it was now my role, to train them into the warriors that I needed them to be. Fighting for their own survival and that of everyone else on this forsaken rock alongside myself and Katiana a year from now.

And I had to admit. Even though those cracks above the clouds might have been the largest event I had ever seen in all my years, I also had to admit that the fifty students that I had been left with, were by far, some of the strongest and strangest that I had ever seen.

They all ranged in age and ability, anything from seventeen to twenty-three. Anything from basic casting magic to advanced enchantments. One of them could even manipulate the air pressure around them to make landing a punch almost impossible.

They were young and they were unfocused in their craft.

Yet to decide what aspect of magic they would study as

they grew older. Yet to find their stride. To identify their talents. The true extent of their abilities.

But all of them were chosen for the same reason in the end. Despite their ranging specialities and the spells they already had proficiency in, they were all equal to one another when it came to one important thing.

Their magical strength.

The aspect of a mage that determines the potential potency of any spell they cast. Beyond just forcing magic energy into it until the spells burns into ashes, a mage's magic strength is what put some mages above others even if they drew in terms of intellect and technique.

But strength alone is not all that there is to a warrior.

You need skill, experience, the will to fight your enemy, and of course, a great deal of luck to go along with that too.

In my experience, I have found that luck is quite possibly the best ally that a soldier can have when lacking in everything else against their enemy.

And learning how to rely on it and how to manipulate it could one day be the only thing that stops you from dying when in your final moments.

But in reality, luck is a conceptual thing. It doesn't tangibly exist. It is pure superstition when one believes their luck to be improving through their actions.

Would it be his bad luck that a soldier thanks in those final moments or would it be his own inability to fight harder? The answer was simpler than you'd think.

When all was said and done, the only thing that matters during any and all bloodbaths of war was our own ability to fight.

Our collective strength and defence, our ability to rely on

each other and not to be hopelessly dependant on our luck to make up for whatever we were missing.

That's how we'd win.

Through training and practice.

A lot of it. All crammed into a single year.

But these students were completely untrained in advance combat when I first met them. Heaps of yet untapped talent and potential steaming out of them all.

They were nothing more than hand grenades in those first few days.

Powerful, yes, but uncontrollable at best.

It was because of this that even though these students were of equal power on paper, in battle, they were all quite different.

Each one of them capable of most things while some of them specialised in magic that the others could never hope to master already.

They were strong, yes. Going places in the Magic World if they kept at it. But In the state that I had met them in, they wouldn't have lasted five minutes once the fighting began.

That is why they were at the school.

That is why I had a school in the first place.

To train them.

And after what felt like an hour or more, each one of those waddling children slowly came walking out of the dorms at last.

With them all settled into their new rooms and hopefully remembering which one they each chose, I trusted that they had remembered what I told them before. That their first lesson would begin shortly after they arrived.

I would later see to it that each student had remembered

their room numbers and had their keys on them too. And I would even make sure to drill in the rules of those dorms too. Making sure they understood how the gender restricting enchantments worked. Ensuring that they understood the consequences of breaking those boundaries or any other of the rules pertaining to their life within the dorms.

The gender restrictive enchantments don't physically stop a girl from entering a boy's room or vice versa but they were still quite effective.

If any student entered a room that did not belong to them, the enchantment would create a small amount of pain in their head until they left. But if they had entered a room belonging to another gender that pain would become unbearable over time.

While one encourages you to leave, the other forces you to. To some this seems a little harsh but to me, it didn't seem like enough.

These students were being trained for war and even if they didn't know about it, I wasn't about to let something as trivial as relationships get in the way of allowing them to reach their potential now.

One day they would all come to understand that everything I did was to ensure that they were ready, to ensure that they survived. And this included restricting their connections to one another of course.

But with everyone done and ready, I waited patiently for each of them to arrive on the courtyard for their first lesion as I had told them too.

I would have normally used the dojo for an exercise like this, but with Julian there to carry them all, I felt it better to kick things up a notch. The dojo simply couldn't handle what I had in mind.

And as they all gathered in the courtyard, I noticed that they had already begun to form makeshift relationships with one another. Standing next to people they knew or that they wanted to know, attempting to create bonds between them and figure out their places on the social food chain.

After this first lesson however, they wouldn't be so sure that these people were their friends anymore.

The school's main purpose was to train these students in battle, the best way to do this was to make sure that they had opponents; who better than their own classmates?

So I stood in the centre of the courtyard in front of the crowd. I said nothing and did nothing. I simply stood there with my arms behind my back, the dorm rooms behind me and a vast expanse of open field between the students and the house behind them. And staring at them with a fierce expression, I waited.

Staring at them intently in fact. Aad as they stared back at me, they also took the time to take in their surroundings. looking at the boundaries of the grass-covered box that they were stood in.

Unlike a normal school or academy, the courtyard was located in the centre of the three main buildings but it wasn't fenced off and had no barriers surrounding it.

It had no stone paths and no seats. No trees and no decorations. My courtyard was one of practicality. Nothing more.

It was a place of learning, not one of relaxing.

This courtyard served only one purpose.

It was an outdoor combat area. The only one within the

school barrier and the only place besides the dojo that was large enough for the students to fight one another without being smashed through walls or into the forest trees.

Given that I owned almost eighty acres of land, the students were most likely confused as to why they couldn't use the fields or the woodland areas as battlegrounds. But the answer was simple.

Those areas were outside of the school barrier that protected them. And thus, with no protection from themselves or to the other buildings I owned, any combat taking place beyond it would have endangered my property.

And god forbid, my house.

One could say that a simpler solution to this would be to just put a barrier around the house but I disagreed. When you think about the power contained within its walls. The priceless and powerful artefacts on display inside, and not to mention those within the vault – and when you consider that not only would this barrier need to protect the house but also hold these objects at bay if anyone ever touched them without realising the power right at their fingertips – then you come to the conclusion that nothing in the world would have been strong enough to hold it back.

The weapons alone could have quite easily broken through even my strongest barriers let alone the rest of the items. Putting a barrier around all of that would have simply destroyed the house rather than protect it.

Should one of the artefacts set itself off one day or if someone deliberately used one of them, the barrier would have contained the blast for a moment, engulfing it and forcing it back towards the house. Killing everyone and anyone inside the barrier at the time.

So any attempt to contain such power would have only destroyed the very thing that I was attempting to protect.

So my solution was to simply enchant the walls of the house to contain as much as I could and then place a barrier around the school should anything approach it.

I didn't have a problem with rebuilding or remodelling the house, I had done it many times before. However, the students didn't know this, they only knew that they were stood in the grass doing nothing.

I don't know what they were thinking but I could guess that they were quite confused at the time.

All they could see were the buildings and myself.

But instead of explaining it, I stood there patiently, waiting for them to figure out what it was that I was waiting for.

Nothing happened however.

I thought that this lesson would have been obvious. The school specialised in combat training and the courtyard was built for fighting on, surely they would have guessed that they needed to start throwing punches.

However, it soon became clear that they weren't going to move unless told to do so. And in the interest of saving time, I saw to it that they got started in another way.

I contacted Katiana telepathically, something that both Katrina and Julian soon picked up on as it seemed by the startled looks on their faces in that moment, and I asked her to fire a few arrows into the crowd.

Knowing what I had just said, both Julian and Katrina were the first to turn and duck down as the arrows flew overhead a moment later.

Non-lethal ones of course, they were formed of magic,

restricting the potency of their structure also restricted the damage output they could produce.

But they were still enough to hurt a man. Perhaps break an arm. But they wouldn't go all the way through. And besides, they weren't aimed with intent. At least not that time.

Those were warning shots. And they were more than enough make those students of mine realise what they should have been doing.

Katiana had teleported out of the house minutes ago and had long since taken up her position far behind my crowd of front facing students. Far out of sight towards our garden gates but still within range for me to sense her movements and for her to aim her shots by watching everyone else.

I could feel her energy as she summoned the bow, feel the strength of her muscles as she prepared to fire. Hear the hum of the arrows as the loosened and saw the fear on the faces of the students as they whizzed between their heads and smashed into glass shards of crystal against the enchanted walls of the school dorms having it no one.

But despite no one being hurt, they were pissed off. One of the students even had the audacity to direct that anger at me. Shouting in my face, demanding that I give an explanation.

"What's the meaning of this?" He said with a look of anger and confusion on his face.

He had only just realised what it was that had shot past him and had spoken out before thinking it through it seemed. He saw an arrow and immediately assumed that it was meant to harm them. In a sense, I suppose that it was but in truth, it was all part of their training. There was no ill intent here.

I had been waiting for that question all day though.

I knew exactly what to say and do after that.

I had done this so many times now that it was almost predictable that someone would ask.

Students, due to their lack of experience or knowledge, are always easy to predict. I had done this exact exercise so many times before that I had memorised every possible thing that they would do or say.

I knew what moves they would make before they had even thought of them. As though we were playing a game of chess, I was several turns ahead of my opponent even before the game had begun.

"This is a combat exercise." I said. "You should have expected there to be some 'combat' involved!"

I allowed them to regroup with one another while they caught their breath and wore off the shock, a lot of them had ducked and dodged in fear once the first arrow was seen, most of them did so in such haste that they all bumped into each other.

As expected.

"Students, your first lesson started ten minutes ago. The purpose and outcome of this lesson is simple. To group you into your classes. In order for this to happen, I need to know what you can do.

There are only two types of students in my school and thus only two classes. In one, those with fighting skills and in the other, those with more support-oriented skills."

I stood there in silence and waited after that.

I knew what they would do and it was only a matter of time.

280

And soon enough, one of them stepped forward to give it a go. Trying to show off.

He had a look of confidence and authority on his face and a clenched fist to his side.

"So this is a fight then?" He said as he opened his arms, drawing ever closer to me by the second.

"In a sense." I agreed. "However!"

He had gotten just close enough to reach me and took a swing; I stepped to my side and knocked him on his ass a moment later.

The rest of the students laughed a little in the process.

"Those who go around starting fights, often end up losing them." I explained to the boy.

He picked himself up off the floor and I pointed to the oak tree far off to my left beside the dojo, telling him to go and stand next to it in wait.

"But, since you struck first and had the courage to approach me while everyone stood still, you will be placed in my class. Go stand by that tree and watch the rest of your class mates as they fail to strike me just as you did." I said to him.

He seemed oddly glad to have heard that. Quickly walking over to the tree and standing there as instructed while I continued to teach the rest of them.

And now that they understood what to do, the real fun had begun.

"There are two ways to pass this test. Either get knocked senseless by me and join my class, or get hit by an arrow for not doing anything and join my wife's class." I explained. another one of them soon stepping forward. "Not so quick lass, this fight is not a one on one. It's a team effort. Work together, protect each other and do your best. Now come on then! I'm not getting any younger."

I waved my hand in the air and suddenly they all sprang into action.

Forty-nine students coming towards me like the march of an army.

But like always, not all of them went in for a strike.

Some of them stayed back, casting low-level enchantments or telling others what to do. Those were the students who were eliminated first. All struck by an arrow, still non-lethal of course, and sent to stand on my left once they had picked themselves up from the floor.

Those who find it too difficult to focus on fighting while worrying about defending their rear are always better suited for support rolls.

My wife's class filled up rather quickly too.

Almost twenty of her twenty-five students had been selected before I had even eliminated my second.

The first few to reach me were simple to take care of, using raw strength instead of magic. Those were the ones who were picked off the fastest. Using your fists would have been a suitable tactic against a more inexperienced opponent but against me, they should have started casting spells straight away.

The first wave of students to take their swings at me were quickly sent off towards the tree before the next wave came forth.

Using barely any effort at all, I avoided their attacks, responded with fire or high-pressure wind to knock them back and when that failed, I sent a pressure wave through the ground. Shaking the very dirt on which they stood until they lost their balance.

This left me with only twenty more opponents to go.

Five of them would end up with Katiana and the other fifteen would be mine.

But at least now that I'd warmed up, they were beginning to try a little harder.

Sparks flew through the air as someone pointed a hand directing two fingers towards me. The other hand was directed to their heart. A stance that I knew quite well indeed.

"Ah. Bioelectric amplification. Impressive." I told this student truthfully, looking at the bolt of lightning that had passed me by as it hit the dorms to assess its potency. "Only class two. Disappointing."

That part was honest too.

Normally if a mage knows enough about that spell to actually cast it, taking their own body's bioelectric field and expanding it, amplifying it into a stronger charge using your own magic energy and then channelling it through their arm to fire at an opponent in battle, they would at least be capable of producing something a little stronger.

But that was a high-level spell. More than I'd expected from level seven students. So, I was still impressed.

Holding back from the fight however, hiding within the remaining students and not making much of any attempt to show off, was Julian and that same girl from before.

They seemed to be working together though. But I didn't know what they were up to quite yet.

Finally though, someone in the group actually started showing some promise. Teleporting left and right to evade my kicks and fists.

His pattern was erratic, no sense to it at all and to make matters worse, I still had nineteen other students to deal with at the same time.

Soon it became too much to simply force them to evade my attacks as they got close to me, instead I actually had to start evading them.

Franticly dodging swing after swing and kick after kick before the ranged spells started flying overhead.

Crystal formations, ice and even fire were zooming past in an attempt to strike me. But they weren't all that well aimed or particularly powerful. However, in addition to those fighters already around me, dodging them still proved to be a challenge.

A few of them were still easy to deal with though.

I sent a few gusts of air beneath their feet to knock them over. To my disappointment and surprise this worked, dropping the remaining opponents down to twelve.

Just seven more to go at this point and I was done.

I saw arrows flying through the group all over the place, desperately trying to hit someone but none of them did.

The students were finally getting the idea, not standing still for too long and keeping a watchful eye of both their front and their rear at the same time.

For a moment, I was impressed. The fact that they could do such a thing without being taught it yet filled me with hope but that hope soon faded once I saw how easy they were to take out.

That was when I noticed who was coming for me next, it was Julian and his newfound friend.

He was out in front firing a barrage of elemental spells at me while she was behind, enchanting his movements and casting a deflection spell to divert the arrows from behind her at the same time.

Dual casting was an advanced skill.

She certainly had potential.

And they made quite the team those two.

I was amazed that they had managed to grasp the purpose of the exercise so quickly. Instead of attacking me one after the other, those two were actually working together. Casting spells to benefit each other and working in unison.

Most impressive.

I blocked what I couldn't dodge and used a wave of unfiltered magic energy to act as a veil in the air and dismantle whatever spell came at me next.

And even with his spells taken care of, I still had the man himself. And with Julian up in front, a few students stood still to watch in awe.

Their mistake.

The arrows hit their mark and finally Katiana's class was full. Leaving these final seven to me.

Normally I would have just ended the fight there but after quickly eliminating all but the final two, Julian and Katrina, I decided to have a little fun.

If these students wanted to prove themselves so desperately at this early stage, then I wasn't going to stop them.

Either way, I was eager to find out just how much Julian had progressed in those years at the academy.

Julian had taken the lead and the other students watching had gotten lazy as a result too. I made it look like I was simply dodging the attacks that Julian fed me but in truth, I had been targeting the other students the whole time. Knocking them down one by one as I avoided the fury of Julian's attacks.

This left me with two, the two that had actually been trying, the two who had been working together and the two who were proving most difficult to take out.

They were a truly impressive pair, fighting in unison with each other. Probably communicating telepathically throughout the ordeal to allow their actions to stay perfectly in sync.

Julian would hit me with whatever spells he could cast instantly and then when I went in for a punch after deflecting or blocking that spell, he would teleport out of the way, leaving behind a perfectly cast defensive shield from Katrina.

Not as powerful as something like Defensive flare or Fatal Mirror but strong enough to block a punch and much easier to cast.

They were more similar to barriers really but they couldn't sustain themselves autonomously and they weren't very large. That being said, it was impressive to see her cast them so quickly. She didn't even speak. The incantations were all in her head.

With how these two were fighting, I could have gone on until someone ran out of magic.

I was holding back immensely of course but even so, they were too. With how little effort Julian was placing into each attack I would guess that we were fighting equal to each other. And at that rate I would have had to up my game to win but I didn't have to in the end after all. Those two hey had a plan and were only just beginning to put it in motion.

I suppose that they had planned to hold back, keep me fighting at a lower level so that I wouldn't have time to react. With no enchantments, weapons or armour, I was weaker to everything. One quick and powerful strike and they could do some real damage. That was a plan that would have worked perfectly if I didn't have such a fast reaction time when it came to recognising danger.

I finally managed to get a punch in and sent Julian sliding backwards. Katrina caught him and then the most peculiar thing happened. They grabbed each other's hands and began reciting a spell, well Julian did at least, Katrina was mute after all.

The power boiling up inside of them was enough to shock me at first and even from the distance that she was standing at, Katiana could feel it too.

It wasn't long after their hands had touched that I saw her teleport closer to assess the situation.

At first, I didn't recognise the incantation, it was being said so fast and with such poor pronunciation that it was like a foreign language. However, it didn't take long to figure out what it was purely from what they were doing.

That stance, the formation of the magic in the air and the placement of the sigils emanating from them, there was only one spell it could have been.

And once I had realised what spell it was that they were casting, I immediately shifted into my Athereon form as fast as I could to survive the blast when it hit.

Final Stronghold, that was the spell.

A spell requiring two people to cast, one to supply the energy required and one to act as a bullet and fire the shot. This spell surrounds the caster in a veil of magic energy, one so strong that it acts as both shield and sword as it surrounds them perfectly like a flowing river of water descending from their head.

But unlike a shield or a sword, should this energy hit someone or something else, it is transferred into them and created quite the fireball as a result there after.

And as long as the caster is surrounded by this veil of energy, many things are possible. They would have speed, more than even the fastest moves that I could produce, enough strength to break bricks and the ability to fly.

Just like a bullet being fired out of a barrel, the mage wearing this veil would travel through the air until he met his target.

It was quite the spell, one so powerful and complex that only a handful of mages that I had trained knew how to pull it off.

I was surprised to see such power in the hands of Julian and even more surprised to see the same power possessed by that girl.

That event was most peculiar.

The spell was so strong that at one point in history there were discussions over banning it. Only the most destructive spells are ever considered to be forbidden and this one certainly qualified as destructive.

It was designed for the purpose breaking through any defence that was held up against it. But despite its destructive force, it remained legal for the simple reason that it was very rarely ever fatal.

If it had a one hundred percent chance of killing its target, it would have been forbidden long before Julian had even been born. I guess that it's a good thing that a mage can survive more damage than a normal human then.

But when I realised what was really going on it was already too late. Julian had stated glowing and was already heading straight for me by the time my shift had completed.

I put my fist out to try and cast a barrier but I quickly realised that it wouldn't have been strong enough to hold out against that spell.

Even my barriers couldn't survive a blast from Final Stronghold and to make matters worse, I didn't have time to place one anyway.

I don't know why I did but the only spell that I could think of, the only spell that I thought would have a chance of surviving the power of that blast was Julian's. The only spell with any chance of protecting me without killing him as a result was Defensive Flare.

A spell that I myself had never even cast before.

I made a fist, said the words and to my amazement it was just like Julian had told me. My body did the rest.

I could feel the new circuits form as it was cast, layer upon layer melding with those that I already possessed.

It was a strange sensation in truth. As if the spell itself had a mind of its own. It was almost as if I wasn't casting the shield, it was like I had cast a spell that had cast a shield for me.

I didn't feel like I had done anything at all.

But just at the last moment, the spell was cast and it was magnificent. The feeling that it created, the sense of protection that it filled you with; it was completely un-nerving.

The shield formed, a shell over five meters wide and less than an inch in front of my hand that was already just a handful of feet from Julian as he flew in.

Even though this was the first time that I had cast the spell, even though I had never practiced it before, it was still stronger than any that the students could have made. After all, I was in my Athereon form, I had five if not seven times the magical strength that they would ever have.

And when Julian came, his fist punching against my shield, the power of his spell was sent towards me. Protecting him entirely as it left his body. And soon after, the blast held within finally went off.

I saw the magnificent glow of red flames as the shockwave bounced off of the shield. Or should I say shockwaves. The power released by that explosion wasn't dispersed as quickly as it should have been.

For many seconds after the initial impact, the flames continued to burn, the whit-hot glow of the explosion continued to illuminate my surroundings and the pulsating shockwaves from the blast continued to bounce violently off of the shield over and over again.

The light dimmed and the shockwaves subsided after fifteen seconds. The spell had stopped being cast and a large puff of smoke and ash filled the air soon after.

Then all I could hear was a telepathic scream.

The word.

'JULIAN!'

When the dust settled, I saw Katrina lying on the floor not Julian. Her arms were out as wide as they could go planted directly in front of him.

She must have teleported in when she realised what I was doing. A foolish and selfless thing to do and it could have killed her.

Normally there wouldn't have been a need to protect Julian, the veil of energy surrounding him should have outlasted the explosive power of the spell but it hadn't.

The spell had been prolonged by something and as a result, his shield had dissipated before the flames had died down. She must have seen it from her end and jumped in to protect him.

If I had realised that he was in danger I would have done the same, but I would have at least tried to protect him with magic rather than my body.

Perhaps she was too drained to do so, or maybe she didn't have time. I don't know. And all I do know is that she jumped in to save him and it had worked.

When I saw her body, the charred skin and clothes, the smell of freshly burned long pig and the sight of her wounds, I feared that I was already too late.

The only word that came to mind in that moment wasn't too impressive. All I could think to say was.

"Shit."

I stopped casting Defensive Flare and lowered my hand, the cracked remains of my shield dissipated quickly and soon disappeared altogether.

Normally I would have taken a moment to express a little surprise when I realised that Defensive Flare was capable of deflecting such a powerful spell but I didn't have the time. Every second was crucial now, Katrina laid on death's door before me and I wasn't too sure that I could get her away from it.

I shifted back to human and rushed forward to help her.

By the time I got there, Katiana and Julian were already finished healing her. That was a surprise I suppose. The wounds looked too deep and devastating to have been healed so quickly but this was Katiana I was talking about. She had spent a lot of time healing my own wounds. She knew how to efficiently get a body back to its best.

But that didn't matter at the time, all that did was that by some miracle, I hadn't lost a student on that day.

She was quite the resilient girl. That much was true.

Being that close to the explosive nature of the flames when it happened should had ripped her apart.

And besides that, Julian would have been fine if she had left him, he had already been moving backwards, just far enough that the explosion wouldn't have affected him too badly beyond the odd burn but still she had decided to protect him.

And while her life had been spared, her clothes had not.

It was a pity too, those robes of hers looked expensive, as if she had dressed to impress that day. No matter, clothes were physical possessions, they could be replaced.

Once I realised that she was going to be alright after a little rest, I dismissed the students with their faces of awe and sent them back to their dorm rooms.

I needed to have some words with Julian and this girl and those words were not to be overheard.

And while she was already healed, she was still unconscious from the pain.

So Julian and Katiana carried her to my office and laid her down on the makeshift sofa I had in the corner. On some nights that sofa served as more of a bed than a chair. Occasionally I would wear myself out so much from training throughout the day that I simply couldn't carry myself to bed. But while I call it a sofa, it was actually just a pile of boxes and a lot of cushions on top of them.

It seated three though. But not too comfortably.

I followed them in through the door and had already started to list the array of questions that I had to ask, one of the most pertinent being where they hell they had learnt that spell.

Julian stayed by her side, holding her hand during most of the conversation.

Unlike the girl, he was fine. She must have shielded him from the entirety of the blast when it hit.

I looked down at him for a moment, not really looking at anything specific but still something about the way he acted forced my eyes to focus on him and her.

That was when I finally noticed the matching gold rings on their fingers. Those two had gotten married at some point in the four years since I had seen them last.

For someone as observant as me, I was surprised to have not noticed this sooner.

I sat down at my desk and Katiana, being a more sensitive person than me, sat down next to Julian and offered some form of emotional support.

I'm not the emotional type though. While I do feel emotions, I have lived so long and experienced so much loss that I'm numb to most of them now.

"So Julian, you can probably guess that we have some questions but let's start with a simple one. When the hell did you decide to marry her? Last I checked she was trying to blackmail you."

Katiana seemed shocked for a moment after that, franticly trying to figure out how I had surmised that those two were wed.

It didn't take her long to notice the rings and soon after that she was filled with an expression of happiness. She was happy for him, glad that he had found companionship and happy to see that he had found someone who he could finally call his family.

Back when he was first living with us, not long after Katiana actually became attached to him like a mother, she was worried that he had never known what family was.

He'd never known his mother or his father, never had siblings or children. She was concerned with his social growth because of this and while she was right to do so, in the end there wasn't a need for it. He had found his companion and had wasted no time in making her his.

Julian smiled in response to my question.

I guess that he had intended to tell us eventually but being forced to explain it the way that he was doing must have been quite unexpected.

"Not long after I met her to be honest. While she initially just wanted to talk with me, she and I eventually couldn't get enough of each other, after the first few months that is.

Once we got past the blackmailing thing and actually got to know each other, we realised that we were a perfect fit and were dating within a month.

We were soon told that in order for relations to exist between students we had to be married or face expulsion. So, we talked about it and one thing led to another and now here we are I guess."

"Well that's one way of getting hitched." I said.

I didn't intend to stop talking there but before I could get to my next question, Katiana had gotten in there first. Probably to stop me from saying something insensitive if I had to guess.

"She risked her life to save you, that says it all. She must really care for you Julian. But tell me, where on earth did the two of you learn that spell. It's not officially listed as something that Academia is allowed to teach." She inquired.

"Final Stronghold?" Julian asked.

"That's the one." Katiana nodded, looking into his eyes attempting to draw his attention away from his unconscious wife.

"It was a wedding present from …the Headmaster." Julian said reluctantly.

I sat there in shock for a moment and then couldn't stop the words from coming out.

"That old fart gave you and her a level twenty-four spell, designed for destroying fortresses as a wedding present?" I yelled.

"While normally level seven mages would be imprisoned for even knowing the spell, let alone using it, he had the Council make an exception in our case." He replied.

Katiana didn't say anything about it but I could see her rage filling up inside. She obviously didn't know anything about this. The Council had kept something from her yet again and this time it was something important.

They had gone behind her back before but never like this. To have granted special permission to a newly recruited mage to use a level twenty-four spell is unheard of and to make matters worse, the head of the Council hadn't even been consulted.

She only found out about it years after it had happened.

I ignored her frustration and moved onto my next question swiftly to try and snap her back into the moment. If she had dwelled on the Councils betrayal for long, she would have eventually done something that she would have regretted later.

"What led him to do this then?" I asked.

I set back in my chair and crossed my arms, I couldn't believe the man. The last time I wanted a student to learn Final Stronghold he refused to even consider it, only allowing me to do so once she had become Crown Mage.

Completely ignoring our wedding at the time.

Katiana was exceptionally strong and more than capable of performing the spell at the time, he only said no because I had asked him.

It was above her rank and if I had asked him to do it, the Council would have used it against him. Going against the law is one thing, but when I'm involved, the Council goes looking for blood and always seems to find it.

"He saw us competing in the school tournament in our first year and realised how well we complimented each other. At least that's what he said, whether or not it's true is anyone's guess." He replied.

Julian released his grip of Katrina and turned his chair to face me. He had obviously come to accept that she was fine and returned his attention back to the conversation at hand.

"Master, I assume that you do not approve of us knowing that spell?" He asked.

"On the contrary, I'm glad that the two of you know something that powerful, it will help in the months to come. However, what I do not approve of is her carelessness. The risk that she took to protect you was reckless and unnecessary. The blast would have hurt, yes, but you were never in any real danger. However... I am confused as to what made the spell last as long as it did. Your protective veil should have outlasted it." I pondered.

"Yes, that puzzled me as well. The last time I cast it, the blast lasted only a moment at best. Something obviously went wrong I guess. Wait!" He looked at me with a sense of joy appearing on his face. Something had obviously clicked inside that head of his. "So you mean, were not in trouble?" He asked.

"Normally using a spell that strong during a friendly match would have landed you cleaning the dojo with a toothbrush for the next week but considering that the aim of the test was to see what you can do, I think that I'll let this one pass. But if in future you two get into a fight that isn't life or death, the use of that spell will land you both being separated, both in the dorms and in class." I said.

"Thank you Master… Wait…" He said, pausing for a moment to think. I could see that he had caught on to what I was saying. "So you're saying, we can share a room together?"

I smiled like an adolescent teen as I said this.

"As long as you cast noise cancelling enchantments on the walls, then just like in Academia, for now I will allow it." I told him.

The rules on relationships in Academia were quite simple. Married students get a private dorm to themselves, separated from the main dorms by lock and key.

Even the corridor leading to the couple's dorms was locked away. Other students weren't allowed anywhere near them. As for newly formed relationships, they are given a little leeway but if the teachers start noticing that the two students in question are becoming too obvious, they are given choice. Break up or marry.

I could see quite easily which one Julian and Katrina had chosen. I could also understand why the Headmaster had felt the need to teach the two of them that spell.

Knowing what he did and that the two of them were going to end up in my school eventually, he must have thought that it was a spell that they would need.

He knew that they would have no problem getting through the entrance exam; he also knew that they would be the strongest pair in the school.

He must have known that they would have no problem graduating, that they would one day be fighting the war on the frontlines.

I understood why they had been given that spell, it was because he didn't want them to die the same way that some of his friends had done back when he fought alongside me on the battlefield.

I didn't quite understand why he would teach them this without my consent, it was a spell that was capable of many things, most dangerous of which being that it was capable of breaking through almost any other defence I had.

There was a reason that I wasn't allowed to use it anymore and it was the same reason why I wasn't allowed to teach it anymore. It was simply too powerful and too uncontrollable.

In the wrong hands, that spell could have even toppled the Citadel. And that thing was built to last. So that's saying something.

But I sat in my chair and took some time to think. It wasn't long after that, that Katrina herself regained consciousness. So my thinking would have to wait. Proper introductions were in order first.

'What? Where am I?' Her voice asked inside my head.

Katiana seemed shocked.

I then remembered that I had never explained just how powerful this telepath was. She probably wasn't too happy to know that there was a student who could break into people's minds so easily.

Julian answered her first. His telepathy had improved greatly over the past four years, probably from talking to her all the time.

'Master's Office, how are you feeling, can you sit up?'

'Yes, I feel fine, I should be able to.' She replied.

Julian grabbed her arm and helped her up. It was then that she noticed my wife and I were also in the room.

'Oh, hello again.' She said.

That was obviously directed at me as she had never met Katiana before so I replied swiftly.

"Katrina.' I nodded. 'This is my wife Katiana."

I waved my hand in Katiana's direction.

"Do say hello dear." I said.

Katiana wasn't as adept at telepathy as this girl, I thought that if I kept it to a minimum, she might be able to cope a little better.

"It's very nice to meet you, Katrina." She said. They shook hands as Julian moved to sit next to her on the sofa.

'You're the Crown Mage… aren't you?' Asked Katrina.

"That's correct."

Katiana smiled, thinking that the girl was impressed, really she was just frightened. Even students still under the legal protection of their masters fear the power and authority of the Magic Council.

'Please don't brand us, we were given permission for that spell I swear!' She pleaded.

Katrina began to try and beg my wife for freedom, not realising that there was nothing to fear. I laughed a little; I should stop doing that I guess.

"Don't you worry child, no one is going anywhere. In fact, we were just discussing your sleeping arrangements." Katiana replied.

'My what?'

"Now that we have been made aware of your circumstances I have chosen to make an exception in the dorm room rules. You and Julian can share a room." I said.

She suddenly stood up and did something most peculiar, she bowed. She was just as formal as Julian I guess. Although it wasn't necessary. Formalities are reserved for important events or when first meeting someone, she didn't need to bother with them over such a simple matter.

'Thankyou sir.' She said.

"You will address me as Master from today on young lady. After all, I am your teacher now." I replied.

She stopped bowing and corrected herself.

'Yes, yes of course, Master. I look forward to tomorrow's lessons.' She said.

"As you should do. Now return to your dorm room, I believe you have some luggage to move. Dinner will be severed in the cafeteria in six hours. You have until then to do as you please. The full list of rules and expectations can be found on the noticeboard in the dojo. You have free reign of the campus too but you are not to leave it. That is all."

Those rules I mentioned, they were unlike any that these students have seen before. Since the purpose of this school is combat training, the rules complimented that.

Rule one. Students will stay within the school barrier unless instructed to leave.

Rule two. Students will observe the boundaries of gender specific areas at all times.

Rule three. Unless otherwise unable to, you are expected to cast your own healing spells should injuries occur.

Rule four. Should a fight erupt at any time, students are expected to stop and continue the brawl in the dojo until a victor is decided fairly and in the presence of at least two witnessed.

Rule five. Lethal spells are forbidden except when used during safe and supervised, practice lessons.

Rule six. You will make no attempt to copy any of the Athereon's spells unless instructed to do so.

Rule seven. Teleporting into and within the dorm rooms is strictly forbidden.

Rule eight. When class is in session, you will leave only when told to do so.

Rule nine. The hallways and classrooms are decorated with real and deadly weaponry. Should you take one of those weapons without permission your punishment is to fight your teacher with it. Last more than thirty seconds and it's yours to keep.

Rule ten. Good luck, only 23 students can pass this course.

The standard rules of the world still applied of course. Forbidden spells were still forbidden and killing another mage would not be forgiven under any circumstances.

Trespassing is dealt with by force if necessary and revealing any part of the Magic World to humans would result in branding within a day of doing so.

As for my rules, they weren't particularly long or detailed by design. This made them both easy to remember and also easier to bend in order to fit any situation as I wish.

But it never came to that, not once during their stay did any of the students break a rule, nor did they attempt to claim a weapon.

Probably out of fear, not wanting to have to fight me at full strength let alone with weapons, even if it was for a mere thirty seconds, I don't think that anyone would have even thought about it.

After all, none of the students had ever used a real weapon in combat before, how could they possibly hope to use one against me in a simple sparring match and actually win?

Even if winning simply meant that you needed to stay standing for a set amount of time, I doubted anyone was willing to give it a go.

Rules were one thing though. Anyone can name a restriction that they want to put in place, it's in our nature. There are always going to be things in our lives that we want to control and rules are just one of the ways that we maintain that control but getting people to follow those rules is much more difficult.

I had the luxury of having every student fear me.

They wouldn't have dared to actually test my limits.

But if any one of those students were to break the rules it would have been Julian. He knew me, better than any of them did. If there was anyone who had the nerve to break one of the rules, it would have been him.

He had the best bet of surviving whatever punishment he

would receive too.

With everything said and done there was no reason for the two of them to stay any longer though. Katrina and Julian left the room shortly after I told them to.

I intended to do the same but it seemed that Katiana had more to say. Something that soon filled me with even more fear on top of what I had already experienced that day.

"She worries me." Katiana said.

"I know what you mean. She is the most talented telepath that I have ever seen, her abilities shock even me." I said.

"That's not what I mean. It's how she acted, how obvious the looks on her face were, how still her heart was. It's almost as if she's pretending to have emotions." Katiana suggested.

"Yes, that bothered me too." I replied.

Then Katiana got up and showed me something, something that bothered me even more than the way the girl had acted. Something that would end up being far more important than anything that had happened so far on that day.

What she showed me, it was so impactful, so undeniably important that if she had showed it to me while we were in the middle of battle, I would have stopped doing anything else at the time in order to deal with it. Even if that meant dying a few times.

"There's also this."

She spoke with fear and sadness in her voice. She held the palm of her left hand up to me. And all I could see was a patch of black and rotten skin, a wound the likes of which I hadn't seen in a very, very long time.

"How did this happen?" I asked.

I panicked a little, grabbed her hand and desperately tried to heal it. Forcing so much energy into the spells that they should have been able to heal anything apart from death.

With so much energy the spells should have regrown limbs but the mark wouldn't go away. I could see her hand shaking as I cast spell after spell trying to heal it. The shaking meant that the spell was entering her body but it wasn't doing anything as a result. All I was doing at the time was wasting what little energy I had left.

"I've already tried that and it's pointless. No matter what spell I use it won't go away." She said, almost crying in the process.

I looked at her face and saw how scared she was. Tears were beginning to form and my efforts were achieving nothing. Not one of the two dozen healing spells I tried had done anything, not a single spell could heal her wound. Even those designed to regrow organs or cure cancer did nothing.

"How did you get this mark?" I shouted.

I grabbed both her shoulders and gave her a small shake. Trying desperately to get an answer out of her. She immediately focused on my face and all I saw in hers was the fear that she felt.

"It happened when I was firing arrows from my bow. After the first five or so, I could feel a slight burning sensation in my palm. By the time that I stopped firing the pain had faded but when I put my bow away... I could see what it had done. There was no burn, no inflammation, just this mark."

I took another look at her hand, this time ignoring the

fact that it was a wound and instead looking at its shape. To my amazement and my dismay, the mark, looked exactly like the grip on her bow.

Never had I felt more fear than in that single moment. Never had I been more afraid for the wellbeing of my wife and I intended to never feel that way again.

"The bow resisted you?" I asked.

"I think so."

Her eyes began to water even more, almost erupting into a barrage of tears. She knew as well as I did what was happening. When a weapon that has been bound to you resists your magic energy, it is a sign of one of three things. A sudden loss of magic energy, pregnancy or an early warning of a corrupted magic growing within her circuits.

All of these can be fatal, even the pregnancy. A mage cannot survive childbirth when that child is mine; neither can the child itself. The level of magic required to keep the child alive is too great, even for a mage as strong as she was. It would have killed her and subsequently the child as well. There simply isn't a way of holding enough magic energy to keep yourself and the child alive, it would need far too much.

But none of those three possible causes were the true source of the rejection. At the time, I had no idea what had caused it but I knew how to make it go away.

I grabbed her hand and held on tight. What I did next was probably a little foolish but it worked. I focused all of my energy into my hands, draining every magic circuit I had. Focusing all of it into a spell that I have never had to use before. One that I had only ever described to her, never showing her the true extent of what it could do or what it costs.

It was a type of healing spell, a very specific and powerful one, a forbidden one. It drains the casters life force in order to heal the target. Or in my case, it would have used up a few hundred of the several million more times I could resurrect myself.

My hands began to glow green brightly within an instant. And then it only intensified from there.

Soon enough she figured out what I was doing. There were very few spells that give off a green hue and only one of them was designed for healing. She knew exactly what I was doing and what it was about to cost.

She said nothing at the time, only scolding me later that night. Every bit of energy I had went into that spell, every single drop that was keeping me on my feet at the time.

The light it gave off was so bright that later that night, the students would ask me what it was.

My body went numb and the spell began to activate. Spirals of sigils filled the room, covering our hands like a snake, casting a spell that no one but myself and Katiana knew existed.

And when the light faded, so too did my strength. I almost fell off my feet but I couldn't allow that. I had to see first. I needed to know that it had worked.

I let go of her hand and took a peek. The mark was gone as I had hoped, but deep down, I could still feel its effect on her.

There was no immediate danger from what I could tell. I didn't sense a lack of magic energy within her, no child in her womb and no corruption in her circuits. But I knew that if one weapon had resisted her, the rest probably would as
306

well.

To keep her safe, I told her not to use any of them for a while but just like all women, she didn't listen.

Unfortunately, I did not have the luxury of comforting her there and then. I had a dinner to prepare, for all fifty of the students and the two of us as well.

I retreated to the cafeteria to begin preparations and to rest, I told her to come and see me if she needed anything but she never did. At the time, I was amazed that I could even walk, let alone prepare a meal for fifty people.

But it was later that night that my lack of energy came back to bite me. If only I had drained my Athereon form to heal her, maybe then I would have been able to help her when it happened. But alas, I had used too much energy and as a result, I was too weak to do anything but watch.

Under any other circumstances, I would have stayed in that room and just stood there, holding her close. But at the time, there were things that I couldn't ignore.

While I was truly worried about her, I knew that she was out of danger for the time being. So I returned to my students and left her behind.

But looking back on it now, maybe that was a mistake.

Then again, how could I have known what was going to happen? I had nothing but the evidence to go on and none of it could have possibly led me to the truth.

All I knew was that something had possessed her weapons to resist her. I had no way of knowing the true extent of what that signified.

How could I have done?

All I knew was that something wasn't quite right with my wife, I had no way of knowing just how serious that problem would soon become at the time.

I only wish that I had. Perhaps with a little more insight on my part at the time, I could have avoided the events that followed.

After all, as someone who is meant to protect others, I should have foreseen that event. I should have known that she was still in danger. It was my job to know, my purpose in life. My reason for being, just as any other husband should have done, I should have protected my wife.

I should have moved heaven and earth to protect her.

To save her.

I should have realised the danger and done everything in my power to remove it.

If only I had looked into the cause of that injury rather than focusing on removing it, then maybe… maybe I just might have saved her from what was to come.

Maybe… I could have also prevented the sacrifice.

The one that I should have never made.

ATHEREAL ENERGY

The late hours of that dreadful day soon approached.

I had no cause to postpone any further. The entrance exam was done with. The students had been separated into their classes and were now busy entertaining themselves elsewhere throughout the school

Exploring the dojo and the classrooms, the cafeteria and the dorms. They had free reign of the campus site. And they were taking advantage of that freedom. Already beginning to practice their magic outside of lessons without my consent.

I could feel them outside the walls of the cafeteria. Practicing their telekinesis and teleportation. Over and over again like they were trying to force their skills to improve right then and there.

I monitored them from afar however.

I could trust that they weren't stupid enough to break the rules on day one. And I could trust that they weren't suicidal enough to try and cast a spell that was beyond them just for the sake of it.

Though, it was entirely my fault that they even had this free time to begin with. I hadn't continued the day to the second lesson after their first.

I couldn't.

Katrina's condition necessitated careful attention in the moment, I had no choice but to dismiss the class and direct my focus towards her recover. And then after that was done with and I would have gone back to the second lesson of the day, Katiana's condition had cost me almost all the magic energy I had recovered since dawn.

I didn't have the energy to continue teaching that day.

But the day after that would be different.

I would set my schedule and stick to it.

There would be no distractions from here on. I swore it.

And with Katiana left behind having been healed of the initial effects of her corruption, I thought she'd be capable of coping on her own for the time being.

Of course I wanted nothing more than to stay with her, to figure out what had caused that mark to appear on her hand all of a sudden and to reassure her that everything was going to be alright. But I couldn't.

While I might not have been thinking rationally when I cast that spell to heal her, I was defiantly thinking rationally when I decided to walk away.

If she had still been in danger, if I had believed there to be an imminent threat upon her life then I might have acted differently. But at the time, there were more important matters to attend to in light of my ignorance.

Some would think it strange for a man to have something more important to do than look after his wife but for me, I didn't really have a choice but to go back to my routine as quickly as possible.

The events of that morning had made it clear to me already that I wouldn't have any time to waste this year.

THE ATHEREON: WINTER'S WAR

There were two Tears in the sky, a barely holding barrier keeping them at bay and fifty untrained students that were nowhere near strong enough to fight against them.

I left my wife alone in my office because in that moment I had weighed the odds and decided to put the fate of the world above her own.

I had ignored the possible outcomes from having that mark on her hand and I returned to my students as though nothing had happened in the thirty minutes I'd been gone.

And if I was to train them well enough to fight against what was coming, I didn't have the luxury of time on my side anymore.

Every moment was important now. And every second both within and without the classrooms had to be well spent at all times.

So I got back to work.

Heading for the kitchen of the cafeteria, keeping my ear to the wind to monitor their activities and making sure that they behaved themselves as that day slowly turned to night.

And as that night crept in, they were surely realising that it was their day of training and I hadn't fed any of them yet.

If I couldn't even get them to trust me enough to rely on me to make their food on time, then how would I have ever gained enough of their trust for them to fight alongside me on the battlefield?

So knowing what I had to do, I made the choice to leave my wife behind that day in order to head for the kitchen. And that was a choice that I have regretted ever since.

I abandoned my wife when she needed me most and I returned to what I should have been doing instead.

Looking after the students.

I might have been left with plenty of time between healing Katiana in that office and the time when I should have been serving the food. However, it seemed that I might not have been left with enough.

With how preoccupied and distracted I was with the wellbeing of Katiana and the imminent doom looming overhead, I ended up taking a great deal more time than I should have done to prepare that food.

I ended up spending the whole of the six hours that I had to prepare and then serve the dinner just cooking it. There was so much to do and so little time to do it in.

If I had been in the right frame of mind then maybe I wouldn't have taken as long but with everything that had happened and the state that I was in, I had been left operating at anything but peak efficacy.

A meal for fifty would normally take a while to cook due to the sheer quantity of food needed, that much was true for both humans and mages, but it shouldn't have taken six hours on our side of the border.

I should have been able to do it in three if not two.

Telekinesis would have allowed my sole person to do the work of ten in that kitchen. Other spells would have allowed the control of the temperature and texture of the food as well. Some would have even provided me with ample time to ignore a boiling pot as the spell prevented the water inside from evaporating off too far.

If I had been cooking as a mage, I could have done all of that so much faster than I did in the end.

But the fact that it took six hours working by hand only further proves that I wasn't very concentrated.

After healing Katiana in the way that I had, I was

practically running of fumes I'll admit.

I had no ability to cast any spell at the time. And certainly no way of speeding up my cooking. No way of easing my exertion in the slightest.

So at the time, I had to do every part of the cooking by hand. Which for a mage, should have almost never been necessary.

Any use of magic would have surely made me collapse though. I was too week to even move at my natural pace at times. Even my muscles were begging me to stop and rest.

And while it is true that I could regenerate magic energy faster than anyone else, that doesn't mean that I can use it without end.

There are always limits to what I can do and this was one of them.

With how much energy I had used throughout the night it would have taken two or more days to recover all of it. And then what little I had recovered was used up in its entirety by the end of that morning.

Even after the six hours I spent cooking, I had barely recovered a smidge of my strength. I was still far too weak to perform at my best.

And it wasn't long after I left Katiana in my office that the time for the students to have lunch arrived. Which gave me even less time to get on top of everything as I now had to prepare and serve fifty cold meals as well as prepare the fifty hot meals for later.

They gathered in the dining hall and crowded around the kitchen window as though they owned the place one by one in quick succession.

Prancing around as though nothing mattered anymore at

first. But I noticed this and soon took care of it during their next lesson.

If they didn't want to respect my property then I would just have to scare them into taking care of it.

I would have said something then and there but I was too tired to do anything about it in the moment. So I allowed them to continue as they were without mentioning it. But I certainly didn't forget about it.

They all took at least one item of food from the display of plates I had arranged on the counter and they each took the odd drink of water too.

But for those who did not choose to drink water or freshly made orange juice, there was the tea. And I severed them so much tea that I was worried I might not have enough left for myself after they were done.

I was curious to find out what had made them require so much of the beverage though. They hadn't exerted themselves too much throughout the morning, there was no way that any of them were drained.

Perhaps they were just drinking it to ensure that they would be at the top of their game for the following day but they must have known that it didn't work like that.

Simply sleeping would have given them more than enough time to recover all of their energy without the aid of the tea. And if they took the time to meditate in a magic circle to amplify their regeneration of magic energy it would have been even faster.

Whatever their reason though, they took their tea and went about their business. Most of them had questions to ask of course, queries about what had happened on the courtyard, curiosities about what that strange light from my office had been.

I answered most of what I could. Doing my best to bury their curiosity about the light and shifting their interest towards the spell that Julian and Katrina had cast.

However, I couldn't tell them much about that subject either. If they wanted to know anything more than what I could tell them then they would have to ask Julian himself.

It was his business after all.

But the lunch period didn't last long and soon the immense chatter that had filled the hall went silent and the students retreated to the dorms.

They weren't restricted to their rooms though. Just the building itself. They were welcome to visit the dining hall if the needed anything to eat or drink but they weren't allowed to stay in there forever either.

There were rooms specifically designed for recreation and the dining hall wasn't one of them.

They had the freedom to go anywhere in the building and do anything they wanted, within reason anyway. And with the wide array of books on offer in the student library in the basement, it must have seemed too good to be true to them at first.

So much knowledge up for grabs free of charge whenever they wanted it. Academia would have never allowed such a thing. Every part of their leaning had to be perfectly scripted and monitored.

But I didn't agree with that.

I preferred that my students choose to learn what they want to when they want to. More often than not it speeds up the process considerably.

But the fact of the matter remained, they would have

never been given that kind of free reign in Academia.

While you're a student within its walls, you will go where you are instructed to go when you are told to do so without question.

The only freedom that they got during the day was at lunch or just before dinner.

So for those students, this was most likely the first time they had ever experienced this form of luxury and once they left, they weren't likely to ever find it again.

With the war looming overhead, invisible to the untrained eye, they wouldn't have long to enjoy it before they would be fighting to ensure that luxuries like that would still exist when the battle was over.

Many hours passed after that.

Dinner came along and went splendidly

Followed swiftly by an even more successful evening. Every one of the students seemed to be fully integrated into their new home by then. And it was a good thing too.

The faster that they got used to life in my school the easier it would be to teach them.

Little did they know though, that there wasn't going to be much time to relax from there on. Because the next day would see the start of their real training.

The lesson that they had had on the day was nothing, it didn't even really count as a lesson in my book. All it did was show me who was best suited for what roll. From there I can sort them into their classes and begin teaching them what they would acclimate to the fasted the following day.

Starting from then they would be learning new and more powerful spells the likes of which they had never seen or could have hoped to imagine.

Doing and seeing things that they could never dream of. Practicing and training in techniques that no other academy would have ever dared teach.

And slowly over the next twelve months, they would eventually become the warriors that I would need them to be in order to help me win the war that was to come.

During the dinner service that night, I gave them all their first drink too.

This would have been the first time that any of them had tasted alcohol by my guess. Being in Academia from the age of fifteen or earlier in most cases meant that you missed out on a few things growing up.

This includes your independence as a contributing member of society of course. The ability to form meaningful and strong relationships with peers not of your own age. And also, this would indefinably isolate you from everything outside of the academy walls right up until the day you graduated as a fully qualified mage.

Put simply, that night was the first time that they had eaten a meal outside of Academia in the past six years. For most of them anyway.

There were exceptions of course. Julian and Katrina were amongst the eldest of them and the youngest would have only been a student there for a few short years. Some of them might have been recruited earlier if their magic developed extraordinarily fast as a child but that was rare.

This meant that while they had all been deprived of these luxuries since joining that academy, not all of them had been missing out for the same length of time as the rest.

Some had been isolated for longer; some had hardly been isolated at all.

It is a tough life, the one lived by a young mage.

Taken from your homes and families at the age of adolescence and thrust into a world that you barely understood without any explanation. Never to see your loved ones again until you graduated or eventually go kicked out for underachieving.

This wasn't entirely necessary though.

While it was true that by limiting what the students feel attached to does make them stick more closely to rules and laws, what it didn't do was teach those students the value of having something to lose.

When you fight, you will be doing so for one of two reasons. For your own gain or for the sake of others.

And a mage that fights not only to save his own skin but also that of the others around him will always be a stronger warrior than his opponent.

Because if you have something, anything at all that you can lose, you will never let yourself do anything but gain victory in your battles. You'll stop at nothing to ensure that whatever it is that you are fighting to protect doesn't end up taken away from you one day.

For the sake of that which you protect, for the sake of the lives depending on you to succeed, you win, no matter the cost, no matter the sacrifice.

Fighting to protect someone or something is the strongest motive a warrior can have. And I needed them to rely on this going forwards. So unlike Academia, I allow my students to form relationships, to tune their social skills and find something in life that is worth protecting.

Whether it be the taste of fine wine, the treasures they possessed or their friends. I taught them all how to find something that they could hold dear and never let it go.

This not only allowed them to fight harder but it gave them a sense of what loosing was.

It wasn't simply a defeat or the loss of their own life. Loosing is what happens when you let others down. Loosing means that your failure will have endangered or even destroyed something that you cared about.

And as a result of teaching them this, it scorched a sense of selflessness into their minds. Something that they all needed to have by the time the fighting started.

The first step to teaching them this sense of heroism, this mind-set that would allow them to fight for that that was not simply just their own, was a drink.

A luxury that most of them had not been allowed to enjoy in the past. The first thing that they would soon come to care for, the first part of their life that would be designed for them to become attached to.

The drink would be the first thing that they would learn to protect, it would be the first part of them that depended of their victory.

After all, how can you drink that which can only be made by people when there are no people left to make it?

And if, in the end after all I try, they still didn't have enough worth fighting for to win that fight, then the war had already been lost.

Not only would I fall on the battlefield to come as a result of their lack of selflessness but so too would the rest of the world. And all because I failed to give them something to fight for.

A simple drink with a home cooked meal. That was where the process of their preparation for war truly started.

Surprisingly most of them seemed to like it, drinking whatever they could get their hands on. Wine, vodka or even beer.

Everything was on display. Everything was up for grabs. All they had to do was take it. And when it ran out, that was it, they didn't get any more that night.

Needless to say, the alcohol didn't last very long. Even a mage cannot resist the enticing attraction of fermented ethanol on their first time.

Just as a human would have done, they lined up and took all that they could carry.

Almost nine whole kegs of my collection had been drunk in a single night. Not that it was dangerous for them to have drank so much. A mage can safely handle two or even three times the alcohol than a human can before it affects them to the same degree.

With the exception of myself, they couldn't possibly have drunk enough to do any damage that night.

And in addition to the drinks, that night I had served them with one of the nicest meals that they had ever tasted.

A very old recipe of mine. Whole roasted lamb.

It was Sunday after all, they deserved a good roast dinner for once. A purely British tendency, that much was true, but it is one that stuck and a tradition that no one I have ever met had disagreed with.

Who could turn down a well plated meal when I was the one who had cooked it from scratch anyway?

Most of them enjoyed it of course. Some who did not have the taste for the texture of lamb didn't fair to well, but all the plates were empty by the end.

They must have been hungry.

But before dessert could be served after I had let their warm food go down, I had some rather important things to tell them.

Minor details, each of them, but all in addition wound up being a rather hefty amount of information about the workings of this course and the details that I felt they should know.

I had given them answers before the questions were even asked. That was the plan anyway.

There wasn't any need to keep them guessing, they had a right to know everything but certain details had to be left out at that time for obvious reasons.

I didn't want them fleeing for their lives after they learnt the truth. Not before they had been taught to stand their ground and fight for themselves.

So I explained that simply by being on this course I had already promoted them to the rank of a level nine mage. But I went on to add by the time they left all those who graduated would be level nineteen at least.

That was the advertised reward of this course. The promise of knowledge and power beyond comprehension in the shortest period of time possible and then at the end of all their trials, they would even achieve a mage rank only beaten by the Crown Mage and myself.

It was a promise.

One that, while true, wouldn't be possible for all of them to achieve.

Some would be leaving the course before its end and some might even be unlucky enough to fall during the final exam. That exam being the war of course.

If any of those who survive the rest of the course were to

falter, even slightly, during the fight to come, they would surely be dead as a result.

But I didn't tell them anything about the battle that was fast approaching, I simply made it seem as though this course was just like any other. It was tough, not everyone would succeed but at the end, they would all be greatly rewarded for making it through.

So I moved on from the obvious gap in the truth and explained some of the specifics on how lessons would be structured.

I told them that all students in my classes would be learning offensive spells and focusing on both fighting techniques and how to effectively deal damage to an opponent quickly and powerfully.

All students in Katiana's class however, would focus on defensive spells and enchantments. Their focus would be supportive combat, the aim of which was to create a more balanced team of warriors by having them augment the movements of the fighters from the rear.

Two classes, one made up of those who deal damage and those who can defend against it. A tactic that never seemed to fail in the scenario that I was training them to fight in.

I explained the rules about using high-level spells on campus next. Focusing on the best practices for such spells as to avoid these students killing anyone accidently. And how and when to safely use a spell that could be fatal to either the caster or the target too.

It was simple enough to get your head around.

During a friendly match, there were no exceptions, no spells intended to kill could be used. But when up against an opponent like myself for instance or during a situation that constitutes such excessive force such as an opportunity to show off, it was permitted.

If a student was in a fight that they were certain they couldn't survive, then I didn't want them to die as a result. It was in those situations and only then that they were permitted to use such powerful spells. For the sake of their own protection only.

And after the more formal parts were out of the way, I when I got on to the more important details. The ones that pertained to myself. And my past.

Such details are not taught in Academia because even they don't know enough to teach people the specifics of who or what I am, let alone teach them what I was truly capable of when I'm at my best.

I explained how the relationship between my human and Athereon bodies worked at first.

Not something that is especially complicated but it's also not exactly easy to explain. The best way that I have ever managed to put it into words is by explaining it as if my other body existed in a separate pocket dimension. Occupying the same space at the same time as the other but never touching it.

I told them that when I switch between the two, think of it as my mind simply swapping between what can be seen and what was hidden.

When this happens, the only thing that remains the same is my personality and memories. My body and everything within or on it is swapped out with the other one.

Muscles, skeleton and appendages. Everything is replaced, everything is different.

It is for this reason that I find it either extremely painful or even impossible to switch when wounded too badly. This is because of how switching works.

The other body takes over the one I am using at the time completely, taking its place as if it had always been there, matching the shape and form of the one it is replacing before it does.

Put simply, if there was a hole in my side or in my arm for example, how is the body I am switching to supposed to match it when only one of them had the hole?

In those cases, switching can cause the damage that I have already sustained to be replicated and amplified on the body I switch to, or it can simply prevent me from switching at all.

When the latter of these events happen, I am only able to go as far as half way and only temporarily. In these rare instances where such action is necessary, I can only hold the shift for a few moments and at great cost to myself. Both in terms of pain in in terms of the amount of magic energy this would use.

However, during this brief moment of time where my body does switch, if only for that one moment, I am able to do things that my human form cannot.

Cast more powerful spells or even just have access to more magic energy if my current body's reserves were low.

Doing this half switch as it were, is not overly useful, but in a fight and when wounded especially, you take your advantages from wherever they might appear.

Even if it meant causing serious damage to yourself or even enduring pain so unimaginable that it cannot be put into words.

But I very rarely performed this form of switch. It was

excruciating and exhausting. But when I do, it is always because it was necessary to do so.

I told them this and I even explained the difference in skill between the two forms that I possess.

I explained that while human, I am essentially equal to any other level twenty-nine mage – not that human mages that powerful actually existed – but when I become the Athereon, I am unmatched, going far beyond what the levelling system can classify.

While the levelling system was designed to organise mages into groups based on the power they possess, it didn't go above level thirty. There was no need, no reason for anyone to want a classification system that approached that height.

No mage in history had ever accomplished anything higher than level twenty-seven. I wasn't even sure that it was possible for a mage to even come within an arm's reach of level thirty, let alone actually get there.

In all my years, one truth had always remained constant.

Human mages have a fundamental limit.

No amount of training would ever allow a mage to reach those heights. No amount of practice or wisdom would have allowed them to gain enough power to do so.

They were limited by what they were.

Human.

It simply wasn't possible for a mage to equal me in strength, their bodies couldn't handle the energy required to do so.

Even I had to obey this law.

By skill, my human form is level thirty but in terms of power, my human body is level twenty-seven. Skill counts for nothing when your body cannot output enough power to support it.

Every spell that existed above the level thirty mark were far too taxing for my human body to cast. If I wanted to do anything more than what a normal mage could, I had to use my other body.

This was something that I left out.

I didn't want to tell these students that there was a limit to what I could teach them, a limit to how far they could progress.

So I allowed them to believe that one day they might even be capable of rivalling my power and then moved on. My purpose was to ensure that these students made it to a level of power sufficient for fighting in the war when the time came. My purpose was to make sure that no matter what, they reached this level of power by the time they needed it. And if I had told them that there were limits to how powerful they could become, I would have severely compromised my chances of completing that purpose.

So I kept the truth from them and then continued to reveal even more details about myself to them. I told them what I could do and what I would never do.

I told them the limits of my power and the lines that I would never cross. Resurrection was one of these lines. Every mage is capable of this but none of them would ever actually do it.

The rules of messing with the order of things were… don't.

In order to bring someone back to life, you must obey the rules of equal exchange. A life for a life.

So in order to resurrect someone, no matter who it was or

how they died, the only way to do it was to take another life in return for theirs.

The only exception to this was me.

I had a way of resurrecting people without sacrificing a life but the price for doing this was much higher. For me, bringing someone back from the dead was something that I was capable of doing but was something that I would never do.

There are some lines that no one should ever cross.

But it didn't matter which method I used, someone had to die in order to bring the target back from the depths of darkness.

There are somethings in life that you must never do, forbidden and unspeakable acts that must never be committed and this was one of them.

My exception to this rule was that I contained a unique skill that allowed me to use the same energy that kept me alive to bring life back to whomever it was that I had chosen to resurrect.

The only problem with this was that I wouldn't have been left with anything for myself. But the result was ultimately the same though.

A life for a life.

No matter what you did to avoid that fact, it still remained. There was no way of bringing anyone back from the dead without killing someone else first.

And after telling them this, I had to counter it with something more positive.

So I told them the rules behind my immortality and my strength. I told them the secret to what kept me ticking and explained that once they were capable of it, life extension spells and the proper use of them could achieve the same result.

While they would never be perfectly un-killable, they would at least have a lifespan equivalent to mine if they wished. Well… not entirely.

But in all my years, never had I met a mage that had wanted to or actually survived that long. In the end, living forever is as much a curse as it is a blessing.

There was a reason that everything in the universe was designed to die, an underling truth of the world that had to be obeyed.

Death was not a curse or punishment, it wasn't an eternal form of torture or a way out of life, it was simply an end.

Throughout your life, there will be events that you will pray to the heavens in order to forget. Losses that you would never be capable of moving past, loved ones who would one day leave you behind.

Events that you would one day do anything in order to change, to rid from your mind. And death was the answer to this.

If you were to live long enough, you would eventually welcome death as though he were an old friend. Going peacefully into that good night and leaving your regrets behind for someone else to deal with.

Death wasn't an escape but it was freedom.

It was a way of ending your anguish and torment and allowing you to find peace. Death was a means to an end that we will all one day seek.

I did my best not to brush over the topic of death and resurrection too lightly though. I needed the students to understand that while they might one day figure out how to do it, it was something that they must never do.

After all this talking, all these revelations about the way that the world truly worked, I must have depressed them somewhat more than anticipated judging by their faces.

But I still continued to speak.

I still continued to explain.

I kept going for over an hour, telling them every detail about me and my abilities no matter how small or insignificant they might have seemed.

I did this because one day, in the not so distant future, when those kids would be fighting beside me on the battlefield, this was information that they would need to know.

If your army understands you completely, everything that you can do, your strengths and your weaknesses, then they can not just fight harder knowing that you have their back but they can also defend yours when they recognize that you're in too deep.

By telling them every detail, I had ensured that they could predict some of the actions that I would take during the war.

It allowed them to strategize and plan out attacks on their feet without even realising it.

By taking away their biggest unknown factor during the battle, they would be able to think for themselves and take actions without having to second guess my abilities beforehand.

I had given them the one thing that they needed in order to rely on me.

Knowledge.

And when I finally finished speaking and they knew

what they needed to know, I asked if they had any questions. And they only had one.

Of all the gravely depressed faces in the room, one was lit up with curiosity. One face amongst forty-nine others that just shouted out that he wanted to know more.

The question was simple, the repercussions of answering it were anything but.

He asked how old I was.

A question that was probably secretly being asked in everyone's mind.

It made sense I suppose. I had told them that I was practically immortal yet I hadn't mentioned how long I had wondered the Earth.

Of all the people to have asked this question, I would have expected the person who had asked it to have been Julian but he had no interest in finding out.

His face suggested that he hadn't been interested in anything that I had said over the past hour that I had been speaking for.

He seemed completely uninterested. He must have had his reasons so I ignored the look on his face and answered the question.

The simplest answer to it was the one that I gave them, I don't know. The more complicated answer is that the definition of a year has changed so many times and that we have had so many calendars in my time that I simply lost count.

I gave them a rough guess, somewhere in the neighbourhood of fifteen thousand years but I couldn't be certain then and am even more confused as to my true age now.

The room of students went quiet after that, I'm not entirely sure why but no one dared say a single word.

I realised that my presence was probably the cause of the silence, so I handed out the dessert that the students had been patiently awaiting and left for the night. Instructing them to clean up when they left.

It wasn't long after I left the room that I heard the chatter begin, they probably just wanted to discuss everything that I had just told them, they could have done so while I was there but they probably would have found that to be rude.

It didn't matter, tomorrow was a new day and I still needed to see to Katiana, her wellbeing had been worrying me for that entire evening.

I went back to the house expecting to find her already asleep or reading a book in the living room but I couldn't find her in either of those locations.

I checked the bedroom, her office, the upstairs living room, the kitchen, the dining room, the vault and still nothing.

I checked everywhere that I could think of to try to find her and found nothing but empty rooms and burnt out candles.

I thought that maybe she had teleported off somewhere but she wouldn't have dared do so without telling me first.

As Crown Mage she was supposed to have a body guard with her at all times. Since I was the most powerful person on the planet and her husband, that duty fell to me.

If she were to be seen in public without me by her side, the Council would never let me hear the end of it.

So I tried to contact her telepathically and still nothing.

I couldn't even sense her presence.

It was as if she didn't even exist for a moment.

I couldn't feel her and I couldn't find her, it was as if she had just vanished. I did my best to remain rational and started to think about where she could have gone, and besides the house, only one location sprung to mind.

The dojo.

Whenever she was stressed or angry, she went there to practice her magic. Normally just her archery but occasionally she would create a few explosions for me to clean up later.

The two things other than my company that actually made her happy, fire and firing arrows. It was a good thing that I had a safe place for her to train given those interests of hers I guess.

But in the short time that I had been searching for her, the students had already finished their dessert and had left the dining room. Or perhaps they had left because the commotion had enticed them to do so. Either way, I had only just started to make my way back over there when I saw it, a large gathering of students surrounding the dojo's main doors.

The rest of them watched from afar, keeping their distance but still saturating their curiosity by observing.

Through the barrier surrounding the school area I wouldn't have heard the commotion, nor would I have sensed it. I had no way of telling how long they had been there but it had been long enough for them to have started taking action by the time I arrived.

I often wondered why none of them tried to summon me when it had all started but I would guess that there simply hadn't been enough time for them to think about it by then.

According to what they said when I first arrived, they had only been standing around for a couple of minutes. While I would have appreciated being told as soon as they knew what was going on, a couple of minutes wouldn't have made a difference.

Just as I approached them, they had started trying to break through the doors by force, not magic. But even magic would have been pointless, once the training barrier has been raised, those doors wouldn't have been opening any time soon.

I told the students to get back. Pushing them out of the way as I forced my way in front of them to get to the doors, giving them a strong tug and finding the barrier firmly in place already.

I tried my best to teleport in but it was useless. I wasn't strong enough to break through one of my own barriers at that time. And this just had to be one of the few that prevented teleportation didn't it?

So I rushed around back and tried the side door, the barrier's strength would have been weaker there and the door itself too but that wouldn't budge either.

I considered breaking in through there since the door was smaller and not expected to survive as much but that didn't mean the enchantments on it were any weaker.

The side door was also steel and the main doors were oak. The best chance I had of getting in was the front.

I returned to the front and tried teleporting again, using brute force and will power to force my way in. To my surprise I was actually able to start the motion. I felt my body go into the bubble and then everything went black. I opened my eyes expecting to see the dojo but I had never arrived inside the barrier. I had simply been deflected off the walls and thrown aside. Only moving a few feet and in the wrong direction.

After everything that I had done during that day, simply teleporting was beyond me. Truly pathetic.

It was nothing more than a barrier, if I had had just another five percent of my energy back I would have been able to break through in a moment but at the time, I was too weak to do anything.

After healing Katiana's foreign wound and deflecting Julian's attack, both my bodies were pretty much drained. And then on top of that, I had almost completely drained myself twice earlier in the day when I created the barrier to hold back the corruption.

I saw no other way through but an assault on the barrier. I would have to break it.

Even though I was weak, I thought that I would have had enough strength to do that at least. So I raised my hand and pointed it at the door, I fired every destructive spell I could think of at it. Fire, Ice, Explosive, even forbidden arts such as Atomic Supposition, the ability to split atoms and use their energy as a boost for your attacks, all that and still nothing happened.

I raised my hand again and began the incantation for Deconstruction magic. The only form of magic that can rip individual atoms apart one by one and disintegrate any solid matter but I had nowhere near enough energy to cast a spell as complicated as that on a door that large.

I guess there was a reason that it had been deemed too powerful to use. It was too draining on the user and also too destructive to contain.

THE ATHEREON: WINTER'S WAR

Then I lost my mind for a moment, the frustration got to me and my own impatience go the better of me and the next thing I knew I was attempting to form a quantum event at the base of the door.

I didn't realise it at the time but such an act would have not only drained me but also completely destroyed everything inside and outside the dojo as well.

Not only would such a spell have warped time and space once formed but it would have also acted like a black hole while it was open sucking anything and everything inside of it until it ran out of power or grew too large.

I'm glad that I managed to come to my senses and stop before it was too late. Even at full strength, I'm not sure that I would have been able to create and then disarm a spell as powerful as that. If I had managed to cast it, it would have just kept eating until it had consumed all the energy required to create it in the first place

Instead of endangering the lives of a couple hundred people in a split second decision to blast through my barrier with the same force as an atomic bomb, I used all my remaining physical strength to bash the door as hard as I could but all that accomplished was a chip in the wood. It didn't even budge.

The barrier was simply too strong for me to overcome in my weakened state.

I tried shifting into my Athereon form after that but I didn't have enough strength to sustain it yet, I was still drained form using Defensive Flare earlier and both my human and my Athereon forms were still weak from saving Katiana.

The spell that I had used consumed a lot of my life

energy and since I had two bodies to sustain with that energy, it had drained them both.

I couldn't do anything in either of my bodies, even if I had had the strength to switch between them I would have needed their collective power in order to get through.

So I thought and thought, going through all the possible ways to break through. Nothing that came to mind was too promising but that was when I started thinking, not of myself but of what the students could do.

None of them had any especially strong spells under their belt. But there were the notable exceptions of just two. And that's when I had the idea, I used all my energy defending myself from Julian, maybe with a bit of a boost, this time he'd be strong enough to break through.

The strength of Defensive Flare had already proven to rival that of even my strongest barriers so maybe he could do it. If he had managed to crack a stronger shield earlier in the day then perhaps he could shatter a weaker one with ease.

Final Stronghold was designed with destroying a fortress in mind, it even got its name from the saying that the original caster spoke before using it.

"This will be your final stronghold."

I'm not entirely sure who said this first or why but the spell was named after it because the original intention behind its design was to destroy anything in front of it.

"Julian, Katrina get over her now!" I shouted at them.

Perhaps I was a little too loud at the time, partially scaring them in the process. I just wanted to get my words out quickly and make sure that they had heard me. I then pointed at the floor and out from the crowd they appeared.

They came as quick as they could, pushing through the crowd and standing beside me. I looked to Katrina and told her what she needed to do but she wasn't going to like it.

"Katrina, since your magic is obviously compatible with Julian's, I'm going to give you a boost, just stand still, this might hurt a little." I said.

I was desperate and didn't have time to think clearly, just like I had with Julian so many years before, I committed a crime to save a life.

I placed my hands on the back of her neck and gave her what little power I had left, even a small amount would have made a difference, she was only a mage after all. With what little I had left, I probably only managed to restore the energy that she had used earlier to fire the spell at me the first time. But it was enough.

She yelped slightly and then her eyes began to glow a bright and menacing golden colour, a rare but natural response to having excess magic energy in the body.

And in that moment, she would have felt invincible.

Unlike Julian, who was completely drained when I gave him my energy, she was almost fully charged and this had sent her way over her limits.

If she didn't release that energy soon, it would have killed her or everyone standing around her when her body finally forced the energy out of its system in a rather explosive fashion.

I then turned to Julian. I looked at him, my face so cold and serious that it stunned him for a moment. He looked scared but was that because of me or Katrina.

"Julian, forget everything that I told you about high-level spells earlier. Break down this door, now!" I instructed.

I shouted at him again in my desperation, giving him an order as if he was already a soldier.

To my surprise he simply obeyed without question.

He didn't say anything, he nodded and took a few steps closer to Katrina. I rushed everyone to a safe distance behind me and nodded to Julian. Then he grabbed Katrina's hands and began the incantation.

With my magic as a boost, this spell would be much more powerful than normal. If I could, I would have done it myself but it's a two-person spell, I couldn't have done anything without the help of the person I was trying to save.

Katrina screamed telepathically throughout the spell, the overwhelming energy flowing through her was damaging every circuit on its way out.

But when it finally hit Julian, he yelled in pain as well. An otherworldly aura of red and blue magic energy surrounded him like fire. It covered him, it consumed him. The energy was immense, the complete power of the two of them combined plus around five percent of mine.

The red hue of energy tinted the air as if he were a spotlight. He was a blindingly powerful explosion waiting to happen, and my only hope of getting through that barrier if he could do as asked and aim it correctly.

And when he let go of Katrina's hands, he was launched at the doors, already going at full speed by the time he had travelled the three meters to reach them.

The nature of this spell, is a strange one, it essentially turns the casters body into a projectile, launching him or her at a target. In this case, that target was the door and subsequently the barrier that had been raised right up against it.

Katrina collapsed shortly after casting the spell, a moment later and Julian had punched his way through the door and destroyed the barrier surrounding it too. Shattering the wood into unrecognisable pieces as they went flying into that room. And then the barrier just after that. Magic dust falling through their air as it crumbled under the force.

And that force didn't just go the one way either.

My barrier did the best it could to withstand it. Releasing so much magic energy in go against it like that had backfired greatly, knocking a few students who were stood behind me to the floor with the shockwave alone.

But when the spell wore off and the dust and debris settled, I could finally see into the dojo and after my eyes recognised what was on the other side, I just reacted.

Sprinting in as fast as I could, barking orders at Julian and the students. Telling them to stay back, to tend to Katrina and keep out of the situation that continued to unfold before me.

I ran and ran towards the dojo as fast as I could, finding exactly what I had feared lying on the floor in front of me as soon as I reached the centre of the room.

It was Katiana. Huddled up unconscious in a ball on the floor. And beside her was exactly what I expected to find. Exactly what I had been hoping not to find.

It was a pile of her weapons. Every single one.

She had tried to see if they would reject her like her bow, and they had. All of them had.

Even her armour.

That too was laid out on the floor, cracked, chipped and deformed all over, as if it had been blasted off of her body when she tried to put it on.

It was ruined but that wasn't important at the time. I could replace the armour but nothing could have replaced her.

The signature of the black energy looming in the air of the room was rotten, corrupt, and poisonous. No wonder the barrier was so stubborn on staying up, it was in quarantine mode, the room was practically toxic.

One breath of the stuff and I felt my legs go numb. Any more and I would have been incapacitated.

I reached my arms out and did my best to absorb the majority of the energy in order to protect the students, myself and the fragile remnants of my wife laying on the floor.

It burned as it entered my body. Scorching every circuit as my body attempted to acclimate it.

The pain was brutal but I could bear it, I had to bear it. If not for the sake of my wife then for the sake of all the students that would have been breathing that stuff in if they had entered the room.

While normally forcibly absorbing magic energy as corrupt as this would have been fatal, my body was different. With how weak I was at the time, I knew that I would have more difficulty neutralising it than normal but I didn't expect it to have hurt as much as it did.

Imagine being burned alive, now imagine that pain being constant for the next five minutes. Then times that by a factor of ten.

Now you're close but still not imagining how much it actually hurt.

Perhaps there isn't a way to describe it, it's not like a

simple human could have endured so much pain for as long as I could.

The initial shock of this pain caused me to close my eyes and almost fall to the floor before it subsided but I didn't. I couldn't afford to pass out then, there were more important matters to attend to.

So when I opened my eyes I turned my attention straight back to Katiana. And now that the remaining energy in the air had dissipated I could see more clearly. No longer did a dark fog cover the dojo, instead only the scattered fragments of my wife's energy did.

All over her body I could see the same black makings as before. Her hands, arms, chest and face. It was spreading by the minute.

I looked around the room to see what had initially set off the protection barrier and that's when I saw the layers upon layers of black crystals in the walls. The same kind that she fired when she lost her temper. It's not officially a spell but neither is it naturally occurring. The only mage that I knew who could do this was her and because of this, I knew exactly what they should have looked like.

Normally there wouldn't have been a problem with seeing the crystals but black wasn't the natural colour of her magic. It should have been green. Black magic symbolises only one thing. Corrupted magic energy, the same as the stuff spewing out of the holes in the sky, only a lot more condensed and powerful.

Unlike the monstrosity in the sky above, her corruption had been developed naturally, not artificially. The stuff coming out of the sky had been made by hand, the stuff inside of her had been made by her body.

I knelt down and franticly I grabbed her hand, ignoring my pain and focusing on hers. All I could feel how drained she was, unnaturally so. As if those shards in the wall weren't fired intentionally. And it was at that point I realised, she was so far gone now that couldn't control her magic anymore.

She was too corrupted for her mind to command it.

From that moment onwards, I knew that if I saved her, she would never use magic again, it wouldn't have been safe for her to do so.

But at that point I didn't know how to save her.

I didn't have enough energy to use my Athereon body despite my attempts to desperately try again and again to switch into it.

And when I finally wasted the last of my energy trying to do this, I came to the earth-shattering conclusion that I couldn't perform a spell strong enough to make a difference in my human one either.

So I stayed knelt there beside her, holding her hand close to me, crying silently and shaking profusely.

I couldn't do anything. I was about to lose her and all I could do was watch.

It didn't take long after I started to cry for the students come in despite what I had told them. They asked what to do, begged me to tell them how to help but there was nothing that they could have done.

None of them were strong enough, not even Julian.

I was just about to accept the reality of the situation when something happened, something that broke my heart even further than it had been already.

Katiana regained consciousness for a moment, and

though it caused her immense pain, she spoke to me.

I knew what it was, I didn't want to but I knew

She was saying goodbye.

"Athereon." She said.

"I'm here."

I sniffled, placing her hand up to my mouth, kissing it, stroking it. The only things that I could do. Because when it finally came down to it, I was powerless. Unable to save even one life, not even my own wife.

"Save your tears, we've both known this day would come."

Despite her pain and how weak she was, she did her best to wear a slight smile on her face. Her breath was shallow and week, she could barely even open her eyes.

"But it's too soon."

I clutched her hand even tighter. Not willing to let go.

"Forget about me." She said. "Focus on the children. Just go! Go and save the world."

She coughed. Seemingly beginning to lose consciousness again. I shouted her name out again and again, begging her to stay there in that moment just a little longer.

But my words fell on deaf ears, she had already begun to fade away and my heart had begun to shatter.

I felt a large sinking weight on my chest and there it stayed only intensifying as the moment continued.

The students tried their best, each of them trying purification and healing spells but even with all of their combined power, the spells they were using wouldn't have done anything.

Only an Athereon could have saved her and I was all out of juice.

I continued crying, slowly accepting the fact that I had lost yet another wife.

And then Julian and Katrina rushed in.

She was up on her feet and seemingly okay.

But the same could not be said for my wife though. All I remember feeling when I saw the two of them was envy. If his wife was fine then why couldn't mine be as well?

"It's my fault." She said.

Initially I ignored the fact that Katrina had spoken and simply focused on the words. My face and mood changed instantly, all the emotion drained from my body and became nothing but rage.

I turned to face Julian and Katrina, ready to throw a punch or swing any one of the swords that lined the walls.

Julian looked just as terrified as she should have been but she just stood there, clutching her arm and limping a little. Not showing any emotions on her face at all as she continued. Acting just like a machine.

"Her proximity to me, it had created a paradox that her heart could not sustain. This resulted in the corruption of her magic energy. This corruption is what has caused the event that is unfolding before you." She explained.

I stood up and walked a little closer to the pair. Still Katrina seemed unfazed by the events or my aggression. Julian was scared but considering what I know now, maybe that was an act as well.

With how well he had been keeping the truth from me, perhaps he had forgotten what it was like not to pretend.

"And what would you know about her heart?" I asked in anger.

"We are the same." She said, placing her hand on her

chest. "We were both created by you, Athereon, many years ago. Like magnets of the same polarity, our magic repels one another. Corrupting her and also weakening me."

I stood there in shock, mere moments away from losing my wife I didn't know what to do or what to feel. I just stopped, stood still and remained motionless as she spoke. The weight of her words slowly baring down on me, crushing what little I had left to stand on.

"Every machine, will eventually fail." She said.

I fell to the floor, realising what I had actually done all those years ago. By saving her life the way that I did, I had doomed her to the fate she now suffered because of it.

But just as I dropped my head and began to give up, my hands holding me against the floor as I sat on my knees, Julian now have me his insight as well.

"There is still a chance Master."

He knelt down in front of me, holding a hand out for me to grab. But I only pushed it away. I could barely even process the events that had occurred so far, how could I have listened to anything else. I simply didn't have it in me to care anymore.

"What chance? The only thing capable of tuning the heart of a doll into that of a mage isn't even possible. It's not here anymore." I told him.

He stood back up and looked at Katrina.

"Athereal energy, that is the price to pay is it not?" He asked me with a smile, turning his head towards my wife's increasingly lifeless body slowly after he spoke.

"How would you know that!?" I asked him in concern.

I spoke in an even more enraged voice than before. I lifted my head and stared at him. The information that he knew, it wasn't possible unless it was true, unless my suspicions had been correct all along.

"Because I used to be just like you." He said.

He then turned back around and finally I learnt the truth.

"Centuries ago, you created two machine doll hearts, one was to save the life of your wife, the other you discarded due to its malfunctions but you never destroyed it. It's link with its twin would have destroyed them both." He said.

I nodded; still questioning every word that came out of his mouth like I would have done to anyone speaking truths that they should not have known.

"One day that heart was eventually placed into the body of a young girl who was dying due to an accident of magic that made it impossible to heal her." He continued.

So it turned out that the sister heart to the one I used to save Katiana had found its way into the body of Katrina over two hundred years later.

To think that something so small and so old could have come back to haunt me then. It had been so long since I made the pair of those hearts that I had almost forgotten that they existed.

After all, it's not like you could tell Katiana had one, I had designed it to mimic human emotion perfectly, unlike the one that ended up in Katrina.

"When I met her, she told me what she was and asked me to save her." Julian continued to explain. "So… I did what I could."

"But how, in order to correct a machine doll's heart you have to give up the part of an Athereon that keeps them immortal." I said.

"But like you I also share this power. Athereal energy

flows through my veins as well as it does your own." He replied.

He knelt back down before me, in an attempt to get face to face and continued his explanation.

"I used most of it to make Katrina as close to human as I could, enough to stop the heart from failing like that of your wife but not enough to take away all of the resurrections that I have left to use." He said.

"Then tell me, tell me how to give her just enough so that it works." I begged of him.

Pleading and praying, I asked him to tell me how to save her but… he wouldn't.

I had ignored everything that he had told me except for the part where he said that I could save her. I didn't even care about what he was saying unless it was a way to stop her from dying.

"I'm sorry Master but I can't."

He stood up and walked towards the now decaying dead body of my wife. I hadn't even noticed that she had stopped breathing until he got close to her.

"It's as she said, you need to save the world."

That was when events unfolded that to this day I still cannot comprehend. I could feel the magic energy flowing within him. It was instantly familiar, almost as if I should have known it but in the spur of the moment, I couldn't recognise him in the slightest.

Though, thinking back on it now, I'm surprised that I never figured it out sooner.

It was only after the fact that I realised this sense of familiarity to the energy within him was because of how similar it was to my own.

The energy that I was sensing began to flow into his back, focusing on the parts where his scars were placed. A moment later and he had done the unthinkable; he had shifted into his Athereon from.

I stood there in awe, looking at his badly damaged armour, his broken, rotting wings and the shackles still attached to his arms and legs.

He looked at me for a moment and that was when I recognised his face.

He wasn't just an Athereon, he was mine.

My own son.

Thousands of years ago, before the fall of our civilization, he was my son. My first and only son.

I didn't have time to react to that, all I could do was stand there and watch as he knelt down once again, placed his hands on her body and began to do what he needed to.

He began to heal her heart. Transforming it from one of crystal to that of a human mage. And seconds later for the first time in centuries, I heard its beat and felt its true magic energy once again.

The power of her own magic quickly removed all traces of her corrupted state. Purifying her every cell. Her skin returned to normal in seconds, her energy became pure once again and her heart was beating.

She was alive. He'd done it.

But this had come at a cost.

Soon she began to regain consciousness and Julian's Athereon form began to fade, permanently.

Before it did, he performed one more miracle, one last act of kindness, he absorbed the remaining corrupted magic from her veins and then fused it with his own.

When his body disappeared, it would take this corruption with it. Never again would the stench of its energy pollute my wife and never again would I get to see my son.

The lights of the dojo began to fade and eventually turn black for a moment during this event. And when they came back on, my wife was fine but Julian was far from it.

His Athereon side was gone, leaving only the human body behind and it wasn't even remotely in a good state.

It was weak, he had probably never turned into an Athereon while he was in it before. It would seem that the body couldn't cope with the strain of transferring his body and person from one dimension to another and the shift had taken its toll on him as a result.

But the other result was that my wife had been saved from that darkness of death. But the cost of achieving that miracle was that my son had to die in her place.

The laws of equal exchange, a life for a life, an eye for an eye, a miracle in exchange for sacrifice.

A selfless and noble sacrifice but it was one that I should have had the responsibility of making myself.

She was my wife, he was my son. I should have given my life to protect them both.

It was my duty, as a husband and as a father.

And I failed in both regards.

What right do I have now to call myself a guardian?

What right do I have to call myself the Athereon?

And how the hell would I even begin to explain this to the remaining forty eight students standing around the four of us in that moment without things getting out of hand?

A FORGOTTEN SACRIFICE

The initial shock of what had transpired was starting to pass. And with its passing came nothing but a period of unending understanding and clarity.

With the shock now gone, with my wife saved and the moment calm, I could finally see. The veil of darkness that had surrounded me for as long as I had known him had been pulled back. And with its absence, with the truth of the world revealed to me at last, I had been left with nothing but questions that now no one could answer.

I had concerns. I felt a great wave of confusion coming over me once again as I realised how much more there was that I wanted to know. So much more that I needed to understand. So much more that I needed to learn.

But… none of that mattered in the end.

I had to refocus my mind and experience the moment for what it was. I couldn't seclude myself within my mind to seek out truths that I knew I would never find.

I had to move forward.

Accept everything and face value and move past it.

And with the shock of the events finally gone and my mind only just piecing itself back together now that the unthinkable had been averted, my focus had also returned to the present.

I was no longer fixated on the past but on the moment.

I could see my wife before me, sitting up on her own, holding the frail yet still breathing body of Julian on her lap, not a clue as to how or why he was there. Simply acting on impulse and protecting him as she would have done her own child as he was cradled within her arms.

And beyond her, towards the far side of the dojo where they had all retreated, I could see the other students staring back at me.

The confused and troubled looks on their faces – the look of fear, for lack of a better description.

They were afraid. But it wasn't a fear of me. It wasn't fear for or of Katiana. And it didn't seem to be a fear of Julian either.

To me, it seemed that the only thing they felt fear towards in that moment, was the fear associated with facings something that they could not understand.

They couldn't comprehend what had just witnessed. Their minds could not come to terms with what had happened. They were left in limbo. No confidence to ask the questions they had and no way to go without asking them.

And there in that limbo, they had been left with nothing but a sense of fear.

After what they had been put through; watching me break no end of laws attempting to rescue my wife, seeing me forcibly infuse my energy with that of another student just to open a door. Seeing the lengths that I was willing to go to in order to protect her. What I was ready to sacrifice just to save her. It went against everything they had ever been taught to believe. Every law they had ever been forced

352

to abide.

How could they not have felt fear?

They had watched my wife die, seen her life fade from her body and witness death for the first time. They had been exposed to corrupted magic, exposed to truths that they weren't ready to learn about the magic of this world.

They had seen the true form of Julian, they had seen what he really was. They had stood witness to a selfless act of kindness as he gave his life to save hers.

So I understood. Because no matter how you looked at it, each of them had seen enough to make any normal man afraid in one way or another.

But none of them spoke even a single word after Julian's light faded. None of them even moved a muscle. They simply stayed in place, filled with awe and drenched in fear.

None of them dared to do anything but watch. Similar to what I was doing at the time. I hadn't moved from my spot on the ground since Julian had saved Katiana, I hadn't said a word either.

I just did nothing, remained in the exact position I had fallen into and made no attempt to escape it. The darkness of mystery had circled me like a wolf would predate its prey.

I had become encased in a box of questions that stood eternal. Never to be answered.

I was frozen there, struggling to make sense of the events. And as I did begin to try to get my head around what had just happened, as I tried to piece it all together and revaluate what I already knew now that I had been presented with yet more crucial information, I began hearing another voice creeping in along with my own.

But unlike the voices of those in my memories, unlike the

voices from the repeating events in my head as I tried to analyse everything I had just seen, this one was different. In fact, I would even describe it as being tangible.

In my head, echoing around and around without end, I could hear her voice. Words repeating without purpose, line after line of speech sounding like nonsense at first but soon it became clear.

The confusion was all a part of its design. It was meant to induce it. To affect the mind in certain ways as to manipulate it to your own design.

But I had a stronger will than that.

So it didn't take long to realise that it was Katrina in my head, her voice being projected telepathically while she also spoke the same words out loud to compliment that chanting she continued to perform.

She was casting a spell.

An unorthodox one at that.

I wouldn't have usually approved of anyone knowing this spell. The implications of its misuse were immense. And the possibilities for it to be abused were even more diverse.

In fact, it was so uncommon a spell that I was initially confused as to where she had learnt it. It's not like you could learn that sort of thing in school. And even if a student could, the mental development required to perform the spell, telepathically invading the mind of every target at once, speaking aloud and mentally at the same time but saying two different passages simultaneously, it took decades of practice to get your head around that one.

And even if a student could, if she missed even one syllable, just one word, and that spell could have had deviating effects as a result.

As far as I knew at the time, only the Council had the knowledge or the permission to use that spell and yet, she not only knew of it down to the most minute detail, but she was also casting it. Flawlessly.

I had no time to react to her actions however. Not that I could have done if I had. My body still felt the raging burning of the corruption I continued to try and absorb was in that moment, just like all those leading up to it. I was powerless.

I was useless.

Even if I could have reacted, even if I could have done something, I'm not entirely sure that such an action would have been wise.

At the time, I didn't understand why she would be using such a spell. I found out only a short while later and when I did, I was glad that I hadn't done anything to stop her. However, I still didn't agree with her using or knowing that spell despite what it had been used to achieve in the end.

"Here me, oh wavering one. To dawn the hour, the night's beacon has come at last. So sleep now and forget thine trials of the light. Allow my voice to lull your highness towards his slumber.

An Funz Elitne Grantenz.

I implore you, kind king, thou art restless of late. Do follow your lady's encouragement. Welcome into your mind the peaceful serenity of the night.

Drem Rwah Pourz Elitne.

Please my king, sleep now. And when you awaken, you will have forgotten all that has transpired here.

Sleep now, and allow your mind to wonder.

Sleep now, and forget."

Those words. Those soothing and calming words. Translated from that of a language far older than any the people of the world speak today. Millenia had come and gone since I had last heard them aloud.

And though translated, those words had come from a language far older than that of the girl speaking them now.

Alone they are meaningless. But together with the right amount of magic energy and mental fortitude as well as a constant and unwavering chant broadcast telepathically, they form an incantation for a spell invented many thousands of years before her birth had even been considered.

And yet there she was, standing there tall and strong with her arms out wide as she looked to the ceiling with her eyes closed. Her words reaching everyone in that room. Her mind breaching all of our own.

That spell predated her almost as much as I did and yet she knew them all.

She knew the pronunciation of the ones that didn't translate. She knew their meaning and she knew exactly how to cast such an intricate spell as though she had done so before.

Line after line of her chant repeated within my head for many minutes before they stopped at last. An almost endless spiral of sentences and paragraphs that made up the required incantation for the spell.

They echoed around over and over again. Filling my mind and bouncing off the walls of the dojo, gripping at my very soul as I heard them, pulling me into the darkness as they did attempt to lull me to my slumber.

The same was true for the others as well, everyone heard

it and everyone felt it. And without the forethought to strengthen their minds or the experience to contradict spells like this one, it was soon enough that one by one, the students dropped like rain in a storm, crashing onto the floor.

The incantation that she had recited had cast a very powerful and forbidden memory-altering spell, erasing everything that had happened over the past hour or so from all of our minds. As if the events had never transpired in the first place, the memories of that night would be gone.

With such a powerful spell being cast by such a powerful mage, it wouldn't be as easily undone as regular memory spells could be. In fact, I'm not sure that I could have removed its block if I had tried. It was so perfectly cast and so strong that I'm not sure it could have been removed.

If a regular mind block is like a wall made from stone, then this wall would have been constructed from diamond. Nothing could have gotten through it. The memories on the other side of it weren't going to be coming back. Not now, not ever.

As soon as the spell had burrowed into the minds of the students far enough to take hold, that would be it. The students would never know of what had happened that evening, none of them would remember Katiana's death, nor the sacrifice that was made to bring her back to life, not even the various laws that were broken in order to try and save her in the first place.

It would all just be forgotten.

My son gave his life to save that of my wife and yet, no one would ever know, no one would ever carry the memory of what he had done to save her.

No one would ever know of the sacrifice he made.

It was such a dishonourable way to be forgotten.

Not befitting of the hero that he was.

His death would be forgotten and the life he saved would live on. It was such an upsetting way to say goodbye, such a pitiful way to be remembered.

I would not have allowed such an event to have been forgotten under normal circumstances. I would have honoured his death; I would have allowed him to be remembered. I would have forced the students to remember if I had to despite the endless questions that would have followed as a result.

I would have done anything to make sure that his memory lived on in the minds of those students but I didn't. I couldn't.

The spell quickly began to take effect on the students. I could feel their minds being roasted over one after another, I could feel their memories, everything that had happened on that night, fading into nothingness.

They were being locked behind unending walls and barriers or just removed all together as the spell did its work.

But no matter how strong a memory spell you use, it would have never affected me, I wouldn't allow it to. I resisted it throughout its casting. I wasn't about to forget that night, no matter what the cost would be I forced myself to remember.

I felt it attempt to grab at my mind but once it reached my defences and my physiology, nothing happened as a result of its presence.

While it did try to rewrite my mind as it did the others, I was able to stop its effects. This was because of what I am.

358

My mind was split between two bodies; the metal fortitude required to control two bodies at once made m mind special compared to that of ordinary humans. Far too complex a mind for any mere memory spell to have affected it unless I wanted it to in the first place.

All I had to do was concentrate hard enough and the spell simply couldn't reach me. Once I felt it stop trying to get in, I relaxed a little and returned to the moment.

And then I realised that it was also having no effect on Katiana. None what so ever. She was more mentally resilient than the students but this wasn't enough to stop such a powerful spell.

There was more to her miraculous resistance to the spell than a strong mind. Then the answer came to me, it finally clicked and I understood why she was immune to its effects, she was different now. The resurrection spell that Julian had used, the way that he had brought her back. It would have changed her.

On some level, some unseen scale that went from human to Athereon, she wasn't as close to her side as she had been before.

She wasn't a mere human mage anymore. If only for the moment, she still had the power of my son flowing through her veins.

In some small way, she was now part Athereon.

A memory spell wasn't going to affect her the same way anymore. Nothing so limited and basic could have done now.

With practice and training, she would soon find that she was more than a mage now. She was more powerful than any mage could have imagined. She was practically invincible now.

If theory serves, she should have gained whatever amount of resurrections my son had left to use. She had been granted life, unending and powerful life.

But even her newfound immortality as one of my kind wasn't enough to prevent what happened to her in the end.

However, in the moment of that spell's casting, I had become hung up on what was happening rather than questioning why.

It was this that finally broke me out of my silence, it was this lack of reason that allowed me to return to the moment.

"What are you doing?" I asked Katrina as she continued to chant the spell. However, despite my attention to the situation now actually becoming focused, I stayed put. Kneeling on the ground, staring at my now conscious wife.

"Making them forget my husband's sacrifice. They do not need to know what happened here tonight. This is for his safety as much as it is for yours." She told me.

She stopped chanting verbally but still continued to cast the spell telepathically while we talked. I don't know what possessed me to do this but I accepted that answer and allowed her to continue.

All I wanted to do in that moment was talk to my wife, nothing else mattered to me. Not one thing in the world, nothing could have broken my focus in that moment, my wife was all that mattered to me. The wellbeing of the students and the remembrance of my son came in second under those circumstances.

I sat there and talked with here for many minutes, telling her every detail in full, leaving nothing out and hiding nothing from her.

I explained what had caused the corruption of her magic and told her that I had absorbed it. I told her how Julian had saved her and I revealed who he was to me.

I told her that he was my son, the only son that I had ever fathered; the one who I thought had died almost twelve thousand years prior to that night.

But she did and said nothing as I spoke, she only sat there in silence, resting Julian's injured body on her lap.

He was practically lifeless but his heart was still beating, there was hope for him yet, however slight.

While we were talking however, Katrina continued her spell, almost exhausting all of her energy in the process as he ensured that every student had been effected to the same degree and that the walls the spell had built inside of their minds would not faulter should she have stopped too soon.

It was only moments before she finished that my pain finally subsided and I could move normally once again.

My body had worked hard and finally it had purified the corrupted magic and absorbed it. I had energy again and Katrina was finished.

I stood myself up and did what I needed to.

I had already figured out that I would need to cover the truth from the students and what I did next would help me in that endeavour.

So I ended my conversation with Katiana once I realised this fact and I began using the energy that I had only just acclimated into myself to teleport every student back to their dorm rooms.

One by one I grabbed them, taking them back to where they would think they should have been and placing them atop their beds.

I did this for many minutes, putting each one onto their dorm rooms until there weren't any more to move.

Then that was it, all the magic energy I had left was gone and I was moments away from falling to the floor and losing consciousness as a result.

But what needed to be done was done.

The students would now wake up in their rooms thinking that they had gone to bed, just as they would have done if the events had never transpired.

So I did one last teleport back into the dojo and ignoring my lack of energy and strength, I tried to take Julian to my office but that was it, I was done.

As I attempted to teleport my way there, I felt my body give up and I started to fall.

I was drained, more so than I had been for many years. But I still knew this feeling all too well.

It felt like dying, if felt cold and dark, the feeling of your entire body going numb at once and shutting down. Your eyes closing and you muscles relaxing. Your body falls and you do too. But unlike death, a mage is only sleeping when this happens. However just like death, you have no control over it when it does.

Katiana saw me as I began to approach the floor and acted as swiftly as she could. She grabbed me and Julian, teleporting us both to my office as I had tried to do myself. Katrina soon followed.

And when we arrived, we did not do so with any grace. The teleport was rushed and we had landed at quite some speed in the absence of my wife accounting the the slight shift in the planet's positioning as we moved.

My body was thrown from Katiana and Julian on impact

but that's all I know of it. My body could no longer stay conscious after the level of stress that I had put it through.

I passed out on the floor by my desk but I managed to keep my mind active, allowing me to communicate telepathically for a while at least.

Telepathy came naturally to an Athereon, it did not require magic or teaching, it was something that we could simply do given practice and as such, as long as we have an active mind, we can communicate even when our bodies cannot.

'Does someone want to explain what's going on?' I heard Katiana ask.

She felt strange, almost like a new person but there was still something about her that was the same.

I was confused by her question, perhaps she hadn't heard me before or maybe the spell that Katrina had cast actually did affect her somewhat. Either way, she had forgotten or was pretending to have and needed it explaining again.

At this point I had no sense of my surroundings what so ever, nothing but my ability to communicate telepathically to go on.

I was alone in that moment, as true as the sky is blue, I had no one to touch and nothing to see. I was inside my own private world. One where it was always dark, always cold and always empty.

'I can do that if you truly wish to know.' Katrina replied.

This was the only way I had of knowing that Katrina was in the room. If she hadn't have spoken then I would have assumed that Katiana was talking to me.

'Well go on then.' Katiana ordered. 'And Athereon, I presume that you're still here?'

While I could feel her inside my mind, that was is. I had no other senses to go on. Nothing but my telepathy and my emotions to rely on. It was only after she had asked me this question that I understood why she was talking telepathically rather than verbally. She knew that I was still there, despite the fact that my body was motionless.

'Don't call me that!' I replied. 'I don't deserve that title anymore.'

That is what I told her as I contemplated my pitiful existence as a guardian. I wasn't even able to protect one single mage from death. What right did I have to bear a title that literally translated to "The Great Protector".

'I'll take that as a yes then.' Katiana said.

While I couldn't tell at the time, I presume that during this conversation Katiana was starting to heal Julian as best she could.

It was a good thing too, she was the only conscious mage left. Katrina had exhausted herself, she wouldn't have been much of a healer in her condition and she knew that.

It probably crossed her mind that Katiana would have to heal him and now that she had his magic energy melded with her own, she was fully capable of saving him.

'Are you ready?' Asked Katrina.

'Yes.'

'Then I shall begin.

When your husband created a machine doll's heart to save your life many decades ago, he did so by making a pair. This is unfortunately due to how they are made; a crystal with two poles, one light and one dark. Whichever was the more promising pole was the one that he used. Breaking it in two and creating your heart with one but discarding the leftovers.

Only one heart would be capable of becoming almost human however. It would give you emotions and long-lasting life but the other would be dark, almost useless.

One was used to save you and one to hide, throw it far, far away so that it could never hinder the life that he had given you.

That heart eventually found its way to me. After suffering from injuries too severe to heal magically, my father sought out any way that he could to save me. Eventually scouring the black markets of the human world in a desperate attempt to find something that our world couldn't' offer.

This is where he found your sister heart.

He sold everything he had in order to buy that heart and save me. His house, his possessions, even giving up his family crest in order to afford it. But as you know, this did not work as intended.

The heart rejected me at first and almost killed me faster than my injuries would have.

After many days of barely clinging onto life, it eventually accepted me. Resurrecting me in a sense but not fully. Due to the nature of the heart, the fact that it was the discarded one of the pair, it didn't have the enchantments and features that yours does.

It didn't give me emotions, it didn't heal my body fully either. Leaving me mute as a result. And it didn't give off the same aura that yours does.

In a sense, I didn't even look human anymore but at least I was alive, that was all my father wanted.

He never lied to me about what I was, so I knew that one

day I would need the Athereon's help to regain my humanity once again.

Despite the fact that I was alive and breathing, I didn't want to continue living if I couldn't feel anything, what would be the point of such a pitiful existence?

However, when I finally got a chance to meet him so many years later, he had brought a friend to apply at the academy. It was faint but I could sense that what I needed existed within him as well.

So, given your husband's reputation for refusing requests of aid, I arranged a meeting with him. After much deliberation and many nights, we became lovers rather than business partners.

I waited patiently for his Athereon powers to reawaken. The more I scoured his mind the more I found the memories of his other half. Slowly I was able to understand that if I just waited, they would awaken on their own.

And when they did, he saved me there and then, not even questioning as to why. It was as if something just clicked inside of him and he immediately infused his power with mine, giving me all the benefits that your heart would have done.

He made me seem human even if I wasn't.

But by doing so, it turned my heart into a polar opposite of what it once was, in a sense, my magnetic field now conflicted with your own, repelling you. When we are close to each other the two resist one another violently. The result almost kills you and severely weakens me as time goes on.

You've felt it once before. When you created the full body enchantment on Julian during his entrance exam, you must have realised that something wasn't quite right with how slowly your magic was returning.

But that was before Julian saved me, afterwards, our proximity to each other endangered both our lives once more. When you tried to use your weapons in the dojo, it backfired, corrupting your magic and making your use of spells uncontrollable.

When Julian realised what I was doing to you simply by being near you, he told me that he might have to do this. He gave up the last of his Athereal energy to save you, to make you truly human once again.

Doing this obviously came at a cost, that cost being that it killed the Athereon side of him. He is nothing but a mage now and will have no memories of the last three years we've shared together as a result of this.'

Images of these events raced and flashed past as she explained them, almost as if she was forcing them into our heads.

Her words echoed around an empty space as my consciousness began to fade entirely but even so, I clung onto my semi-conscious state for as long as I could. Everything that she was saying, the truths that were being revealed, I had to know them.

'Why did you wipe their minds?' Katiana asked.

'Because Julian won't and cannot remember what he was. If he ever does his mind will burn and he will die. It's the true cost of sharing a human form with an Athereon, you cannot survive without the other and the other cannot survive without you.

His mind is resetting as we speak, going back to how it was three years ago when his powers first awakened.

I have already begun to fill in most of the blanks with

memories of my own but every memory he has of being an Athereon will be gone and he can never be allowed to remember them.

So to protect him, I erased everyone's memories of tonight's events. For their protection as much as it was for his. Unfortunately, that means myself as well, we share a psychic link, him and I. If he were to ever find those memories within me, then I would never be able to live with myself.

I would have allowed him to die.

But I swear to you now, if he ever remembers, so will I and the first thing that I will do upon my return is kill anyone who was responsible for it.' She explained.

Her voice faded after that, I'm not sure if that's because of my own mind shutting down or the spell that she cast to change her own memories kicking in.

All I remember feeling was a mixture of two emotions, grief and happiness. I had gotten my wife back but had lost what remained of my son in the process.

Now all that I had left of him was the human side that I called Julian.

Explaining how an Athereon body works is complicated so bear with me for this next part. It is not something that is simple or short.

At one point in history, we lived in one body only, nothing but our Athereon sides. That was what we were, nothing more.

But then, seeing that humanity would one day rival our own species as the dominant race on this planet, someone figured out how to share that life with the body of a human and blend into their world while still remaining a part of our own.

And since that day, all Athereon's have lived a shared life. On one side, we were human, on the other, we were Athereon.

The process of achieving this symbiotic relationship was complicated in the beginning but we soon perfected it.

At first, we had many failures. Deaths in the thousands.

However, those that worked in the end, were perfect.

By implanting all of our Athereal energy into a human body, we were able to copy ourselves. And after some time, should the human have survived being infused with that energy, it would awaken with our minds in control.

We would be Athereon at heart, able to control magic and communicate telepathically as normal but we would be purely human in body and soul.

This method was considered unsightly to the Athereon people at time. It was almost abandoned. But it was only after the first two of these shared existences decided to make a child that we realised the true use of this technique.

Because an Athereon child this is birthed from the womb of one of our own while in human form would be born into a life of a shared existence.

They would have two bodies but one singular mind.

And ever since this discovery was made public, that is how Athereon children were born. All of us look human but we are far from it.

But that wasn't how Julian had become the human side of my son. There still another way of making an Athereon, one that not only allows for true immortality but also allows for an Athereon to be born human and then awaken their powers later in life.

It was rare for this to happen but should an Athereon require a new human body, due to the loss of their own or the inability to use it anymore, they could implant all of their power into a baby, a new-born child or one that was just about to be born if you could find one. But it had to be extremely strong for it to survive.

By doing this, the previous body that the Athereon had been living in would perish and the Athereon side would live in limbo as it waited.

The baby would be nothing more than a mage at first, he would be born knowing nothing of what he was, and would continue to exist as a normal human being until the power within him broke its way through.

However, this was an extremely complicated ordeal.

Until those powers awaken, the babe would live as a human and would be nothing more than that. He would make connections, form relationships and even think as a human would have done.

He would have had no idea of what was inside of him until the powers awakened. But when they did, it wasn't as simple as giving a human a handgun and calling him a soldier.

When the powers awaken, they take the human form over completely, overwriting him and replacing him with the mind of the Athereon that had implanted his energy into that child in the first place.

There were several drawbacks to this method of creating an Athereon though. The mother dies shortly after childbirth due to the immense amount of magic energy required to keep the child alive.

This was because in order for this to work without side

effects, you actually had to implant your energy into the child during the birth. While the babe is still passing through the birth canal.

It has to be done while that child is still sharing the life-force of its mother. But if not, then the child would never have enough power within them to live and would simply die from trying to survive the absorption of your own energy. And then you too would be dead as a result.

But if you implanted your energy during the birth, just before the child begins to crown, then it should work. Provided that the child was strong and so too was the mother, your energy should be easily accepted into the babe and then that's it. All that's left to do now is wait.

For how long? No one knows.

Sometimes it's only until adolescence, other times its after thirty years or so and in extreme cases it happens only when the human side begins to draw its final breath.

If you were unlucky enough to end up with that final option you would have only seconds to save yourself before a resurrection would be necessary.

When the powers do eventually take over, the Athereon does so as well. In short, that human child becomes the Athereon in both mind and body. Melding their memories and feelings together as one. Creating a slightly different person as a result.

It was more like reincarnation than it was resurrection I suppose.

But this was the only way that an Athereon could cheat death should they need to.

It granted them with a fresh body and a slightly increased supply of resurrections to use.

I had only ever done it once and that was because I needed to. It was not something that I would ever choose to do gain if I had to.

It was many centuries ago that I attempted this. And I didn't have a choice in the matter.

I was being hunted by every mage on the planet and needed to lay low under a new name and with a new face in order to hide myself until the kill order against me had been forgotten.

So I implanted all of my power into the new-born body of the man that I now wear. I wouldn't normally do this but it was necessary.

I would have never stooped so low under normal circumstances but I had to. The mother was a friend of mine, already close to deaths door as it was. She begged me to let the child live and I made a deal. Allow me to resurrect myself within him once he was strong enough to hold me and he would live.

He would have a life of his own for decades.

He would live.

I swore that to her.

And she accepted. And now here we are.

I now wear a man once known as Terrance, a boy born into a world that denied him and someone who I thank immensely for allowing me to survive.

But I couldn't allow my memories to change when I finally awoke within him. So I took precautions to make sure that my mind would be intact upon awakening.

However, in order to do this. I had to kill Terrance.

When I first started to reawaken, there is a split second when both minds exist at the same time before they fuse with one another.

So I took advantage of that moment and scorched every cell in Terrance's mind to allow myself to be reborn as the man I once was and the man I am today.

This was cruel I know but it was necessary.

Terrance was ninety-five when my powers awoke, he had lived his life and it was time for me to return to mine.

When this form of resurrection is done correctly, the baby would be fine, no problems or signs of the procedure being performed would be left behind. It would have no weaknesses or wounds.

The baby would be just as strong as you were the day that you were born and then once it was strong enough to hold you, the power you placed with it would take over and you would be reborn as a new person in a new body.

It's a risky way of achieving immortality and it didn't always work.

In my son's case and my own, it had.

I didn't want to accept this when I first figured it out but knowing what I know now, I had to.

While I didn't understand all of the details, it was the only explanation that made sense.

I believed my son to have perished when the rest of the Athereon's did. I'm glad I was wrong but I was sad that I never got to find out until it was too late.

I never even had to chance to say goodbye, to say that I loved him or to say that I had missed him.

I had been deprived of all that and in return he had saved the life of my wife.

I didn't even know what this new version of him was like. Was he exactly the same as he always had been or was he more similar to Julian?

I had no way of knowing and now I never would.

But somehow, he had not only survived but had also escaped the war. He had survived every war after that as well. Somehow, he had managed to survive for the twelve thousand years since that day and then he had implanted himself into a child that would one day become him.

To do this he was very careful about who the mother was. He had to be. Not only did the child have to be strong but so too did the mother.

So he chose the most powerful mage alive at the time and kidnapped her so she could give birth to himself.

He must have known that she was probably the only mage in the world strong enough to parent a child capable of holding him.

But that said, he had done this out of desperation. Something must have happened to him before he created Julian, otherwise he wouldn't have needed to do it.

Athereon's are immortal, the only reason that you would want to cheat death like this would be if someone had figured out how to kill you.

Whatever his reasons though, he had succeeded and I got to see my son again but only for a brief few moments before I lost him once more.

I would have never expected that to happen without actually seeing it. Nothing that you could have told me would have made me believe that my son was alive, let alone that I would see him again.

In all the years since our civilization's collapse, only two of us had survived. Myself and my partner.

Knowing that another of us had managed to make it

through the ages only made me curious, I couldn't shake the feeling, the thought, the fear. What if he wasn't the only one?

Could there be more of us out there, living amongst the humans or the mages? Were there more of us out there right now? And had I met them already?

That was all I could dream about as I slept on that floor.

For many hours I laid there, not capable of waking myself up or even communicating telepathically, all I could do was think and I did a lot of it.

I thought through events over and over again until I understood them.

It took me many, many hours to come to the conclusion that I finally found myself at.

Everything that I had just told you about how Julian had turned out to be my son, had taken most of that night to figure out.

But in the end, there wasn't anyone left to confirm my theories. But there wasn't anything to disprove it either. So I believed it to be the truth and went on with my life, mourning the loss of my son for weeks to come.

When I eventually awoke, the sun was starting to rise and the student's classes would soon begin.

Sadly, none of them would know the sacrifice that was made to save my wife, not one of them would ever know that my son gave his life to save someone else so selflessly.

He will forever be a hero to me but his sacrifice will be forgotten just like the rest of him, simply lost to time.

I woke up in an empty room, no Julian, no Katrina and no Katiana.

I was still quite week but I had enough energy to contact

her. Turns out that she had never gone to sleep – I was curious to find out how she planned on coping for the rest of the day but that didn't matter in the end.

She coped just fine on her own as it happened. After a couple dozen cups of tea anyway.

But she had used that time well. Spending those twelve hours beside Julian's bed as she healed him the best she could.

He would still be sore but at least he wouldn't know why. The internal damage caused by losing an Athereon body, it's not unlike being hit by a grenade but without as much carnage.

He would have had internal bleeding, broken bones from head to toe, swelling in the brain and maybe even intestinal problems. Healing him would have taken many hours at least.

She had then teleported both him and Katrina to their room, making it seem as though they had fallen asleep in each other's arms.

She had spent the rest of the night and most of the morning repairing the dojo, cleaning up the blood and mess, fixing the doors and removing the black shards from the walls and even doing her best to replace the broken display items with ones of similar design so to not confuse the students.

If anyone had asked as to why the dojo needed repairs, we would simply say that my wife got a little carried away while sparing, nothing more.

But while that day was mostly normal to my standards at least, one question popped up in my class and then later in hers. One question that I hadn't expected so soon.

"Master, is it true that Julian cast a forbidden spell last night?" Asked one of the students.

I will never forget that question, it was unfounded and purely a rumour but luckily for all of us, they seemed to accept the answer I gave them without needing any further convincing.

"Where are getting this from then?" I responded.

The boy looked at me as if I should already know but then answered anyway.

"I only ask because no one remembers going to bed last night and Julian seems to be a little bruised. I wonder, did you do something to him and then wipe our memories?"

That was a tough one to be honest, I hadn't really expected that kind of question so soon but my answer was well formed if just a little rushed.

At least I knew that the students weren't stupid.

They were spot on with their deductions and reasoning.

If they hadn't been born mages, I would have placed them as detectives in the human world but as far as I knew then, there was nothing stopping them from doing so themselves when the war was over.

"Actually, that was a test. Last night I laced the dessert with a tranquiliser to see who here had the best immune systems. Julian's surprisingly resilient body passed the test flawlessly. The rest of you did not.

We then spent a few hours teleporting you all to your rooms and we used the rest of the night for sparing.

To be honest, my wife might have gotten a little carried away, she almost destroyed the dojo again. Julian was badly hurt as a result of this I'm afraid, both mentally and physically. To protect him from further harm we put a

377

sleeping enchantment on him while we healed him. Side effects might include amnesia or numbness, so unfortunately not even Julian will remember for a while."

I later gave my wife a rundown of that same story for her to answer the exact same question later in the afternoon during her class.

They might not have believed the story in its entirety but they never asked the question again, that's all I know and all I can tell you.

Kids have a mind of their own, it's natural that they won't believe every word you say but at least they never told me if they did or did not.

Unfortunately for Julian, the gaps in his memory would never heal despite what I had said in my lie. And he would be forced to spend the rest of his years never being able to remember the sacrifice that he so selfishly made.

Never being able to remember who he was to me, who he was to himself or the man that he could have become. He would forever be yet another forgotten hero, going through life like everyone else, not knowing the full extent of how important he was to me and the bond that we once shared.

That night, I had come far too close to losing the most important thing in my life but instead, it was revealed that something far more important still existed and I ended up losing that before I even had a chance to contemplate what it was.

That night could have ended with the loss of my wife but instead it ended with the loss of my only son.

For the second time in my life I had let him die. For the second time in my life I had been forced to feel the pain of his loss.

Never did I expect such an event to occur once, let alone twice. For a father to outlive his son, there is no greater punishment for a man.

He was supposed to live, he was meant to live. He could have become so much more than he was and yet, that opportunity was taken from us both.

He had too much good in his heart, he was always ready to sacrifice himself for the sake of others and in the end, the sacrifice that he had to make in order to save my wife was not one that he should not have had to bear.

It was my responsibility to protect them both, and I failed.

That day was and remains to be, one of the worst twenty-four hours in my life.

If I knew then what I know now, I would have made this sacrifice myself.

She was my wife, my love. She my responsibility to protect and he was my son. I should have done everything that I could to protect them both.

And I failed.

I will not allow this to happen again.

The next time that my wife needs protecting, I will move heaven and earth until she is safe.

It is my duty as her husband and as the Athereon. Protection is my purpose and I will not fail that purpose again.

At least, that's what I told myself at the time anyway.

DEVELOPMENTAL LEAPS

Despite the traumatic and life changing events of that first evening, I had to move on from it. For the good of this world and everyone on it I was required to move past my loss.

So I forced myself to.

Doing my best wouldn't be good enough. I couldn't simply try and ignore the past. I had to bury it. Occupy my mind and body to the point that I couldn't spare the time to think back on that night.

So I did the best of someone better. I put it behind me and I looked forward. Focusing immediately on the tasks at hand and the threats soon to come. The dreadful and nightmare inducing event that quickly approached with every night that passed me by.

I couldn't afford to spend time mourning. I couldn't take the time to cry. I couldn't take the time do anything.

I had to act as though nothing had happened.

Mourning my loss could come after. I didn't have the luxury of spare time to waste on such a pointless way of living. Mourning was for those who had been broken not for those who had to hold their ground.

And while anyone could have argued that having your

wife die and then be brought back from the brink of that eternal rest right in front of you while the son that you had thought to already be dead dies again right before your eyes was important – while they would have been right to say so to almost any other man – that night's torment paled in comparison to the devastation that would follow should I lose this war.

The results of my defeat, they would not be isolated to just one of the two worlds. The Magic World would fall, the walls would crumble with it and then the carnage would spread across the globe. This corruption slowly engulfing everything. Living or otherwise.

There was no fighting it. No defending against it. No hiding from it.

It would sweep across this planet as a blanket of death expanding with every life it absorbed. Slowly seeping into every corner of every map. Killing relentlessly and dispassionately. Not one man or woman would be spared. Not the children or the elderly. Not the innocent.

No one.

This force that I pushed back every twenty-six years was one that could wipe out all life on this world within a single decade should I have ever failed in my purpose.

The world needed my protection in order to survive.

The world needed me at my best.

It needed me focused.

So I couldn't allow myself to mourn.

I couldn't even take the time to weep.

Because those cracks in the sky, there were still there. Growing slowly every day that I left them open. The war waiting on the other side of them quickly approaching faster and faster with every hour that passed.

I was running out of time with every second I wasted.

And if I intended to lead these warriors of mine into battle against the forces waiting to burst through into this world, I would need to train them. I would need to ensure that they were prepared for the fight.

Whether they would release it or not in the coming months, they were being trained with a purpose. And that purpose dictated that I give each and every one of them my undivided attention. It dictated that I push them until they break and then push them eve harder.

I needed to beat these children into the ground, make them realise their limits and their weaknesses and then continue to beat them down until they learnt to push past them.

I needed them to know what it was like to feel weak, to feel defenceless. Because only then would they learn how to become stronger. How to overcome their bounds. To fight back against a force that they believed impossible to defeat.

These students were being trained with a purpose alright. And that purpose was so that they could one day save the world from the darkness that had threatened it for almost as long as I have walked upon it.

They were being trained so that one day sooner than they would expect, they could become the heroes that they all deserved to be. But not the heroes that they would be remembered as.

So I accepted what had happened as fact.

I ignored my questions and I forget my confusion.

I looked beyond what had happened. And I moved past it.

And after what had happened, life went back to normal. As though nothing had happened at all.

Katiana going about her business as normal, the students acting as I would expect and even Julian completely unaware that there had ever been a change.

But there was something different.

Something that existed in the subtext of every conversation I had with Katiana since that night. Something that hid in her actions and my own inability to notice them.

Slowly over the course of the following days, she and myself began to grow distant from one another. I wasn't entirely sure why by the time I noticed it.

I kept asking myself if it was because of something I had done or something she had?

Or was it a combination of both?

What she had gone through wasn't the first time she had been knocking on death's door in her life. In a certain light it was something that she had experienced before. But the last time it wasn't even close to how it had happened this time around.

She had experienced death once before, that was true despite how much I wished it wasn't. But the last time it happened it wasn't anything like this.

When I first placed the crystal heart inside of her, she died there on that table. Her own heart had been removed, the arteries were bypassed, connected to one another with their walls enchanted to aid blood flow autonomously once the crystal took over.

She was dead on that table as I worked. Only for a few minutes in the end but even so, her heart was silent and her brain functions were almost non-existent.

Installing the heart was a simple matter.

Once it has become fully integrated, there would be no need for a normal blood circulatory system, so attaching it to the major arteries of the heart wasn't required, they would circulate on their own.

But what was required to make this process a successful one, was drastic action and superhuman reflexes.

In order to install the crystal heart into her, I had to remove the defect ridden one that she already possessed. I had to kill her, cut her open, pull out her heart and then place a new one inside of her before her brain was starved of oxygen for too long or her core body temperature grew too cold.

It all had to be done in less than four minutes.

That was all the time I had to do the work of fifteen mages with just two hands.

But I had been preparing for that operation for weeks.

I had practiced on corpses. I had gone over everything in my mind a thousand times. Timed myself down to the second. Over and over again I had made sure that I could do it.

And then when I had no other choice but to go ahead and do it, Katiana laid down on that table, she said goodbye to me as though it would be the last time and I simply smiled at her. Telling her that I'd see her soon.

After that, she was put to sleep and her heart was removed.

A minute later and her arteries had been rearranged, her chest cavity had been enlarged to fit the crystal and fifty seconds later that too had been placed inside of her.

Three minutes in and the hole in her chest would be

closed and healed shut. Twenty seconds later and I turned the new heart on and watched as it went to work.

Healing the residual injuries caused by installing it and integrating itself with her body exactly as intended. Automatically melding itself with her central nervous system, connecting to her muscle tissue and fat to become a permanent part of her body. And then before even ten seconds had passed since that moment, it would begin relighting her fire and waking her up like nothing had happened.

It would exist within her, generating magic energy on its own and giving her body and mind everything that she needed from it.

A fully working and aliment free body sustained by a heart of crystal. The heart would begin greeting pressure within her arteries and veins, moving her blood around little by little to keep oxygen moving throughout her body. And as for her muscles and skin, they were both operated and sustained directly by the heart. Her entire body was kept going like clockwork.

Machine dolls are normally built to simulate the life and behaviour of a human, not to actually become one. Most of them never achieve anything but simple forms of consciousness, nothing similar to that of free will but close enough to pass as human upon the first glance. They make up our workforce, our guardsmen. Our cooks and cleaners.

Automatous people doing labouring tasks for mage kind all over the Magic World.

But whilst they looked human, they couldn't feel.

They couldn't even think for themselves.

But if you place the heart of a machine doll into an

already living being, and if you were to try hard enough to mask its presence, that human is resurrected as something more than human.

They would no longer need anything more than one meal a day, no more than a litre of water a week and would have abilities far beyond that of any human.

Enhanced reflexes, inelegance, stamina, concentration and even enhanced vision. All far above what a human possessed even at the peak of their performance.

But it came at a price.

Human machine doll hybrids, were forbidden.

One of the few crimes that if broken was punishable by death.

It was a taboo far beyond any other in the magic world.

The creation of higher beings, it was something that no one wanted. They would have been too difficult to contain or control, too intelligent to be trusted and too powerful to defeat.

Artificial humans were only forbidden out of fear for what they might be capable of. Like so many other things, it only came down to something that might have happened. Not something that would.

And by saving Katiana in that way that I had, by curing her disease and replacing her failing heart, I had broken the only law in the world that I had until then always obeyed.

But I had to do it, no spell I knew of at the time could have stopped the infection from spreading, nothing could have prevented it from reaching her heart and stopping its beat.

It was only a century after saving her this way that I managed to invent a spell that could have saved her but I couldn't have done it any sooner.

The technology wasn't there to allow me to understand the disease in full. I only knew what it did, not why or how. It took me one hundred and six years to do it but I finally managed to invent a spell capable of curing cancer.

But it was too late to undo what I had done to her.

The change was permanent.

Or it would have been if I wasn't an Athereon.

Athereal energy can do many things, it can bring its host back from the dead a finite amount of times or it can be used in larger quantities to create miracles.

By expelling it from our systems, we can resurrect others or even turn a crystal heart into one of flesh and blood it seemed. And in Julian's case, when he used what small amount of energy he had remaining to save that of his own wife, it could even be used to rewrite the very function of that heart.

I had thought about using some of my energy to make her human again many times in the past but I never went through with it.

I didn't know how much it would use, how many of my resurrections I would have to sacrifice in order to do so or if I could even survive doing it in the first place.

I suppose that if I had known how much energy it actually required to do this, how small an amount of my resurrections would have been sacrificed, I would have done so gladly.

But I didn't know and my son gave up his resurrections in my place. Giving up the only thing that was keeping that side of him alive all this time in order to save my wife after he had already saved his own.

My son did a selfless thing in order to save her, he gave his life in order to save hers and even managed to leave Julian behind after doing so.

I respect him for that.

And if anything, I loved him as a father even more.

But never again will I be able to speak his name, I couldn't.

For two reasons really.

First was the language barrier. Athereon names were primal, more like the incantations of a spell than they were words but they couldn't be translated to English.

Athereon incantations didn't translate to anything, they were more like feelings than they were sounds. They had tones, not syllables. His name could only possibly be expressed as a sound, not a word.

So much like my own, I cannot tell it to you, not without being there in person.

Not all of us were named this way however.

Some of the newer generations, the ones many centuries younger than myself or my son, had names based on the human languages of the time and as such can actually be translated with some effort.

The only reason that my name any my son's weren't based on human languages at the time was simple, they hadn't invented a language more complex than grunting yet.

It was only when they first evolved to a point that speech and language became possible that we started learning it in order to understand them.

After some time, we even started naming our children in this language, it was easier than expressing feelings through monochromatic tones I suppose.

But even so, I only wish that there was a way for me to tell you our names, it would be nice for me to know that you could carry our memories as well but that much isn't possible.

So to that end, my son might as well share the name of Julian. He had been resurrected into his body and mind after all, he was as much Julian as he was my son.

But as for me, I remain the Athereon.

It is fitting I suppose.

It was my rank, my title and my species.

What more did I need? It made an almost perfect name.

While I did still wear the body of Terrance, I never bonded with his mind, I never became him and as such I am not him. While I might still use that name to identify myself amongst humans, that is not and has never been my name.

I am the Athereon, that is my name and it will remain to be so until the day that I eventually die.

Julian had become the name of my son the moment that the two of their minds bonded. And even if he had only managed to live for three years under that name, that was still what he chose to go by. So that is how I will remember him.

But he never did get to tell me what he was. He only got to say goodbye in the end.

That was what had saddened me for a time.

But I moved on. I had to.

But the same was not true for my wife.

Because what he had done to save Katiana, the sacrifice that he had made, it had torn us apart slightly. But I wasn't sure exactly why it had.

She had experienced death and I had lost my son, we

both had grief to deal with but there was nothing that should have affected our relationship.

It was only eighteen days later that I finally found out what was creating this divide between us and once I knew what it was, I put a stop to it.

It was late at night when she confessed what was making her want to avoid me. She said that she felt responsible for what had happened. That she blamed herself for the loss of my son.

Once I knew this, I fixed it straight away.

I explained to her that I had gotten over the loss of my son thousands of years ago. That while the loss of him again might have affected me slightly, it wasn't something that I would be hung up on for long.

That what he had done to save her was his choice, his gift to me. That she hadn't been to blame for it and that I would never blame her for it.

I told her that if anyone was to blame, it was me.

I should have destroyed that other heart the moment that I made it. I'm not even sure what possessed me to discard it. If anything I should have locked it inside my vault to keep it close to home

And after hearing what I had to say to her through whisper as we laid face to face in bed, she livened up a little. Accepting my comfort once again and seemingly going back to being the same woman I had married all those years before one again.

But even with the slight improvement, once I understood what had been weighing her down it suddenly clicked. And now I could see that she had been through enough that she wasn't coping well on her own.

I managed to settle her down. I did my best to prove to her that nothing had changed. And after weeks, finally we went back to how we were. Talking about random things all night. Laughing at our little in-jokes and even playing tricks on each other as we always had.

But what had changed permanently since that day was only one thing. She never saw Julian in the same way after that. If anything, the event had brought them closer together than ever before. It was almost as though she actually felt like a mother to him now, she was married to his father after all.

She would often ask me about my son.

What kind of man he was, what he was like, who his mother was and how we had met and what life was like back when I lived among my own kind.

She had never asked these questions before, but now, she was too intrigued not to know. So I did my best to explain it to her and she listened.

She listened and listened until the early hours of the morning some nights and even staying up all night just to find out more of what I had to say.

There were so many stories to tell her.

So many legends of my kind.

So many myths.

I could have gone on forever.

But I couldn't.

The following morning after the night that I sorted out our relationship was day nineteen into the semester.

Nineteen days since the cracks had opened, nineteen days since the students had arrived and nineteen days since the part of Julian that was my son had perished.

Every lesson was becoming increasingly difficult. An ever-evolving challenge that stood above the one that came before it day after day.

The students were working harder than they ever had done before and surprisingly they were actually coping well the increased workload.

As if what they had been learning previously was holding each of them back, they seemed to be craving the knowledge that I offered them each day and practically begged to be challenged on a daily basis.

So I gave them what they asked for, increasing the difficulty, trusting that they understood more than I had expected them to already and cramming more into my lessons on top of that as well. All the while, focusing on their continued progression above all else.

And they were progressing well.

They were learning and practicing the spells I taught them with every new lesson rigorously. Making progress however slight it might have been with every day that passed.

But soon enough however, the pace of their progress would be meaningless. Whether they had learnt how to or not, they would have no choice but to fight and they could not afford to lose.

The students had come so far in such a short amount of time, and while I was impressed compared to the students I had taught in the past, even that pace of theirs wasn't enough.

It had only been nineteen days and although they had learnt so much already, they hadn't even started learning what they needed to know.

They had all impressed me in their own ways but I didn't have time to take pride in how far they had progressed just yet. I needed to remain firm and stubborn. I needed to be a harsh and strict teacher in order to cram as much information into their skulls as I could before the time came for them to use it in the field.

A lot of students didn't seem to react too well to this approach at first but they soon settled into it and began moving forwards yet again.

Even Julian was making tremendous progress, despite how much weaker he must have felt at the time. Not that he had any idea as to why it happened. He must have noticed that casting spells took more out of him than usual but he never said anything about it and simply carried on amazing me with his natural talent for mage craft day in and day out.

Even if he didn't have Athereal energy in his veins anymore, he was still a very powerful mage.

I could see in him exactly what I had always seen. That deep down, underneath all that apprehension and lack of confidence, he was quite possibly the strongest mage on the planet.

At first, I suspected that this was simply a result of him sharing a body with my son, however, since that part of him was gone now and he was back to the way that he was before, it was obvious that him being athereon had never made a difference.

He was stronger than anything that I had ever seen before. Even without athereal power in his system, he was extraordinary, even capable of rivalling me at times.

I could see that my son had made a wise choice, he truly was the only mage alive capable of merging with an

Athereon after all.

So I could only wonder, did he have a part in making sure that he would be strong enough in the first place?

He must have been very careful with who the father was, no ordinary mage would have done the trick. His mother was the second strongest mage on the planet at the time so the father must have been equal to her in order for their offspring to be as powerful as Julian.

However, no matter how many times I would think through his past, no matter how many theories I made or conclusions I come to, there is no one left alive to confirm them.

They would always be nothing more than theories and a theory without available proof to back up or confirm it, isn't worth wasting your time on.

And by the end that nineteenth day, every one of my students knew at least nine level twelve offensive spells. These spells included elemental attacks and the creation of gravity altering fields, ideal for fighting what we would be up against when the fighting started.

After only two and a half weeks I was a little surprised to see that they had mastered so much already but I knew they could do better and I was going to make sure that they did.

Learning spells and practicing them is one thing, to actually fire them at another creature without failing to hid your target and keeping a clear mind as to not corrupt the spell as you cast it is another.

Similar to how a farther coaxes a child into killing their first dear, I would have to ease them into the idea of killing something as well.

I would start with rabbits, give them a taste for what

burned flesh smelt like when you shoot it with a ball of fire. Give them a glimpse of the brutality of having your internal organs pressed out of you as one hundred times the regular gravity flattens your body to that of paper.

And then I would move them onto something larger. Foxes and then dear. And after that, to get the idea of targeting a human with your spells, I would have them practice on lifelike machine dolls as well.

Humanoid creatures with artificial hearts. That's as close as I could get to the real thing.

By default, they don't have a sense of emotion or pain but if you put enough effort into the creation of the heart, they can look and feel just like any other human when you murder them cruelly like these students would need to.

However, I didn't see a need to have the students being trained to kill artificial beings that could think and feel just yet. All I needed them to train to do at that point was fight against opponents that looked human. After that, I'd start teaching them to fight against something that could move.

Before finally, something that could fight back at random.

I'd be simulating free will but not actually containing it. Living machine dolls are outlawed in most parts of the world. People see them as living creatures at times. It can be easy to make that mistake I suppose.

However, since I needed these students to get an idea of what killing felt like and I couldn't have them killing each other, I ignored the law and created several dozen anyway.

While there were often exceptions made in the law to allow the creation of anything but a hybrid, I didn't have time to go through official channels, so I made them
396

regardless. It wasn't like they were going to be 'living' for long

Needless to say, these savages obliterated those dolls without question or second thought by the time they faced their third or fourth try.

It seemed as though killing came a little too naturally to them. Or maybe it was just because they didn't see their opponents as living creatures.

Either way, it didn't matter, the students had shown they could take life away from a create that looked and felt like a human and that was all I needed to know.

My class was now one step closer to becoming the warriors that I needed them to be but they were a long way off from being ready for the war just yet.

Katiana's class had been learning fast as well.

Despite what had happened to her, Katiana hadn't allowed those events to affect her teaching. She was just as ruthless as she had ever been and with her natural magic energy now bouncing around within her once again, she was far stronger than she had been in quite some time.

Each of her students could now produce a perfect Defensive Flare on demand, some of them could even do so twice in the same hour.

They had also been taught enchantments that would work on both themselves and their partner in battle. Enabling enhanced reflexes, enhanced strength and even allowing for an enhanced defence.

While these were only basic enchantments, the impressive thing about them was how efficient they were. Only taking mere moments to cast and not even using a noticeable amount of magic energy to sustain.

Basic yet practical.

Even a simple spell can be more than enough when used in the right way. You have no idea how useful a simple fire spell can be when in the right hands.

Where do you think the legend of dragons came from?

Illusion spells mixed with basic fire casting, it was quite efficient and every effective. Even to this day you still hear stories of the fire breathing winged lizards.

Not one of those stories will ever tell you the truth though. I'm not sure that there's anyone left alive that could tell you that anymore but I will.

The legend of dragons was formed because a mage wanted to have some fun.

However, legends don't win wars, soldiers do.

And now that my class had learnt some more advanced fighting techniques and spells to go along with them and now that Katiana's could protect themselves as well as others, it was time for the next step.

Partners.

Now that my students were learning how to actually fight and her students could now defend and enhance the both of them, it was time to partner them up.

Since the end goal of the course was to train them to fight as one, teaching them how to fight alongside others was vital.

So I went about making my observations of their fighting styles and abilities. It took some time but I eventually had a good idea of who would work best with who.

The only problem was that the only obvious partner for Julian was the one that he already had, his wife. This would leave two extra supportive's, as I liked to call them, without any offensive partners.

I couldn't have them partnered with each other, this wouldn't have given them any kind of offensive abilities, they would have been sitting ducks.

Well defended ducks that is but even the best defences won't last forever.

So as a solution to this problem, what I did was simple, two of the pairs became a trio.

Surprisingly this went well in both instances. The two trios seemed to get along with each other in combat just as well as the other pairs.

Far more efficiently too since they had three spell casters in total who could do anything at any time.

So, from there on, everything that I had those students learn beyond the theoretical uses of their techniques, was solely intended for them to use on the battlefield.

Once I had given them partners, that's when I finally started training them for the war.

And while some didn't like the fact that two of the groups had an extra member, I didn't care. It simply meant that the others would have to try a bit harder when taking them on.

You can't expect every opponent in life to be fighting fairly. Some would have advantages over you and some would be at a disadvantage. Realising and overcoming the limitations of not only your opponents but also yourself only helps you to become stronger fighters in the future.

And once the pairs had been made, the lessons lasted longer and the training got tougher.

Days eventually turned into weeks and lessons soon turned into repetitive nonsense.

Everyone was exhausted, only being able to rest when they were asleep, only relaxing when they had finished the day.

They were being worked harder than ever before and it was all for a very good reason, they were capable of it.

These students weren't chosen at random, they weren't sent to me by accident, they had all been in the top two classes at Academia, a school designed for the training of powerful mages just like myself and Katiana.

If they couldn't take what I was throwing at them then they had been seriously over estimated by their previous teachers.

But that wasn't the case. They were strong, smart and quick to learn new techniques and skills.

I was impressed by their progress every step of the way and even by the end of the fiftieth, my students had learnt well indeed. Now capable of basic summoning magic and some more advanced teleporting skills, they were pretty much ready for what was to come next.

Not that they had a choice, at my school it was do well or fail miserably. If they couldn't handle it, then they were out, sent back to Academia and forced to tell others that they had been kicked out for underachieving.

The same could be said for Katiana's class as well, all her students could now cast high-level healing magic as well as remotely place enchantments on allies.

A few of them knew some basic attack spells too but that didn't matter at this stage.

How you chose to fight in a battle is up to you, whether or not it works depends of what it was that you did.

So while what I was teaching them was what I would

prefer they did on the battlefield, if they had an idea or a different style that they wanted to try then I didn't have a problem with it, as long as it didn't get them killed.

But with almost all of the students ready for the next step, I had some arrangements to make in the dojo.

After all, if they had made it this far already, then it was about time I put them to the test.

It was time once again, for the tournament to begin.

And the prize?

Graduation.

On the spot.

No questions.

However, that did mean that the students left standing at the end had to fight me at full strength and win.

I wasn't too hopeful of their chances but, if they had come this far, they'd at least be far more capable than they were on day one.

So, it was about time I found out just how capable they really were.

TOURNAMENT

For the next three days, I permitted the students to relax somewhat. Something that, due to the way I had been structuring my twelve-hour long school days and cramming in more and more into every lesson that passed, they wouldn't have seen coming.

I allowed the students to go about their business as normal for the mornings. Their lessons with myself and Katiana lasting from nine till midday as they otherwise would have done in the classrooms. But in the afternoons, they had no set timetable. No lessons to speak of.

It was a rather prolonged break period for them at the time. No practical lessons of any kind. No practice.

But that did not mean that they took the time to sloth about and take in the scenery. No. They used this time well. They even seemed to be enjoying themselves.

Practicing their techniques and spells over and over again.

Sparring with one another.

Even competing to see who could do the most damage to my barrier before it self-repaired. Forming small cracks and chips in its wall over and over again until everyone had had a go. Examining their sizes and depth and then timing how long it took for the barrier to recover.

They damn near blasted a hole large enough to walk through one or two times. But it was a good way of gauging their individual strength. So, I allowed them to continue.

But eventually, these small games lost their effect.

The children needed something more exciting, something more hands on.

So within a handful of hours on that first day of having the afternoon off, a fighting contest of sorts had broken out on the courtyard.

It was almost ironic considering what I had planned.

But I guess that they were all thinking about it by the time I gave them that break.

Who wouldn't want to know, the school's purpose was combat training, naturally they would want to find out who was the strongest pair.

When I realised what they were up though, the intensity of their spells and the shouting that I heard through the dojo walls giving it away within minutes, I sent Katiana to keep a watchful eye on them all.

I was half expecting there to be a dozen separate matches at the same time. Everyone fighting someone else. No order to it at all. But to my astonishment, even though I hadn't sanctioned the fights, they were still following every one of the rules that went with such sparring sessions.

Not one single person used a spell that was beyond them and none of them used their magic with the intent to kill their opponent at any time.

In fact, the most serious injuries that came from these fights were bruises and broken bones. Easily healed within an hour and not at all life threatening.

And the experience that each of them gained through this practice session, that was invaluable.

Most of the fights were one on one as it turned out. Most of my class had wanted to compete with one another for a while and in a similar way so too had those from Katiana's group.

But after an hour or two, those smaller, organized battles soon turned into all-out battle royals. The fights now consisting of up to nine students at a time. Students from both classes put up against each other. Last one standing winning the round.

Katiana had nothing but praise for the students when she reported her findings. And I admit, I agreed.

Learning to fight each other is one thing but holding your own up against eight other opponents was quite impressive at this stage of their training.

The special awareness and quick thinking that each student would require to dodge and counter every one of your opponent's attacks was more than I would have expect from them.

But even if most of the students were standing out in their own way, none were doing so more than Julian and Katrina.

Their fight was the most impressive of them all.

I couldn't help but go and watch it myself when I recognised their magic energy in the atmosphere.

But it wasn't the two working together that I sensed out there beyond the dojo walls. It was their unbridled wrath emanating from their magic and their minds as they traded blows with one another that caught my attention.

With how close those two were at the time I didn't think

that I would ever be able to convince them to go head to head against one another but it seemed that I didn't have to.

Those two were born fighters.

They both had excellent and very impressive hand to hand combat skills, almost similar in terms of speed and efficiency to that of a black belt in jujitsu.

And they were evenly matched too. Looking like they were going full tilt from the off. Seeming as though they intended to take each other's heads off with every blow that the other blocked or dodged at the last second.

And that was just their physical fight.

The magical one was mesmeric.

I couldn't count the number of spells they both threw around during that fight. Elemental casting and manipulation. Gravity altering fields. Teleporting back and forth to dodge or land a hit. Casting defensive flare and weaker variants of other protective spells to block the other's stronger attacks.

They were both using the most sophisticated combat techniques I had ever seen. And none of them were even close to what I had been teaching them.

With every trade of their fists, punching hard and fast at every turn, landing strikes that were painful enough to look at let alone feel. It was like watching two eternal enemies go head to head. Not lovers.

Those two must have really enjoyed themselves during that one. I can say that I certainly enjoyed watching it.

And the surrounding students didn't seem to mind the spectacle either it seemed. They could do nothing but watch in awe as the two most promising people in the school went up against each other in the background of their own fights.

But it was quite the tremendous fight to observe.

Either one of them was capable of winning yet they continuously drew with each other whenever I saw that one of them had an opening to knock the other down.

It looked as though they were fighting for fun rather than to win but if that was truly the case, then I wouldn't have wanted to see them when they were fighting for real. The savagery from that friendly match alone was enough to make my stomach churn.

But whatever their goal, it showed me what they were capable of both with and without their magic.

Nevertheless, that was the first day. The second was much of the same though Julian and Katrina stuck to working together for that one. And then the third day almost no one fought a single match.

They instead practiced and exercised in their pairs.

And with that third day over, my renovations to the dojo and the addition of several hundred more layers of enchantments within it were complete.

It was now ready to host the tournament once again.

Though this time, it would be unlike any that the students had ever seen before. Whoever won this tournament would not only be declared as the strongest team in the school but would also be the ones most likely to help win the war.

The tournament itself was not meant as a way to thin the heard or anything though. It was simply a way of determining whether or not they were ready to move on to the next stage, the part of my training course where I introduce them to armed combat and all the additional training that goes with it.

DANIEL FREARSON

But I suppose that 'tournament' wasn't a fair description of the event that I would be holding this year. In truth, it was more like a 'winner stays on' style of fight. Whoever stood atop the rest would have been the pair that had not been defeated. And if they outlasted everyone, then that proved beyond doubt that they were the strongest fighters we had.

And the rewards were nothing to scoff at either.

The rewards at the end of each stage were simple, whether you won the match or not it really didn't matter, your reward would still be the same. However, the way that I worded the reward section of the tournament rules made it seem like each round that you survived would allow you to acquire more impressive and stronger armaments than the others.

The rewards themselves were actually pretty basic, I wasn't going to go around giving the students the strongest armour and weapons when they've only been training for eight weeks.

In a sense I suppose you could call the rewards 'training gear', that's what their intended purpose was after all. To be used during training.

At the end of each round, a victor would obviously be declared and a loser would unfortunately be sent to sit back down with the rest.

It is these losers that get the reward for completing that round, the ones who won go on to the next round thinking that what they'll receive would be better than what they had just passed up by defeating the previous two opponents.

Each reward was a set of two items.

A complete kit of basic yet still sturdy battle armour and a weapon that fit the role of each student receiving the
408

reward.

If that student preferred distanced combat, he or she would receive a bow or perhaps even a throwing weapon but should the student prefer more hands on, close range combat, they would receive a sword, whip, dagger or even a pike as their weapon.

To them it would seem as though I had been handing out the weapons randomly. The students would have believed I was giving them a weapon that I thought would suit them best when in reality, they themselves have made the choice already.

Every step of their training so far had been closely monitored. Their fighting style, their attitude, their physique, everything had been taken into consideration when I made the choices for what weapons would suit them best.

But obviously if someone survived until the final round, they would expect to get something a bit more impressive and a lot stronger than the previous contestants had been awarded.

That was where the variants in the design of each reward came in. Each weapon that I had chosen to put up as a potential prize for these students had been handcrafted years ago to look more impressive than the one next to it.

It is only when you compare them in actual combat you realise that essentially all of them were the same. Be it in overall strength or the enchantments placed upon them, their weapons were identical despite their outward appearance.

Armour worked the same way, however the armour itself had been designed slightly differently than in previous years. While the armour was just like the weapons in the sense that each piece was designed to look better than the one sitting next to it; they differed in the enchantments placed upon them.

However, instead of attempting to amplify the spell being cast through them like a weapon, the armour sets were designed to enhance your survivability in combat.

This was done in any of three ways, sometimes in all three at the same time. It would either enhance your stamina, your ability to store magic energy or it would simply enhance your ability to withstand a punch or the bite of a knife.

Armour enchantments are tricky to predict, you never really know exactly what a student needs until they begin using it. That is why when I gave each student this piece of armour so early in the year.

They would have free reign to place whatever enchantments they were capable of writing onto it after the fact if an improvement was needed. The same went for the weapons as well. They could enchant them on top of what they've already been enchanted with or simply keep them as they were, the choice was up to them.

This tournament had two goals at its core though. It was a way to introduce students to the idea that everyone was your enemy and it was also a way of making students realise there is more to a fight than simply winning in.

Simply by participating you would be rewarded, both in knowledge and in apparel. What they would learn during the contest would be invaluable and the weaponry they received as a reward would be vital to completing their training.

410

And this tournament would consist of twenty-four matches. The first twenty-three would be a face-off between student and student, eventually leaving us with just one victorious team at the end of it all.

This team would be the one who had beaten every previous victor. The one team who had proven themselves stronger than everyone else by defeating the ones who had defeated those who came before.

And this one team who stood at the end of these twenty-three matches would get the honour of facing me as their final opponent. Not only in an unrestricted combat scenario with me fighting at my best from the off, but also an armed one.

It is this that the students were truly fighting for.

They were not going into this tournament thinking that they were going to become the strongest pair in school. They went into this tournament knowing that if they managed to beat everyone else then they would get to fight me in a way that none of them had ever seen done before.

It was this that each student strived to achieve.

A chance to not only prove themselves against their fellow pupils but also a chance to prove themselves against me.

But if for some unknown reason a victor is not declared or if someone is eliminated by forfeit or by force, the tournament rules and regulations would be changed accordingly.

If one pair was missing then another pair would get a chance to fight twice, but if by some miracle the final pair left standing actually managed to take me down in combat, they would be immediately graduated.

They would be given the rank of a level twenty-four mage as promised. They would be given an armour set equal to the one I wore and weaponry the likes of which they had never seen in their lifetimes and then sent on their way.

If someone managed to beat me, the rest of the course becomes mute. The entire point of this course, the reason I trained those students the way I did, was so that when they leave they are not only ready to fight but are also capable of doing so on a level equal to mine.

In all the years I had run this tournament at the school, all the times that I had faced off against the power of promising students, never had this victory been achieved.

No one had ever beaten me.

And unfortunately, even though I'm mentioning it now, this doesn't happen. I simply wanted to mention what would happen if someone were capable of winning.

But no one ever has been so lucky or so powerful.

If any of them could have been capable it would have been Julian but even he wasn't strong enough to beat me when it came down to it.

But that came later.

First, the tournament had to be announced.

It was one o'clock on a Saturday afternoon when I finally gave the students the news. It was then that I placed all the posters around the school informing people of the rules, regulations and requirements to compete in the tournament and it was then that I told them the tournament would begin in less than twelve hours.

I have always found that if you start an event like this as late in the day as possible, even at night if you can, the contestants not only fight harder but are also more on their game.

Put simply, by starting this tournament as late in the day as I possibly could without risking my students being tired; I allowed them to not only fight at their best but also to do so while their minds were clear and thinking at their best.

The students were quick to react to the news though. Rushing to the dorms, discussing fighting styles and even going as far as to make little pacts to ensure that the next person or even a group of people could be victorious based on who they thought had the best chance of taking me down if they won.

Little did they know that the order in which they fought would not be the order in which they were ranked as they had assumed.

The order in which they fought would be simple, two pairs go up first, one pair is then defeated and is sent off and replaced. I would then make it seem like I had randomly chosen the next pair and they go up, this continues until the last pair is chosen and the final victor is declared.

By doing this, it not only gave each student a chance of showing their skills against one another but it also showed who had the greatest endurance during battle.

It's one thing to be able to win the first fight after all. But it's another thing entirely to be able to keep that up for twenty-three more rounds.

Even if I sent the strongest pair of students up first and they somehow ended up remaining the unbeaten victor for five or even six matches, they wouldn't be able to do so forever.

Eventually one of two things would fail them, either their

endurance or their magic. It is always one of these two things that determines the point at which someone has fought to their last punch.

When your stamina fails, you can move no longer.

When your magic fails you, if it does so fast enough as I have told you in the past, you can faint or even completely collapse into a coma from the drain.

But I was sure nothing like that was going to happen. The students had never been pushed quite that far. A lot of them didn't even know their true limits yet.

From what Katiana had told me of their practice fights in the yard, it seemed as though when a student becomes tired or is incapable of continuing to fight, they will simply forfeit the match.

While it is admirable to recognise and accept defeat, it is also worrying that they would give up so easily when their opponents might have been in the same state that they were.

But enough explanation for now, now it's time for the tournament to begin.

Five nineteen in the evening,

I left it as late as I could.

However, if I had waited any longer I might have collapsed from being too tired myself.

As I've mentioned previously, I can go without sleep for upwards of three days, something that at that point I had already done.

I wasn't kidding when I said that I spent three days on the renovations to the dojo, I meant three whole days when I said it.

I wasn't talking about three twelve hour stretches, what I meant was that I had taken three whole days to do it in addition to all my other duties.

I spent those three days with no sleep and little food to go on. I only took the one break and that was to watch Julian fight his wife in the yard.

Beyond that I was teaching my lessons as normal and cooking breakfast, lunch and dinner on time each day too.

My body was beginning to grow weary from the exhaustion by then. So I needed to get this thing started before I myself needed to go to bed.

So I summoned the students, sending them all cryptic telepathic message.

Within this message were details of how to not only prepare yourself for the tournament but also how to enter it first.

The first two teams to complete these requirements would be the first two to arrive and the first two to face off against one another.

I'm not entirely sure what I said exactly. Then again I was tired at the time and the message itself was cryptic but I do know that it contained instructions on the requirement of wearing the sparring uniforms and that the students were to teleport into the dojo as soon as they could.

Within five seconds, a record by my account, the first two teams had arrived.

Not to my surprise, one of them consisted of both Katrina and Julian.

However, the team they were facing off against, that was what surprised me.

Students Lila and Trevor, both excellent fighters in their own regard and as a team they probably equalled Julian himself in terms of power alone.

The fight between them impressed me too.

I was stunned, watching as they fought each other in ways that I have still never seen replicated to this day. Never before and never since have I seen such raw fury.

Both teams wanted to win and both teams were prepared to do so.

While they mostly stuck to the techniques that I had taught them, the ways that they implemented these techniques into the fight was most peculiar and quite uncommon as it seems.

Ever since that day, I have never seen anyone fight in that same way, no matter what I tried, I simply couldn't teach people how to do it.

Trevor was an expert at all things ranged, be it fire, ice, wind or even teleporting, he was best at what he did when he stood as far away from his opponent as possible.

Lila on the other hand she was the golden child in my opinion. Being one of the youngest students at the school, she was only seventeen at the time, I would have expected her to be one of the weakest, but her defensive skills and enchanting style, at times it rivalled that of most mages I knew that were ten times her age.

She was quick at what she did, casting three or even four layered enchantments within seconds, being able to cast the most impressive display of defensive spells I had ever seen at the same time and doing all of this while not only staying almost completely silent but also while not moving her feet an inch.

It is unusual for any mage to stay perfectly still during the casting of a spell but for her it seemed to help. It's an unconventional fighting style but since her role in that fight was to hold back from the front lines to aid and protect Trevor, I didn't think that it would be a problem, at least I didn't think it would be a problem until the fight actually began.

After many minutes of waiting, the final few students arrived and took their seats, gasping in awe at the sight of my newly renovated dojo.

They took in everything that they could as they waddled over to the chairs.

They realised that things didn't quite add up rather quickly as it happened. The room seemed larger on the inside than it should have done, most of them probably just thought this was an illusion but in truth the room was actually larger.

A special kind of concealment magic that allows you to hide a larger space within a small exterior shell.

It's nothing too fancy but when you need to host large tournament events and don't want to build a completely new dojo to host them in, it comes in handy, especially when you're trying to smuggle objects through checkpoints.

It's not easy to find contraband when you can't see it because it's all being concealed within a matchbox.

Even something the size of a coin could be used to conceal something bigger as long as you could carry its weight. Not even magic can make an object weightless, you still have to carry most things unless you're using magic to make it move.

Nevertheless, the students all took their seats, some of them actually took them as in that they moved them from where they were and placed them elsewhere to get a better view.

I was opposed to this at the beginning but when I realised it really didn't matter where they sat as long as they could see the fight and had easy access to the main ring, then it really didn't bother me in the end.

Julian and Katrina had already taken up their positions on the tournament floor. Standing within their clearly marked zone and waiting patiently for their opponents to do the same.

It took them a minute to figure out what was going on though. Most students in the dojo now had never actually seen a tournament circle quite like this one.

Not only was it designed to be large enough that ranged mages could actually flourish within its area but it had also been designed to be not only long but also narrow.

A traditional tournament circle would be an actual circle extending up to fifteen metres in diameter. But this one was a more elongated shape.

It was thin and long. Three metres by twenty. That's all I can say about it. It was designed to allow mages to fight at range or in close quarters combat without allowing them too much room to move.

The idea of this fighting style is to restrict the movements of the contestants in such a way that they are forced to almost stand still during the battle. This is a little unorthodox for most but you soon get used to it.

Not only was its purpose to teach the students to fight even when boxed in but it also prepared them for yet another scenario that they might have to face some time soon.

Changing up fighting styles like this on a constant basis allows your students to not only realise that there is more than one way of fighting an opponent. But it also teaches them how to fight in certain situations that, while they might not think they are ever going to encounter, they might well do during the war that was to come.

And finally, after a little bit of waiting, the students who were watching had quietened down and the tournament was ready to begin.

On display behind me to the south side of the dojo was a large rack going wall to wall. Upon this rack were fifty sets of trainee's armour and fifty weapons to go along with it.

As I said, each one had been catered for a specific student, and while they would think they are simply getting a random weapon when they walked up, they themselves had chosen it weeks prior to this event.

I stood at the side of the tournament ring in-between the two opponents, from there I erected a small yet powerful barrier to protect the spectators from any magic that may deflect off in their direction. Best not to have the spectators receiving more wounds than the participants.

But since it had been weeks since Julian had knocked down the previous barrier protecting those within the dojo, I had yet to get around to replacing it. So this was all the students had to protect them.

The barrier that used to stand in that building takes weeks to set up. I didn't have that kind of time though. So I would just have to live without it for the time being.

And while I stood with my back to the weapons and armour, a challenger on either side of me at the edges of the ring, and the students ahead of me in the stand, Katiana was there too.

Standing next to the entrance. There on standby in case

anything needed to be done. Be that damage control or emergency healing; she was there in case something happened that I could either not deal with or could not have foreseen.

But with everyone in their places, I raised my hand into the air and explained the specific rules of this fight.

Every fight was different and each student required different rules to determine a clear and fair victor.

In Julian's case he was forbidden from using Final Stronghold, a spell so powerful that it was even able to break through one of my own barriers as well as a fully enchanted and fortified door.

And in the case of Lila, she was forbidden from using illusion magic. Not because it was illegal or that it would have given her an unfair advantage but because the type of illusion magic she used was most commonly used to give people nightmares rather than win a battle.

While in a true battle it would be quite useful to terrify your opponents, I did not feel comfortable with her giving all of my student's terrifying dream sequences because she had cast a spell that was a bit too powerful to control or contain.

After I was done explaining the rules, the two teams of students bowed to one another. Signifying the not only showed respect for their opponents but also that they were prepared to get on with this fight.

I looked over to Julian and still, even though it had been over a month since that night and the events that took place during it, all I could think about was the time he saved Katiana's life, the time that he had given up his own.

I did my best to clear my head and return to the moment.

My hand was still raised in the air and I felt that it was about time to move it.

So I forced my hand downwards as fast as I could, waving it in the air and allowing the fight to begin.

The two teams began to prepare their magic, storing it in their fists and their legs, activating enchantments and preparing to cast spells.

I thought about what Julian might be planning, he always seemed to have something up his sleeve when it came to a fight. The first thought that came to my mind was that he would probably try and use Defensive Flare to deflect the first wave of bombardment upon him.

But that wasn't what he did.

I then thought that he might try using a technique that I had mentioned to him but not actually taught, casting a fireball in your hand and then using teleportation magic to throw that fireball in the opponent's face from a distance.

This allows you to bypass any shields or enchantments they may have cast around themselves and even allows you to bypass Defensive Flare if aimed and times correctly.

But again, this was not the case.

Instead I turned my mind to the possibility that he had planned something with his wife, perhaps she intended to use her ability to read minds to get a sense of what the opponents were planning.

On the other hand, perhaps she would simply continue to cast defensive spells on Julian until his opponents had run out of magic energy.

This didn't happen either though.

In the end, he simply stood there, allowing his opponent to take cheap shots at him. Each one landed, striking a hit, dealing serious damage to Julian's body and magic energy as each one made contact.

The first barrage of projectiles were fire based, low level but frequent. Like an assault rifle, each shot might not have actually dealt decent damage but overall the amount of shots fired into the enemy was overwhelming.

But Julian simply stood there and took it. Not moving a muscle, not reacting in the slightest, he just stood there and allowed his opponent's attacks to hit him.

When the dust and smoked cleared from Julian's face and chest, Trevor was shocked to find Julian still standing there with the same disinterested look on his face.

And only when he switched from ranged to close quarters combat to try and circumvent whatever defence Julian was using was it that I realised what he had planned.

Knowing that Trevor was proficient at ranged combat he needed to create a scenario in which Trevor would approach him and close the gap so the two could fight in Julian's own comfort zone.

This was an intriguing plan, they created a situation in which Trevor believed that Julian was simply going to stand there and allow himself to lose, this situation forced Trevor to feel as though he could get away with punching him physically rather than magically.

And this had two effects. It made Trevor's movements easier to predict and also put him further away from his partner resulting in her having a delayed reaction time to anything that happened and also a less clear view of what had happened too.

The ball was now on Julian's side of the court and what he did with it was most intriguing.

Other than the specific rules that I had mentioned before the fight began, there were no other spells that were banned during this fight.

Julian, Lila, Katrina and Trevor could do whatever they wanted. And Julian had planned for this. I could feel the level of magic energy building up within his chest, an uncommon place for anyone to want to use magic as it's not an offensive position but unlike what I had expected, Julian wasn't on the offensive.

Instead Julian had switched rolls, allowing himself to take that damage, hurting him both physically and magically but what it had not done was force him out of the fight.

When Trevor got within punching distance, something happened, something that happened so quickly I almost missed it.

Both Julian and Katrina teleported to each other's positions at the same time. Allowing Julian to be behind Katrina, casting whatever protective enchantment or spell he needed to and it also allowing Katrina to not only surprise Trevor, in a way that put him off his guard but also allowed an uninjured and unhindered opponent to enter a fight against an opponent who had already exerted himself on someone he believed to be an easy target.

He had forced his opponent to narrow his view.

He had made Trevor fixate on himself and allow him to forget about his partner. Opening the stage for her to prepare and then execute whatever plan of attack she had come up with in the meantime.

A surprising tactic. And a very successful one.

The fight didn't last much longer after that moment.

To my amazement, Katrina actually managed to fight on a level that was almost identical to Julian once she took over. Knowing him he probably trained with her for many months while they were in Academia.

And mere moments after her teleportation cycle had ended, her fist was firmly in the air, striking Trevor's jaw on the way and leaving Trevor himself flying through the air on his way to landing on his ass.

With no enchantments and no magical energy in that fist whatsoever, she had punched him with pure physical strength. The surprising thing about that was that she seemed pretty frail for a girl of her age and skill.

While she only looks to be a nineteen-year-old girl, as I had recently come to realise, she was in fact closer to the age of Julian himself thanks to that heart of hers.

Machine dolls do not age after all.

The fight didn't last long after that action.

Lila panicked and cast too many protective spells at one time to protect Trevor. Caused a conflict between those enchantments as they tried to take effect and resulting in nothing happening at all.

And since they had all been cast at the same time, all she had done is waste time and energy in her panic. A truly amateur move if I've ever seen one.

After realising her mistake and how open she had left herself, she quickly attempted to cast another spell but by then it was too late.

With Trevor on the floor, an uninjured Katrina took her chance to mess with his mind.

I'm not entirely sure what she did to his head but whatever it was it screwed him up pretty badly. He laid hunched on the floor crying in pain and possibly even agony after she was done with him.

And when I asked her what she had done, all she said was that she had shown him himself.

But since Trevor could no longer continue in that state and since Lila was too puzzled to react, I didn't see a point in forcing her to take a punch before the battle was over. So I declared Julian and Katrina the victors of the first round and then I teleported Trevor back to his room and put him to sleep.

Unfortunately, with a spell like that, the only thing you can do is sleep it off. Mind-altering spells can last for many hours, even days. The best option you have is to stay unconscious and let them pass if you can.

And after realising that these two we're not going to be as easy to eliminate as everyone had assumed, the following opponents upped their game.

Each one trying and fighting harder than the next but none of them could defeat those two, not a single pair of students in the entire school even came close to defeating those two in battle.

Not even when it came time for the groups of three to have their turn did those two go down. Be it Julian's exceptional ability to fight or Katrina's ability to read minds, those two never came close to losing.

Perhaps I should have changed up how this tournament worked once I saw their winning streak. But at the time I chose to do it this way, I had foreseen no problem with it.

Every member of the school would have their chance against the two of them and every member of the school had been swiftly knocked on their butts as soon as they tried.

There was even one pair who ended up being fried in the process. They had thought that if they projected a constant stream of flames towards Julian and Katrina they would have eventually ran out of magic energy to block those flames with. Obviously those two students never actually paid attention in class because then they would have known that Julian and Katrina are quite adept at casting Defence Flare, a spell that not only deflects and reflects the spells cast upon it but also amplifies them as it does so.

The resulting injuries were not pleasant but it was nothing that Katiana couldn't heal. And luckily that only happened once. The smell of burning flesh is not exactly one that you want sticking around in your dojo if you can help it.

It took three hours for the two of them to win the rest of their battles though.

Twenty-three matches and they still stood undefeated.

A little worn out by this point but after their close teamwork and Katrina casting ranged healing spells slowly in the background during their simpler fights, neither one of them was wounded in the slightest.

They were tired, drained and nearing their limits.

But finally, after the last pair of students had been fought off, I allowed everyone to go and claim their weapons and armour.

I told them that the numbers labelled upon them were the rounds in which they had fallen.

Rather than placing names on each armour set and weapon and making it obvious that each one was catered to a certain person; I placed the round numbers on them to make it seem like each reward was tied to a specific round.

However, what they didn't know was that I had remotely

changed those numbers depending on which round I chose each pair in.

No matter who I had chosen or who had won, they would have always been receiving the same reward.

Each student picked up their armour, picked up their weapons and went on their way back to their seats where they were about to see something truly spectacular.

They were about to see not only the first example of armed mage combat but also the first example of me during armed combat.

I took up my position while Julian and Katrina picked up their weapons and armour.

I had chosen a very special blade for Katrina, one that not only worked from range thanks to its ability to emit deadly beams of burning light into the direction of an opponent but also worked quite effectively up close due to its enchantment allowing it to break almost any material known to exist.

Thankfully, that didn't include my armour, otherwise I would have just given them a weapon that could actually have hurt me.

The blade I had chosen for Julian was even more impressive. It was a large two-handed sword engraved from pommel to tip with enchantments of all kinds.

Not one single exposed part of the sword wasn't engraved with enchantments. The handle, hilt, blade even the tang - the piece that actually connects the handle to the blade – that too was engraved with enchantments.

Its use was simple, hit them hard then hit them again.

The enchantments upon this blade were slightly more powerful than all the others but its drawback was its size and how slow it was to use.

While it was stronger in both physical aspects and magical aspects, the blade itself was difficult to wield, resulting in an equalisation of its destructive capabilities compared to the rest.

Because while it could hit hard, it did so while being pretty slow and easy to parry.

The armour was nothing special. Plate armour with leather straps that slipped on over their clothes. It was the same as everyone else's. But that being said, it did look a little nicer with its gold and red tinted patterns decorating it from head to toe.

All in all, the armour itself was just like all the others. They had the same enchantments, basic protection stuff, nothing too fancy, and a little bit of stamina enhancement mixed in.

Since this was an important fight and I'm sure they didn't actually care about how they looked, they slipped the armour on top of their existing clothing. It probably wasn't too comfortable but in addition to the protective nature of the sparring uniform, the armour probably protected them just well enough to withstand my attacks.

I shifted into Athereon form, stretched out my wings, extended my magic energy as a pressure wave to show off a bit and then I began to choose my weapon.

Since this body was quite literally fused to the armour it wears; I don't have a choice as to which one I wore during battle. But I did have a choice of any weapon I wanted and I knew exactly which ones to choose.

For dealing with Katrina I placed my left hand out in the air and began summoning my bow. It was very similar in the shape and overall design to the one my wife had. Since they actually shared the same maker you would expect that they looked alike. Not a perfect replica but just like hers, it was small yet very powerful.

The spectators behind me gasped in confusion, none of them ever seen a summoning spell used on a weapon before. I would have actually been teaching it to them anyway but at that moment it was their first experience with a mage who could successfully perform a summoning spell on something as large and complicated as an enchanted weapon.

Summoning works similarly to how teleporting does, in the sense that you have to imagine the destination and also create a bubble around yourself.

However, in this case you have to imagine the weapon and then create a bubble around it remotely. Teleporting it from wherever you have been storing that weapon and then placing it in your hand.

It's nothing too impressive, the most important aspect of any summoning spell is the weapon that you're choosing. For me it was simple, Katrina had shown a weakness against ranged attacks, so for her I summoned my bow and placed it in my left hand ready for use later.

For Julian, things were a little different.

He had not shown a weakness in any area that I could see, meaning that the weapon I chose didn't have to be specific to exploit any of his flaws but it had to be versatile.

I needed to choose a weapon that could not only fight at range if needed but also up close and in any other situation that might have occurred during that fight.

To that end, only one weapon sprung to mind and it might not have been the most appropriate choice given that

429

this was a friendly match. Such destructive force should have only been used during real battle scenarios. But nothing happened in the end so I suppose that the risk wasn't as prominent as I had expected.

The only weapon I could think of that would do everything I needed it to might have been slightly too powerful to have used in such a confined space as that dojo.

The blade I summoned is known by many names but more recently it has been known by the name of the Chaos Blade but in truth its name actually translates to the Blade of Flames but you tell me, which one actually sound more impressive?

I placed my right arm out to my side and began summoning the blade. This one took a bit longer due to how I have to store it. In the wrong hands this blade is capable of causing great destruction and even in mine it was still a little difficult to control.

In order to safely store this weapon, out of reach of anyone other than me, I kept it in one of the deepest floors of my vault. A lead lines box twenty-three meters below the house.

The only thing stronger that that blade was down there too.

But that sword wasn't one that I could ever take out.

Even holding it was too great a risk. The thing could destroy entire continents at full strength. So it was a good thing that no one would ever get a hold of it.

And with the blade that far down and encased in lead, no mage other than myself could possibly have known that it was there. But it also made teleporting it out pretty difficult.

Summoning this blade takes time and time was not a

luxury that I had. Before even the handle of this blade had been materialised, Katiana had already lowered her hand declaring the beginning of this fight.

But from the looks of it I wasn't going to get very far.

Julian had already teleported in front of me before I could even cast any of the defensive spells I could think of. I simply had to stand there and take a few punches as he jabbed at me to test my armour.

And by the time that he actually had the idea of swinging his sword at me, my blade had already been summoned.

With my right arm now usable, I sprang into action. Hitting his blade with mine as hard as I possibly could without breaking the two of them.

This sent his blade flying in the air and made it obvious to me that these kids would also be requiring basic weaponry training on top of the more advanced techniques I had planned on teaching them.

I would have hoped that they'd at least know how to properly hold a sword.

Nevertheless, with his blade out of his hands, he attempted to use a spell that I didn't really agree with at the time. Now that I think about it was probably justified, he was up against me after all.

The spell he used was called Insight.

It's a spell that reveals all magical circuits and enchantments placed within a body. It's not difficult to perform but it does leave your opponent open to very specific and targeted attacks the likes of which his wife was just then preparing to perform.

With my weaker areas and now visible to her senses, she held her sword up in the air pointing the tip of it towards

431

me. I wondered if she'd already figured out how its enchantments worked but I didn't have to wait long to find my answer.

A moment later, Julian just beginning to back step from my position as I rearranged my footwork to react to Katrina, a beam of light was launched towards me. While not travelling at light speed per se, it still travelled at a quicker speed than most would have been able to dodge.

Four inches wide, strong enough to pierce steel or sever a head from one's shoulders, it was coming from me faster than anyone would have been able to deal with. But me being me, I put my footwork to good use and rolled out of its way just fast enough to avoid it.

And with my body moving now as I avoided that attack, I headed straight into Julian. He hadn't expected me to roll forwards, he was probably expecting me to go back.

This through him off his guard just slightly enough that I was able to defeat him within a matter of moments.

I was swift to act, I spun around on the floor and knocked him off of his feet, sending him falling out of the ring, disqualifying him but not Katrina.

She was still standing and was still armed.

I would have expected more from him but by then he was running on fumes. It only made sense that he didn't have much fight left in him.

But his wife on the other hand, she soon became quite angry at me, possibly because I had just knocked her husband on his ass or maybe it was because I wasn't as easily defeated as she had predicted.

The two of them knew that I was week and tired, they probably thought that with weapons in hand they would have an actual chance of defeating me. But I am not that easy to take down. Even when I am tired, I was still a better fighter than the two of them put together.

I saw my opportunity to act though, so I threw my sword in her direction to force her to have to block it with hers. And now that her sword was no longer facing me as she protected herself from mine, I turned my attention to my bow. Pointing it towards her and pulling back on the string.

With this bow you don't need arrows, the shots that it fired are formed purely of magic and as such they become ever more powerful depending on who's firing them.

I drew the bow back and fired one arrow directly at her.

It moved so fast that she didn't have time to react. By the time that she had tried to dodge it had already landed, hitting her in the shoulder but not knocking her over or kicking her out of the fight.

With this being a magic arrow it doesn't actually cause physical harm unless you wanted it to. Instead, I had used an arrow that was intended for fighting against mages and as such it only caused pain should you hit a target in a muscled area.

It was these muscles that you would feel the pain in, stimulating them in such a way that it probably felt like I was burning her alive.

A bit cruel sure but necessary in this situation.

The shoulder I had managed to hit was her right one, incapacitating her entire right arm as the arrow dug into her muscle beneath the skin.

And while she attempted to swap her sword into her left hand, I teleported in close and just gave her a little kick. Again, not enough to cause physical harm but enough to knock her out of the circle and declare me as the victor.

I had expected more from those two to be completely honest but considering that that was their twenty-fourth battle in a row, I'm not surprised that they relied on their weapons to do most of the fighting.

They were probably almost completely drained of magic energy as it was. My fight most likely finished them off.

But alas, I was impressed with them, they had earned their title of being the strongest pupils in the school and had also done me proud.

I was proud to be their master. I was proud to be their friend. And I was proud to be their teacher.

And with the tournament over, the students would soon retire into their rooms for some much-needed rest.

By the next day, there wouldn't be much lefty to do now.

The only thing that was really left on the syllabus for the rest of the entire semester was training them to use their weapons and teaching them how to perform a perfect summoning spell.

Passed that, there isn't much other than preparation.

The war would be just around the corner by then.

After teaching them how to use and summon their weapons, the whole teaching part of this course would be pretty much over.

Once they learnt how to summon the weapons that I had given them and how to use them, that'd be it. I would no longer be teaching them theory in classrooms but instead I would be observing them as they spent the following six months preparing themselves as combat ready warriors and as battle-hardened mages.

Over the next few months, the only thing that they would

be doing would be fighting, be that against each other or against me.

The second half of the course is purely a constant and unending fight. This builds up their stamina and strength, prepares them for the unexpected and teaches them to think on their feet.

While this was not a teaching style that often worked, it was one that I approved of. The only other solution to this problem would be to train each one of them individually until I was happy to say that they were ready.

But that takes time and time was the one thing that I did not have much of.

So instead, I would be training them as a group. Focusing on all of them at once and not letting any of them fall behind.

I had to get them ready for what was to come and I didn't have a lot of time to do it.

Their final test, their graduation for all intents and purposes, was to be the war itself, and that war would be coming a lot sooner that I had thought possible.

Soon enough that perhaps, none of us were ready for it.

But we wouldn't have a choice.

Once that barrier came down, the fighting would start.

No questions, no delay.

Once the Tears opened fully and that army came through, whether we were ready or not, we'd have to fight.

And come victory or defeat, we wouldn't stop until the last breath was drawn.

But would that be ours?

Or theirs?

TIME RUNS OUT

Something changed after that night.

The clash of mine and Julian's swords, the feeling of our magic energy filling the air, the sensation in my core as I watched the fear in his eyes faulter to his will. In that moment, I could see that something had changed.

The boy I had met years before was no longer standing before me now. His body had matured, his muscles had grown twice their size, his endurance had excelled any expectations and his abilities were beyond anything he might have imagined the day that we first met.

Before me now stood a soldier.

A man with a strong mind, heart and body.

Ready and willing to learn. To train. To fight.

And he wasn't alone.

Now, day after day, endless night after endless night, the students and I would train together tirelessly. Strengthening their bodies and their minds. Preparing them for the challenges and the horrors of the fight to come.

A little shuffling around with the fighting pairs came first but after that, the students seemed to settle into the idea of fighting side by side with one another no matter who their partner.

The first steps are always the hardest. And theirs were far harder than most.

They lacked even the basic footwork and stances in order to wield the weapons that I had granted them. They didn't even have the foundations to begin practicing grip and technique.

It took me a week just to get them to a point where I could trust placing those weapons back in their hands.

But slowly, day after day and little by little, they were beginning to make astounding progress once again.

Their magical abilities were suitable for what they would face. Their understanding of enchantments and protective incantations more than sufficient for keeping themselves alive. And their hand to hand skills more than enough to keep them standing if they ever lost hold of the weapons I had placed in their hands.

All that was left was teaching them how to use their weapons.

Be it as a catalyst for their spells, as a means of attack or as a means of defence, this students needed to understand all manner of weapon techniques in order to survive what was coming.

Summoning those weapons to their hands, holding then firm and then trusting that their bodies would know what to do as they slashed and stabbed at anything that came near them once that barrier in the sky crumbled into dust.

They needed a lot of work.

But then again, every mage does when it came to this stage.

Magical talent is something that the academies are intended to flourish. Weaponry and fighting tactics were my job. And once those students each had their respective weapons in their hands, it became apparent that once again, only a few even had the faintest idea how to make use of them.

And worse yet, getting them to work as a team was even more challenging.

It was almost as if the students weren't able to see each other as allies in the beginning. They didn't seem to understand that they were much stronger working together than they would ever be apart.

I suppose that issue was my doing in a way. So far in their training, I had mentioned nothing of the war and simply stated that they would be competing to stay on the course.

I hadn't told them the truth behind why they were being trained and as a result, they didn't trust anyone but their partners for quite some time.

In order to make sure that they were working as allies rather than enemies, I had to put them in situations where two of them wouldn't be enough.

Katiana and I had to fight them at the same time in order to make them see that having someone there to stay by your side isn't always enough when your both outclassed and overpowered.

By forcing them to realise that they could not defeat the two of us by themselves I eventually managed to get them working as a team.

But even this small amount of team building wouldn't be enough to cement the level of trust and teamwork that I would need them to gain in the end.

When the time came, if I didn't have every student

willing to work and fight together, then we wouldn't have a chance.

There wouldn't have been a point in fighting if I couldn't get them to fight together.

If you cannot rely on the person behind you to have your back or if you yourself didn't have their trust, then you have no chance of winning.

You would be forced to watch all sides at all times and even for a fully trained warrior, that much was impossible against the numbers that we'd be fighting.

Every fighter needs someone to watch their back. You focus on the front, and they protect your rear. This has been and will continue to be the best and most reliable fighting style that I had ever taught.

It worked every time without fail. But in order for it to do so, the students needed to start trusting one another.

A month since the night of the tournament soon passed and the time had finally come to continue their training to the next step up.

Since that night, I had mostly spent my time teaching those kids how to wield their weapons. Teaching each of them the techniques that were ideal for each of their various fighting styles, the strengths and weaknesses that their weapons had too. But most importantly, I had painstakingly taught each of them how to properly summon those weapons.

While it was more than a little bit difficult for most of them at first, they eventually got the hang of it.

They weren't able to do it very quickly or consistently but they had all done it at least once.

And now that they could summon a weapon, no matter

where they would be or what they were doing, they would always be able to defend themselves.

All they had to do was remember where they had left their weapons and summon them if they ever needed to fight. Even on the battlefield if they must.

Summoning your sword when it gets separated from you is much faster and a lot safer than trying to find and retrieve it on foot when you have no way of dealing damage otherwise.

So with that accomplishment made, they were now ready for much, much more from me.

So I moved on to their armour.

While I had been adamant that they wore it during their weaponry training, a lot of them decided that protecting themselves was a secondary concern when it came to those practice sessions.

It took a few days to convince them of its importance at first but I eventually got them into the habit of wearing it all the time. Putting them through more vigorous and intense training each day made them endure more injuries. The idea of being hurt if they didn't have something to protect themselves was what it took to convince them in the end.

They believed that if they didn't wear it, they wouldn't be able to survive my hits. Which was true. But if I was actually trying to kill them, there would need far more to protect them that just those flimsy pieces of armour.

However, my method of forcing the students to see sense was quite effective as it turns out.

Surprising them at every turn with battle after battle, no warning and no choice but to participate, that seemed to get them into the right mind-set in the end.

The idea that you are never truly safe even while at school.

That's what I needed them to understand.

And I did this by launching sneak attacks at all hours of the day. While they were asleep, after lunch or during it, even during lessons if I must. I started fight after fight until they finally got the idea.

I needed them to know that they were far safer wearing the armour than they would ever be without it.

After they realised that these random fights wouldn't be stopping any time soon, they all started wearing their armour for protection.

It was fun in the beginning.

During their lunch break I would make it look like I was simply patrolling the campus but should a student catch my eye on that walk, I would draw my blade and start swinging.

They didn't know how to react at first but eventually they all wanted to be chosen.

They would keep their weapons by their sides as much as possible and have their armour tightly strapped to them just in case.

They would wait in the courtyard rather than go and get food too. Just so that they might get a chance to fight.

They saw it as a reward I guess, being chosen at random to have a one on one fight with me.

I saw it as a vital part of their training but as long as they understood what it was that I was trying to teach them, then I didn't mind.

And now that they wore their armour pretty much all the time, it meant that they had learnt of its importance and it
442

meant that when the day came for them to fight, they wouldn't have a problem with putting it on.

So now that they were wearing it, I taught them how the enchantments worked and how to add new ones on top of them to either compliment or enhance the ones already there.

While I didn't expect them to be using those armour sets in combat, it was still important that they knew how to improve them.

Moving on from that I focused on teleportation based combat. Since the strongest pair of students had already shown evidence that they had somewhat mastered it, it was important to teach everyone else how to do the same.

I taught them how to time their teleports, how they could charge the action and then store the energy in their chests to activate it instantly later.

It took a lot of concentration to pull off but it allowed for a much faster teleport than normal, provided that your mind can keep up with the change in surroundings in the middle of a battle without ending up dead.

Coupled with how to pull it off, I also taught them how they could use this skill to think outside of the box and surprise their enemies.

To catch them off guard or even avoid them all together.

I even taught them how to bypass most types of defensive spells, simply teleport the spell you cast behind their shield after it moves away from you.

The result is a short range, fast moving bullet – for lack of a better description that is.

It didn't matter who you used this on, no matter what their skill or size, no one would be fast enough to doge

443

something that fast when it was already that close.

Then I moved onto how to teleport during a physical activity like a fight.

While most teleportation requires you to stop moving in order to cast the spell, there were exceptions to this.

A lot of mages find it tricky to get their head around teleportation while moving given the added variables and math required to track your position. And those students were no exception to this.

It took a week to train the first two how to do this and with the exception of those two, Julian and Katrina, it took everyone else several more attempts and many more days.

But they managed to get there eventually.

Teleportation techniques during combat aren't always effective and can't always be relied on due to how easy they are to interrupt or deflect but I taught them how to do it anyway. Even if it didn't help you offensively, it would at least improve your defence.

I taught them how to teleport back and forth from spot to spot and confuse your enemies mostly. Landing strikes in quick succession but not staying put for long enough for that enemy to retaliate.

Not everyone was capable of this, it proved too taxing and draining for most students to use. And most of the ones who could, only had the ability to do so five or six times in a row before needing a rest.

This was understandable, teleporting over and over again requires quick thinking and a lot of concentration. It wasn't something that I had expected everyone to be able to do but I was glad that at least some of them could.

But unfortunately, teaching them this took many days

more than expected and ate up a lot more of the precious time I had left than I would have liked.

But they got there in the end. All be it at a slower pace than I had expected.

But as a result, they could now wield and summon their weapons, they understood the importance of their armour and had mastered basic teleportation combat.

With that out of the way, I finally moved on to one of the most import things that I could teach them.

Offensive enchantments and how to place them on their amour and weapons.

While Katiana had taught all the supportive fighters how to cast defensive and enhancement enchantments, she hadn't taught them how to strengthen their attacks or how to use the enchantments already on their armour and weapons yet. That level of power behind their punches would have been too much to defend against before.

But now they had the skill and the experience to protect themselves when sparring against someone with that level of power. So I taught them that part too.

Teaching them some of the strongest enchantments that I thought they could handle and then showing them how they worked in combat.

It didn't take long for the students to like what they were seeing either.

Compared to an enchanted attack, what they had been doing was nothing more than poking at the enemy.

With enchantments and some quick thinking, a mage's strike could literally send someone flying or cut them in half with as much effort as lifting a finger if used correctly.

And depending on the mage, one could even

theoretically level a city with a single swing of their sword. Although, that too depended on the sword.

Not many would be able to survive the level of magic energy required to do this before breaking. But that being said, it wasn't impossible.

And once they understood this, they would be ready for the next step. Their reward for making it that far, the effective middle point of the curriculum, would be an immediate promotion to rank fifteen and some real armour.

No more of the pathetic trainee's armour that I had given them already.

But they had to make it that far first.

Teaching them about enchantments took a couple weeks on its own. And over the course of this subject, the students had been practicing hard. Starting more and more fights in both the dojo and the courtyard.

Almost all of them were using the enhanced techniques that I had recently taught them. Teleporting all over the place at a rapid pace, wielding their weapons like they actually knew how to and even managing to summon their weapons at will during combat should they be separated from them.

It was at this time that I finally saw true hope for these students.

They had come a long way, both physically and emotionally. They were no longer scared of fighting, every one of them could hold their own now and all of them had shown a great improvement in their magic energy endurance too.

So the next step was team battles, three or four sets of pairs against each other.

This opened them up to the idea of more coordinated large-scale battles, just like the ones that they would face during the war.

But I didn't get to that part.

I was less than a week away from teaching them this when it finally happened. The day that I had been dreading for five months. The day that I had thought would come later.

But it was now, after one hundred and twenty days since their opening above my home, that the cracks in the air turned the sky red. And it was then that I had to change my plans on the spot.

I was running out of time and I knew that wouldn't be able to train them as much as I had intended.

We were only half way into the course and they were nowhere near ready.

I was supposed to have more time, I was supposed to have them ready to face what was coming before this happened. IU was supposed to have whittled them down to a select few. But alas, even my worst predictions were too conservative.

I had expected to have another two months at least but luck it seems, was not on my side.

Five fifteen P.M. That was when I felt it, the first signs of my barrier failing and the corruption steadily breaking through it at long last.

The students were busy fighting recreationally at the time, enjoying a much-needed break from the hard day of training beforehand. Neither them nor myself had anticipated what was about to happen.

But how could we have?

They were acting as though it had just been an ordinary day. They were fighting together, laughing together, working together, nothing was out of the ordinary and yet everything about that day was anything but normal.

We were ill prepared and starved of time.

We weren't ready.

The sun hadn't even fully descended when it happened, I could still see the slightest cusp of its light on the horizon before it was obstructed by the blinding light beaming down from above.

I had felt slightly off throughout the day but I hadn't managed to put a finger on why that was. But when the first signs of the barrier failing appeared, my finger was on it straight away.

Why I hadn't been able to recognise that feeling was anyone's guess, I should have known what to expect and I should have prepared for it.

First the ground shook violently, then the birds flocked away as fast as they could and finally, as the temperature dropped and a great pressure gripped at our hearts, the sky began to bleed.

The first few layers of my barriers had given in, breaking one at a time in quick succession as the pressure grew too far. And with those layers gone, the barrier was finally stretched thin enough that it was allowing the corruption to begin to seep through.

My barrier was holding, barely, but not enough to hold back the forces against it now. Because now that it had been weakened, enough of that corruption was spewing into the atmosphere to finally have an effect on the world.

I felt them break one by one, like shockwaves from explosions coming out of the sky as the first three layers shattered.

Three loud crashes could be heard in the sky shortly after, thunder without lightning, the all too recognisable sound of my own impending doom. A sign that I had run out of time.

The barrier was servery weakened and wearing thin.

It had begun to collapse and more and more of the corruption had begun to force its way through the Tears. The two of them now opening wider and wider by the hour, expanding their influence and placing more and more pressure on the paper thin shell still barely holding them back.

They had opened so wide and become so powerful that almost every mage would be able to feel it now. Some of them Might have even been able to see it.

It must have looked like the night sky had just disappeared all of a sudden and was then replaced with a blinding white light.

But for those who could see it, they could see all of it.

Its influence on the environment, its size and its power, the light that it gave off and the feeling that it created.

For those who could see it, they must have been terrified.

And due to how powerful they had become and how fine-tuned their senses had become recently, every one of students could see them now too.

They finally knew what I was hiding.

So I had no choice but to explain everything after that.

The sky had started to rain blood red water after all, that's not something that you can just ignore. Add that to the fact that there were now two large holes in the sky that blinded anyone who looked directly at them like the sun and I defiantly had a lot of explaining to do.

The first drops of rain stated to fall not long after the shaking stopped. And due to their nature and origin, the barrier around my house and land recognised them as a threat. Refusing them entry. Deflecting them off its surface violently every time a drop hit its surface.

The barrier sparked and shook as each droplet hit its shell, the sound of gunfire soon filled the air as each drop of water was turned to dust, shattering just like a bullet hitting a wall.

Red lightning screeching across the dome of my barrier. The energy of every one of those drops desperately trying to break through. The barrier holding them back. Spreading the load all across its surface. Illuminating us now with red flashes of light amidst the white of the Tears above us in the sky.

It looked like the end of the world.

Which was quite fitting.

Since it was.

I immediately teleported out of my office and into the courtyard as fast as I could after the shaking finally subsided. I had been monitoring the students from my window, but this situation needed to be dealt with head on.

I didn't have time to waste.

"Everyone, inside the dojo, now!" I screamed, pointing at the dojo with a violent thrust of my arm as I grabbed everyone's attention.

I had little time to react and I had to make sure that the situation remained under my control.

If the students had been left to stare at the sight by themselves, they would have started running before long.

But I couldn't have done much better.

I had been inside the school reviewing the student's progress while Katiana prepared their dinner for that night, we weren't prepared for that to happen at the time. It was many weeks earlier than it should have been.

No, it was months earlier.

The students immediately did as I said, teleporting their weapons safely to their rooms and rushing inside.

I did a quick head count and only one person was missing.

Julian.

I contacted him telepathically but received no response. Realising that he more than anyone could look after himself, I ignored his absence of a while. I would have to find him later.

The students in the dojo with me proceed to stare out to the windows running along the celling of that room. Looking up at the holes in the sky and the streaks of blood red water running down the dome shaped shell of my barrier.

The rain was more crystalline than mere water, as if the sky was raining ruby red gemstones. But when each drop hit the barrier they shattered and became the fluid that the students saw running down the side of it.

"Students. The time for me to explain has come." I said, not even slightly gaining their attention.

Truthfully, I would have preferred to tell them from the start but now that they were at least partially combat trained they were more applicable to the information I intended to tell them.

"Master, the sky. Why is it cracked?" Asked Trevor, walking up to me with his new partner not far behind.

While I didn't think so at first, it turns out that Robert ended up being a much better fit for his fighting style than Lila.

So I swapped Lila with Robert and put her with Dilian, someone that seemed to have a better fitting approach to combat than Trevor did.

"Everyone, listen closely now." I said louder.

I was only moments away from beginning my explanation when Katiana suddenly teleported in with Julian in tow. He wasn't in good shape.

As expected, Katrina screamed telepathically at the sight of him and ran to his side.

It turned out that during the initial shaking, the floor above him had caved in on his head.

I questioned why he was in the school in the first place but it didn't matter.

Katiana was a skilled medic and Katrina knew more about his body than anyone, they would have him back in one piece before long. However, this did mean that I would have yet another blood stain to clear up in the dojo again.

Had that accident occurred on any other day I would have rushed in to help him as well but on that day, more pertinent events were occurring.

The barrier around the Tears hadn't given up completely. I estimated a week at best before the fighting began. But it was going to take all of that time for me to get the students accustom to their battle armour and what it was capable of.

First though, I owed them some answers.

With all that was happening, a few of them had become quite unsettled. But that was nothing compared to what they would soon have to face.

"Students, settle down." I said.

They soon quietened down a little. Enough to hear me at least. But still, the sound of nattering remained, senseless chatter in the background that distracted them from the moment.

"I have known that this day was coming for months now but I hadn't expected it to come this soon. In the sky above us are two interdimensional portals, known as Tears. These portals lead to a place that you would not understand or want to know about. But traveling through them now comes a form of magic that every mage knows to fear. Spewing out of those holes in the sky, is an overwhelming and un-ending supply of corrupted magic energy.

This is why the rain is red. It's the world's natural response to having that much corrupted magic in the atmosphere. And it will only get worse.

Soon there will be volcanic eruptions, tsunami's, earthquakes. You name it. Every natural disaster that you can think of will come as a result of this magic.

However, this is not the worst of it.

On the other side of these portals lies a vast army. I have come to simply call them the Corruption in my time fighting against them. They are formed from corrupted magic and feed off it to gain strength. They are very hard to kill. This is what I have been training you for. This is the fight for which you have been chosen to play a role in."

As my shoddy and not very well worded explanation started to sink into the minds of the students, it shocked them and created a sense of distrust between us.

I had been lying to them from the beginning and now that they knew, I would have been surprised if they could find it within themselves to forgive me.

"All of this, the combat training, the battle tactics. It was all so that we could fight in a war we knew nothing about?" A voice said in anger. Yet again, those words came from Trevor, he had always been the punctual one.

"I have been training you over the past months so that you could help me win a fight that I know everything about!" I replied. A bit forceful I admit but that's the only response that came out.

"Then tell us what we need to know." Said Dilian.

"Fine. But you will be wishing you hadn't said that in a minute or two. The portals open once every twenty-six years. They don't always open in the same spot but once they appear, they'll stay there so long as the army behind them has stuffiest numbers to maintain the spell that created them.

This army feeds off of corrupted magic and so do the portals. Destroy enough of one and the other goes away as well. Naturally, the easier option is to take on the army since the portals are too high up to launch a reasonably sized attack. However, I should tell you that the corrupted magic that creates these portals, isn't natural. It was formed artificially over twelve thousand years ago. By my people."

I quickly looked over to Julian to make sure he wouldn't hear any of this next part. He was still unconscious but at least by that point he was stable.

"The Athereon. These words serve as my title, name and species. My people lived many thousands of years ago. They were the true parents of modern-day magic and they are the reason that it is still threatened to this day.

On the eve of their destruction, they sealed the army that had laid waste to their civilization by encasing them within the corruption. After realising that even this wasn't enough, they sent all the corrupted magic that they had created into another dimension, through portals much like the ones you see above the sky.

The spell they used was immense, taking many thousands of them to cast it. And by the end, the cost of saving the world in the way that they had was the near extinction of my entire species. They sacrificed so much in order to save the world. Leaving me and one other behind to protect and oversee what was left of it.

They never realised that the corruption would eventually come back, so I have been fighting this war every twenty-six years since that day as a result.

But as of three hundred years ago, I have been doing this alone.

That is why this school exists and that is why you exist. To protect what remains of the world from this threat and help me in sealing those portals once again!"

Most of them went silent, taking in the shock of what I had just told them. They seemed dazed, almost terrified by the news.

What was unexpected however, was the conversation and head nodding that erupted within the crowd afterwards.

I couldn't hear exactly what they were saying but I didn't need to. Trevor elected himself as spokesperson for the school. Asking me one simple yet earth-shattering question.

Answering this question, much like the one Katiana askes our guests upon their visits, determined whether or not they would help me or if I would be forced to go it alone.

"Master. If I'm understanding this correctly, then it means that you have been fighting this war for over twelve thousand years? A war... against a people who live off a magic type that can kill us all? Then... if that is true, I have to ask, how have you always won?"

I stood there speechless for a moment. My mouth gaping slightly and Julian regaining consciousness as Katiana approached me, I was frozen.

I soon snapped out of it and answered this question honestly. And what I received in return, still to this day shocks me.

"I've never done it alone." I said morbidly, momentarily mourning the losses of all those who've helped me in the past to stave off the end of the world on days just like this.

That's all I could say, I told them the truth.

I had never done it alone, not even once.

Originally, there were two of us. Two Athereon's. That's all we needed to fend them off. Our collective magic and fighting styles were more than enough to win each battle. But those times were long ago and I will never go back to them.

Ever since the day that I lost my partner I have been fighting this war with the help of mages. Be it just my wife and the Headmaster of Academia by my side or an entire army of fully trained students form my school, for the past three hundred years, I had always needed help.

While I was stronger than any mage on the planet at the time, I was still nothing compared to my partner. She used to be the one who did most of the fighting, I was simply her support.

It was her and some of her more trusted friends that took care of this fight while I was locked away within the body of Terrance.

Once my consciousness remerged, we fought this fight alongside one another as we had done in the past.

And while our bodies might have changed, our mission had not. We were to protect the world and that was exactly what we intended to do.

But alas, three hundred years before the day that I began training these students, she left and I have not seen her since.

I looked for her obviously but I never found her.

No matter what I did to try and locate her I never did manage it. And so was forced to fight this war alone for the first time in history.

It was that day that I became the last of my kind.

Not knowing where she was and unaware of my son still being alive, I claimed to be the last and I begged the Council for support.

And so they gave me their army.

But those times were long gone, I didn't have a full army anymore. And myself, Katiana and the Headmaster would never manage this one alone.

So this time I had students.

An army trained by me personally. A group of mages that I could rely on along with a wife that I could trust.

I had all I needed in them to win. And I needed from them was for them to want to help.

So that's why I was so shocked when Trevor finally said

what he did.

Trevor looked back at the students behind him and they nodded slightly. He turned back to me and gave his verdict. Just like a judge in court he was about to seal my fate.

"Then we fight. Just tell us what to do." He said.

They stood there, trembling slightly, all of them terrified at the idea of fighting in a war but they had made their decision and surprisingly so had he.

Then more miracles continued to occur.

Not only had the students just agreed to fight in a war that they didn't know existed a matter if minuets ago but they had also agreed to help me.

Me, the person who had told them nothing of this and kept it to myself while I trained them.

But while this one event shocked me, the one that followed it only amazed me even more.

Julian coughed as he picked himself up off the floor, he seemed week but nothing that he had overheard had sparked anything in his mind.

For now, he was safe.

"What he said." Julian shouted. "If there's a fight that's truly worth fighting, then I'm in. Katrina too."

That's all he said upon his awakening. Baring a strong look of confidence of his face and a look of determination on his wife's.

I looked at each of them and thought hard about what to do. They weren't fully trained but if I split them into large enough groups then maybe, just maybe their collective numbers and a great amount of planning would be able to do this.

"On behalf of my wife and myself I would like to offer

you our thanks. We knew we couldn't handle this one alone and questioned ourselves every time we discussed telling you. We truly appreciate the help." I said to them, bowing to show that I was being sincere.

Katiana remained speechless, standing beside me not doing much other than looking beautiful as ever. It was only when I looked down at her that I realised what I needed to do. Something that I would have done eventually but since we were now completely out of time, I needed to do it there and then.

"First thing we need to do is form a pact." I said.

"A pact?" Asked Lila this time, not the most surprising person to have spoken out but still not who I would have expected.

More surprisingly is was Katiana that answered this question before I could, she must have felt as though she had been quiet for long enough I guess.

"A pact is a very special form of bond between two or more mages." She said. "By forming one with my husband and me, it will allow for many things to be possible. First, he will know where you are at all times, allowing him to teleport in to offer aid at any point.

Secondly it will allow him to keep an eye on how you're doing, monitoring you magic energy levels and you physical wellbeing.

And finally. It will allow him to perform a very rare and powerful summoning spell. I'll let him explain this one." She said, looking at me as she stepped back a little.

I stretched my arm out to my side and summoned the Chaos Blade for demonstration. A few seconds later and it was in my hand and I could explain how this summoning spell worked.

"This summoning spell is very different from any that you have ever read or heard about. Not only does it require the use of a sword or enchanted weapon to act as a catalyst but it also requires a great deal of magic energy to cast.

But in return, it allows its caster to summon all those who are bound to them at once. Put simply, a pact with me allows for me to summon you, anywhere on the planet and at any time. All in one go." I told them.

"All right." Trevor said. "What do we do?"

So I directed them to hold hands and form a circle. I joined that circle and so too did Katiana.

The link was prepared, the formation made. So, all that came next was the actual pact.

I began by passing a constant flow of magic energy between us all like links in a chain. The students wouldn't have been able to feel it so I said nothing about it. I didn't have time to explain every part of the procedure or ask for permission.

"Students, repeat after me." I said.

I recited the oath required to for the pact line by line as I cast a summoning circle on the floor.

The circle was massive, almost ten meters wide. Consisting of five inner rings and one thicker outer ring. These rings acted as both protective barriers and summoning sigils, containing all the necessary inscriptions for the summoning.

The circles were formed from my imagination, I simply imagined how they should look and then I made them by passing magic energy into the floor with my feet into that exact design.

After they were placed and activated, the circles did their part and acted the same way that magic circuits would have. Casting the spell.

With a spell this powerful and complex, it not only takes time but also requires so much magic energy that the circles will glow as the spell is cast.

Just like any other spell that required that level of magic energy, a lot of it is given off as wasted light energy due to its potency. There's a natural limit to how much energy had be efficiently passed through one body part at a time.

Since I was in my human form, the light was blue. A bright and brilliant blue that filled the room. If I had been in my Athereon body, the light would have been yellow, a blinding golden-yellow that would have shone as bright as the sun.

And with the circle starting to activate, I began to recite the oath and form the pact.

"I vow to be all that is good in this world."

The student's said the same of course.

"I swear to uphold my promise as a protector, a philosopher and a mage."

Again they repeated what I had said.

"I have made mistakes, I bare regrets.

But I do not go asking for forgiveness.

I do not seek redemption or salvation.

I only ask."

The final few lines were approaching and my marker had almost finished implanting itself within the students. The magic energy I was placing into not only them but also the spell had begun to take its toll but it had to be done. Whether or not I was still conscious afterwards wasn't

461

important at the time.

"That you hear me now.

Brothers, sisters, friends, comrades and allies.

Become my warriors.

Act as my shield, serve as my sword and together I swear.

We will be a true force for justice in this world.

Protect those in need.

Fight against darkness and reveal the light."

They recited those final lines and then Katiana told everyone to get in the centre circle on the floor.

They did so quickly and I finished the spell. Completing the pact and getting them ready for the next time we would have to do this.

I drew my sword from its sheath on my hip and forced it into the outer ring of the circle. Placing as much magic energy into it and consequently the circle itself as I could.

The wood cracked and chipped as the magic energy scorched its way through. The blade of the sword growing warmer by the second. Fire soon to be erupting from my palms.

But either everything in place, I finished the oath, forming the pact and activating the summoning. But with all of them already within the circle, it wasn't the students that I was summoning, it was something else.

"Everyone listening to me now, listen well.

For Athereon summons you.

Honour your oath to me and come at my behest.

Now!

COME TO ME!"

I removed my sword from the ground, creating an

explosion of magic energy that surrounded the students and myself.

The light was blinding, too bright to see any part of the students kneeling within it. All I could see was light, it was so bright and so powerful that it dwarfed that of the sun.

Looking at it for too long would have certainly cost me my vision.

But soon the light faded and the intended result had been achieved.

The students had been pacted with me, they were now bound to me in a way that is incomprehensible to most. We were linked together permanently, just like all my previous students had been before.

But unlike them, these students were young and strong. They hadn't had time to grow old or get out of shape.

They were exactly what I needed and as such I replaced the pact that had been formed with my previous students with the pact that I had just built with these.

The ritualistic spell that I had just performed was a single action, but in the end, it did the work of fifty-two separate spells in one.

Firstly, it had formed a bond between us that would never fade unless intentionally broken. But also, the words used to form it are the same required for the summoning. Because of this, I had performed a summoning at the same time as forming the pact.

But I had not intended nor had I needed to actually summon people, but instead I had summoned their new armour.

This summoning had not only removed their clothes, but it had also replaced them with their new battle armour.

Magnificent and custom made, gold tinted, blue dyed titanium and steel chest plates matching the new leggings and the braces on their arms.

A full set of priceless enchanted armour. Capable of withstanding most attacks but not all of them.

Of course, some of the students probably didn't like the idea of having their clothes remotely ripped off of their bodies, especially the girls, but it was necessary.

And besides, everything had happened while that blinding light was still shining, no one would have felt or seen anything even if they had realised that there was something to see in the first place.

With the exception of Katiana, who already had a perfect set of armour on in the first place, all fifty students had been redressed in the clothing that they would soon be fighting in/ And whether they knew it or not, they needed to get used to its feel as quickly as possible.

For all I knew at the time, they would be dying in this new armour. It would be better if they felt comfortable in it before they took a dirt nap in it.

And with that crucial step out of the way, all that was left to do was teach them how this new armour worked and how to use its enchantments.

The pact was complete and the war was looming just around the corner.

A patient predator, carefully stalking its prey.

Ready to pounce.

Now I just how to be sure we'd be ready when it did.

ELEVEN DAYS

When man first learnt how to make fire, how do you think he felt? How to you suppose he reacted?

When the first primates of this world had evolved to a point where they were capable of harnessing something so destructive and powerful as those golden-red flames, how do you think that affected them?

Those primitives, these predecessors to the humans of today, would they have believed that the power before them had come from a god or other supernatural source rather than believing it to be a natural one?

Would they have been able to comprehend its complicities, the raw and unmatched fury that was the flame before them? Did they even know what it was that they were seeing?

Do you think that it made them feel safe or powerful? That perhaps the creation of this force had given them a sense of control?

Do you think that just because they could now create and manipulate the flames that they trusted them?

Simply because they had the power, this did not make them powerful. But, would they have known this?

No. Because those first few creatures who huddled around the flame would not have understood what it was.

They wouldn't have felt protected. They would have been unchanged. Feeble, weak and vulnerable.

And they couldn't control the flames, only create them.

Fire is a natural and unforgiving force of destruction. By learning how to create it, they had only opened the doors towards their damnation.

My mother used to tell me this story, the story of the first apes who learnt of fire.

It was so long ago, many thousands of generations before my birth. Many tens of thousands of years before I even knew how to walk. But the story of it remains.

It was a historic event that my people refused to forget.

The story of how the creatures we now call humans went from being one of our more disappointing evolutionary cousins to a prosperous species that would one day rival our own.

This tale has made its way through the ages thanks to one thing. One simple and irrefutable concept.

It was a bedtime story.

The same one that my mother used to tell me when I was no more than two feet tall.

And before her, the story had been passed down like legend throughout my family and many families like our own.

It was safe to say that almost everyone knew it.

And it was a safe bet that everyone found some meaning in it too. And no matter how many years passed and how much more progress those hairless apes made; we never did forget the day that the made that first step.

THE ATHEREON: WINTER'S WAR

The day that they first harnessed the power of fire on their own

It was too important. Possibly the most important event in both our histories. The moment that humans finally understood how to control something that out powered them hundreds of times over.

It was the moment that humans went from nothing more than hair covered pink skinned monkeys, to a species capable of grasping at the truth.

It was at that moment, that humans finally joined us as the rulers of this world.

The story of those three hairy men who discovered the power of flame is something that I know well. As though I had witnessed it myself, I can recall every detail.

They had been smashing rocks together in order to make some form of tool to cut up meat from their fresh kill. Sparks from the iron rich stone lit the sky around them, falling to the ground and igniting the pile of dry leaves beside them.

It was these three men who first discovered the flame and it is to this day, both the worst and most beneficial mistake that their species has ever made.

They screamed in fear and circled the flame as if it were a predator. They feared its power, its uncontained fury and destruction.

And while they had seen flames before, lightning striking at trees or the sun scorching the grass at their feet, they had never created them until that moment.

As the story goes, one man believed the flame to be a demon walking amongst the living and tried to kill it, stomping on the flames and burning his legs as a result.

That man did not survive those injures, they had no

understanding of medicine or healing back then. And while he might have been alive for quite some time after the initial injury occurred, it was the infection that followed soon after that killed him in the end.

The other two simply stood by and let him die as it set in, but they didn't have to wait long. The infection took hold quickly and he died within the following three days.

The man who had created the flame ran to the west, journeying far until he came across a cave full of his own kind. He explained how to create the flame, showing them the stones that he had carried to them and crating another flame in the leaves outside.

From there, word of how to create the flames spread quickly and before long, every man on the continent at the time knew how to make fire.

But the final man stayed behind, staring at the blinding yellow light before him.

He sat on the ground and observed it for many hours until it died down.

He was curious.

He was not afraid; he was not quick to spread rumours and he was not foolish enough to touch it.

He simply studied it, taking in the spectacle and sitting in awe as the fire burned.

My mother used to tell me that only three types of people exist in this world. She said that those who go into situations looking for a fight, only relying on violence to guide them, often end up getting burned.

She told me that some of us would be quick to act and spout lies rather than truths because we didn't understand what we had seen. That men like that often end up
468

forgotten.

But there were some, some rare and marvellous people in the world, who wanted nothing but to study the situation at hand.

She said that is was these people who made the difference, the people who understood the situation rather than fearing or spreading lies about it.

She said it was these people who knew how the world worked and that they were the smartest of us all.

She said that out of the three, she would have liked me to become like this man, the one who stayed behind and observed. Not the fighter and not the teacher, she wanted me to become the scholar.

However, I would have to argue that she was mistaken with her assessment of these three men. I would say that there was a fourth option.

The man who understands the topic and teaches others about it, the man who fights and trains others to do the same as he can, the man who not only observes but also documents the events. I would say that the man I became in the end was a mixture of the three.

I was a fighter, a teacher and a scholar.

I was a warrior.

The time that I spent with my mother was shorter that it was supposed to be. It was the curse of being Athereon that was her downfall to her life in the end.

The price that every mother had to pay in order to become one, the one thing that you absolutely had to give up in order to create offspring. Was life.

You had to give up some of your immortality in order to create the child. And the caring woman that she was, gave me so much of her energy, so many of her resurrections, that she left herself with almost nothing to survive on.

She said that this was so that I could live my life unhindered by petty things like a limit on how many times I could die. But little did she know then, that when the Athereon Empire began to fall and we started dying permanently for the first time in our history, the remaining resurrections that the fallen had left to use, began to pool into the remaining survivors.

With every soldier that fell, the ones left alive would be given an even slice of their remaining resurrections.

And when the war was finally ended and both sides seemingly defeated, the remaining resurrections were divided between the two remaining survivors, or more accurately, three survivors since I later found out that my son had survived as well.

Normally, we are born with somewhere between five and nine thousand resurrections each, depending on how many our mothers are willing to give up. But as for me, I was born with sixty-three thousand resurrections to use, leaving her with a measly three.

It was pneumonia that used the first of these three.

It was an illness that we hadn't encountered before and at the time, we didn't have the knowledge to cast spells strong enough to cure it.

The next resurrection was used after she had a heart attack. A rare occurrence for our kind but still more than enough to kill you.

And the final one, the final life that she had left to live, was used up with time.

She was old by the time she had me, older than most had

expected to be possible. With over nine thousand years in her past, she had simply ran out of strength to go on.

When you reach a certain age, for my kind at least, keeping yourself healthy and young takes more and more energy than it used to.

Eventually using so much that you're not able to sustain your physical form past that point.

And when this point is reached, you die.

If you have any resurrections left to use then you can bring yourself back but the same problem would remain. You would be too old to survive and you would die yet again.

So in the end, she had simply reached the point of no return. And that was it. I had to bury my mother that day. But if I knew then what I know now, I shouldn't have had to.

If she had left herself with enough resurrections to survive just another hundred years then she would have been fine. She would have been around when it was announced that a spell had been invented to keep us young and fit permanently, without the use of our own strength.

If she had left herself just enough more lives to make it that far then I would have had many more centuries with her before the war started.

But she had given me almost all of her resurrections when she finally welcomed me into the world. And as a result, she died far too soon.

And if she had known, if she had known that it would be a waste, if she had known that after the war I would be left with millions, she might have lived longer.

She might still be with me now.

But that wasn't in the cards.

My mother died. And I lived.

And I kept living.

Never before had an Athereon had such an endless supply of deaths to cheat. And never again will this happen.

With my son dead, one would assume that the remainder of his resurrections would fall to the last of us but that was not the case this time.

He died because he had used them all.

I don't know how many times he must have died before he did this but by the time that I finally found out that he was still alive, he had only three to five hundred resurrections left and he used all of them to bring Katiana back from the grave.

I estimate that he must have used six or seven hundred on Katrina but that means that he only had just over a couple thousand when his powers awakened within Julian.

To have lost so many lives in such a short amount of time, I'm not even sure how he could have died so frequently.

He should have had millions left to use and yet, after a mere twelve thousand years, he had been left with a little over a handful to use. And he had used them all.

One selfless act after another, he used his remaining power to reclaim some of his wife's humanity and bring mine back from the dead.

Whatever it was that caused him to die that many times over the years must have been relentless.

To have killed a person over three million times, I can't imagine what could have done such a thing.

He would have had to have died almost three hundred

times per day for over twelve thousand years. Such a feet would have been easy if he were human but he was Athereon, despite our ability to come back from the grave, we are still very hard to kill in the first place.

Ordinary blades will not cut our skin. Bullets cannot penetrate our muscles. Punches take more force than mere strength alone can give you to leave a mark.

My kind do not go down without effort.

But that didn't make us impossible to kill.

And as I of all people should know, there are many ways to keep us dead once we're down.

So just like my mother, my time with my son was cut far too short.

Time... Huh?

That was the thing.

Time is the only constant in the universe.

Time is the one thing that Athereons, humans or nature hadn't created, because it had always existed.

Unlike language or math, time had always been there and it will remain until it finally runs out.

Time is the one thing that an Athereon is supposed to have an endless supply of and yet, mine too was beginning to run out.

From everything that I had to go on, I estimated that we had week at most. A week until the fifty young warriors that I had been training would have to show me what they could do in battle.

The barrier had lost at least five of its nine layers before the second round of shaking finally stopped the day after the first three collapsed.

The rumbling of the earth beneath us lasted many hours

on that day. And initially, standing there witnessing it, experiencing the next two layers fail and crumble, I believed that only one layer had been broken.

But then the shaking came again just an hour after the second round had ended. And it was much stronger than the last round of quakes. It lasted multiple hours and went on throughout the night.

And unlike the first few, these quakes started moments before the collapse of a layer. They were a warning that it was about to break. And then after it had, they lasted for upwards of four hours after it had shattered.

And during these quakes, I didn't think that they were going to stop, I feared that they were a sign of the barrier failing completely but they soon subsided on their own.

I still had time.

But the barrier was now half as strong as it was before and the corruption was pouring out of it like water through a leak in a dam.

All forms of whether abnormalities soon formed as a result. The blood red rain poured without end for days leading up to the final collapse.

Even when the sky was clear of clouds, the rain continued.

The wind picked up so violently that I had to alter the way that the barriers recognised threats to keep it out.

The temperature spiked and levelled over and over each day, creating overwhelming heat waves and then unrelenting chilled winds. Keeping those out was a challenge.

The best I could do to keep the students safe from this madness was dampen them. Within the protected area of my main barrier the temperature did not rise as far and did not drop as low as it did outside.

However, even though we were practically unaffected by the weather, we were all under the influence of the dark energy that poisoned the air.

I did my best to keep it out but my barriers were meant to protect us from physical threats, not magical ones.

It was because of this that instead of teaching the students anything battle related, I focused on training the students on how to resist the effects of this dark energy first.

But before I could get to that, I had to evacuate the village. With how violent the weather was becoming and how powerful the earthquakes had become, the humans living there weren't safe anymore.

And when the fighting started, I didn't want to have to worry about protecting them from its fallout.

The earthquakes and the rain are easy to explain as a natural event but humans are not so easily fooled forever.

If one of them were to pay close enough attention to my house then they would notice that everything was centred around it. Not to mention that every time it rained now the liquid was running down the side of an invisible dome covering my land.

Try explaining that to humans.

Moreover, if I left it too long then eventually the portals would have been large and strong enough for humans to see and if anyone had noticed, I wouldn't have been fighting the battles alone anymore.

I would have had every army on the planet asking for a piece of the action.

I thought it best not introduce the humans to the idea of

magic at the same time as a war on this scale.

But the village was the only source of human civilisation within a couple hundred miles or so, removing them from the battle would buy me more time at least.

And as for the rest of humanity, I had taken care of that centuries ago and so too had the Magic Council.

Those walls I mentioned before, the ones between us and the humans. They weren't another way of saying we had a massive border defence, they were actually walls.

The largest continues ring of magic barriers ever created, it took over a month to do and over three thousand mages to create. But when we were finished, the result was a powerful, five-mile-high wall.

Covering every part of our world and securing it from the humans.

Simply going anywhere near it would effectively force you to turn around. It changed your thinking, altering your thoughts and convincing you to walk away.

That's what happens when you go near it anyway.

Touching it would result in excruciating pain, forcing both mind and body to turn tail and run but if you were in a tank or plane, they would spontaneously blow up.

Nothing from the air or from the ground could possibly get it unless we wanted it to.

And in addition to its practical defence, it also had a secondary and more easily concealed one.

On the human side, looking at the barrier would just show you mountains. No buildings and certainly no people.

To humans, that's all that we were, a massive field of linking mountains covering three of the world's largest nations. But on our side, we can see through it just fine.

It was the best and only way to keep the human world away from ours.

There was only one exception to this wall however. A single path, hidden to the untrained eye, that would lead you into our world. Partially at least.

The only time that this is ever used is when the armies of the world decide to visit me but as I've said, once you leave the village and return down this path, you forget all about me and my house.

To the human world, everything that was happening was perfectly natural and nothing was out of the ordinary but on our side, we were about to fight a war.

A war that they would never know about. It would be a forgotten page in their history. As though it never existed at all, it would be a war that they couldn't feel, hear or see. A war that they couldn't be a part of, a war that was best kept as a secret, both from them and from most of the mages on this side of the walls.

The only way that humans could have found out about it was if the various men and women living in the village down below were to run and tell someone.

The barrier around the town only stopped you from remembering me and my home. It had no effect on anything else.

If they saw the Tears, they would surely have run as far as they could to find help.

So I evacuated the village and after a lot of hypnosis and patience, I convinced them to run before seeing anything at all. I made them all believe that some disaster had destroyed their village and that they weren't to return for another month at least.

By the time the hypnosis wears off, the battle should have already been won. And upon their return, they would forget everything that I had told them to leave in the first place and return to their lives as if nothing had happened.

So after six hours of talking to every single member of the village, they all left. Huddled close to one another and squeezing into any vehicle that they could find.

And with them gone and out of harm's way, I returned to teaching my students.

Katiana had started going through the subject while I was gone but ultimately, she needed me there in order to teach them. I was about to train them the process of resisting corruption, in order to do this, you need someone who knows how to control it to be there.

And while I can manipulate it to a certain extent, I still couldn't fully control the corruption, otherwise I would have closed the Tears myself the moment that they had opened.

It was still quite difficult to do this in such a short amount of time. But rushing through it was the only way to get to the other side.

We were hard pressed for time and if the students couldn't even survive breathing the air, how could they have done any fighting?

So I did what I could, teaching all of them in the art of strengthening the mind. Telling them how to identify signs that the energy was affecting them and how to resist it.

I spent a full day and a night doing this.

Sitting in the classrooms and exposing them to the corrupted energy a little bit at a time until they could handle the environment that now existed outside.

For humans, this energy would pass straight through

them, barely affecting them physically or psychically.

To them, the energy that was now seeping into the world was nothing more than a weather system. They had no clue as to how much danger they were in because they had no idea how ultimately blind they were.

They couldn't see the Tears yet, they couldn't feel the energy and they couldn't taste that which we could lingering in the air.

To them, everything that was happening was purely natural but to a mage it was so much more.

To a mage, the Tears were a well-known occurrence but not but a few knew their real significance.

To the outside mage community, the Tears were a phenomenon that occurred every twenty-six years and wreak havoc on the environment for a while until they close by themselves.

To a point, this was an accurate description but for those who knew the truth, it was nowhere near it.

The Tears were not natural however they were reoccurring. They were not simply going to go away on their own and they did a lot more than mess with the weather when their appeared.

Every time that my barrier around them finally fails, a horde of creatures that can only be visually described as demons, would rain down from them, unleashing what the Bible spoke of as Hell.

In all the time that I have fought this fight, in all the thousands of years since its first occurrence, the only people to have documented it among the human world were scholars.

Sensitive enough to magic to be able to see the spectacle

but unfortunately religious enough to eventually write about it in the Bible.

No matter what your feelings are about that fairy tale of a book, it is undeniable that some if not most of the stories within it were based in reality.

In fact, a lot of it was based on spectator accounts of the miracles that I used to perform.

Back then, I was much younger, ten thousand years younger in fact. My purpose in life was to protect and guard the human race. I never realised that in doing so, I would strengthen the people's belief in religion because of what I was doing to save them.

In those days, I would heal the sick, protect the week and fight this war in full view of passers-by.

How foolish could I have been?

Everything that I did back in those days only further confused the people with events and miracles that they did not and could not understand.

The humans had no knowledge of what magic was and even less understanding of what I was.

They called me an angel at first, then a god, then a charlatan and then a demon.

I went from the humans most trusted and famous friend to their most hunted enemy in a matter of decades.

They feared what they did not understand and before I knew it, they were rebelling against me.

It was at that point that I decided living in hiding would be best.

Only revealing what I was during this war or any other event that required my attention.

I only acted when I was needed, never when I was

wanted.

There were countless humans who requested my aid, many of the sick and dying who needed saving but I did nothing about that.

I could have helped them all but in doing so I would have done more harm than good.

They would have been stoned for even talking to me. Burned at the stake as a witch for surviving events like the plague and hung for attempting to disprove their religions.

If I had gotten involved, I would have put everyone that I saved in even more danger of dying than the ailments that they had sought to heal.

I was tasked with protecting, not saving them. And unless I was left with no other choice, I wasn't meant to kill them either.

It was not my place to intervene, despite how much I wanted to or how much I could have done to help. So I stayed in isolation, strengthening my skills and learning new ones.

Fighting the war as it happened every twenty-six years and doing what I could to keep the truth from the rest of the world.

And for the most part, this way of living went remarkably well.

Me and my partner, fighting together on battlefield when needed but then going our separate ways when it was over.

I respected her privacy and let her live her own life, only contacting her when we were required or when she needed me. But soon, this wasn't enough for her.

She wanted more, she was capable of more, and she thought that she was entitled to more. She created and destroyed entire civilizations in her selfish lust for power, fooling the people of the dessert to worship her and building great monuments in her image out of sand and stone.

She became a queen. Idolised as a goddess. But soon she was seen as nothing more than a monster.

The people of her nations rebelled against her and soon erased her from the history books.

She was ruined, thrown to the curb by her own people.

So she acted in kind, burning down their cities, creating plagues, tricking others into fighting with her in a war against the people that she once ruled.

It was then that she revealed her true nature to me and it was then that I stopped contacting her altogether.

Despite this lack of contact, she still turned up every twenty-six years to fight. Every time she was wearing a different body and had a different accent.

I could tell what she had been doing. She had been traveling, all over the globe. With what she was capable of, I didn't know if she was resurrecting herself within others or simply changing the body that she already possessed.

Either option ended in the same result. She was swapping bodies quite frequently but I never spent enough time with her to find out why or how.

She continued to do this for many years, creating many stories in her wake. Every now and again, I would hear a rumour about some healer or witch moving from town to town. She was always a woman, always of a similar age but varying greatly in her appearance.

While I didn't approve of her lifestyle at the time, I know now that it did the humans no long-term harm. They soon stopped believing in witches and the stories about my previous partner soon faded all together.

The only reason that I talk about her now is that she was the one who first alerted me to the possibility of humans containing magic energy.

It was just a few months after we had last seen each other on the battlefield when she just appeared in my house, with a scared and half-dressed young girl in tow.

With little explanation and no warning, she simply threw the girl into my arms and left.

Dazed, half asleep and greatly confused, it was only when I finally took a proper look at this girl that I realised what she was.

She was the first human that I had ever seen that could actually generate, store and use magic energy.

As far as I knew at the time, she was the first of the human mages. And she was the reason that the world today exists as it does.

It was her descendants and people like her who opened my eyes to the possibility of humans one day doing the job that I had been left here to do.

Fast forward eight thousand years or so and here we are, living in a world containing both humans and mages, coexisting in almost perfect harmony.

Some humans know about us but every mage knows about the humans. We are the ones who pass through towns unnoticed, undetected and without leaving a trace.

We exist in our world and live in yours and none of you are even aware of it.

The outsider living in your home, the stranger walking down the street, the weird kid at school or even the girl you have a crush on.

We are everywhere and we are nowhere.

We are so spread out now, our reach extending far beyond yours and still we are invisible to you.

Humans and mages exist apart from one another but depend on each other to survive.

We eat your food, live in your homes and even clean your streets for you. Without even realising that we are there, we avert disasters; we save lives and protect the unprotected.

We help to fight in wars that you know about and hide the wars that you know nothing about.

We have always been there. Since the day you were born to the day you die; we were there, protecting you. Mage kind is all that keeps humanity from extinction these days and we do all of this without asking for anything in return.

Humanity owes us a great deal and none of you knows anything about it.

Every day one of us dies, either at the hand of a human or from the blade of another mage but that doesn't matter. We die knowing that nothing we ever did in life was done in vain.

We protected you from the beginning and will continue to do so until the very end.

So every twenty-six years, myself, my wife and a selection of personally trained warriors fight to protect you.

A group of kids, anywhere from eighteen to thirty, doing everything that we can in order to win a war that you don't even know about.

And I had trained the newest batch of fighters as best I could. Giving them their weapons and armour, teaching them the skills to wield those swords and carry that metal.

I taught them how to fight and none of you would have ever known about the sacrifices that they had made to get even that far.

Being denied access to their parents or families, never leaving the barriers protecting the schools unless given permission to do so and never having relationships unless also being given the rarely obtained right to.

These kids had gone through school having been deprived of so much, just so that they could one day be strong enough to protect a species that didn't even know they existed.

However, despite their lack of luxuries and their lack of freedom, they had grown into exceptional adults and I couldn't have been more proud of them.

They had come so far, seen so much and learnt an outstanding amount in their short time at my school and now it was time to get them ready.

In a matter of days, we would be fighting a war. A war that would not only decide the fate of our world but also the fate of yours.

We should have had many more months to prepare but our luck and our time had finally ran out.

We were rushing and I had no way of being certain as to when the final few layers of the barrier would fail.

It could have been five hours or five weeks.

There was simply no way of telling but everyone would know when it finally started. Everyone would feel it and no one could mistake what that feeling would signify.

A heavy weight pulling tightly on your chest, a shortness of breath and an overwhelming feeling of fear. All of these would be the signs that the barrier had broken and that the war had begun.

For me, I would know a little sooner than they did but not by much. Since I had created the barrier, I was tied to it. I could feel the claws of the corruption desperately digging their way through and I would feel it when the remaining layers finally shattered.

Not knowing when this day could come though, I taught them as quickly as I could.

Prioritising what they absolutely needed to know first and then moving on to what I wanted them to know should I still have the time.

So we started with their equipment. They all had their new armour and their weapons in hand and were swiftly learning how to use them.

Constantly practicing and preparing themselves for the fight that was to come. But I was rushed, so I skipped most of the advanced techniques and went straight to parrying and attacking.

Ignoring advanced swordplay or bow tricks and simply giving them the skills needed to survive the fight.

We only needed to win, we didn't have to show off or avoid ever being wounded, so I did what I could to ensure that we had the best chance of making it through even if it meant some of us would be back at death's door by the end of it.

With the pact made and fully established, I could feel everything that the students did at all times now.

Their emotions, their energy levels and their pain.

I could monitor it all and keep an eye on them as long as I was concentrating hard enough anyway.

With the exception of those strong enough to resist my

attempts of peeking in, Julian, his wife and mine, I had full knowledge of what everyone was doing and where they were.

This would prove to be vital during the endless slaughter that we foolishly called a war.

Normally the formation of the pact comes last, literally.

It's usually performed at the graduation ceremony six months after the point that we had made it to.

It was there that students are promoted to level twenty-four and it is there that I say goodbye to the twenty-seven of them not graduating.

Those twenty-seven would leave at level nineteen, still higher than most mages in the world but still not the result that they were striving towards all this time.

And it is only after finning the herd like that, that I would normally decide whether or not to tell the students the truth about why they were trained and ask them to fight in the war.

And it was always a choice. Any of them can say no and walk away but never had I seen this happen.

However, the choice of whether or not to tell them depended on whether or not they needed to know.

The past two wars before the one that I faced at the time were barely considered to be bar brawls. They were extremely simple and very short. No need for additional aid and no need to tell anyone else.

Katiana, the Headmaster and a few of the Council's best fighters helped me with the last one. The previous Crown Mage joined in and helped us all the time before that too.

But on those two occasions, the enemy was week and I only needed someone to watch my back and catch anything

I missed. Nothing more.

However, on both of those occasions, there had only been one crack in the sky, one portal. Never before had I seen two of them at the same time, never had one of them been so large and never before had my barrier started to fail so soon.

I didn't know what this would signify or what horrors would await me when the fighting began.

Ignorance is bliss.

Isn't that what they say?

If only in this case that was true.

If I had known what awaited us on that battlefield, then perhaps we could have been more prepared. But I knew nothing about it.

I was going off the information I had from the previous wars, but never had any of them been as challenging or as gruesome as this one.

So I went on as I had done before, training them for the fight that I expected to face, not the one that I got.

To my amazement, the remaining portion of the barrier stayed in tack for eleven days.

Eleven days, that's all the time that I had to rush through the rest of their training.

One of the students asked me why we didn't simply reinforce the barrier.

"If only we could." I told him.

When you reinforce a barrier, you momentarily weaken it during the attempt. So if I had made any attempt to reinforce or even protect the barrier surrounding the portals already, the corruption would have surely broken through during the procedure.

How I wish I had taken that chance now.

Maybe if I had, we would have been gifted with enough time to train for what we were actually going to be fighting against.

However, I had never expected my opponents to be capable of what they did, I never saw that first strike coming and to this day I remember the feeling of overwhelming shock when it finally happened.

I had spent the final week of our training preparing them for this battle. Teaching them the battle tactics we would use and the formations that they had to remember.

We went over every eventually that I could think of. Preparing for the worst-case scenario and imagining how it could get worse then preparing for that as well as anything worse than that.

After a week of this, I thought that they would be ready, I thought that we had a chance but nothing I had prepared for actually happened when the barrier finally failed.

Nothing I had planned to defend against came to attack us because what happened to us in the end war far, far worse. So much so that what it cost me, was much more than I would like to admit.

We went into that fight prepared for whatever they threw at us but we were hopeless against what finally came.

I kept thinking that if we had had even just one more day to prepare, just one more day to train then maybe we would have done better.

I kept thinking that I had done more to prepare them, then maybe it wouldn't have been as bad as it was.

But I was foolish to do so.

Thinking about what could have been wasn't going to help anyone. What happened, happened.

No amount of training would have prepared them for that. Even five years of training with me as their one and only teacher wouldn't have done enough. We simply didn't have a chance.

And in the end, we just got given a bad hand.

It was luck of the draw and we were defiantly not lucky at the time.

As a result of this, we managed to get through the first few minutes with few casualties but beyond that moment, we lost so much more than we already had.

Had we lost any more, we would have lost the war.

Had we not played that hand to our best, we would have all died.

But in the end, in a way, we already had.

BOMBARDMENT

Two nineteen in the morning, December tenth, nineteen seventy-one.

The night that the war started.

The night that we lost too much to bear.

And the night that the red snow and ash began to fall.

The night that ended so much and started so much more.

I had felt the barrier slowly fading for several days beforehand. I went to bed each night knowing that it could fail the moment I closed my eyes.

But even knowing that it was starting to fail, even knowing that day by day it grew weaker and weaker at an ever-increasing pace – I still didn't have enough information to form a definitive estimate of when it would fail completely.

I expected it to do so every day I looked up at that brightly lit sky. And with every day that passed, the irritation, anticipation and impatience within me only continued to grow.

I was thankful that I had more time, but I was terrified every hour that I awoke because I knew that at any moment these children, my wife and myself would be thrust face first into this war.

And then when it did happen, it happened at night.

Dawn was fast approaching over the hills. Midnight had come and gone. The students had been sent to be already but refused to do so. Insisting that we remain in the courtyard for as long as their endurance could last them. Demanding that they keep practicing.

So that night, as with all those before it recently, I hadn't turned into bed at a sensible hour. Instead I kept up with our training routine as I had since the day I changed it.

I had begun giving the students less time to sleep each night to get their bodies used to the feeling of exhaustion. I had granted them less time to eat, preparing rations rather than meals to save on time wherever possible so that I might use every hour of the day as efficiently as I could.

We started having shorter and more demanding lessons. Sparring sessions were scrapped and replaced with live combat training. Longer battles each day. More and more opponents each time. Slowly upping the difficulty until I was as close to the real thing as I could get.

And while I couldn't create a perfect replica of the army for them to fight against in these mock battles, I could at least make rough estimations of them.

Using a combination of projection magic as well as pain inducing magic fields, I made rough copies of what I had seen before. Mere shades of what they would actually be fighting against but they were anatomically correct and they hurt like hell if they touched you.

I did my best to approximate their behaviour too but my mind didn't work like theirs. All rage and impulse. They acted on emotion and instinct. All I could do was mimic them, and it was far from perfect.

But it was enough to give the students an idea of what their opponents would look like and it would give them at least some modicum of experience when it came to fighting against them.

And while it wasn't what I would have liked to do, cramming so much training into such a small amount of time, I was able to get the message across.

Practice battles against up to ten of these creature at a time did the trick as I had hoped. And all I had to do was define their basic parameters, move each one manually as the students fought and then see where improvements had to be made

Fighting against the students like this was taxing. Both magically and mentally. Creating ten shades of these creatures takes a lot out of a person on its own. But mixing that in with movement and the tactics of battle and I was left more exhausted that I had felt in a long time after each battle.

But giving them a somewhat accurate representation of the army we would soon fight to practice against did at least relieve their anxiety.

However, no matter how sophisticated the dummy, it will still never be anything when compared to the real thing.

An actual copy of those creatures was impossible to create with the magic that my body could use. If I were to somehow use their own magic, the corruption in the air, giving that a form and a mind would be theoretically possible. But... it would be no different than just opening the barrier now.

Put a real one of those things in the same room as those students before they knew what to do against it and it would have killed them.

Perhaps not all of them. But it would have taken a few of them down before it followed.

And besides the obvious risk to the students, there was the risk to my own life to consider.

Corruption might be something that my body can purify in small quantities, but the amount that I would have to use in order to make this a reality would be beyond anything I could cope with.

That and, once the corruption is spread throughout my system in an attempt to cast any spell, I would never be able to use my magic circuits again.

They'd misfire and burn to ash if I even attempted it.

Corruption wasn't named that for nothing.

It is an invading force within your own magical body.

Once inside, if you cannot eject or purify it, it will spread without end until it has consumed you.

The best thing you can hope for in that scenario is a quick and painless death. Because if you're unlucky enough not to receive one, then god help you.

So I made do with what I had and I taught those students everything I knew of how to fight against these creatures for as long as I had to so.

And by the end of it, they had all come so far. They had all learnt so much and matured into the true warriors that I had needed them to be. But it still wasn't enough.

Because when it happened, I thought was ready for anything. But it turned out I was ready for everything except what actually took place.

Even though I knew that what we had prepared for wasn't going to happen, I could do nothing about it in that moment. I simply had to hope that the students had endured enough training to be able to cope with what was to come.

But from that moment on, they were no longer kids, they were no longer students, they were no longer tools or mere weapons. From that moment on, they were my warriors, they were my friends, they were my army.

And at last, the war had come.

I looked up the sky when I felt it. The sudden pain in the back of my mind that I had been expecting for days before that moment. And as soon as it was felt, all I could do from then on was stand back and watch.

And I watched alright.

I watched as this black mist that we mages called corruption ate its way through the final shards of my barrier and exploded out into the atmosphere the moment it was gone.

It was an ever-thickening cloud of black smoke building up inside of a box. Increasing in size and pressure by the minute until it finally broke through.

Corruption so concentrated and powerful that it was actually able to manifest as a physical substance.

How could I have expected that?

I don't know why I hadn't noticed sooner. That black cloud of corruption building up inside the barrier. If I had seen it, just the once before that moment, I would have at least had some warning that it was time.

But by the time I had noticed its presence, the barrier had already begun to break. There was nothing left that I could do. It was beyond my control.

And as I stared up at this phenomenon and watched it

eat through the strongest defence I had in seconds, all I felt from then on was fear.

I felt fear. As I watched the thing that had been protecting the world for months finally came crashing down, I was afraid. I was scared.

And I continued to watch.

I watched as my strongest barrier was shattered right in front of me like it was nothing.

Black dust started to fall, shards and fragments of the now corruption rich barrier as they came from raining down upon us.

The last thing that my barrier ever did was create a glowing blue tint in the blood red sky.

Beautiful.

Were it not terrifying.

And as the dust of those final layers started to fall, it reacted with the corruption in the air. The last few seconds of magic energy they had to spare resisted till the end. Fighting off as much of the corruption as it could but then exploding into nothingness as the last of its energy was depleted and the battle became forfeit.

It truly would have been a beautiful display to behold if it weren't for the real truth. The truth behind what had created it in the first place.

Something so horrendous and devastating could never be described as having beauty despite how amazing the experience was to witness.

And what followed the explosive display above us was a series of nothing, followed by an even more prolonged period of yet more nothing.

At first, only the corrupted magic energy came through

the Tears in the form of an ever-growing black cloud of menacing power covering the sky.

But slowly, as more and more of this energy spewed out of them, the two portals began to grow. Faster and faster as more and more corruption came flooding through.

And when the two at last touched in the heavens above us, they did the unthinkable.

The two portals began to merge, growing exponentially right up until their boarders finally met.

But when that convergence took place, we had already gotten ourselves into position.

Katiana by my side as she should be, followed by Julian, Katrina, Lila, Trevor and Robert directly behind us.

Behind them was everyone else.

Weapons in hand, armour worn and their blood pumping. Magic energy surging. Their minds wide awake their muscles quickly being soothed by the adrenaline in their systems.

It was clear to see that we were ready for whatever followed.

Or so we thought.

I had positioned the strongest fighters at the front of the group to allow a quick and easy takedown of the first wave as I had in the past.

However, although history had begged to differ, that wave did not come.

Instead of the corrupted remains of an ancient army raining down from the sky, I saw only light.

I beam of pure light being projected straight down towards us.

The clouds swarmed towards the now singular Tear.

The air rushed in.

Everything went silent.

And then a moment later a great pillar of light was heading straight for us.

Possibly a hundred meters wide and beyond powerful.

The colour of it… the light it emitted was yellow. A golden yellow at that. A most disturbing sight indeed. Far too similar to that of Athereal Energy. Too similar to be a coincidence and yet, mixed in with this colour was the black darkness that was the corruption.

Two differing types of magic existing at one time in a singular beam of light as it raced down from the heavens. That shouldn't have been possible.

But I saw it.

With my own eyes I stared deeply into it.

Watching as it approached.

The corrupting acting like a thick black haze the entire time. Surrounding the beam just as fog clings to mountains. And like a cloak of darkness shrouding the light beneath, the corruption engulfed the beam completely. Surrounding it with its power and its own dark intentions.

The pillar or light now raining down from the sky was no accident. This was a spell. An attack. And as unbelievable as it was, it had been fired intentionally.

Like a missile; it found its target and attacked.

However, unlike a missile, it was a constant and unending beam of pure light heading straight for us.

Heading straight down from the hole in the sky, it stuck the very top the barrier that covered the eighty acres of my land and shattered it just as easily as a brick would break a window when thrown

The barrier that had protected my home for centuries. Gone. Just like that.

But I understood how.

That beam of light wasn't just heat.

It was made of pure magic energy exactly as I had feared. A pool of magic that outshone anything I could have compared.

It was undeniably stronger in both scale and scope than anything that I had ever seen before. But disturbingly enough, its shape and use was far too similar to something that I had theorised before.

It looked like the spell produced by the Planetary Firing Rings.

But a spell that powerful couldn't have possibly been in the hands of the corruption. They didn't have the intelligence. They didn't have the magical talent. And yet, I could not deny what my eyes were seeing.

The beam was almost identical to what I had theorised the PFR would look like when used.

It had never been fired before, and I sincerely hoped that it would never need to be, so if this was the same thing, it was the first time that I had ever seen it. And the sheer wrath of that attack frightened me to my core.

The rings had been created as a last resort, a means to an end if all else had been lost. It was purposely built to only be activated if one of two things occurred, either I had died defending the world against the army that I now faced or that I had turned against the world.

Should either one occur, the rings were to be activated and the resulting beam of energy would have hopefully been enough to eradicate anything in its path.

Whether that target be myself or the army on the other side of this portal, it didn't make a difference. If the time came that it had to be used, then I would have wanted it to work. So I designed it to be powerful enough to destroy anything imaginable.

But the blast from this weapon I created under the watchful eye of the Council – it would have split the planet in two if not fired carefully.

That is why it had never been fired. The risk was too great. And even if I could create something similar on my own, the destruction caused would be beyond anything that I had ever required in the past.

So that was why I had never seen anything quite like it before. And that is also why, when I saw this beam of light raining down from above, I just stood there in fear.

Even if it wasn't the actual power of the rings being fired against me, it was at least close enough to look similar to it in both power and scale.

It was incomprehensibly powerful in fact.

More devastating than the combined strength of every mage put together, the intensity of its raw energy was only matched by the Athereon armies of old.

It was the only comparison that I could make, nothing else existed at the time could have possibly created such a powerful weapon, not even the power of corruption itself.

And the PFR, the only thing on the face of this earth capable of such power was impossible to use unless a total of three thousand separate Council members signed off on it.

I wasn't about to let someone with ill intent use it just because they had managed to gain access to it of coursed. In order to fire even one of the rings you needed express permission from fifty Council members by way of a spell requiring all of them to cast it. But in order to activate all of them at the same time, you would need over half the might of the entire Citadel to agree with you and cast the spell in union.

This was the only way to fire it and this was exactly why I knew it hadn't been fired. The rings themselves are impossibly well hidden, no one could have found them by chance. But the spell required to fire them, that takes a day at least to cast.

But even though I knew that it was impossible for this weapon to now be facing me, I knew that whatever this attack was, it was too similar in power and malice to have not been a coincidence.

It had broken through my barrier as if it was nothing. Shattering the one thing that had protected my land for as long as I had.

For centuries that barrier had stood. Withstanding the attacks of man and mage alike.

Nothing had ever broken through it before.

In fact, I didn't think that anything could.

It took fifty mages to create it and two Athereon's to reinforce it.

I didn't even think it was possible for it to crack let alone for it to shatter in an instant like it did.

And with that last line of defence gone, the beam continued to head straight down, not even seeming weakened by the pile of magic dust that my barrier was ultimately reduced to.

It continued to travel down even more, hitting the land directly below the centre of the portal and exploding into a fireball of corrupted magic energy expanding in all directions at an impressive rate just a nano second later.

I had little time to react, the barrier around the school buildings would only last a mere moment up against such strength.

I stood there thinking as I watched in awe of the violent devastation that was the black flames approaching us.

The blast had originated almost a kilometre away but the resulting explosion was growing and expanding too quickly for it not to hit us.

I shifted into my Athereon form and shouted my orders.

I needed to do something quickly and I could think of only one thing that stood a chance without also draining us all completely as a result. Therefore, I did what I could and willed it to work.

Using as much energy as I could spare to protect us. Draining my Athereon body before the fighting had even begun.

"Everyone, Defensive Flare. NOW!" I screamed.

I raised my hand and began to cast. My armour and wings began to glow as a pure golden hue surrounded me thanks to the overwhelming energy that surged through me in that moment.

It was a strange feeling at the time, having the combined power of all the students flowing through me as I cast the spell. It was a result of the simultaneous casting. I had seen it before.

With all of us casting the same spell in such close proximity, it allowed the spells to merge into one unbreakable shell of protection, forcing all the energy through the strongest mage in the group who would be responsible for sustaining the spell until he willed it to collapse.

We have a name for spells like this, we call them Miracles.

Not because they were one but because the first time that it happened, that's just what someone called it and the name had stuck ever since.

When a group of mages cast a Miracle spell, it is quite the sight to see but at the time, we couldn't take note of its appearance. Only how well the spell had worked.

The shell formed about a foot in front of me, expanding by the second just like the explosion we intended to defend against.

And the power of that blast was overwhelming, creating a feeling of true fear within my very soul.

I stood there and sustained the spell for as long as I could.

A moment later and the school barrier was no more.

A split second after that and neither was the school.

The power of that explosion was about to come crashing into us and I just had to hope that I was ready to face it.

The sound of the two forces colliding echoed through the air.

Shaking and barely withstanding the power of this attack, the shell began to crack like glass. The initial impact had subsided after a moment, leaving us with nothing more than a paper towel for protection but at that point that's all we needed.

And with the actual blast out of the way, we only needed to survive shockwave after shockwave of energy heading towards us.

It was blinding at first and then deafening as the explosion passed. Leaving only pulsating waves of energy in its wake.

The ordeal lasted for many seconds, passing slowly, feeling like ten times the time that had passed.

The cracks in the shell continued to expand as the energy waves hit it but sooner than expected, those too subsided.

It was just moments after the final pulse of energy hit it that I quickly stopped casting the spell and returned to my human body. I needed to give my Athereon form every moment that I could to recover, I knew that I would be using it again soon and I needed it to be ready.

And when the smoke and corruption cleared enough to see, all that was left of my land was pure devastation.

Just a small patch of untouched grass and the fifty two of us standing upon it.

We had survived the onslaught but nothing that I owned had.

The shell protecting us faded a second after my hand was lowered. And with it gone, the dust clearing and the heat rising, it allowed us to have a front row seat from which to experience the destructive force of that singular beam of light.

One attack, that's all it took to destroy everything that I had held dear for the eons that I had existed.

All of my land, the fields, the house and the school, it was all gone now, leaving nothing but charred and broken earth behind.

And after the initial shock of what they were up against had finally faded, I told the students what to do. I gave them their orders. And then we got to work.

We shook off our fear and marched forward into the smoke and ash.

It was thick, too thick to see through properly.

Anything could be hiding within it and we all suspected what would be there somewhere.

The army that we were there to fight, by now they'd be down on the ground and waiting patiently for us to approach them.

During all the commotion of that initial attack they must have jumped down. We wouldn't have been able to see them, for all we knew they were in that beam of light or maybe they had fallen down while we were blinded by the explosion.

Either way, we knew that they would be there and we only needed to find them.

"Students. Training's over, it's time to fight." I told them.

They soon took up their positions, forming the two large formations that we had practiced. Thirty students with Katiana and twenty with me, including Julian.

These numbers were devised because I was easily worth twenty of these students and Katiana was worth about ten. This gave us both the combined strength of forty soldiers. In theory at least.

The archers and the ranged mages stayed back and slightly off to the side. The students most proficient at close quarters combat were at the front and the edges. Creating a circle in the middle for the healers and supportive fighters to stay protected but still within range to be useful.

Katrina and Julian followed behind me creating a triangle of fighters behind them. Each row becoming more spread out than the one before it.

This formation wasn't ideal but it was the best we could do under the circumstances.

We cut through in a straight line and hope for the best.

That was the plan.

So Katiana and I headed for the centre of that blast, the point where the light had hit the surface of the world below.

She headed north and I headed east, eventually turning towards one another so that we could fight whatever we found on two fronts to divide our enemy between us evenly.

The smoke and ash was blinding, making it hard to see anything, hear anything and at times it even made it hard to even breathe.

But no matter the condition, a soldier fights.

So I followed the plan to the letter and began turning towards Katiana's position when I thought that we were in the right spot.

And as I began striding forwards again, that was when I saw it.

The ash and smoke faded away and revealed a clearing in the centre of it all. And there in that clearing before me, only a short distance away, was ten, no, twenty thousand soldiers.

More than there had ever been at one time before. More than I even knew existed.

We stood at the top of the crater with the army pooled below.

And how nice they were to have prepared the battlefield for us. Creating a large circular dish for us to fight in. How thoughtful.

But I didn't have time for sarcasm in the moment.

I had to remain focused.

THE ATHEREON: WINTER'S WAR

I had been keeping my sword in a defensive position in front of me before that but when I finally saw the army that stood before us, I dropped it to the ground out of shock.

Some of the students did the same but we didn't have the luxury of time to waste gawking at our foe.

While we had only expected five thousand per wave, we knew that we could still handle these numbers if he tried hard enough to pace ourselves.

And besides that, we didn't have a choice but to rush in now.

We could all see and hear what was happening on the far side of that army and just from the sound of it we could tell what it was.

In front of us on the north side of the crater, I could see Katiana's position, she had already started fighting, drawing the attention of the soldiers towards her. Leaving them open to a surprise attack from us.

We noticed this opportunity and rushed in as fast as we could.

Running down the hill of the scorched dirt, firing spells and arrows as we approached.

And like grenades, we detonated those spells at their feet sending upwards of twelve of them flying at a time.

The arrows we fired never missed their targets either. Then again, how could they? The enemy was packed so densely that if you missed one you would certainly hit another.

And with that aggressive start, before we had even gotten within a hundred meters of them, we had already taken care of almost two hundred or so of the enemy.

We were making progress but we needed to do much

better than that of we wanted to win this round before we all grew too tired to continue.

So we kept going. And as we approached the bottom of the crater, we noticed that it was almost flat, as if it had been sculpted that way.

We hadn't expected that. And when we got to the outer edge of the army, we were suddenly on equal footing to one another. And with that we had just lost our best advantage.

But it didn't matter.

We fought nonetheless.

And as I looked to my enemy with every kill I cared into their numbers, I noticed that the soldiers seemed different than I had seen them before.

More animalistic, weaker even.

They seemed to have less awareness and less armour, they even felt weaker than they should have. My blade seemed to simply pass through them as if they were made of paper rather than bone and metal.

I ignored it at first, simply continuing to run towards the thousands of enemies before me.

And when I reached them, I quickly noticed why they were indeed weaker than they should have been.

They must have used almost all their collective power to fire that beam at me. Not much had been spared to sustain their physical forms.

So while they appeared to be made from bone and armour, in truth, nothing so strong remained of them now. And as for remains, that's all they were. Nothing of the original army was left anymore. They are simply made from corruption and as such were nothing more complicated than the projections that I had created to train with.

Judging by how weak they had left themselves; the beam must have been intended to eliminate me in one strike. Why else would the fire something so powerful before attacking on foot?

Since it hadn't hit me as they probably hoped, this meant that although there were several times more enemies than normal, they were still as powerful as they would have normally been if there had been half the amount.

So a pleasant surprise as it might have been, despite their numbers, the overall challenge of that battle hadn't changed at all.

And when we finally reached the front line of enemy troops, our assault began.

They had no ranged troops facing our direction, making it exceptionally easy to eliminate the first thousand of them as we went.

We ran through them like a knife through butter. Almost nothing obstructed us as we made our progress.

We were all sticking to physical attacks to conserve energy and with how oblivious this army appeared to be we were simply ploughing through like it was nothing.

I stared at their faces and figures before I struck each one down. Black, shadow-like figures. That's all I could describe them as. They wore armour made of bronze, not even containing an single enchantment. Their bodies seemed to be nothing but bone and smoke, almost as if the corruption keeping them alive had engulfed them down to their souls.

That was all that was left. After thousands of years trapped in that dimension, the corruption would have taken them whole by then. Nothing of the army that once laid waste to my people remained, only their figure and their numbers.

No intelligence and no physical presence.

They were more like plants than anything.

However, most plants don't tower five to seven feet tall and carry swords now do they?

They might well have been nothing but corrupted remnants from another time. However, they were still more than worthy opponents for myself.

While one on one it would have been child's play, with these numbers, that might have actually had a chance of winning.

But I wasn't about to let that happen.

Corruption has no place in this world and corruption is exactly what they were; twisting and poisoning our magic energy every time we touched them.

It felt like someone lighting a fire beneath your skin when it happened.

So we tried our best not to touch them with anything but our weapons and spells.

And with our training finally having a chance to pay off, we were cutting through the first thousand in the first few minutes. And it was going surprisingly well too.

After that point though, they had figured out what was going on and a lot of them had turned to face us, surrounding our front line of fighters like the way a wave covers a beach. Engulfing everything but the back of us, we were locked in tight and still we pushed on.

With every step forward another seventy of them would have fallen. Impressive work so far.

Ahead of me stood eighteen thousand more soldiers to kill. Behind me, other than the clashing of swords and the firing of bows, I could hear the supportive fighters chanting their spells, casting enchantments and healing our wounds as we moved.

Our formation was working.

We were winning.

I felt invincible in that moment.

As though I couldn't be stopped.

So with that confidence fuelling me, I just continued to fight, cutting through anything I could reach and then firing waves of magic energy when I couldn't touch them.

With a simple swing of my sword, when used in the right way, the enchantments converted my magic energy into a light-based attack. Creating expanding waves of nothing but power, cutting down ten or twenty of them at a time before it dissipated into the air.

However, similar to how Katrina's sword functioned, it couldn't be used over and over again without weakening both myself and my blade.

So I switched from ranged combat to hand to hand by the second. Chopping down the ones up close and devastating the ones at range when I had the chance to divert my attention.

Katrina and Julian had figured out what worked best and how to do it by then. They were teleporting about like madmen. Only staying in the same spot for less than a second, they invaded and destroyed the enemy lines moment after moment, clearing the way for us to progress.

But even that wasn't enough.

We had made too much noise and too little progress.

By the time the first thousand had been slain the enemy archers and ranged attackers had noticed us too. Turning their attention and fire towards our position.

Julian and Katiana were forced to return to the group and act as shields. Casing a spell known as Duster over our heads to protect us from arrows and spells as they fell.

This spell wasn't too complex and was easy to maintain. It took the incoming attacks of whatever touched it and used that as the fuel to sustain itself. Breaking down any material and dissipating any magic.

It was a veil more than a shield. But with the two of them casting it together as we moved, it was just like holding an umbrella above our heads.

So long as it was there, we'd be fine.

And just like an umbrella, carrying it was only a slight inconvenience.

But with half of our best fighters now acting as shields rather than swords, our progress slowed but still we kept moving. Not allowing anything to stop us letting anything stop us.

Arrows, swords, even spells, anything and everything that got too close to us now would be turned into nothing more devastating than glitter falling through the air.

With the exception of pure magic energy anyway.

Spells did still get turned to dust but only their physical aspects, the energy contained within them was subsequently dispersed into the atmosphere with every strike.

We could have absorbed it if we wanted but this was corruption, not even I could have absorbed that much and lived to tell the tale.

So we continued heading through the army and towards the north side of the crater, slowly making progress towards Katiana and her group with every second.

Over two thousand of them had died on our side at this point but it was then that we noticed a problem.

The enemy on the outer rim was easy to deal with on purpose. They had thought it through, as if they actually knew how to think anymore.

They had placed their weakest soldiers on the outer edge and placed the stronger fighters further in.

When we realised, it was already too late.

Suddenly I swung my sword and it was stopped in its tracks, getting stuck inside one of the footmen. It was in that moment that I knew something was wrong but it was a moment that had come too late.

I watched as one of our group was pulled from the line and sliced apart violently.

I saw Julian teleport over and cut down the soldiers that had done it but he was too late to save him, we had had our first casualty.

Julian fought out of rage, like a savage beast, singlehandedly taking out another hundred or so in a matter of moments as he swung his blade back and forth. But it was too late, that man was gone and we had to keep going.

I didn't have time to mourn, I simply ordered Julian back to his position and we pressed on.

The line adjusted and filled the gap and we continued killing.

However, it was obvious now that the enemy was defiantly stronger than before.

They were now able to actually anticipate and deflect some of our attacks, making it take two or three seconds per soldier to best them.

Despite this, we still pressed on, completely unaware of

the horrors that awaited us, we just continued to fight.

Not simply for our own survival, nor for the sake of the homes that made up the village down the hill either

Today, we fought for the sake of everyone and everything.

We were fighting to save everyone.

And we'd continue to do so until the end.

Even if the world would one day forget our existence, we were still going to save it.

The war had only just begun and I intended to win it.

WHEN ANGELS FALL

Over twenty-five minutes had swiftly passed us by since the initial bombardment upon my home. Just twenty-five short minutes. That's all the time that had passed since we went from being a group of trainees to being a bunch of blood-stained soldiers fighting a war.

A war that thus far had us all deceived. Believing that with our strength – with our focus, and with our numbers – we might actually be enough to win.

But we didn't see through this lie in the moment.

We only saw what would happen if we failed.

For this was a war that would ultimately determine the fate of the world.

If we lost here, chaos would engulf the world as it tried to pick up from where we left off so many thousands of years before. But if we won, if we made it out of this fight, we would be rewarded with peace.

A blissful and ignorant peace.

No one knowing hat we had done to win.

No one knowing what could have happened had we not.

And while it wouldn't last forever and wouldn't prevent all other conflicts while it was in effect, this peace would at least keep us safe from the annihilation that we would have faced as the alternative.

If we won, the world would be saved, the people would survive and soon enough everyone could return to their lives as though nothing had happened.

But in order to win, we still had a long road to walk down.

And although they had taken everything that I owned, my possessions, my house, my land, my school, my past – they hadn't taken our lives.

We could still fight.

The field of battle might have been re-sculpted. Everything we had known might have been destroyed. The devastating power of this army might have increased. But we were still standing. We still had our weapons. And we could still use them.

So that's exactly what we were doing.

With those very weapons in hand and armour strapped to our bones, we were as prepared as we needed to be.

We had our formations, our training and our trust.

Trust that allowed us to count on one another.

Trust that meant we had each other's backs.

And with all of that put together, it was a safe bet that we weren't about to go down without even trying to make a stand.

Even if none of us had been fully prepared for that initial attack, none of us had been adversely affected by it. We were hot headed and full of adrenaline.

Fighting wasn't going to be a problem.

And even if their numbers had grown. We could handle them.

From what I had seen in the past, I had told the students

that there would be five to ten thousand soldiers to face off against in the first wave. Shortly followed by a quick reprieve and then the second wave. Three thousand soldiers. Then a few hundred less in the third wave. Perhaps not even five hundred by the time the final wave made its way down.

And even when their strength had been higher than expected, never had I had to fight off more than six waves before. So that was what I prepared them for.

I trained them for the fight I expected. Not the fight that I received.

And with twenty thousand of these savage beasts on the first wave, I didn't even want to guess as to what awaited us on the next one.

Their army was stronger than it had been in the past. And not just that, it was also vast, diverse and organized. I had never seen that in the Corrupted before.

It was as if they had some leader pulling the strings but that shouldn't have been possible.

The first thing that corruption does to you before it fully takes hold is mess with your mind. These beasts that I fought, the left-over remnants of the people that they once were, didn't have one shred of rational thought left in them now.

Their minds were mush, nothing more than animalistic rage and basic fighting skills remained within them anymore. But I couldn't argue with what my eyes were telling me. That they were organised for once.

They had formations, layers upon layers of increasingly more powerful fighters as we approached the centre.

This army wasn't as soulless as it should have been and yet, there didn't seem to be anyone on the ground calling the shots. They didn't seem to be protecting any one position, they didn't seem to have any sense of what protecting each other even meant.

They simply attacked, not caring for what they hit or if they even landed a strike. The weapons and arrows that flew through the air had no purpose attached to them, no drive to wield them. They were just being swung at random, with the enemy just hoping that they hit something.

They no longer had any way of communicating with each other either. They only grunted and panted like the dogs that they were.

And despite their appearance and somewhat humanoid shape, they were anything but human.

Whatever species that these shades once belonged to was long forgotten now.

It was often speculated during the original war some twelve thousand years ago that these creatures might have at one point shared a common ancestor with us much like humans do but they were far too different from us for me to accept that.

Due to the powers that they used to possess and their shape, many believed that these beings were once us. A failed evolutionary branch from whatever beings came before the Athereons.

I suppose that in a way, these things were almost like cousins to me, sharing some part of history however distant that it was.

But of course, I might not have known who they were during the original war. I might not have even accepted what they were during this attack in nineteen seventy-one. But I do know now.

I know exactly what they are.

But where they came from didn't matter, all that did was that we knew how to kill them.

When they were still alive, they were quite difficult to take down, it was because of this that they were able to destroy everything that my people once had.

Something about their magic made it impossible for an Athereon to resurrect themselves once dead. Whatever these things were, they had evolved to be a perfect weapon against us.

And when we finally ended that war and sealed them away within the corruption that we had based off of their own dark energy, we never expected them to be capable of returning.

We thought that we'd won.

But then they came right back.

They returned over and over again and with every time that I thought them, I noticed that they were slowly becoming less and less like living creatures and more like mindless beasts.

And now, after thousands of years of decay, they had devolved into the lifeless creatures standing before us.

However, I didn't care.

While I was curious and desperate to be able to study one, I knew that I couldn't take that chance. They needed to be stopped and that was exactly what I was doing by cutting them down as I marched.

So I and everyone else pressed forward.

The students behind me following closely as we took each step through the mud.

We sliced and diced through everything in our path, not

letting anything slow us down or get in our way.

The plan was to head through the army until we reached the other team, from there we would from a circle and fend off anything that was left.

However, in order to put this plan into motion, we had to reach the other group first. And with such a great distance to cover and so many enemy soldiers in our path, I questioned whether that was even possible now.

With almost two and a half thousand dead behind us and almost a two hundred meters of penetration into the army of undead before us, we had made our mark.

Taking out almost a tenth of the enemy as quickly as we had done filled every one of us with confidence. Even though we had just lost a man, we pressed on valiantly, with hope and triumph in our hearts and determination in our eyes.

We moved forward as quickly as we could, taking out every enemy in whatever way we could.

Spells, tricks, a sword or fist to the face, you name it.

We were doing whatever we had to do so that we could win.

If the enemy's numbers had not been so vast then I might have been able to wipe out an entire wave at once... but only at a great cost to myself.

There was only one spell that I was capable of casting that would have done the trick but its range was too limited to eliminate such a vast crowd of enemies.

I have mentioned this once before actually. The formation of a quantum singularity, a black hole for lack of a more accurate description. It was a point of gravity that was so devastatingly powerful that not even light could have escaped, but it would have been too small and its effects not strong enough to work against so many opponents.

Even if I had saved enough magic energy to create one, it would have only worked against half of them. After that, there would be almost ten thousand of them left and I would be out of action for a day or two. The others would have never survived.

I had only ever used it twice, and both times were during the final waves of this war. On both occasions it proved too much for me to handle and I fell unconscious as a result but that wasn't an option this time.

It required a great deal of energy to create, let alone sustain, with almost all of the energy of my Athereon form gone and still recovering from protecting us earlier, I had no choice but to focus my efforts on physical attacks.

If I had worn my human body out too quickly and forced myself to have to use my Athereon form, I wouldn't have lasted long while I was in it.

Athereal energy might have been able to bring me back if I fell, but it couldn't be used as a substitute for magic energy.

Out of all the various miracles that could be performed with its power, regenerating magic energy wasn't one of them.

The only reason that Katiana had recovered all of hers when Julian brought her back was because of how he did it.

He gave her her natural heart back and as such, it immediately started generating magic energy for her.

And with so much of his own energy dedicated towards keeping her heart going, that regeneration was fast.

But there was no way of knowing if I would even be capable of returning if I had died here.

These creatures had been capable of stopping our resurrections in the past, I had no way of knowing whether or not they still contained this power.

So I was forced to be cautious.

To keep in mind that during that fight, my life mattered just as much as everyone else's. I had to protect my students from harm where needed but I couldn't afford to allow myself to be reckless.

So I kept to tactics that I knew to be effective. Physical attacks and sword swings, I couldn't afford to take any further risk that that.

I had lost so much already and had only two things left to protect, the people fighting by my side and the planet itself, I wasn't about to lose those as well.

So onwards I strode, slashing the shades before me with my sword and killing anything that stood in my way.

Slowly but surely, I was winning.

With Katiana in view directly in front of my position, I knew that my goal was within reach and wasn't about to allow myself to be cut off from reaching that goal.

And as I slowly drew nearer to Katiana and her group, I started to be able to hear it. The sound of her fighting, the sound of her winning.

From our position, I couldn't directly see her through the densely packed army but I had felt what she had done thus far. And I could easily see the sparks and blood from her team's fighting as it all went flying through the air.

Through our pact, I could feel her more and more the closer we became.

I could feel her anger, the sense of loss weighing down on her chest and each of the scratches on her arms.

I knew what had happened.

While I could not see it, while I could not hear it, I knew what it was. Her emotions and the condition she was in said it all. Someone had gotten too close and a student had jumped in to save her.

The level of pain that she was in, both physically and mentally meant only one thing. That student had died protecting her.

She was no longer fighting for survival, nor because it was her purpose or her job. She was fighting for the same reason that the students in my group fought for.

Revenge.

Losing someone who was meant to be under your care, there isn't a way of describing the feelings that such an event creates. So instead of feeling it you turn to anger, a fiery rage that burns deep within your soul.

This builds and builds until you stop noticing it and start to accept it. Using it to your advantage and fighting on.

With adrenaline pumping through your veins, the need to avenge that lost one and the sword in your hand was all that you can focus on.

You do all that you must to make sure that that death was not in vain, to make sure that it doesn't happen again and to win the fight that they had died to ensure that you could win.

And soon enough, I started feeling all of it.

I could feel every beat of her heart, every swing of her sword and every drop of sweat on her face.

She was fighting as hard as she could and it was working. The level of corruption in the air slowly subsided by the minute. As each soldier fell, the magic supporting them dissipated into the planet and the portal grew weaker as it suffered yet another loss.

Or at least, it was growing weaker for a while.

At first.

But I didn't notice.

I was too busy fighting.

And as we continued to fight, taking down as many as we could, it arrived.

And in that one moment that saw the end of our push, our victory quickly became impossible.

We could all see that we were winning, the corruption in the air slowly being absorbed by the planet and the battlefield slowly pooling with the blood and bones of the fallen. But even so, nothing could have stopped what transpired from happening.

Most of the soldiers evaporated when they took enough hits, like an apparition in the night, fading when the light floods the room. Many thousands of them did this, leaving a space where they once stood for the ones behind them to move in but some of them didn't.

Some of the larger ones, the stronger ones, refused to disappear. As we cut them down, they fell to the floor and that was where they stayed.

Like any other creature in the world when they died, they laid there motionless, bleeding profusely and being trod on as we pushed forward atop their bones.

But it didn't matter how their stayed dead, as long as they did. And while I knew that eventually these creatures would be reabsorbed by the portals and sent back down in the next wave, I at least knew that once they were down, I didn't have to worry about them again for quite some time.

So on we pressed, every step getting us closer to the other team and with each one of those steps, we took out more and more of those unsightly abominations, slowly making a dent in their numbers and whittling them down.

This progress was good, I expected to win that first battle within the first few hours, I saw no reason to expect anything but a victory.

And then after that victory, I knew they there would still only be more to come. There always was.

Despite their initial numbers for the first wave, I knew that by the following day, they would re-emerge and the fight would start all over again.

Repeating itself until we had exhausted the magic energy keeping the portal open.

So no matter how many we faced in that initial fight, I knew that there would be more. I just didn't expect what that actually meant.

I heard it long before I saw it.

The sound of the sky cracking open once again.

The sound of raging thunder and the crackle of a lightless lightning.

The sky reacted like it was a wounded animal about to die. Doing all that it could to stop what was happening. Clouds soon covering overhead, the temperature dropping rapidly and the blood red rain finally dying down as a new whether system built up to replace it.

The wind subsided and the silence of the world became unending. The only thing that I could hear was us. The only sound that filled the air in that moment was the fight, nothing else.

No animals, no storms, no wind. Just nothing.

In that moment the sound had stopped, the moon had been clouded over and all that illuminated us was the light from the portal overhead.

That was when I saw it. A light, far brighter than the portal above our heads dancing across the sky, blinding us.

I stood there in disbelief for a moment but that helped nothing. No matter how much I was surprised by what I saw, no matter how much it scared me, the truth remained.

There was now another portal opening in the sky above us. So I directed my attention away from the fight and to the stars, gazing up at the snow and ash as it began to fall. The smoke and blood above me made my eyes sting at first but I bared the pain and focused only on the sky.

Not even making a single gesture towards protecting myself or the others. I simple stood there in awe and forget about everything else.

Within a moment I had seen it, it was small, easy to miss but it was there and it was blindingly powerful.

A portal, no more than three meters wide, directly below the first one. It was dead centre of the first but was around two or three hundred meters below it.

The only reason that I could see it was that the edge of it was coloured. A slight tint of purple covered in the black shade of corruption.

It was quite different from the white light being emitted from the main portal and was far more powerful.

It was emitting far more energy than one that size should have been able to produce. And in response, the air grew thick, reacting to the toxicity of the magic flowing through it.

For a time, it was hard to breathe/

And then. Then it happened.

The same glow that appeared before the initial attack shot across the sky.

It was another beam of light. All be it weaker than the first but this time it wasn't aiming straight down at my barrier in an attempt to finish me off.

This time, it had targeted a position to the north.

Initially I thought that it was heading for its own army but then I realised, that was Katiana's position.

This time I was sure of it, there was no doubt in my mind, someone had made a copy of the Planetary Firing Rings. That was the only explanation.

There was no mage, no Athereon, no force of nature that could have created that kind of an attack without them.

To think that someone had not only managed to replicate its function, not only managed to charge it with the necessary magic energy but also had managed to do that from within the corruption itself.

That shouldn't have been even remotely possible and yet, that was the only possible answer. There was no other way, no other spell that could have created such a powerful attack.

It was intentional.

This was planned.

The beam that I saw was thinner and far more precise than the first but still equally as devastating.

I knew then and there that this was no accident, no mere random attack; it was a precision strike, aimed directly at my wife and the students fighting alongside her.

Time almost stood still in that moment and all I could do was watch as it approached her position.

I stood in silence with dread in my heart and a scattered

wasteland of thoughts and ideas in my mind.

I felt fear, more heavily that I had ever done before.

I knew that if I lost her during this fight, it would have broken me. Left me no more than a mere shell, powerless and still.

I would have just given up.

I knew that I was out of options, completely powerless to do anything in that moment to prevent it.

All I could do was drop my sword and fall to my knees as I watched the light race across the sky.

It was too late; nothing that I could do, no spell or ability that I possessed would have allowed me to travel fast enough to save her.

It was moving too fast and there was too great a distance between us.

Seconds soon became hours in my mind and all I could do was watch. I didn't even care that I was about to die as well, I just couldn't move, I couldn't think and I couldn't act.

In that moment, I couldn't do anything.

Julian and Katrina rushed in front of me to cover my position, breaking formation and putting us in a standstill.

And now that we were still, we were stuck.

The enemy surrounded us completely, forcing us into a circle limited to basic attacks and defensive spells only without the necessary room to move around.

We didn't have the space to do anything. I heard Julian shout out my name over and over again but I paid no attention to it. I simply knelt there, experiencing the loss of my wife yet again.

I was useless; I had no way of getting to her, no way of reaching her in time. Even teleporting wouldn't have been fast enough.

I just did nothing and watched as the light finally hit her position. I just willingly sat there and watched my wife die for the second time.

But from the time of the portal opening and the beam being fired, only three seconds had passed, and another two seconds had passed for the beam to hit its target.

That was all the time I had to react, just two seconds. Teleporting would have used four at least, flight would have used thirty and running would have used a whole minute. There was no way of reaching her, not unless I could find some way of moving faster than the speed of light without needing any acceleration to get up to speed.

I was too far away and had too little time to respond.

I was useless.

And then it was over.

The ground shook violently as the explosive force erupted into chaos. The yellow glow of the energy filled the disc of the crater and the orange fury of the fire ball quickly spread outward.

I saw no less that fifty enemy soldiers go flying through the air when it hit, even more as its shockwave moved through the army and then that was it, I had lost her, again.

Just like that, in less than a handful of seconds, she was gone.

Like a laser, the beam of light continued to fire, burrowing deep into the earth with every passing second, digging a hole like a drill as it continued to plough over what remained of my wife's body.

I stayed still and just allowed myself to feel the loss of my wife. After all, what more could I have done? No matter how hard we fought after that moment, no matter how much we did to make sure that we won, nothing would bring them back.

They were gone.

She was gone.

It didn't matter what miracles I might have been capable of, I couldn't turn back time and I couldn't completely rebuild a disintegrated body.

Knowing how powerful that attack was, I knew that there wouldn't be anything left, I knew that she was gone. Both body and soul, now out of my reach for the rest of eternity, not even resurrection magic could have saved her from such a fate.

Nothing I could have done would have been enough. She was gone and the beam of light continued to rain down from the sky as though it still hadn't hit its target.

I just sat on the floor, soaking up the blood and mud with my cloths and staining my skin underneath.

I just sat there and watched as the students tirelessly continued to fight.

I could see in on their faces, the feeling of loss, the look of awe, the grief and the anger building up inside.

They weren't going to be able to cope for long.

They were scared and they were weak.

It was then that I began to give up and it was only after that moment of grief suddenly passed that I saw it, the light that continued to fire upon her position; being deflected and aimed at the very army that had fired it.

Cutting through them like a laser bouncing off of a mirror, it just kept going. Nothing in its path to slow it down. Then it started moving. It went left until everything in that direction was gone and then changed to go right.

The light was now targeting every enemy on the field, mowing them down like they were nothing. Blasting its way through until it hit the wall of dirt from the crater we were fighting in.

Then I heard something, something that struck me hard like a fist made of iron hitting my face. It woke me up and made me react just in time. If I hadn't heard it, then I would have gotten them killed.

I heard a voice in my head.

I heard her voice.

'Get down!' It screamed, echoing around the empty space inside my head.

It was her voice, my wife, inside my head.

I didn't take the time to think, I just reacted.

I relayed the order to the students and watched as the light missed us by a matter of inches.

As it passed over our heads, we all got a taste of its power too. The energy that was eradiating from that beam, was more than simple corruption.

It was, Athereal.

Just as I had feared, the light was far too powerful to simply be random and I knew it.

Someone had invented it and who better than someone like me?

Someone whose natural born affinity for magic allows us to create spells at will.

Who better than an athereon to be the death of us all?

And as I laid there on the floor, drenched in the muck of the blood-stained dirt, slowly being covered in falling snow and ash, I had time to think.

I thought and thought for many moments before I realised my mistake.

If she was dead, then why didn't I feel her die?

That was my one mistake, in that moment when the beam of light fell, I was consumed by grief and all because I had failed to realise that I could still feel her heart beating.

If I had only taken the time to evaluate the situation more closely, I would have known the truth.

If only I had acted as a calculating soldier rather than a scared husband, I would have realised, I never felt the blast hit her body.

And then as the light stopped firing after it passed over us, it was then that I could see it. I stood up and cast my gaze over to her position.

And all I saw was a perfectly cast Fatal Mirror front and centre.

No one else over there could have been capable of sustaining it for as long as she did.

A large plane of perfectly reflective glass hovering in the air just in front of her body.

Fatal Mirror, a spell so powerful that it can deflect anything, as long as you are capable of paying the immensely taxing price for casting it.

If anyone else had tried casting it besides her, it would have probably killed them. But even so, even with my wife's own magic energy to power it, she shouldn't have been able to keep it up for as long as she had. Even she wasn't capable of that much.

But I didn't care, the plan had worked and the beam had cut down almost fifteen thousand of the remaining forces.

Leaving just a thousand or so to the right of my position

that she'd missed.

So my group ran towards them, cutting and punching as they went.

They hid their emotions and simply continued to fight as if nothing had happened. Relying on their newfound high spirits and rushing to the end that they now saw on the horizon.

The remaining students of Katiana's group did the same. Leaving her and Lila behind to recover.

They made quick work of the remaining forces of course. Celebrating valiantly as they killed the last one.

However, I knew that this celebration was premature, there was still more to come and if that blast had taught me anything, it was that this fight was unlike any other that I had faced before.

If only I had had some real back up, then maybe I could have avoided the outcome of that fight, maybe I could have saved them. If only I had known where to find her, then maybe I could have avoided this whole mess before it even began.

But in that moment, I didn't think on such things. I only picked my sword up from the ground, shook off the blood and then sheathed it. Focusing only the task ahead, I pulled myself together and started walking. Gathering my thoughts and feelings as I went.

Thinking that we had won the first wave at least, I rejoiced and congratulated my students. I contacted Katiana telepathically as well while I continued to make my way towards her.

She was alive, that was all that mattered.

Her condition and where the beam had come from was of

no importance to me in that moment. All I cared about was the fact that she was still breathing. As long as that remained true, I could repair any wound that she had sustained, she just needed to be breathing.

'Don't you ever scare me like that again!' I told her.

She laughed I assume but couldn't do much else, she was running on fumes after that. The Fatal Mirror spell would drain most mages to the brink of death but for Katiana, she was strong enough to avoid such a risk. However, she had kept the spell going for far too long.

She was empty, still conscious but overall powerless.

I saw Lila kneeling beside her offering support, possibly even a healing spell but I was too far away to tell.

I was only half way there when I noticed.

Since the army had been destroyed the portals should have started to fade already. That should have been it for that wave but there was more to come and even I couldn't handle it when it did.

I was only just starting to wipe away every feeling of dread and loss that I contained. I was just starting to grieve for the fallen students in both groups when it happened.

Something that I could not have foreseen.

The fight resumed.

Out from the smaller portal they came, three of them, falling out of the sky above me.

The first thing that I saw were their wings.

Four glowing white wings on all of them.

Gold highlighted armour adorning heir bodies and then the weapons, one sword, one bow and one spear. Again, I stood still, not quite knowing how to process such an event.

Corruption flowed out of them as if it were endless.

It darkened the sky and almost completely hid the portals behind it.

It was so thick, far too thick for it to be coming from only three combatants but the truth remains. It was.

In that moment, I did not feel fear, I did not feel anger or loss.

I felt nothing.

I was simply confused.

The three of them seemed unconscious, simply falling from the sky and quickly approaching the ground. They still had their skin but were most certainly under the influence of corruption. But even when shrouded in that darkness their light still shone through.

Yellow energy filled the sky, making them seem almost seem like holy entities falling from the heavens.

Julian had noticed it at the same time as me and teleported over to my position.

Due to the growing levels of corruption in the air, the teleport took just over a second rather than being instant. Yet this wasn't the last of it.

The air grew even thicker and soon it was obvious, teleporting was going to be next to impossible before long.

"Master... are those, Angels?" He asked, looking up at the sky.

I watched closely, looking for any sign of movement as they continued to fall. And then all of a sudden, there was. The three of them stopped their decent and began to hover. Their wings flapped violently and they righted their orientation.

It was only after they stopped moving that I could tell what they were for sure. And it was then that my confusion turned to fear.

I saw their heads turn left and right, scanning the battlefield. They were looking for something, turning their heads in all directions trying to find it.

Then they did.

Katiana and Lila.

When I saw their gaze focus on her I reacted as fast as I could but it wasn't fast enough.

"No. They're Athereon!" I shouted.

I forcibly teleported over there as quickly as I could but I was delayed due to the thickness of the corrupted magic still lingering in the air.

The teleport hurt, as if I were being ripped apart by a savage animal and then being cruelly put back together piece by piece as I forced my way over there.

With how much energy it took to get there, I would guess that as I left a bright blue light went off from where I was standing.

It would have lasted less than a second but I would have been as bright as a flash of lightning before it faded. Teleporting so violently has its consequences but I didn't care.

The pain and the energy required to pull it off didn't matter. I was desperate and needed to get there as quickly as I could.

But by the time that I got there, it was already too late.

Lilia was cut in half, lying face first in the blood-stained dirt a foot away from the rest of her. Not even her armour had survived the blade, it was beyond anything that I could have protected her against.

And when I looked up from her corpse that laid at my

feet, only moving my head slightly, that was when I saw it.

The cooling corpse of my dead wife, a silver great sword impaled in her chest and blood everywhere.

My heart sank.

I ran over to her as fast as I could, ignoring the three men standing behind me and trying to make it in time to save her but it was already too late for that, she was gone.

Blood was draining out of her and nothing more.

No magic, no heartbeat, no consciousness.

She was dead.

I desperately tried to resurrect her, not even giving so much as a thought as to what it would cost me to bring her back but something resisted the spell.

No matter how forcefully I tried to cast it, not one single drop of my energy would enter her.

And that was when I noticed, the blade that she had been killed with, it was infused with the same dark energy that the army possessed.

She couldn't be brought back after that.

It was the same energy that was capable of killing an Athereon, permanently.

With so much of it within her, there was no way of bringing her back.

She was gone for good and there was nothing I could do about it.

Just looking at her I could feel the pain that she had gone through and it was too much to bear.

Then I caught a glimpse of it, a small glow of magic energy emanating from her chest.

I reached in to grab whatever it was and what my hand finally found was a pendant.

One that I had never seen before.

It was red, a deep and dark red crystal in the shape of a heart.

It was strange, it felt alive, irradiating with pure magic energy.

I took the chain off of her neck and rapped it around my hand. Whatever this pendant was, it was infused with her magic energy and I wasn't about to let go of it.

But as those short moments ended, so too did my delusion.

Because in my haste to get to her I forgotten to notice, that she hadn't just died, someone had killed her.

And that killer was standing right behind me, ready for a fight.

It was only when I looked more closely at the sword impaled into my wife that I noticed its construction too.

Is was ancient, a relic from another time entirely.

It was a blade that I had seen before though, it was the blade of the king. My king. It was an ancient and very powerful war relic from the days when the Athereon Empire still existed.

It was an Athereon's blade.

I turned my attention to the men as soon as I was sure, shifting into my Athereon form out of anger and forcing as much energy as I could through my sword ready to impale it into each of their chests one at a time.

I held Katiana's pendant in my hand as tightly as I could, the chain wrapped around my knuckles and not going anywhere, the heart shaped crystal dangled from my palm and continuing to give off a slight glow from the magic energy within.

538

Even if it was petty, even if it meant nothing, I held that pendant as though it was her body. I wasn't about to let go of it and whether or not it was possible for this to be true, I believed that by holding it, it was as though she was by my side the whole time.

So I polled my energy and my thoughts, preparing myself for a fight against three of my own.

I had no chance.

Even with my old partner by my side we still would have lost.

I was weak compared to her but even so, she was still no match for them. So in a sense, I was the worst choice when it came for going up against three of my own on any day.

I wouldn't even have a chance if it were just two of them.

One on one, maybe, but three, I was a dead man walking.

That was when I looked at his face, the one who had done the deed and… it just clicked.

The sword, the three men, the armour… I realised that I knew him. Or at least I used to.

He was once a friend and if we had met on any other day, I would have treated him as such. But this time he had done the unthinkable. He had murdered my wife.

But I knew who he was and I knew his friends as well.

I knew them more than well enough to know… they'd kill me in an instant.

The three were known as Trinity, the strongest fighters in the war and previous protectors of the king himself.

They would have been on the front lines when the palace was overrun.

However, this didn't explain how they were there in that moment.

Nothing that I knew about the war suggested that anyone other than my partner and myself had survived.

Obviously, this wasn't accurate though. My son had made it, so perhaps others were out there as well.

However, such thinking was for another time.

It didn't matter how they were alive, the only thing that did was the act of murder that they had just committed.

I looked at the two others behind him and thought about my chances some more. Then I cast that thought away.

I didn't have time to think rationally.

My wife had been killed senselessly.

It was high time I repaid them for that.

I didn't care if he was once a friend. What Winter had done, could not be forgiven.

So I prepared for the fight and all but willed myself to win.

Whether or not I survived it, this man was dying.

No matter the cost.

KATIANA ILLISIDEL

I promised myself that I would avoid expressing my emotions while writing these words.

I told myself that I would not shed tears, that I would not lose my train of thought as I detailed every event that led up to my life as it exists now.

However, as these memories surface, I am discovering that my intent to keep myself calm and collected during this is no longer possible.

Because what I am about to disclose onto you, what I am about to relive as I write it down, is too much for a man to push down without showing through the cracks.

Even now, the emotions connected to those events have begun to flow and I fear that I may be unable to avoid expressing them as I continue.

I guess that this is just another example of my broken promises. No matter what I do to ensure that my word is kept, no matter what lengths I go to in order to make sure that I do not betray others or their trust in me and my abilities, something always gets in my way.

I promised myself to avoid getting emotional and I have failed in that endeavour. I promised Katiana that I would protect her life above all else until the day she died a natural and peaceful end. And once more I have failed in that.

I promised my son that I would come back for him once the war was over when I left that day. But it never ended for me. It never ended for anyone.

I promised the Magic Council that in exchange for their pardoning or continued ignorance of whatever lines I crossed, I would strive to protect them and the world they have governed in my place these past three thousand years without complaint for as long as I was required to do so.

And I was about to break that promise too.

But what I promised Kat, what I promised my wife on our wedding day in my vows and what I promised her the day after when our pact was formed. That was a promise that had been broken twice.

In the past, I'd gone to lengths that the Council might well have taken my head for if they knew. I had replaced her heart. I had used forbidden magic. I had killed countless thieves and assassins looking to make a name for themselves by targeting the Crown Mage.

I had done so much to keep my promise.

And yet, this now, her body fallen to the floor beside me on that dark battlefield, this was the second time I had failed to protect her from the powerful jaws of the dogs dragging her away.

Twice.

There shouldn't have even been a first time.

And now this was the second.

She was everything to me, my whole reason for being could have been explained in just two words while she was around. All I had to do was say her name, nothing else mattered to me then.

Not this world, not its people, nor my own existence.

All that mattered was that I kept her safe, that I made sure she was alive and happy. I needed to keep that smile on her face. I needed to keep this woman walking the streets of the world. I needed to.

Like an obsession, I couldn't let myself fail.

And yet.

I had.

I swore to uphold my vows to her on that alter and yet, sickness and health separated us on more than one occasion. Corruption had taken her once and then a blade imbued with that same power had taken her again.

I was powerless to save her on both occasions and now, this time – no amount of Athereal Energy, no number of my remaining resurrections, no spell known to exist - nothing could have brought her back.

Even if my son still resided within Julian, he wouldn't have been able to help again. Not that I would have let him do so even if he could.

I had lost him twice already, I wouldn't have let myself lose him again.

But out of everything that I could do, every spell and act of god that I could perform and every miracle that I have been known to grant in day's past, it wasn't within my power to save her this time.

It was far too late to do anything but feel her loss by the time that I finally reached her side. By then she was already gone, already beginning to grow cold before my eyes as I held her hand. And there was nothing that I could do about it.

I can do so many things with the powers of magic. I can

do even more with just the powers given to my own kind at birth. I can destroy or form mountains at will, grow a garden from nothing but sand and even resurrect the dead given the cause to do so. But turning back the hands of time wasn't something that I or anyone else was capable of.

Whatever happens in life is fixed.

Events cannot be undone.

The clock cannot be wound back.

So once something's gone. It's gone forever.

Always.

There were still methods of bringing people back from the dead that I hadn't tried yet, forbidden, dark methods of resurrection that were outlawed even back when the Athereon Empire's Magic Council still existed.

And when the weight of my loss finally started to sink in, I immediately thought about using them on her in a desperate attempt to save her. But with the blade still impaled in her chest and three combat trained warriors from my own species standing in my way, I wasn't going to be able to do anything but put myself in an early grave.

For a moment, a mere second at most, it was strange.

It was as if time had slowed, almost stopped.

I could see the specs of dust floating in place before my eyes, the flakes of snow as they hovered above the ground and the ash as it spiralled in place, reacting with the wind as it fell to the floor.

I could think in real time, see and react as if nothing had happened but for that one moment, everything was still.

It was as though time had stopped for everyone but me and though this aspiration was certainly a fabrication of the mind, it was still exactly what I needed.

The light emitted by the portals continued to shine and illuminate the battlefield despite the smoke and clouds above. And in this light, everything below was revealed in perfect clarity as the fight waged on.

This purple haze of light in the air revealed the blood drenched dirt, the piles upon piles of bodies and the corpses laid before me.

I had been given a chance to have some time to think and I took it. I didn't move a single muscle, I simply looked at my wife and took some time to recollect on our lives together.

What more could I have done?

Her life had come to an end and try as I might, I couldn't do anything but focus on its beginning.

I thought back all the way to the day that we first met. The day that a chance encounter changed her entire life and brought a certain light back into mine.

Back then, she was nothing more than a mere human walking down the street without a care in the world. She had a normal life. She didn't even know she was anything special.

But that all changed when she met me.

That was how it started for the both of us. That day she just happened to be walking down the same road that I was, wearing her black robes and not taking any notice of others as she quickly made her way towards the catholic church at the end of the road.

She passed me by within a hair's width of my arm. I hadn't even glanced up at her before then. And had she not been so close to me in that moment, I would have never noticed her.

Any other girl would have just slipped me by even at such a close range, they wouldn't have given off anything that made me look. But she was different.

Her arm brushed up against mine and that one moment of contact between us burst through my sulking stare towards the ground and opened my eyes wide as I realised what I had just felt.

The untapped power lying dormant, locked away and discarded within her body. She was nothing more than a fifteen-year-old girl and she was already as powerful as most level seven mages. Without ever even being trained or even using magic in the first place, she outclassed them all in raw power and magic energy endurance alone.

When I felt this power within her, I couldn't help but ask her to stop, grabbing her arm and holding her in place before she could run away.

She turned her head towards me with anger expressed on her face at first, probably thinking me a thug of some kind at the time, however, when she finally made eye contact, she fell to the floor in fear.

With power that strong inside of her, it only made sense that she would be able to sense mine. To her, I would have looked more like a god than a human. That was what she called me after all.

She immediately started praying. Believing that she was about to be judged, she desperately began to repent.

It made sense.

Back then, times were different. The only place for young girls like her to go during the day was church, or as I liked to call it, Catholic Condemnation School.

There she would have been taught by nuns and then

beaten by them after and even during lessons. She would have had the life of a maid forced upon her and she would have accepted it without even thinking. And all so that she didn't have to live on the streets.

Times were rough for people like her back then. Not being born into a wealthy family was as good as being born homeless straight away. No one would have treated you like a person, let alone like the beautiful young girl that she was.

I looked at her as she prayed to me, slowly taking in every detail as I made up my mind.

She simply sat there on the floor and begged me to be forgiving; she truly thought that I was her god in that moment and she feared that I was as vengeful as the Bible would lead you to believe.

She looked younger than she was, that's what I saw in her first of all. Almost a year or two at my guess.

She could have passed as a thirteen-year-old rather than someone who was undeniably fifteen based on bone structure and the progress of her development into womanhood.

She had her hair in a bun and hidden behind her head too. Almost as though she was ashamed of it. And after later seeing what it looked like when it was in full view dangling down from her head without even one strand out of place, I could never figure out why she would want to hide it.

Every detail about her was pure perfection. Nothing, not one thing about her was worth changing and there was defiantly nothing that should have been hidden.

And the one other detail that stood out that most was her skin. It was remarkably clean for someone back then. As was the rest of her in fact.

She didn't look like she had been living in poverty, she might have even passed as one of the noblemen's daughters or as the maid to a wealthy family if she had been wearing the correct attire but she hadn't been born into that life as it seemed.

And nothing could hide the clothes that she wore. Hand-me-downs, tattered and old. Possibly from another family member or even stolen all together.

They had no place on a girl like her.

If she had been born into a mage's family, then she would have been sent to a school long before I ever came across her. She was old enough and defiantly strong enough.

And that strength alone should have attracted someone's attention before me too. The Magic Council had people in the world who looked out for human born mages.

Perhaps this was one they missed?

Or perhaps back then they didn't have enough of a watchful eye?

I reached my hand out towards her and asked her name.

She cautiously took it and I helped her up.

It was then I learned those two words that changed my life and it was shortly after that that I took the chance to test her. I wanted to make sure that I wasn't wrong and that she understood what she was as well as I did.

So I asked her what she saw when she looked at me.

She replied in fear, truly believing that I was a god, she told me that I was such a being. Saying that she could see my halo, an aura of pure energy surrounding me and extending into the heavens.

For some, this is all that they see and as such that is all that I allow them to see. But for her, she could not only see my power but also focus on the rest of me through it.

She had allowed herself to believe that I was her god and while I was somewhat opposed to this I made no effort to correct her at the time, I just allowed her to think this, it would have taken too long to explain what I actually was in the moment.

I grabbed her hand again and forced a little magic energy into it, to humans this wouldn't have been noticeable but for her, she yelped in pain.

Proving that she was not only a mage but also extremely sensitive to magic. I had barely even stared when she reacted. It should have taken two or more seconds for the magic energy to build up. But she reacted instantly.

With that and what I had already felt in her, I didn't need any further proof. She was a mage and she belonged elsewhere. A life of poverty is something that only humans and criminals should have to live, mages were above that.

I questioned her further before making my final decision, asking about her family and if she knew anything about magic. She told me that she had neither. No family and no knowledge.

So it was then that I made her an offer, one that would change her life for the better and forever shape the course of mine.

"Tell me, Katiana Illisidel. Were I to take you away from all this, show you what life can be in a place far more wonderous and magnificent, would you have any reason to stay?"

"No my lord." She said, still thinking me a god. "Nothing."

"Then why not take my hand?" I asked her, extending

the limb towards her person. "And I will take you a place where you will know only happiness. And learn things that you couldn't imagine in a thousand years."

It took her only a moment to decide. She grabbed my hand with a smile on her face and that instant I teleported her straight back to my home.

Under any other circumstances, this would have been considered as kidnapping but for her, I was saving her life.

And when we arrived, she was struck with fear once again but soon that fear faded and all that was left was a very curious young girl staring out the window at my garden.

So I explained some things.

"You're not human." I told her. Grasping her attention in an instant. "And neither am I."

She turned to me, pulling her hands to her chest, mere moments from beginning to pray once more.

"I'll tell you everything." I said softly, walking over to my sitting area to rest on the sofa. "Please, sit."

So I told her everything I could.

What she was and what I am.

I informed her on everything I thought she'd be able to understand about the world of magic and I made sure to enforce the point that she belonged in it.

She thought that I was telling her she was a witch. She feared a burning at the stake. But I quickly informed her that she was far more than that.

She wasn't a sinner. She wasn't evil. And she wasn't party to the devil's contracts.

She had simply been born with the power to do anything that she wanted, be anything that she wanted and go anywhere that she could imagine.

It took some convincing for her to trust me but after many nights of trying, she finally started opening up.

So I allowed her to live with me for a few years, showing her all the wonders of this world as the time passed and training her well right up until, like Julian, she was ready for an entrance exam.

However, at the time, such exams were easier and getting her into Academia took only some simple paperwork. There was no test. Only a gruelling from the Magic Council when I presented a mage trained beyond that of level ten to her very first academy.

That's it.

That was how I met the woman who would one day become my wife.

A teenager living it rough and a man walking down the street.

A simple tale with earth-shattering consequences.

The world would not be as it is today without her in it and I would not have become the man I am now if I had never walked down that road so many years ago.

It would seem that fate had a sense of irony.

For a man who didn't need to walk down roads in order to get to his destinations to have had his entire life turned around by walking down one just that once. Given the chances, what else could it be but fate?

It's too improbable for it to simple be a chance encounter.

She was the most fascinating girl that I had ever met and I did all that I could to make sure that she would never return to her old life again.

For almost three hundred years we were married and in

all that time she never feared death, she never thought that she was going to have to experience it and then this happened.

I got her killed and I couldn't do anything to save her.

She was already dead when I got to her and in truth, she had been dead for centuries. Ever since the day that I asked her to fight by my side.

I shouldn't have done it, I should have kept her safe, I should have put everyone in one group and fought as a team.

Yet, what I should have or could have done was of little importance in that moment. All that mattered was her and now that she was dead, I had some much-needed vengeance to enact.

And three brothers who I needed to kill.

Even if I didn't survive, this was still something that I just had to do.

And I wasn't backing down.

Even without the death of my wife, they were still a part of that army.

They had to die.

So I had to do everything I could to make sure they did.

Even if they meant sacrificing it all.

I would return the favour to each of them.

Slowly.

Very, slowly.

WINTER'S WAR

I had been given just enough time to recollect over our lives together before that moment faded and I was snapped back to reality.

I quickly realised that time had resumed its motion and that the man standing before me was still there as before.

I knew what I had to do, I knew what I needed to do in order to make it happen it but I didn't know how.

I knew I needed to kill him. I knew I would need to take off his head to keep him down. But given the differences in our number and fighting skills, I didn't know how to manage that alone.

So I continued to stand still, ready for anything, staring into his eyes, sizing up my opponent, looking for anything that would have given me the upper hand.

There he stood; mere steps away from my dead wife and moments away from his sword.

I looked at him and his two brothers, trying to make sense of it all.

Winter, the apparent mastermind behind everything. Followed closely by the expert archer known as Janus and their brother, the spear-wielding brute called Uriel.

Those three were supposed to have died thousands of

years ago.

They were the three strongest warriors that the Athereon army had and they were far stronger than me in every way.

I understood how they were alive but not why.

Corruption can do many things but it cannot kill an Athereon on its own. It's power only sustains its hosts. It keeps them breathing and controls their movements until something else kills them. And after that, free of corruption, the host finally died.

How they had ended up within the corruption was beyond me. I watched as the front lines fell that day, I watched as each of my men were slaughtered one by one outside the main gates of the Ruby Palace just a dozen feet from the edge of that disc above the Spire. And I could do nothing to stop it.

I was under direct orders and had no choice but to obey.

I had thought them dead all this time. Their position had been overrun many times over before the end but even knowing that, it didn't change the fact that they were still there.

All three of them standing before me.

It shouldn't have been possible.

When we sacrificed everything to stop that army from devastating the world any further, those three shouldn't have been affected just like everyone else.

The corruption was designed to only target the enemy soldiers. It was constructed using their own magic in the first place. Our kind shouldn't have been compatible.

There wasn't any reason to suggest that it would have taken our own people with it. Why would it?

And I should know, I was the one who buried the bodies

and then the city itself after the fact.

Knowing that the humans were better off not knowing of our existence, I did what I had to do to hide it.

I sealed our city away under a blanket of stone, water and ice.

The bodies of our fallen and the city itself now lie on the bottom of the deepest ocean with a protective barrier keeping back the tides.

Those three should have been down there with it.

In fact, I was almost certain that they were.

When Tao-Avolantis fell, I was sure that only two of us were left.

I would have known if we weren't alone.

I would have heard the stories.

I would have felt their magic.

For the three of them to have been within the corruption all this time without my knowledge, it only begged the question, what else didn't I know about the end of that war?

But despite my questions and what I knew to be true, the truth and the three of them still remained.

They were real, so something that happened back then must have transpired without my knowledge.

Some part of the ritual to seal the corruption had been done incorrectly perhaps.

No, it had to have been.

There isn't another way for corruption to be absorbed by an Athereon unless they wanted it to.

Or maybe that was it.

It had been their choice.

When the army began to storm through the lower town having killed our king and our strongest fighter's that made up his guard, those three must have still been alive. Holding onto life somehow amidst the chaos.

Knowing that we intended to seal that army in corruption if all else failed, they must have thought that they could absorb it to survive.

That's the only explanation that made sense. Why else would those three have willingly been consumed by a force that was beyond their control?

Knowing this didn't change anything however.

My wife was still dead and I was still moments away from joining her.

I knew that I didn't have a chance but that didn't matter, I was still going to try.

So I prepared myself and assessed the situation and thought about a plan.

I tried and tried but the image of my deceased wife was all that I could focus on and it was only made worse when Winter went to draw his sword from her chest.

I watched him grab the handle, desperately wanting to cut his arm off as he reached for it but I knew that I couldn't. If Janus didn't fire an arrow fist, Uriel would have thrown his spear, I could have been dead within an instant and Winter would have only been wounded.

So there I remained, observing rather than acting, just like the coward that I was at the time.

He latched onto the handle and ripped the sword from her body. Blood and organs rained through the air and her lifeless corpse was left behind to rot.

He showed no care for her, no respect for the dead and no regard for how much that made me want to kill him even more. Perhaps he was counting on that. Knowing deep down how much I cared for her and trying to provoke me to gauge my response.

He walked away from her body and re-joined his brothers, leaving her lifeless shell to flop onto the floor like a toppling tree, covering it in even more blood and dirt than it was already. Defiling it tremendously, the image that now consumed my mind was too much to bear.

I was consumed by hate and anger, the feeling of loss now wiped from my mind, leaving only the inferno that was now burning throughout it.

I looked back at the three of them. I saw how they acted as a team.

It seemed as though, even when driven completely insane by corruption, they still acted as brothers.

It was remarkable that even one piece of their former selves remained but even so, it didn't matter if deep down three of my own people were in there somewhere, they still needed to die.

So there I stood, completely motionless and still, not saying a word and not doing anything out of the fear that gripped me.

If I had attacked then and there, then I might have been able to hurt him bad enough to leave a debilitating mark but nothing more. Janus would have killed me not long after the initial strike.

No. Instead, I held my ground, and waited for an opportunity to attack.

I looked at them, assessed the situation and ran simulated fights in my head over and over again as I waited. I knew that I could probably handle Uriel one on one but with the other two there, I wouldn't have a chance to defend in time and then I would be dead.

Janus was simple, he had not one single skill in close quarters combat but the other two were still a problem.

I am the best at what I do. There's no one else who can fight better that me, except for the three of them put together.

One on one I could probably kill any of them in the right circumstances but as a team, they would have killed all of us by themselves.

They didn't need to send in the pawns first. They were capable of doing it alone.

Their magic and their fighting skills were unparalleled back in their day. I suspected that this probably still reigned true even now.

That was when I realised, the beam attack that had been used twice already. It was coming from them, their collective power fused into a light-based attack and amplified through the corruption. If that was how it was done, if it took the three of them to cast it, then that meant that none of them could do it alone.

I would have to separate them to keep them from using it again.

However, even this would be difficult.

They were younger, stronger, faster, smarter and all of them had been trained to fight by myself, personally.

That was my role back then. I was the barracks commander under the direct command on the king's right hand. It was my job to train the new recruits and send them into battle before and especially during the war.

And those three were the only group to ever be trained as a trio. Each of them had promise on their own but as a team, they were unbeatable.

So now I stood in silence, holding my sword defensively waiting for an idea to hit me. But that's when something else did.

A sword.

Narrowly, I was able to deflect using my own and some quick reflexes but it shook me out of my confusion and I did what I must.

The sword had been thrown by Winter.

A random blade he'd picked up from the ground.

Done only to grab my attention.

And he certainly had it now.

But in those conditions, the others were too far away to teleport to me soon enough, too week to survive Janus and his arrows from range either, and too slow to doge another beam if they were to go up against it.

So I did the first thing that I could think of.

I summoned them using the pact that we had formed.

I thrust my sword into the dirt as I knelt down into it and released the built-up magic energy within it in full.

A moment later as the pain of using this spell built up within me and I was truly pissed. Blood fuelled rage clouded my mind and probably effected my judgement for a moment. I replayed the entire attack in my mind and noticed something that filled me with even more anger.

This method of assault, the tactics that those three were using, they were darn right cowardly.

Sending pawns to the battlefield before you visit it yourself, how armature.

Everything these men were doing; the attack, the tactics and the signature of their strikes, they were all things that I had taught them over twelve thousand years ago.

If their goal was to kill me, then they would need to try a lot harder than that.

However, if their goal was to make me angry, fill me with grief and make we an easy target, then they had just succeeded and were about to feel the full extent of my wrath as a result.

I tightened my grip on my sword and continued the summoning. I was under attack and defiantly in danger of dying, I needed help and to top that off there where over six billion people depending on me to win.

They had no chance of surviving if I were to fall then and there. The armies of both the human world and ours might have been able to fight off the corrupted soldiers without me but with three Athereon soldiers now in the mix, they didn't have a chance without my aid.

If I lost now, then that was it, the world was a good as gone. Nothing would have been capable of fending off three of my own kind.

Not even the Planetary Firing Rings. Those three were surely capable of surviving a direct hit or two given their magical abilities and besides, it had never even been fired before.

I had one chance to end this war and it was now, so I took it and did what I must in order to win.

Failure was not an option this time.

So I placed both hands onto the blade, awakened almost every magic circuit that I had left in my upper body and formed new ones everywhere else, jolted my system with so much magic energy that I could feel the drain in my very soul and started the summoning ritual with haste.

The first part was simple, the circuits in my back manifested as a semi-transparent shield around my body, giving me the time and protection to carry out what I had started.

I knew that they weren't going to simply let me gather reinforcements and I knew that I wasn't going to be able to summon them fast enough without needing protection.

So I erected a shield around me, similar to a barrier but more focused and not as long lasting, however it was still weaker than anything like Defensive Flare or Fatal Mirror. If they had used a sufficiently powerful attack then it would have failed and I would have died anyway.

And during the entire time that the shield was erected, I heard no less that fifty-four attempts to break through the barrier around me.

I could see the sparks of the blade striking the shield dance across the sky, the flakes of magic energy bouncing off of the shield as they hit. The blue glow of the hexagonal plates that formed the barrier shaking and fading as each hit stuck their surface.

I could see that they had run out of ideas.

None of them were doing anything other than hit me as hard as they could. Not even trying to use their magic. Almost as if they didn't know how to.

So I took a deep breath, forced as much energy through my circuits as I could possibly bear without damaging their structure and channelled it all through my hands and into my sword.

The enchantments that were etched upon the blade started to glow and from there the energy was transferred into the floor. Taking form as a summoning circle almost twenty metres wide this time.

The ancient symbols and shapes that made up this circle are far too complicated to describe so I won't bother. All you should need to know is what you already do. It was made up of five inner circles and one outer edge, each circle containing a row of symbols and patterns dating back to the time of the ancient ones.

The outer ring of the circle lit up and erected its own protective shield, preventing any entry or exit to or from its core.

The rest of the symbols lit up in a similar manner, their blue glow dwarfed that of the portals and the stars above me, lighting up the area with the energy created by my body.

I tightened my grip even further, pushed the sword into the ground just a little more and began.

Magic energy being forced out of my body and into the sword in a dance of bright blue flames surrounding the blade and engulfing the ground around it.

I lowered my head and began the summoning.

Reciting the lines and completing the incantation.

To the others, it would have felt like telepathy as I summoned them. However, it was more than that.

When someone who is pacted with me hears this call, they need to answer it.

To choose whether or not to help.

But they still had to want to help me, I couldn't force them to. But that time, they did not refuse. And with those willing soldiers summoned, a few seconds later I had what I needed.

I had my army and I was ready to avenge my wife.

The ground shook violently as they appeared, the corruption in the air dissipating slightly as it contended my own energy for the right to inhabit its space and the students standing before me.

They knew nothing of what was going on at this point. To them only twenty seconds had passed and all they had seen was me standing with my sword raised, pointing it at the three men before me.

They didn't know that my wife was dead and they didn't know about Lila either.

They were completely out of the loop.

But despite this lack of information, they were quick to adapt to the situation, surrounding me in a layer of people like a shield.

They raised their weapons and pointed them towards the three figures before me.

Julian by my side followed closely by Katrina, they both stood there staring at Katiana.

I didn't have time to explain, so I let my face do the talking.

They could see the pain and anger upon it and they wore similar looks on theirs. They knew what to do and they didn't question it.

Katiana was more than a teacher to these students. She was more than the Crown Mage too.

To them, she was a friend, a caring woman who listened to their problems.

Every one of them cared for her in some way but Julian even more so. He knew her more personally that the rest of them, she was more like a mother to him than she was a teacher or authority figure. She was one of his closest and most cared for friends and he was furious.

It was Julian that I worried about most during the following fight though. He had seen her dying before but he didn't remember it. At least he wasn't supposed to.

I knew that his wellbeing was at stake, not simply because of the fight to come but also because if his memories returned, he would have been dead shortly after. Irreparably so.

Nothing that I was capable of at the time could have possibly rebuilt a brain when it's been as badly damaged as his would have been.

So if he remembered, then that would be it, he would be gone, just like she was.

But now that I had my students, I regained my confidence.

I knew that I had a chance now and I took it.

I stood myself up, removed my sword from the ground and held it tightly in my hand. The enchantments written upon it were put there by Katiana and I was going to use every one of them to kill that murderer.

"Listen well, Winter." I shouted. Walking through the crowd of bruised and bloodied students to get to the front. "This is the last chance for mercy that you will ever receive. Surrender now and die with dignity, I promise to make it quick." I said.

He grunted, saying nothing in response.

He had no intention of giving up, I knew I still had only a slim chance of beating him and so did he.

Whether he had thought it through or not, he was still willing to fight me.

So I returned to the fight.

If he didn't want mercy then I wouldn't give him it. It was time to start moving so I used telepathy to dish out my orders. Telling the remaining thirty-seven students to divide and conquer.

I told them to direct their efforts on Janus first then evade Uriel until he was taken care of. After that, wear Uriel out and attack from range as soon as they saw an opening.

The man in the middle, the man behind this entire thing, he was mine.

And when I was done telling them what to do, none of the students argued with my orders, they simply nodded and began spreading out.

I knew that they could do it but I also knew that some of them wouldn't be making it back. They were up against the greatest spearman and the greatest archer that the Athereon military every trained.

They could win if they tried hard enough but it would have been more than difficult for them.

I had trained those students to fight on equal terms to me but I never had the chance to finish that training. They were incomplete and one slip up now would have been their downfall.

The three brothers must have realised that I was ready to act and they started to move in response. Janus flew off to a point in the distance and Uriel began to ready his spear.

He was going to charge right at them. Not even using an enchantment. Not one spell.

If they were this ignorant of their own magic then I'm surprised that the three of them were even able to create that beam of light in the first place.

Relying on physical attacks and not even using the

simplest of spells. The corruption within them must have consumed their magic circuits by then. It shouldn't have been possible for them to do anything more powerful than fire magic yet somehow that had managed to not only create that monstrosity of a weapon but also fire it twice.

At least I hoped that they were behind it.

If not, that meant that there was still someone or something far more powerful waiting for me on the other side of that portal.

"CHARGE!" I shouted.

And off they went.

Firing arrows and spells at an impressive rate to confuse the enemy. They ran to the left of me, leaving only myself and Winter behind to fight in single combat as planned.

Uriel had already began to run, picking up speed very quickly, and heading straight for the students.

However, in that moment, I had turned my focus to one man and one man alone. Winter.

I didn't even think about checking on how the students were doing during our fight, I simply focused on killing the man before me.

"I beg of you Winter, do not do this, all you will do is fail." I said but no response came.

He didn't even seem to be capable of understanding my words. And I knew why.

English didn't exist when he died.

At least, not in its current form.

So I tried again in Latin, then again in Sumerian and a final time in the language of Athereons but nothing got through to him.

He simply grunted and made slight facial expressions as
566

each world left my mouth.

I didn't know if he couldn't understand language anymore or if he was purposefully ignoring me.

Either way, my patience and his had come to its limit. Before I got the chance to try and get through to him again, it was too late, he had already started the fight.

Winter came at me with his sword, hitting me as hard as he could.

It was a strong hit but not enough.

Our two blades collided and the fight began.

His blows bounced off my blade as each swing struck. This happened over and over again for many moments, as if he just kept trying the same thing over and over expecting different results.

The results remained the same regardless. No matter how hard or how fast he swung his sword, it would always be deflected off of mine.

With Uriel and Janus occupied, I focused all my efforts on Winter. This was his war and he was going to lose it. I was going to make sure that he did.

Even without proof, I blamed him for everything.

All of my losses, everyone who had died fighting against that army time and time again, the pain and suffering that I had gone through in order to fend of attack after attack and keep the world safe.

I blamed him for all of it.

I saw no evidence to suggest that it wasn't Winter and as such I held him responsible for everything. I knew that this war was his doing and I was prepared to kill him over it.

But even if this belief had ended up being a lie, he was still responsible for killing my wife and for that, he would pay dearly.

A barrage of blade strikes filled the air as we fought.

Ringing metal and sparks were all that you could hear or see. I knew that if I could outlast his initial onslaught of attacks then I might have a chance of overpowering him. So, I stayed defensive. Channelling my power into my sword and absorbing every hit that he threw my way.

Unfortunately, this was more difficult than I could have imagined. The level of corrupted magic coming out of him, the smell and feeling that it created was overwhelming. It distracted my efforts, almost making me slip up at times.

I realised then and there that this would need to be an aerial battle. From the ground, we were too evenly matched and the corrupted stench of the bodies we were fighting amongst wasn't helping efforts either.

So I stretched out my wings and gave them a flap, knocking Winter off his feet for a moment only to then have him flying as well.

No matter what you say about my people, no matter what stories you hear or legends you tell. One thing always remains, we can all fly.

Now airborne, the fight became more fast paced. Every slash of our swords resulting in one of us being thrown back a few feet in the air. His attacks were fast, they hit hard and they were erratic.

No sense or strategy to them.

No spells or enchantments backing them up, nothing to suggest that he was even trying. He was nothing but rage fuelled muscle now. Not a single part of his consciousness remained.

The corruption had consumed him completely. He was

nothing but an animal now and I intended to put him down like one as soon as I had the chance to do so.

I would avenge my wife.

I would have justice for what he had done.

So I fought at my best. Using ranged spells where I could and deflecting his strikes as they came.

They continued to grow weaker with every hit too.

He was slowing down but not fast enough.

As the fight droned on, my rage continued to fuel my muscles and his slowly faded. He was tiring out, far too quickly for him to have only been fighting a single opponent though.

A man like him should have been able to fight at his best for well over an hour straight yet he was seemingly tired after the first few minutes.

It wasn't right, he shouldn't have been so easily worn out. But then I stopped to think about it. If he had fired that beam twice now, that would have completely drained him, that was why he didn't use magic. And if he had done this in such quick succession it would have certainly worn him out already.

It would seem that those strikes, however powerful and unexpected, had worked in my favour.

If he was that tired after only a few minutes of fighting me then the other two were surely feeling the same way.

After realising this, I stopped worrying about the students. If he was this week already then the other two must have felt similarly and would have been far easier to take down than I had initially expected.

But no matter how exhausted he became, he still continued to swing his sword at me. Despite his efforts, he hadn't hit me yet and soon even I was growing weary of the battle.

Deflecting blow after blow without making a single retaliatory strike had begun to take its toll on me.

We were fighting at such a speed and pace that I almost missed the moment when the others took down Janus.

Injuring him and knocking him out but not killing him, only someone as strong as an Athereon or as corrupted as Winter could have done that.

I looked down only for a moment, I couldn't afford anything longer than that. I had a flying sword coming at me every other second at the time.

With Janus out of the picture, they focused on Uriel as I had told them too but they had already lost another three people.

I didn't have time to morn, we were so close to winning, just minutes away from the finish line. Only a little further left to go.

So I returned to my fight in the air and took it even higher.

Flying up and up until I was mere meters away from the portals above my head.

I could hear its buzzing energy, feel its dark corruption and I knew that up there, things would work in my favour yet again. I had the high ground, or would it have been the high air?

My fight with Winter slowed down a little at such an altitude, he was getting increasingly tired by the second and I was getting close to an opening.

He took another stab at me, missing by inches rather than the millimetres he normally did and it was then that I saw my chance and I took it.

He was wide open; both of his hands on his blade and nowhere near mine. Therefore, I went in for an attack, not striking or impaling him with my sword, not using a spell or other incantation. Instead, I forced a portion my magic energy into him.

I slapped my hand onto the crystal in the centre of his chest plate. The corruption within immediately flooding into my body. The heat as my magic energy resisted its flow built to the point that I felt as though my blood was on fire.

But in that moment, pushing against the corrupted flow of magic into my body, I realised what I had to do. What I had to do to end this fight. To end it all.

Corruption corrupts.

But briefly… it can be controlled.

So with my body resisting him, I forced every magic circuit within it to redirect my magic energy into my palm.

Against the unrestricted flow of my own magic, corruption can not contest. And against my will, no longer could the man whom had become its host.

I pushed my magic energy through that palm with all the force and urgency that I could muster.

And a moment later, I had flooded his entire system with it.

The look in his eyes is something that I will never forget. Pain and shock. A moment of unbelievable pressure building up within his body. Forcing him to soar across the sky as the impact of my energy sent him flying.

His crystal cracked and chipped, his sword fell from his hand, his wings turned dark and his head tilted back towards the stars.

571

Exactly as expected.

As soon as my energy had hit his heart, it had created a conflict within him for dominance. My magic energy staving off its own corruption at the expense of its own existence. Fading away into nothing and taking the corruption attacking it along for the ride.

Two forced fighting within the same body to survive.

And no matter how strong the corrupted magic energy within him would appear to be, mine was stronger.

It always would be.

Because I willed it so.

And as that war waged on, Winter remained silent. Incapacitated for as long as that battle continued. Granting me all the time I would need to kill him once and for all.

And as he started to scream in pain, his hands stretched out to his sides and his fists clenched in pain, I approached with haste. My blade aimed true. The tip mere moments from striking his face.

And that was when I saw it.

Staring into the eyes of my enemy as I went in for the kill, I saw something that I hadn't expected. A flicker of light emanating from his core.

Some part of him was still in there after all.

And I was about to kill it.

Even after all this time, some part of his consciousness remained intact, un-effected by corruption and unaware of what he had done.

Somewhere deep down within him was the old Winter, the man that I once knew and my friend. And I was mere seconds away from impaling it.

But I didn't care.

I ignored what I had seen. I kept going.

My sword striking true, penetrating through his skull and exploding out from the other side.

And after that, I gladly watched him fall back down to Earth having now lost the ability to do anything at all. No way for him to move. No way for him to die. So long as the war within his corruption infused body continued, neither side would let go.

He would continue to experience the pain of my attack until my magic energy either stopped trying to kill him, or the corruption stopped trying to sustain him.

He wasn't dead yet. But he would be soon.

I would make sure of that.

So with Winter out of action, Janus knocked out cold with wounds keeping him from ever waking again and Uriel practically dead already by the time I had done this, that was it, we had won. Victory over this fight had been ours in the end.

But at what cost?

The initial wave had been defeated, the people pulling the strings lied bloodied on the floor. There was nothing left now. We had done what I believed to be impossible.

We had won.

The only thing left to do was to make sure that the portals closed before the next wave arrived.

And if possible, keep them closed.

I began my descent as Winter fell from the sky, gliding down from my height and approaching the ground below exhausted and drained.

And that was when I noticed. As I drew closer, that weas when I finally saw it. I had been so far up and I was so occupied that I hadn't noticed at first. I hadn't even felt it. Perhaps my proximity to the portals interrupted our link but even so, I should have known.

I should have noticed that below me, almost two kilometres down, many more students had died and all that was left were the last surviving members of my school.

Sitting down in the mud and blood, crying at their losses and licking their wounds. Uriel's body lying not too far from them. There they were.

Their enemy was very badly wounded, so much so that not even corruption could have fixed that.

He wasn't going anywhere.

Neither were most of my students.

A further nine of them laid in ruin.

Broken armour and blades. Not a drop of magic or life within them.

I had lost a grand total of twelve students during that attack and thirteen before that.

I had lost too many.

Half of them.

And it was all my fault.

I was supposed to do my best to protect them during this fight and instead I left them alone to die.

So as I lowered my altitude, still too distracted by the loss of Katiana to take note of the students right away, I looked at the bodies.

And then I saw him.

The one that stood out the most.

Julian.

SACRIFICE

I have suffered the loss of many things throughout my long life upon this Earth.

The earliest of my losses, that of my friends and family. The soldiers I had trained over my many years of service to the king both during and before the war each lost their lives over time.

Loved ones come and go like the wind. The frail nature of humans and mages, their short lives and the ease at which each one can perish.

Possessions have been taken from me over time.

Stolen or lost to the aether, forgotten and buried or completely destroyed.

Even my own child.

I have lost more than you or anyone could possibly imagine in all my years. But never had I lost anything without at least trying to protect and preserve it first.

That was until the day that Katiana died.

During the calm before the storm that followed, I had lost her. Bloodied and mutilated, lying dead on a battlefield littered with the bodies of the fallen from both sides, she had been taken from me and I never even got the chance to so much as think of trying to save her.

I was handed her death after it was already done.

By the time that I had reached her, I was too late to do anything but immediately mourn her death. I was unable to do anything in that moment to save her. And just like the last time, I had to accept that fact.

Never before had I been so powerless in my life. So useless.

I was once the most powerful being on the planet, capable of raising the dead, creating miracles and protecting the weak. But in that moment, on the day that she needed me at my best more than ever, I was not the man that I should have been.

So much of my power has faded now, I'm not as strong as I used to be. Many spells that I could use in my youth were now too taxing to perform. Many feats of mine are now impossible once again.

And in my prime, I would have been able to save her in a heartbeat. I could have moved so fast that you wouldn't have been able to see me coming as I flew across that battlefield and beheaded Winter before he could do the deed.

But on that day, the day when I needed that power to save her, I couldn't do it.

I was too weak to save even one mage.

I was too useless to even save my own wife.

What right did I have to call myself a protector when I couldn't even do the one thing that every husband is supposed to do?

Despite all that I could have done, what I should have done, the one thing that I couldn't do was save her from dying.

THE ATHEREON: WINTER'S WAR

When I first saw that Winter and his brothers were heading for her, I didn't do enough. I just acted as I would have done in any other moment, I teleported over as soon as I could but that wasn't fast enough.

I should have known that something like that was going to happen, I should have been by her side the moment I realised that she was alright.

I should have gone to her the moment that I saw them falling from the sky. I should have been there to protect her but I wasn't.

I wasn't even there when she died.

By the time that I managed to reach her, she was already gone and I was left with nothing but the pendant that she was wearing to cling onto.

Never before had I let anyone die so carelessly.

Never before had I not been there to save them.

Never before had I let someone die without even trying to save them.

And to make matters worse, I had just gone and done it again.

Less than an hour after making that mistake for the first time, I allowed history to repeat. Abandoning my students, not even staying by their sides as they died.

I had realised my mistake the first time but had done nothing to ensure that it wasn't made again the second.

When I decided to seek revenge rather than a victory, I made a choice, a choice that cost me far more than I had already lost.

I knew that the students wouldn't be able to go up against the two brothers without casualties but I didn't care at the time.

I only wanted blood and that was exactly what I got.

I needed to face off against Winter by myself and in order to do that, I sent many of those students to their deaths, without even considering them as being important whilst doing so.

In exchange for sacrificing the lives of my own students, in exchange of giving them an order that I knew would get most of them killed, all I got was blood.

Blood that now stained my hands.

An eternal reminder that I got them killed

That I could have saved them.

If only I had wanted to.

When I gave them the order to fight, I did so without realising what it would cost me, I simply wanted them to keep Janus and Uriel busy while I killed Winter. I didn't even care if they won, I just needed them to buy me more time.

Time, it seems, was all I got in return.

Time to think, time to reflect, time to mourn and time to kill. Because I used every second of the time that the students bought me to fight Winter, I never even thought about helping them when they needed me most.

I simply wanted revenge and all that got me was even more dead bodies to avenge.

I should have felt each one of them die, I should have sensed their pain and their fear but I didn't. I did nothing to save them or even make sure that they were alright. I pushed those feelings aside and ignored them. Telling myself that it was my proximity to the portals that interrupted our connection but that wasn't true.

I felt it when it happened and I decided to ignore and

forget it. I could feel each one of them fall to the ground, the life fading from their bodies and the pact we shared shattering like glass thrown to the floor.

I could have done so much more than I did, yet I chose not to.

I knew that I might have been able to save them, I might have been able to protect them but I didn't. I simply thought of them as an army and ordered them into battle as such. Not even stopping to realise that that army was made up of people. That it was made up of friends.

I sent them into a fight that I knew they couldn't win without casualties and I just didn't care.

Just as I had kept the truth from them during their training, I only wanted them to fight. I never even thought about the fact that they were living people, not simple weapons for me to command.

They deserved a choice and I didn't give them one.

They must have known that even together they were still no match for a fully charged athereon and yet they followed my orders anyway and they continued to follow them to the death.

I got them killed and I didn't have to.

I only saw a chance to get revenge and maybe even end this war for good and I took it.

Winter was a tactician back in the day. The only man on the battlefield that understood troop layouts as well as I did. The only person in our entire army at the time who could have thought on his feet and actually achieve victory no matter what he was up against.

He saw events in a different light than most, he saw them objectively. He could evaluate every situation as though he had all the details laid out before him. He could think tactics and fight at the same time, dishing out orders as he cut down his opponents.

He was and still is, the most talented fighter that I ever got the chance to train. His mind was his ultimate weapon, not his sword and not his brothers.

In the end, the only thing that he needed to win was his head and he used to use it so well.

He used to be one of my most trusted advisories, answering only to the king himself, Winter was the one who used to pull the strings, not me.

It was my job to train and fight alongside our army, not to command it.

Winter on the other hand. His job was to evaluate the situation and strategize, to come up with a plan and then put it in motion as swiftly as possible.

It was his job to tell everyone else what to do, and he did it so well.

That was until that final day of the war anyway.

No one could have won, no amount of men or magic power could have possibly fought off what we were up against and yet, he did so well considering what he was up against.

While he was unable to defeat them, his tactics and troop deployments managed to keep their army out of our capital for five years.

Five whole years, that was how long he was able to keep them at bay. But even after all that time, even after all that death, we were still going to lose.

Their numbers were too great and ours too miniscule.

In a last stitch effort to win, he fought on the front lines as they invaded the palace before storming the civilian streets below.

He and his brothers killing hundreds of them before they lost their ground.

He was doing the absolute best that his skills and his mind could allow but it was hopeless in the end. We were never going to win, and we knew it.

It is for this reason that I placed Winter at the head of the snake. It is his background and his purpose that led me to conclude that he must have been the one calling the shots.

While it is true that I was never privy to the full picture, I had seen enough and knew enough to deduct that he must have been the one in charge.

The tactics used to fight against me, the way that the army acted, how they were laid out and how they had struck first, every part of it was something that he had done before.

They were all things that I recognised, all tactics that he had used in the past and all tactics that had worked before.

Hitting the target as hard as you can to weaken them and then sending in the troops, that was one of his hallmarks, a strategy that only he was known for using.

The way that the enemy soldiers were layered, the way that it got increasingly more difficult to fight them as we approached their centre as though they were protecting their commanding officer in the middle, this too was something that he was known for doing.

In fact, every part of this assault, everything about how it was orchestrated to the signature of its attacks, they all screamed out at me that only Winter could have devised such a plan.

He was behind it all, he had to be, or at least, he had to be ordering the soldiers around.

Even if he wasn't at the top of the food chain, he was at least high enough up the ladder for him to be responsible.

Whatever had driven him to want to help these creatures was beyond me but what I do understand is this. No one, not one living person, could have organised this battle in the same way that he had done.

He was the only person who could have come up with this plan and the fact that he was now right in front of me only proved my theory even more.

He was responsible, he was to blame.

This was his war, his fight and his loss.

And when I first realised that it was him who had killed Katiana, when I saw his face and the armour that he wore, I knew.

I knew that if I could kill him there, if I could put a stop to his involvement in this war, then maybe, just maybe, I might be able to end it for good.

But in order to do this, in order to get revenge and maybe even put an end to this repetitive nonsensical war, I would have to distract his brothers.

So I gave that task to my students and whether I had actually realised it or not, I had sent them to their deaths by doing so.

Even though they had managed to complete the task that I had given them and against all odds managed to defeat both opponents, they hadn't managed to do it without significant losses.

None of them deserved that fate. None of them should have had to die on a battlefield such as that one; none of them should have been put in harm's way to begin with.

They deserved more, they deserved better.

They had their entire life ahead of them when we met. They had decades left to live by the time I sent them into that battle. And I stole that future from them all just so that I might get my revenge.

I ruined their entire lives the second that I took them on as my students. I am the reason that they died there like that. If they had never met me, if I had continued to fight this fight in secret, then they would have still been alive and all that I would have lost would have been my own life.

I never needed their help, not really.

There were ways that I could have won the war by myself but the cost, the requirements for casting spells that strong and devastating were too high.

Almost every spell above level fifty, every spell that only an Athereon can cast, required blood. They required a sacrifice.

It's true that I could have won the war all by myself this entire time but I would have had to kill countless others to do so.

That was something that I simply couldn't bring myself to bear.

I had been spared from death by the Athereon Court so that I might become an eternal guardian over the populace of the Earth.

My single reason for being, the only reason that I have been allowed to live for as long as I have done, was so that I could protect humanity from events such as this.

How could I have stayed true to my oath if I went around sacrificing their lives in order to save everyone else?

How can someone who is meant to protect do so if it

means that he has to kill some of the people he is meant to be saving?

The needs of the many, out way the needs of a few.

That is how the saying goes, but I couldn't do it.

It might have only cost me a hundred or so lives each time I cast those spells. Only one hundred others in order to win each battle. But I couldn't make that sacrifice.

My purpose for being was to protect humanity.

Not to kill it.

So, yes, I could have done it alone but the casualties would have been ten or twenty times greater as a result.

After all, the last time that a spell that powerful was used, it took the lives of my entire species in order to cast it.

In order to stop the army that was at war with us from destroying everything that we sought to protect, we gave up our own lives so that we could seal them away.

We killed ourselves so that the army didn't do it first.

That spell, the one used to both lock them in corruption and then seal it in another version of reality, was immense. Far too complex to replicate and far too costly to justify using again.

Even if I could muster the strength to cast it, it would have taken the lives of millions for it to work. And even if I could have cast that spell, there was no guarantee that it would have worked any better than it had done the last time.

So I did what I had to in order to spare as many lives as I could.

I took fifty students from their home in Academia and began training them as soldiers. Warriors to fight in a war that they knew nothing about, all so that I wouldn't have to sacrifice anyone else.

If I hadn't given them those final orders then we might have won the first stage of the fight with nothing but minor casualties.

Before the Trinity fell from the sky, we had only lost a few, I wasn't happy that we had lost even one life but the fact that only a handful of them had fallen as opposed to all of them was better than the alternative I guess.

However, when I sent them into that last fight, a fight I was sure they wouldn't win, I did so without any regard for their lives.

I could have kept casualties low but I chose to raise them, just so that I might enjoy a few brief seconds of revenge.

It was my fault that they were dead and they knew it as well as I did. Guilt would be my punishment and the loss of my humanity would be my sacrifice.

I would have to live with the knowledge that I had allowed them to die for the rest of my days.

So at least I had a lot of them left.

I glided down from the air slowly and took in every detail of the situation below me as my descent continued.

I had caused all of their suffering and all of their loss and now it was my duty to bear the pain. So I didn't hide anything from myself.

I took it all in.

And it was only when I got within a few hundred meters that I could see Julian's body clear enough to make it out. And as the realisation that it was truly Julian who had died hit me, I looked closer. But the truth still remained.

He was dead and it might as well have been me who

killed him. It was my fault the first time and I did nothing to deny or change that fact this time either.

I saw Julian's body lying on the ground clutched tightly by his wife. And there he stayed, motionless. He was far beyond saving when I got there. So just like Katiana, he was dead and nothing I could have done would have been bringing him back.

Katrina was in ruin, crying profusely, a look of loss on her face that I knew all too well. It was the same look that I had worn only minutes before. The look that I was forced to wear when I found Katiana's body in the way that it was.

It was a look of despair, unimaginable pain and loss. It was the look of someone who had just lost their partner. It was the look of someone having their love ripped away. It was the look of your heart, shattering.

The look of someone who had just lost the person that they loved too deeply to put into words.

It was the look of grief.

The look of a woman who had lost her husband.

It was a look that I had seen far too many times before and a look that I had worn far too regularly to count.

It was a feeling that I understood but was the only one that I consistently hoped to never experience again.

I had lost too much in my life, too many loved ones, too many friends.

It was a feeling that I was tired of experiencing.

It was a feeling that I for once, never expected to experience again.

It was when I met Katiana and taught her the ways of magic, then again when I kept her form dying with that artificial heart, when I taught her the secrets of immortality, every time I never expected to lose her.

I thought that she would live forever.

I had hoped to spend an eternity with her by my side and yet, that future was not mine to live.

I never thought that I would ever lose her but I had. Not a single thing that I had done to keep her from death had protected her in the end.

Nothing that I could have done would have protected her from that blade. Nothing could have kept her alive, no defensive spell and no amount of healing magic. But that doesn't change the fact that when her time had come, I wasn't by her side to protect her.

I wasn't there to hold her hand.

I wasn't even able to say goodbye.

So I continued to glide my way down and finally I spotted where Winter had landed.

To my disappointment, he was unconscious but still alive.

I knew that he was behind it, him and his brothers. They had to be, I needed them to be. With all that I had lost, all that they had taken from me, I needed them to be the ones pulling the strings, I needed someone to blame.

And as I approached Winters body, I realised that he wasn't as dead as I thought he was. I had expected to find the life within him to be slowly fading but instead I found that it was getting stronger by the second.

It seemed that even with a raging war within him and a hole in his head, the corruption was still keeping him alive after all.

My magic had sparked every corrupted circuit within his body and all of them were now retaliating against the corruption that had taken hold of him so long ago. But my intention was not to save him, it was to kill him and in fact, it should have done more than kill him already now that he had that wound. But something, some part of his mind or some effect of the corruption refused to let him die so easily.

I stopped flapping my wings as I hovered above him and allowed myself to drop the last few metres from the air, landing me only a few inches away from the feet of Winter's body. He was badly wounded from head to toe but still alive.

But that wouldn't be for long.

Broken bones littered throughout his body from the impact, blood spewing out of his mouth from my own attack., Armour dented and malformed too much to recognise it anymore and irreparable damage to every one of his internal organs.

Even the crystal on his chest plate, the colour of which had turned black from the corruption contained within it, had cracked to the core.

Those crystals were special. The one part of us that was always unique, a marker to identify one another, a physical representation of our names.

Mine was elongated and thin, not as large as some but longer and brighter than most. His was in the shape of a diamond, originally a deep yellow colour but now it was nothing but black from end to end.

There was an old wife's tale back in the day. Mothers and fathers would say this to scare their children into submission, threatening to break their crystals if they misbehaved.

The saying suggested that should this crystal ever break

or become separated from you for too long you would die as a result.

Feeling excruciating pain and then simply stop breathing on the spot. Considering that during adolescence our armour and our crystals are literally grown by our bodies, I almost believed it.

If the armour was a part of our bodies just like our bones and organs, then the crystal must have been linked to us in some way, perhaps there was truth behind this story in some way too. But considering that I was going to kill Winter anyway, I didn't want to waste my time in order to find out.

With how badly he was injured, I would have been surprised if could still move if he ever woke up. Either way, I quickly kicked his sword away from his reach just in case he tried to grab it should he manage to wake up by some dark miracle.

Realising that I needed to make sure that he wasn't going to escape while I was gone, I thrust my sword into his right shoulder, going all the way through the arm and his bones, cementing him firmly to the ground.

Anchoring him in place as the blade ripped through both of his wings on that side.

He wasn't going anywhere, even if he woke up.

There was no way he would have enough strength to pull the blade and with his circuits the way that they were he wouldn't be going anywhere without wings.

So I left him there, knowing that for the moment he was staying put. I would kill him in due time but I had more important things to do.

I planned on savouring the moment of his death but I needed to see to the others first.

The initial feeling and want of revenge had passed and now I was beginning to see things more clearly.

I had responsibilities to uphold and no matter how devastating the events had become, I had duties to fulfil.

So I walked over to the students that were still breathing. Some of them were badly hurt but they were already healing each other when I got there.

However, there weren't that many of them left to heal. They had been reduced to a pitiful sixteen, only sixteen out of the fifty that I had entered this fight with.

Too many had died and they shouldn't have had to.

I said nothing as I approached, only giving a look of remorse to those who cared.

I looked around and saw only what I needed to see, the faces of the survivors and the mutilated bodies of my fallen students.

I saw exactly what I needed to see and it hurt.

Then I looked over at Julian and noticed something else.

He wasn't wounded.

There wasn't a single scratch on him that would have caused death. Nothing about his body suggested that he was dead but I knew that he was, I could feel it.

So I walked over to Katrina. And mere moments away from asking what had happened, she raised her head and looked at me. Showing me the depressing look of loss on her face. A look that told me she knew exactly what had happened.

And knowing had filled her with even more remorse.

Because it was her fault.

I stopped walking when I was within arm's reach of her. I said nothing, I did nothing. I simply stood there and looked at her, waiting for her to explain what had happened.

There was something off about her though, she was completely drained, more so than she should have been.

The fighting hadn't gone on for long enough to have drained her that much. She had done something, I was sure of it. There was no other explanation for her magic energy levels being so low.

"He remembered." She said.

She had spoken, something that she had only ever done once before to my knowledge.

Choosing to speak for the second time since I had met her must have signified something. It was in that moment that I realised why she never spoke verbally unless she had to.

It was Julian.

When he fixed her heart, even though he hadn't done it fully, it was enough to make her practically human. It would have given her her voice back and even some of her emotions.

But unfortunately, only the athereon side of Julian would have remembered doing this, only he would have ever heard her voice.

That is why she never spoke after that night.

She was doing it to protect him.

If he had heard her voice after locking his memories away then it might have killed him. And with her magic energy practically gone and Julian dead, she had no choice but to speak. Telepathy would have knocked her out and there was no longer a need to stay silent anymore, the person that she was protecting was dead.

But that didn't explain why she remembered that night, she had said that she intended to lock her own memories away as well, she shouldn't have remembered any of it.

Maybe it was because she saw Julian die that she remembered, perhaps it was because of the devastating event that she had witnessed that the block on her memories had crumbled but I had no way of knowing.

I just stood there and gave no response to what she had said. I just stood, perfectly still, not expressing emotion or offering support, I just stood and took some time to think. Only offering the look of a man who has lost too much to express any emotion other than solace.

I had no intention of sharing my feelings and she knew it. So she looked back down at Julian, stroking his head and repositioning his blood-stained hair.

"His mind burned the moment Uriel started fighting us. And in the confusion, Uriel threw his spear at my love. That's how we were able to beat him, in that one moment when he was unarmed.

By the time I turned around, he was already gone.

I healed his wound but it was too late, his mind was gone. My Julian, why? Why did this have to happen when we were so close to winning?" She said tearfully.

She then erupted into an even more serious state of crying. Burying her head into him. Holding him as tightly as she could not willing to let him go.

I walked away from her then.

I knew that I couldn't do anything to help a grieving wife. Even if I wasn't moments away from breaking down myself, I was the last person who should have been comforting her.

Instead, I thought about what my next step should be.

I knew that I would have to resurrect some of the

students but I couldn't do all of them, I didn't have enough power to bring back thirty-five people. I could bring back two maybe three but at what cost and how would I choose?

Would I bring back Katiana and Julian then randomly pick the third?

How could I make that choice?

How do I choose one student over the other?

They were all worth saving.

But even so, resurrection magic takes a toll.

If I had used it, I would have needed a year of recovery time at least. I wouldn't have been able to do anything, I would have been bed ridden for months and then after that, I would have been permanently weakened due to the amount of Athereal Energy required to save them.

Even bringing back three, just three simple humans, would have taken over a third of my remaining resurrections to pull it off.

I would have been so much weaker than I was already that I probably wouldn't even be capable of protecting myself after doing it.

So instead, I continued to assess the situation. I inspected the landscape and the weather. Desperately looking for another option.

The dirt of the ground was charred and stained with blood as far as the eye could see. The sky was littered with thick black clouds, no stars or the moon, only the white light of the portals illuminating the battlefield below.

Then I looked at the remains of Janus and Uriel.

They were beyond saving but they weren't dead either. Janus was missing an arm and a leg, almost all of his body was covered in blade marks and nothing of his armour remained.

It had been splintered off of him, whatever the students had done to take him down had been powerful enough to break it.

That much alone was impressive but even more impressive was that he was still breathing. No matter how powerful the mage, no matter how cleaver or how quick, no mage can kill an athereon, not permanently at least.

While Katiana had managed to put me into a state close enough to death that I had to use a resurrection in order to recover before, she had never actually stopped my heart.

No mage could have done.

An Athereon body is too resilient for that, no matter what you throw at us, we almost always get back up.

Janus now laid on the steps of death's door but it wouldn't open for him, he wasn't ready to die, something wasn't allowing it.

I couldn't tell at the time but I soon learnt what it was.

It wasn't the corrupted magic energy within them, it wasn't their minds and it wasn't their athereon bodies. The only thing keeping the three of them breathing was the portals overhead.

The corrupted energy within the three of them was different than the rest, it had a strange taste to it, I guess. And there was a reason for that. The magic energy that resided within them was directly linked to the portals, and as such, it was keeping them alive for as long as the two holes in the sky stayed open.

Janus should have been slowly dying from his injuries, the lack of blood alone should have done him in but the portals refused to let him die.

However, they couldn't save him either. Corruption can do many things, all of which dark and horrific but it cannot heal. It might have been keeping them alive but it wouldn't have saved them.

Janus would die eventually, but it would be centuries before that amount of magic energy would fully dissipate from his body to allow that to happen.

Uriel on the other hand was mostly intact, only one noticeable injury to the back of his neck. Where a blade had pieced his upper vertebrae and cut his spinal cord.

He was paralysed and useless, he could have been healed but why would I have done that?

The two of them were nothing but corrupted remnants of the people that they used to be. They weren't even people anymore. They were nothing but animals.

Other than their appearance, nothing of their old selves was in there, only corruption. I didn't expect to find any form of magic energy within them, no form of energy at all to be honest, I only expected there to be corruption.

However, when I took a closer look, I found something that I didn't expect to be in there at all.

It was so faint and so well concealed that I would have missed it if I hadn't gone looking for it.

But within them, pushed so far down that it could have been written off as some kind of a fluke, I could still feel the athereon part of them clinging to life.

A deep and week energy that was trying its best to keep them alive. It was resisting the corruption within them and losing.

It was so desperate to resurrect them that it was wearing out by the second from constantly trying.

I didn't have long before it would be gone for good.

That was when it hit me.

The idea that ended up costing me my wife for the second time that day.

It had been almost two and a half hours since the initial attack on my barrier. It had been over two hours since the fighting started and far too long since I had lost my wife.

The fighting had gone on for long enough, we had lost enough. I was going to end it and if my theory was correct, I knew exactly what to do.

My species invented this energy, I understood how to control it and that was when the idea struck my mind. The strongest mind within the collective controls the others. The strongest mage within the Corrupted controls the portals.

So if I became that mind… I could close those portals, permanently.

"Athereal Energy…" I whispered, walking closer to what was left of Janus.

I thought hard about what I needed to do and in the end it didn't matter, what I needed to do and what I wanted to do were the same thing. It was only how I did them that mattered then.

The others looked at me, a flicker of hope in their eyes. Even though I hadn't said what I was doing, they knew that it was something.

Either they had heard me say what I had said or they had seen the lightbulb light up above my head when I got the idea. It didn't matter. The students knew that I had a plan and they were eagerly waiting for me to put it into action.

I could feel their eyes on me as I started to do what I needed to.

But I ignored them, I didn't need to explain myself and I didn't need an audience. They would understand what I was doing soon enough.

So I knelt down next to Janus and placed my left hand on him. I raised my right arm and pointed it towards the deceased students now rotting on the ground.

I focused on the ones with the simplest injuries first, I wasn't about to waste too much energy on the difficult ones before doing the others.

I didn't have a lot of energy to do this with and I wasn't even sure that it was going to work in the first place, so I did my best to remain efficient and save as many lives as I could.

I was about to act as a transference device. A conduit.

I was going to pass the energy I needed from him through me, filtering out the corruption and firing the Athereal Energy out of my palm and into the students.

I was going to bring them back to life in the same way that Julian had done when he proved that Athereal Energy could resurrect more than just dead athereons.

So I bit my lip and started absorbing all the energy within his body in one go. The corruption, his life force and the Athereal Energy still lingering within him. I sucked every drop out of him.

I didn't have a choice, it was all fused together within him, I couldn't draw out one without the other following it. I only wanted the Athereal Energy but the corruption followed as well as the human life force within him.

If I had been able to single out his energy then the human side of him might have survived but so too would have the corruption and then the portals would have never closed.

But Athereal Energy was all that I needed out of the three

anyway.

It's the energy that keeps athereons alive no matter how long they live or how badly wounded they get. And it was this energy that would bring them back, it was this energy that would do what I couldn't.

It was this energy that would save them.

And in order for me to be able to hold this much power I had to remain in my Athereon form, literally forced to wear it as the energy came flooding in, preventing me from switching even if I wanted to.

Draining all of this energy from him resulted in his death. With nothing to keep him in one piece anymore he died. Before my eyes, he turned to ash, disappearing in an instant as the last of his energy flowed into my arm.

It felt like someone was skinning me alive while I was slowly being roasted on a fire. Every part of my arm felt like it was being shredded and sliced apart while my internals felt like they were burning. The corruption was fighting hard for control over me and I was fighting just as hard to resist it.

I had no choice but to endure it.

My body would eventually be able to purify the corruption as it had done before but this time there was a lot more of it and that meant that it wouldn't be over anytime soon.

Still I bared the pain and focused all but the corruption into my right arm, expelling it, forcing it into the bodies of the students.

Once inside of them it would spark them back to life almost instantly. Re-growing their organs and limbs but not healing them entirely.

I couldn't spare enough energy to do that much, there were too many dead to bring back with what little I had to work with.

And even using it as efficiently as I could, there still wasn't enough energy for all of them, only resurrecting the first eight was possible and only barely.

But it worked.

Using the energy that made my people immortal, I was able to bring them back to life. But I wasn't done yet.

They were still injured but the rest of the students rejoiced at the event and began healing them moments after they gasped back to life.

The energy from Janus faded and I lowered my arm. I could barely stand after that, the corruption slowly taking hold of my muscles and circuits.

It was far too strong to fight.

I knew that I wouldn't have long before it would become a permanent part of me. Even if I wanted to, I couldn't do anything with it anymore.

It was inside of me and I had no choice but to carry it, there was simply too much to control.

Nevertheless, I continued.

I had more students to save and Julian still hadn't been revived yet.

I bore the pain and forced myself to stand, stumbling over to what was left of Uriel and beginning to do the same as before.

But he was weaker, more corruption than he was athereon. I could feel how weak he was but even so I absorbed everything. I couldn't stop once I had started. Even after I had drained him of all Athereal Energy, the corruption just kept coming. I was powerless to stop it and even more powerless to resist it.

My body was beginning to crack, the corruption was too great to purify but even so, I fought it off for as long as I could. I focused what little energy I had to use into my hand and pointed it towards the students.

I could only bring back one more with what I had and I chose Julian.

The energy resisted him at first but soon it flowed through him as it would have done any other. I guess the resistance was caused by the latent Athereal Energy fragments still lingering within him.

Having a foreign Athereal force placed within him must have caused some form of reaction deep within his fractured mind but even so. I wasn't going to let that stop me. I forced the energy into him as quickly as I could before it dissipated. And before long, he let out a cough and opened his eyes.

A moment later and his hand was placed on Katrina's cheek. He had only just been brought back to life and his first thoughts were for the crying woman in front of him.

It was exactly what I would have done to Katiana if I were in their position at that moment. But the roles were not reversed.

That was their moment, not mine.

Nothing will ever make me forget the joy and happiness in Katrina's eyes but something did distract me from it. This time the effects of corruption had started taking an even larger toll.

I felt my legs go numb as I stood up. Felt my armour resisting my magic as I walked back over to where I had left Winter.

THE ATHEREON: WINTER'S WAR

I knew what was happening and I was desperately racing against the clock. Sooner or later, I wouldn't even be myself anymore but I kept going, there was more to do and I wasn't going to go down so easily.

I am the Athereon, a name the literally translated to the great protector. So if I was about to die, then I would go down saving lives, no matter what it cost me.

I reached out and grabbed my sword. Simply touching the handle made my hand burn as it resisted my energy. But there was one more source of Athereal Energy that I could use and I wasn't going to let the corruption stop me so soon.

I pulled the sword from his shoulder, resulting in the same black marks appearing on my hand that Katiana had once had on hers.

And when the tip of the blade finally exited Winter, I saw something in him that angered me. I saw life.

Somehow, he was regaining control over the corruption, using it to heal himself. That black smoke slowly leaving his body was closing his wounds.

It shouldn't have been possible. Corruption doesn't heal, it only sustains. There shouldn't have been a way for him to do that but that doesn't change the fact that he did.

I watched as the holes from my blade slowly closed themselves and as I realised he would only grow stronger after doing this, I acted quickly from then on.

If he had figured out how to use corruption to heal himself then his body would soon be removing the Athereal Energy within him, he wouldn't be needing it anymore.

So I placed my hand on him and drained everything that I could find.

The corruption, his life energy and his Athereal Energy.

I pointed my palm back at the students and resurrected another three of them; those were all the bodies in range that weren't too badly injured.

There was nothing that could be done for Lila or Trevor, she had been cut in half and he was decapitated, no amount of energy would have fixed that, nothing could regrow half your body parts like that. And nothing that I knew of could have stitched two parts back together.

There weren't any more bodies left in range for me to bring back after that though. Except for one.

I had just enough energy left for one more and Katiana was lying right next to me.

I don't know what I possessed me to leave her for last but that didn't matter. I pointed my arm at her and focused, forcing out as much Athereal Energy as I could.

But in the end my efforts were pointless.

The energy resisted her completely. Not one drop of it had entered her, it had only deflected off into the atmosphere.

She was now truly dead and nothing that I could do would have brought her back.

The way in which she had died, the weapon and the energy used to kill her, it was designed to kill my kind and keep them dead.

No amount of Athereal Energy could have saved her and as a result, no matter how hard I wanted to try, I knew that she wasn't coming back.

And after the last few specs of Athereal Energy left my hand, that was it, the corruption had taken hold.

I was no longer in control of myself after that.

But as a result, both my goals had been accomplished.

I had resurrected as many as I could have done and now I was physically linked the portals.

While I would have liked to bring back Katiana as well, I knew that I couldn't. But it didn't matter, I would be joining her soon enough.

My face tuned white, devoid of all life and emotion.

My wings blackened and my armour exploded away from my body. Rejecting me completely.

The shards of metal, not unlike steel or titanium, scattered off all over the place and revelled the scars that were hidden beneath my armour's shell.

My spine was on the verge of collapsing as the connecting bones ripped their way out of the disks. My clothes were shredded, my wings were bloody and my mind was clouded by the growing void of the darkness that would soon engulf it.

A black empty space covering every thought and emotion. I was being absorbed. I was becoming exactly what we had just lost so much in order to fight.

I was being turned into what we all feared.

I was becoming a threat.

But I accepted this fate, it was less than I deserved and I would have gladly put myself through worse.

Julian was quick to get back on his feet when he saw the shards of my armour flying through the air. Knowing that something was wrong he forced himself to stand. Barely able to stay conscious, he did this for me, putting myself through pain and in danger of further injury just so that he could help me.

I saw him rise from the ground, not taking his eyes of me for a second. I knew that he was going to try and save me but I wasn't going to allow it. I had only just brought him back from the dead. He had been given a second chance and I wasn't going to let him waste it on me.

"Stay back, son." I said.

I could only just control parts of myself at that point. My mouth being one of them. So I forced myself to speak no matter how much it hurt to do so.

My mind was a wasteland, I couldn't even make sense of my own thoughts anymore. I couldn't even feel my human body anymore.

I had been separated from it and was now stuck in my Athereon form.

Becoming quite dangerous as a result.

'Athereon!' He yelled.

Trying to break through the corruption that was consuming me with telepathy he tried to work his way inside my mind.

I felt him fighting the walls of my prison but it was pointless. Nothing that he could do was going to make a meaningful difference. I had absorbed the corruption of three athereons now. No one could have helped me win that fight.

"Don't worry now. I'm doing what I must." I told him.

What none of them had realised, not one single person had bother to check and see, was that the portals in the sky were still open.

They would stay that way until the last of the corruption was destroyed or sent back.

That corruption was now residing within me and I had control over what happened to it.

Or so I thought.

"Athereon, no! You don't have to do this." He pleaded.

I had resurrected him after he had already remembered being an Athereon; of course he understood the situation at hand.

He had his memories back now.

He remembered being my son and he knew everything that he would have done if he were still conjoined with him. He understood how the portals worked and how the corruption was linked to them.

He knew what I was planning.

It was at that moment that I realised that he might be able to think of a way to save me.

So I just looked at him and smiled. I couldn't do much else. My body was slowly being walled off from my mind. I didn't have time to chat.

"No... You can't! What will happen to the world without you in it?" He said. Limping his way over to me, desperately trying to stop me from continuing.

"I'm sure that the two of you can handle it." I replied.

If anyone in the world was capable of replacing me, it was him. Not only was he an excellent fighter but he had spirit and knowledge.

He knew more than any other mage now and with Athereal Energy now flowing through him ponce more, he might not have been an Athereon but he was the closest he could be to it.

This might have even given him his immortality back.

His wife, Katiana, was still using a machine doll's heart, a slightly more human one but still artificial. This would give her a lifespan of several thousand years at least.

And I had made my decision; the two of them would

have made perfect replacements for myself.

The world didn't need me anymore.

Besides, if my plan had succeeded, it wouldn't have needed any one of us ever again. If I was right, my actions would end this war for good.

Julian stopped moving and stood in wait. He was thinking I assume but he wasn't acting. He hadn't figured out what to do yet but it didn't matter, the time had come.

I began to attempt expelling the corruption, dissipating it in the air around me.

This would close the portals in theory but also drain me of everything in the process.

This was it, I was about to die saving the world, as I always expected myself to do.

But the corruption was too strong. I clung to my body. It clung to my mind.

I couldn't get rid of it.

I couldn't do anything at all.

I was just as powerless as before.

After expelling the last of my energy resurrecting the students, I was done for.

I could feel the corruption taking over the last of my mind and all I could do was collapse.

For whatever reason, I had decided to do exactly what I knew wouldn't work.

How had that decision appeared in my mind?

The corruption was too strong to force out, I knew that but I still tried.

I wonder, was this the corruption's doing? Had it taken over my min enough for it to have forced me to weaken myself?

All I had done by forcing out my energy was make it even easier for the remaining corruption to take me over. Under any other circumstance, I wouldn't have been so foolish but in that moment, whether it be the loss of my wife clouding my judgement or the corruption messing with my mind, I had only sped up my decent into darkness.

Just as I began to fall backwards, I accepted my fate and welcomed death, expecting the students to kill whatever remained of me before it was too late.

But Julian and Katiana had other ideas.

They stopped my fall, catching me before I hit the ground.

They held me still, sitting me up and putting their plan into action.

They placed their hand on what was left of my armour, the blue crystal on my chest that was slowly turning black and then they began absorbing the corruption from me. Distributing it evenly between them, saving my life but dooming themselves.

I told them to stop but they refused, sucking every piece of corrupted magic from my body, leaving me just an empty shell.

An immortal shell mind you but completely powerless.

The only thing that I still had to hold onto, the only thing keeping me conscious and preventing me from falling into the shadows of my mind was the pendant rapped around my hand.

I could feel its power, chipping away at my mind little by little.

It was comforting, so familiar and so soft.

It was her energy that I felt. The sweet scent of her power

forcing its way into me. Her final gift to me, her final act was her creating the pendant that saved my life.

The glow from the heart shaped crystal finally stopped shortly after and then that was it, the thing was empty. Completely devoid of power.

By the time that his had happened I had already regained control over my thoughts but not my body.

"From this side of the portal, corruption is king." Julian told me. "But from the other side…"

"We can be instead." Katrina finished in his place.

They thought that they could control the corruption, use it to teleport themselves on the other side of the portal before sealing it from there and keeping it closed.

"Don't." I coughed at them in my weakness. "Just… just let me die."

But it was too late.

They slowly laid me down on the ground and did what they planned to do despite my objections.

Standing side by side, holding each other's hands as the black power of corruption travelled through their veins. They locked eyes with one another and a moment later they had left.

They teleported off in a flash of blue and black light. And an instant after this, a great roar strode across the heavens and the portals disappeared.

Collapsing inwards and sealing themselves.

I don't know what happened on the other side or if they ever got there and I though at the time that I never would. There was no way of telling from here and no way of getting them back without risking another war.

They were gone.

The portals were closed.

And I had been left alive.

I did not approve of this sacrifice.

I had been willing to make it myself but that was a very long time ago and all I can do now is exactly what I have been doing.

I carry the memory of everyone that I have lost inside of me and I will continue to do so until the day that I eventually die myself.

No matter how many millions of years that I might have left to live, I will remember them as if they had just died yesterday.

Julian and Katrina were the real heroes on that day, not me.

I was just the person who got everyone that he cared about killed.

My wife, my son, my students and my friends.

I should have died on that day but instead I was forced to survive so that I might continue protecting this world, just as I have done for the past twelve-thousand years.

Even if it wasn't up to me to make the choice, I would have still preferred it if I had died instead of them.

They had their entire lives ahead of them.

Thousands of years left to live.

I on the other hand was already old.

I had done my time.

There wasn't any need for me anymore, they could have taken my place and the world would have spun on without issue.

But instead, they took my place in death so that I might takes theirs in life.

Not a moment goes by that I do not remember that day, the day that my two closest friends gave their life to save mine.

The day that I lost my house, my wife and my life.

The day that this endless war, finally drew to a close.

THE AFTERMATH

The war was over now, the fight had been won and victory declared.

It had taken only a few short hours to resolve the battle but, in that time, a great many things had happened, a great many friends were lost and a great many truths were revealed.

I was the one who had put them into that fight, the one who had trained them, the one who had killed them. It was because of me that my students died in such horrific ways, that Julian and his wife exchanged their lives for mine and it was because of me that my own wife died in the disgraceful way that she did.

I am to blame for what we lost and yet I was denied the death that I had chosen and accepted.

I was forced to survive, forced to live so that I might fight another day.

I had decided to go out on my own accord, to die with dignity and join my wife in whatever awaited me on the other side but I was forced to stay.

Julian chose to save me, sacrificing his life and that of his wife's for my continued survival.

It was him, he was the one who saved the world from

disaster. It was he who prevented the horrors that awaited it if we had lost and yet most will never know of this.

The war had always been a well-kept secret and that battle had changed nothing in that regard.

Julian, Katrina and all those who fell alongside them would soon be forgotten as well as their sacrifice.

Their deaths would be covered up and no record of how they really died would exist for very long. The only person who would be able to tell you what happened would be me and it wouldn't be legal for me to do so.

Outside of the Magic Council, the senior staff members of Academia and those who were in the battle, none would know of it.

No one, not one other person would know what it took to keep the world safe on that day and no one would ever know the sacrifice that was made to save it or me.

Knowing this, I still couldn't do anything about it.

I had no say when it came to matters pertaining to the world of mages. I am but one man, I have no power to speak of.

With the Crown Mage dead and none readily available to replace her, the Council wasn't even capable of doing anything either.

I couldn't do anything to change the laws that were set in place. Despite how much people needed to know, I couldn't tell them.

While there would soon be a public memorial honouring Katiana, there wouldn't be anyone there to tell you how she died.

Every mage in our world would mourn her death but none would know how she died. She would be granted a royal send-off but the body was mine to bury.

They only thing that they would be lowering into the ground would be their memories of her and an empty coffin.

I would be forced to keep the circumstances of her death a secret as well as the rest of it. Every detail about the war, why the students were trained and why so many of them died. Every part of it would be a closely kept secret, eventually forgotten to time.

To have put all of those students through those events. To have forced them into a situation that they weren't properly prepared for, to have gotten over half of them killed and then not be able to tell anyone. It was more than simply appalling.

It was disrespectful.

Those who gave their lives in battle should be remembered as heroes, not forgotten and hidden under the rug in the way that they were.

They should have been given the honour of going down as the heroes that they were. They should have been respected as people who died saving the world. And they should have been remembered.

But instead, they were forgotten.

Only a few people knew of what they had done to save everyone else. Only a handful of mages on the entire planet knew the truth and that wasn't good enough.

They died protecting the world and yet the world would never know that it needed saving in the first place.

To think that such a society existed, one where those who die protecting others are swept under the rug, one where wars that decide the fate of everyone alive are willingly ignored.

To think that a society that I had helped to build could have been so misguided.

It's not right.

However, the students did more than save everyone else, they did more than protect themselves and what was theirs, they did more than go down as heroes.

They became legend.

I carried on with my life spreading stories of these fallen heroes throughout the human world and my own.

Telling others of their sacrifice through any means that I could.

I told them verbally, through a book or letter.

Scripts for plays or films, I told as many people as I could and soon their story was known as nothing more than fairy tale.

But at least people knew it.

Though people did not believe the words they read or heard, they at least knew them.

Even if it wasn't real to them, the names of the fallen would be in their hearts, for the rest of time.

I created a story that almost everyone knew, one that no one could ignore and one that stood the test of time. For the rest of my life I told their tale and for the rest of my life I carried their legacy.

However, all of this was much, much later after that day than it should have been. The first time that I ever told the tale of that day was over one hundred years after it happened. Well after their story should have been heard.

I would have told it sooner but I was more or less occupied for that whole time.

So much happened after the portals closed and there was

much to deal with.

I eventually told their story yes, but it took me a while. There were a lot of consequences as a result of that night and the first of them directly followed the event.

The two portals had been left open for only a few short hours but in all that time, the overwhelming force of corruption was seeping out of them.

It took quite some time to finally take effect but once it did, the resulting chaos that it caused, erupted around the world in full force.

Weather systems that no one had ever seen before swept across the land. Tsunamis, volcanic eruptions, tornadoes, flash freezing, earthquakes and every other natural disaster that you could think of happened and then even more.

This unending chaos lasted almost a year as the world fought off the last few specs of corrupted magic hovering around in the atmosphere.

So much energy had been released in such a short time that I was surprised the weather systems didn't last longer than they did but with that being said, it's a good thing that they didn't.

With so much corruption polluting the air, it was difficult to use magic outside of the safety and comfort of a barrier that entire time.

The only places safe enough to use a spell were the schools. Not many mage households had barriers strong enough to hold back corruption, let alone the amount of it that there was to deal with.

Never had I seen corrupted energy so wide spread.

Never before had I ever seen so much of it at one time and never before had it been released in the way that it was.

Not long after Julian and Katrina teleported off into oblivion, the portals started to close. Releasing extremely thick clouds of corruption as they did.

The structure of the portals seemed to collapse in on itself. Almost as if it was being sucked though a tiny point in the centre, releasing their immense energy as they grew smaller to compensate.

It wasn't an expected result of them closing but never had a portal been closed so quickly before, I didn't know what would happen until it did.

And when the portals finally closed all the way, they did so in an explosive fashion. I watched as the white light of the portals faded into obscurity and then into the finest of points. A saw a small yellow flash as they finally closed and then nothing but fire.

The sky had erupted into a barrage of flames and light. As far as the eye could see there were bright yellow flames and a black cloud surrounding them.

The corruption itself was lit like the flames on a gas burner. It moved quickly and headed in all directions. Spreading outwards like an actual explosion and sending its heat and flames down towards us.

I laid there on the floor, unable to move or even speak anymore. My body was numb and my mind was a desolate wasteland of damaged cells.

I couldn't move, let alone use magic.

I could barely stay conscious.

And with all that I had gone through, I hadn't been badly wounded enough to use any of my resurrections. I cannot use them whenever I like, I can only do it as a result of entering a state of consciousness close enough to death that my body uses them for me. I had no way of recovering any faster than I could do naturally.

I was a sitting duck.

In that moment I felt as though I was going to die all over again, that the students I had just brought back from the dead were going to be killed all over again as well.

Luckily though, the students were quick to react.

Forcibly teleporting off one by one to get to a safe distance.

I knew that the teleport would have hurt like hell and they did too. With that much corruption in the air, they were lucky to be standing.

I was amazed when they started to disappear. I was glad that they had enough strength left over to run. However, what I hadn't expected was what they chose to bring with them as they fled.

I saw each of them reach down for something before teleporting but I couldn't figure out what until they grabbed me.

They were grabbing the bodies.

They picked me up last, not long after teleporting off with Katiana and their classmates. Even when running for their lives, they had enough compassion left in them to retrieve the bodies of their fallen.

At least they would get a proper burial when the time came.

However, out of every one of those bodies that they grabbed, the few that they did not were that of Winter and his brothers. Uriel was still mostly intact and Janus had turned to ash. But even so, their bodies were still miracles compared to a mage, they should have been disposed of properly but the students didn't know that.

They only took the bodies that they cared for, nothing more.

They didn't know that I had left Winter alive and because of this, they had left him behind like all the other enemy soldiers that littered the crater.

I remember thinking that he would die from the explosion if they left him but I couldn't have been more mistaken. I should have known that such a simple thing wouldn't have killed him that easily.

And when we landed a few seconds later. Only a few hundred meters from the old border of my barrier, I fell into a coma.

Due to the levels of corruption that I had absorbed, my body was in ruin, barely even keeping my heart going. Couple that with how drained I was when Julian pulled that corruption out of me and the result is a coma.

When I finally came to, three weeks had passed.

And in all that time, I had been in my Athereon form.

This had created many problems as I slept.

No one quite knew how to heal me, not one nurse could figure out my biology enough to lend aid.

In the end, I was only in that coma because I had to heal myself naturally.

If only I had been woken up, even for a second, I could have shifted into my human body and then the coma wouldn't have been necessary.

But I never woke up during my time in that bed.

With all the wounds that I had sustained, both externally and internally, the medical staff must have thought that I was dying.

THE ATHEREON: WINTER'S WAR

I was covered in scorch marks, slashes and scratches, broken bones and damaged circuits. Burnt wings and a badly injured mind.

To anyone who didn't know what I was capable of surviving, I must have looked like a corpse. But I am athereon, I do not die so easily and as long as Athereal Energy flows through either of my bodies, I can survive almost anything you throw at me.

Now that I think of it, three weeks was probably the longest time that I had worn my Athereon body in thousands of years.

I wonder what they fed me during that time.

I don't think that I had eaten in my Athereon body back then, well, ever.

I have always eaten whilst human, with my human sense of smell and taste. I don't even know what foods my Athereon body can digest.

But alas, I will never know.

All I do know is that I was in a coma for those three weeks and when I awoke, I found myself sitting in the same hospital bed that Julian had once used.

The fifth floor of Academia's infirmary. Room five oh five, the room that was labelled for "Private patients only".

I wasn't expecting that to be where I ended up when I first opened my eyes. I had expected a safe house or maybe even one of the few mage rooms hidden in human hospitals.

No matter what I had expected, the truth remained, I had ended up in Academia and within moments of waking up I was greeted by a visit from a very distraught Headmaster.

The time between me waking and him arriving was too short for him to have known, so he must have just been checking in on me.

That would explain the look on his face when he walked through the door I guess.

After many hours of talking we eventually covered everything that we needed to.

It was difficult at first. Talking that is.

My mouth was dry and week but then I realised that I had been in my Athereon body for long enough and switched back to my human one. Once in it, I had a perfectly well-maintained body at my disposal, no injuries, no scars and no headache.

It was exactly as I had left it.

Even wearing the same blood-stained clothes that I had worn on the battlefield.

Normally I would have swapped them for something in my wardrobe by summoning some clothes to wear but I didn't have a wardrobe anymore.

I didn't even have a house.

Throughout the conversation I was deciding what to do next, where to go and where to live. I didn't have any modern currency to use. Nothing that would have been accepted at any market. I hadn't had a job in centuries and I hadn't lived in a human household in millennia.

I knew that whatever I chose, it wouldn't be the easy choice.

The easiest thing to do would be to rebuild the house that I had lost but so much had happened there. So many memories both happy and sad, so many feelings and so much loss that I couldn't bring myself to do it.

I would never live upon that hill ever again.

After all, I didn't need to anymore.

THE ATHEREON: WINTER'S WAR

With everything that I had to go on, I came to the conclusion that the portals wouldn't be opening anymore. They had been forced shut, for the first time in history. As far as I knew, that meant that they would be staying that way. Which also meant that there was no need for me to live atop that hill ever again.

However, before I could make plans for the future, the past needed filling in.

So I spoke with the Headmaster for many hours, questioning him, gathering every piece of information that I could from him and filling in what he didn't know with my best guesses.

He told me what had become of the students, where and how they were.

It turned out that each of the surviving members of the group had been raised to level twenty, the highest all but the Crown Mage can become without myself promoting them.

They had mostly gone their separate ways, changing their names and cutting ties with each other. Most didn't want to be found and even less of them wanted to remember what had happened on that day and I didn't blame them.

I understood this, after all that they had gone through, it made sense that they would want to abandon their past. They had the right to forget it, I would do the remembering for them. After all, that was my punishment, to have to carry the guilt and the loss of that day for the rest of my life.

A public funeral was held for those we lost.

However, the true cause of death wasn't so public.

Everyone attended.

The other students, the friends and family of the fallen and even the Magic Council.

However, the council wasn't there just for the burial.

They had come to the academy to oversee the construction of the memorial dedicated to Julian and Katrina in the main courtyard and to make sure that it didn't say anything on it that was too revealing of the truth.

While no student would understand why they were being remembered, those who had ordered its construction would and they knew of its importance.

Even going as far as to place a plaque on the front of it reading.

"In memory of those who gave their lives to save ours."

It was a shame that not one member of the public would understand what they had done but at least they were being remembered.

It was a pretty sculpture of the two. Julian standing strong at the front with his head held high and his hand clutching a sword in the air. Next to him stood Katrina, holding onto to him tight and her head facing his.

Even in death, the two of them couldn't get enough of each other. It was a truly beautiful piece of marble, befitting of their memory.

While a few details weren't accurate, such as the difference in their height or the shape of Julian's sword, it was at least somewhat similar to how they acted in life.

It was nice to see them again and while they didn't have a grave to visit, I visited the statue every year on the anniversary of their deaths to pay my respects.

It was the most times that I had ever visited the academy outside of having students. Every time that I visited, every single time that I showed up on that date, flowers and candles in tow, the courtyard had been sealed off from everyone but me.

The academy understood how much they meant to me and they respected that I was better off being alone during those few minutes every year.

Rumours and theories of why I would visit them every year soon spread around the school but they didn't need to. If they had only asked then I would have told them. I would have said that I was there to pay respects to my friends, people who had given their lives to save mine and people who I had loved as though they were my own son and daughter.

But I was never asked why I visited them, mainly because I never stuck around long enough.

Within ten minutes of arriving, I would have said what I was going to say and would have teleported off.

Visiting the graves of my other students and then finally that of my wife.

It was the Headmaster who told me where Katiana's body was being kept.

In accordance with her will, she was being preserved until I had the chance to lay her to rest myself.

And that was exactly what I planned to do when I went to retrieve the body but it would seem that fate had other ideas first.

It wasn't long after approaching her body that I realised, the pendant that I had placed in my pocket was reacting to her presence.

It knew that she was there and some small part of her was creating a kind of feedback between the two.

I held the pendant up to her and it started glowing.

For a moment, I thought that this meant she was still

alive but she was undeniably dead. So instead I took a closer look at this pendant and tried to figure out what it was and why she had been wearing it.

It was only during this closer inspection that I realised how densely the magic circuits within it had been laid. It looked odd, formations that I had never seen before, giving off a strange feeling of comfort as I looked even deeper.

Realising that it was littered with millions of magic circuits I decided to place a little magic into it and that was when I felt it, I felt her.

When my magic entered the shell of that crystal, I felt her presence, her life force, her mind.

I knew what it was but had no idea what to do with it.

Within this heart shaped crystal was a miracle in disguise. Contained within its complexity was something that I had never seen before.

It was an exact copy of her mind.

Every thought that she had ever had, every memory, every feeling, every experience. Everything that made up the mind of my wife was contained with its shell and I couldn't comprehend as to how it had been created or why.

Even to this day I have no idea why or how it was made but I could guess. The only way that I could think of doing something like this would be to perform an Imprintation spell onto it.

But that didn't explain how or why it was made.

The magic circuits contained within it, they were far too complex. Far too intricate and far too small for a mage to have made them.

I cannot deny that there was some amount of beauty within its structure but I couldn't figure out how it was made either.

My best guess as to why it was made was so that she would have a backup, a way of cheating death if she needed to.

There wasn't much that I could do with something like this at the time but if I ever found an opportunity to resurrect her, if by some miracle I was able to one day bring her back to life, then I would have a copy of her mind with me when the time came.

However, I never actually expected to be able to use it.

I only carried it around because it was a part of her and now it would always be with me. A piece of my wife, immortalised in crystal, never dying or ageing. Just like myself.

For every day to come after that one I would wear this pendant around my neck, not daring to remove it in case it got lost.

After some time alone with her body and this pendant, I had to move on. I needed to decide how I was going to bury her. Someone so important and special deserved a proper resting place and that was exactly what I gave her.

I took her home.

While its name and shape might have changed in the past four hundred and sixty years, I knew where she belonged.

I buried her in her hometown, in the catacombs of the church she had once prayed at.

I buried my wife in the place that I had once saved her form.

I buried her in Rome.

Deep in the catacombs of Vatican City is a room.

Unknown to the public or even to the pope himself, there

exists a sealed room filled from wall to wall with coffins.

The remains of all those dear to me are buried there.

That was how we met after all; I had just finished burying a friend of mine when I passed her in the street.

It was only fitting that the place I would normally bury someone so important just so happened to be the place where I had met someone as important as her.

So there she was laid.

Placed into her own marble coffin and then into the stone chamber along with all the others. Unknown to any within the church, she was there. As close to her god as she could have been.

And even though I didn't believe in his existence, I still gave them the best chance of getting into the heaven that humans so desperately strived towards reaching.

Even if it wasn't real, I still tried.

They all deserved the best in life and even better in the afterlife, if there was such a thing. So I buried every one of my friends there, whether they were holy or not, they deserved a proper resting place in the house of God.

I had planned her burial within a few seconds of being told where her body was and as I sat there, slowly accepting the news I soon realised something. The Headmaster had been stalling.

Everything that he had said so far had taken too long, he was avoiding something and it was beginning to become obvious.

So it soon became clear to me that the Headmaster had even more distressing matters to tell me and he was just as afraid of them as I was.

But soon he continued on, telling me that the students

would never see me again but I could tell that this was not the cause of his stalling.

I knew that the students wouldn't want to see me again and I already come to accept this, after all, I got them into that fight but he was being more specific.

It wasn't that they were unlikely to see me, it was that they had requested not to.

None of them wanted to see me.

I had expected something like that to happen, it always does.

While this time they had made the choice to help by themselves, it was myself who made them the offer in the first place and it was also my fault that their friends were all killed during it.

Looking at the Headmaster's face and seeing the look of silence upon it, I expected him to leave after that and let me finish recovering but he had even more to say.

Words that I had expected but never wanted to hear.

Words that would come to consume me for the rest of my days after that moment.

Such impactful words and yet, I already knew that he was going to say them.

Some part of me, however deep down I had hidden it, had already come to the truth and all he was doing was confirming it.

He looked as though the words were hard to say, almost as if he didn't wat to say them. He regretted them before even opening his mouth.

Never had I seen such a look on this man.

Never had I seen him so ashamed and afraid before.

It was quite the moment but it wasn't appropriate to

enjoy the look he was making at the time. What he told me after that was far too serious to find any satisfaction in the look on his face.

"This next part is not to leave this room under any circumstances. Understood? When the clean-up teams cleared away the remains of the war you fought last month, they found all but one of the bodies." He paused as he lent over the bed, getting closer to my face and locking his eyes with mine. "Athereon, the missing body. As far as the description that the students gave, seems to have belonged to Winter.

As far as we know, he's still out there, somewhere.

The Council has placed the burden on you to find him. He is part of your species; he is your responsibility. After all, 'It was your war'." He said regretfully.

He hadn't wanted to say any of the words that had come out of his mouth but he was right. The Council had probably forced him to say that.

The tone of his voice suggested that nothing he was saying were in his words. I knew that he didn't see the battle as my war. He had fought in three of them himself and knew that if I could have ended the endless cycle of blood and loss then I would have done centuries ago.

The only people who would have referred to it as being my war, would have been those who were now struggling to maintain their control.

The Council.

But other than that, I agreed with every word.

If an athereon was still out there and was as strong as Winter, then I was the only person capable of dealing with him.

Unless my partner came out of hiding but that wasn't all that likely at the time.

Winter was probably nothing more than a mage now but even so, as I have said before, the human side of me is still stronger than any mage on the planet and he was literally infused with corruption now.

I wasn't even sure how much of him would be human before I found him.

But with him out there, none of us were safe.

But all I could think about and wonder in that moment, sitting there in a hospital bed hearing more bad news after more bad news I just had one question.

How much did Winter remember?

Had he regained his sanity or was he still the same animal that I had fought on that battlefield?

I couldn't help but wonder if, when I did try and kill him, would he understand why?

After that, the Headmaster left without ever letting me say a word in response, not that I would have done.

But he did leave me with time to think.

I had plenty of time to think.

The realization that the person responsible for killing my wife was still out there soon hit me during that time.

Whether it was because I had been tasked to do so or because I wanted to find him, I was going to spend every waking moment looking for him until I did now.

He was the one responsible for the deaths of thousands, I was sure of it and more importantly, he had killed my wife.

To me, he was nothing more than a murder, a blood-stained war criminal.

I intended to put him in the ground the moment that I

found him. No matter who or what got in my way at the time, he was going to die by my hand, be it in a well concealed space or in the middle of a human city.

I was going to kill this man.

I didn't care about keeping it quiet.

Little did I know then, that the next time we did meet.

It would be as friends.

To be continued

THE ATHEREON
DAY OF REUNION

Out Now

Printed in Poland
by Amazon Fulfillment
Poland Sp. z o.o., Wrocław

61884101R00374